No One Else Could Heal Her

HIYODORI

Contents

Part One: Hunting Season

Part Two: The Originator Exam

PART THREE: THE CLEMATIS GAMBIT

PART ONE
Hunting Season

PROLOGUE

BACK WHEN I WAS A KID—way back before I met Wist—I had no real grudge against mages.

Those of you who know me might find this difficult to believe. Asa Clematis? *That* Asa Clematis? The infamously petty, vindictive, mutinous, mage-resenting Asa Clematis?

That's me. Growing up, though, the only mage I knew was the lady next door. A Class 1-1, too weak to make a living with magic. A mage who worked as a corporate middle manager.

Young Clematis liked this mage lady because she let us neighborhood kids go tearing through her backyard day after day, summer and winter, morning and evening. She never complained.

No, my animosity toward mages didn't start with my neighbor. But it did take root years before I ever set eyes on Wist.

It started with Yarrow's warning.

Yarrow: an older girl in the neighborhood, and the only healer other than me. The rest of the local kids were subliminals—technically identifiable as either mages or healers, but too low-level to actually use magic or heal aching mages.

Anyway, I worshiped Yarrow. Followed her everywhere. Dusted off my grubby knees and wore cute floral sundresses to match her.

She was soft-spoken, and slow to speak. Long black hair. Dark eyes. Always tall for her age.

You might notice a superficial resemblance to Wist. I'll say it as many times as I need to: I do *not* have a type.

People in the neighborhood thought Yarrow and I looked like sisters. I disagreed: I, for one, had a massive crush on her. I sobbed my little heart out when she left for Guralta Academy.

But I also bragged about her to whoever would listen. Guralta was a rare co-ed boarding school, dedicated to training mages and healers alike. It also happened to be one of the most prestigious educational institutions in the entire country.

Over the next couple of years, I aced all my healer aptitude tests. I was angling to get into the same academy. If I were lucky, I'd have at least a year with Yarrow before she graduated.

Then came the news that Yarrow was dropping out. We'd never go to school together. Yarrow would never graduate.

An S-Class mage in his thirties had chosen her for bonding.

Yarrow only came back to visit the neighborhood once after leaving school. She would've been around sixteen at the time.

She looked incredibly mature to me, with her long skirt and elegant sun hat.

"Let's go on a walk," she told me.

I babbled like a blue jay as we slipped into the yard next door to my house. The one belonging to that nice mage lady.

A merry wind swished at the leaves of my neighbor's soaring trees.

Yarrow caught briefly at her fine-woven hat to keep it from sailing away on the breeze.

Dappled shadow and sunlight washed over Yarrow's face, her long shining hair.

As I chattered at her, I realized something.

No matter how the wind tugged at her hat, no matter how wildly the shadows of the trees played across her, no matter what I said or didn't say—Yarrow's expression never changed.

She'd worn the same fixed smile from the moment she greeted me to the moment we paused in the shade.

My voice dried up in the back of my throat. Yarrow's smile remained pasted on her face. It looked like it hurt. It looked like—

She took my hand.

My heart didn't skip a beat. Not in the way you'd expect. The air around me felt like a straitjacket. My stomach pinched inward.

Yarrow kept smiling.

"Clematis," she said through her smile.

I couldn't answer.

Her fingers tightened. "You got into the academy?"

I managed a nod.

Her lips faltered. A tiny muscle under her eye twitched. And then she was right back to the same beautiful, radiant, welded-on smile.

"Don't be like me," she said.

There was that voice I'd adored so much. So soothing, so sweet, always with undertones of a whisper. She couldn't yell if she tried.

I attempted to say something.

Yarrow spoke over me. "Don't be like me," she repeated. "If you bond a mage, you'll never be alone in your own head."

Her smile flickered, hardened. "If you excel as a healer, you won't be able to avoid getting bonded. Don't be like me, Clematis."

Years passed before the next time we spoke face to face.

Sometimes I saw Yarrow and her bondmate in the news. Sometimes I saw her around the city, always from a distance. She looked calm, peaceful, happy. The very picture of a healer who had it made.

Yarrow was one of the lucky ones, bonded to a top-tier mage. Yarrow would be set for life.

Whenever people said that, I recalled her clenching my fingers like she wanted to break them. I saw the gleam of wetness in her eyes as she smiled like her life depended on it.

I felt sick.

By then it was too late for me to avoid following in Yarrow's footsteps. I'd already tested into Guralta Academy. And the government gave a full ride to all successful applicants, mages and healers alike.

It was supposed to be an incredible honor. Such an honor that there was no possible way to back out.

I instead became determined to do everything in my power to avoid getting noticed or chosen by any mage.

I ditched the lovely dresses I'd worn to emulate Yarrow. I shaved my head. I stopped talking in the same dulcet tones as her.

I became abrasive, and at times downright obnoxious. On healer assessments, I aimed for aggressively mediocre results.

In a matter of months, I transformed into the exact opposite of the high-achieving teacher-pleaser I'd been all throughout my childhood.

Surprisingly, I kind of enjoyed it.

I liked this new grating version of myself, even if no one else did.

At first I thought of my scowl and my furiously unattractive wardrobe and my off-putting attitude as a set of weapons I would carry with me into the battlefield of boarding school.

Later, it dawned on me that this was just as true and valid a version of myself as the diligent student who'd dreamed of getting into the same academy as her neighborhood crush. Maybe this unpleasant Clematis was the truest Clematis of all.

But a funny thing happened on the way to becoming utterly unlovable.

I met another dark-eyed girl. One right around my age. There was a major difference between her and Yarrow, however.

This girl was a mage.

And not just any mage, like my harmless Class 1 neighbor. No—this girl was an S-Class mage.

The highest class of all. The same class as Yarrow's tyrannical bondmate.

She infuriated me like no one I'd ever met before in my life. The more she frightened me, the more I wanted to kick her in the knees; the more I wanted to tear her to bits. I couldn't stop wanting more chances to rip into her.

Her name was Wisteria Shien.

1

START AT OSMANTHUS CITY. Our fair capital. My hometown. Head southwest down the coast. Picture a narrow barrier island with a long, long bridge binding it to the Osmanthian mainland.

Now picture me and my parents. Three short figures. We shuffled awkwardly around the tram station located at the base of the bridge to Guralta Isle. I didn't want to board that squeaky tram. I didn't want to cross that bridge.

Unlike my parents, I'd always had incredibly sharp magic perception. From here, the skinny island appeared to be engulfed by a miasma of lingering magic.

It was still early spring, cool and windy. Yet Guralta Isle glittered like a heat mirage. The mere sight of that magical haze turned my stomach.

My parents noticed nothing unusual.

You can come home if there are any problems, they assured me. You can come home anytime you want.

The lump in my throat felt like it might split me open.

"Wow. Thanks," I said with maximum sharpness. "I feel so much better now."

"Clematis—"

"Hey, what's the worst that could happen? Oh, yeah—there goes the scholarship. Here come the penalties. You get to be on the hook for all four years of tuition. Even if I get kicked out on my very first day."

My mother tried to cut in again. I spoke right over her. "Yep, I'm sure you can afford it just fine. I'll drop out the second I get sick of school. What a relief!"

I stubbed my toe on my luggage as I trundled it onto the tram. I sensed my parents watching me for as long as they could, until the moment the tram lurched out of sight. I refused to look back.

I'd never spent more than a night or two away from home before. It was a sour parting, and it was entirely my fault.

The clouds above looked like paint smeared across the sky by an angry hand. The tram exuded high-pitched squeals as it scraped across the bridge to Guralta Isle. I wrestled with the urge to hammer my fist on the nearest window. Anything to make that sound stop.

First-year healer students—me among them—got summoned to Guralta Academy a full week before anyone else. Supposedly this would give us a chance to get acclimated to campus before any mages arrived on the scene.

Our orientation started in the beginning of April. It was still too chilly to take a dip in the ocean without the aid of a full-body suit (or magic). I'd never fished or surfed in my life. Only mages could partake in stylish sports like surface racing and water tumbling.

And at least in that first week at school, it's not like they left us healers enough free time to go craft sand sculptures. I could almost forget I was on an island, if not for the constant faint hint of wild salt tainting the air outside.

I won't bore you with the particulars of orientation week. I spent most of it calculating exactly how poorly I could score on exams throughout the year without getting expelled.

My parents had raised me comfortably enough that I'd never had to be too aware of where money comes from or where it goes. Still, I understood that even a single year of academy tuition would catapult my parents deep into debt.

Too deep to ever climb out.

Since I was already stuck here at school, I needed to ensure that the government would keep picking up my tab. I'd fulfill the bare minimum of my academic obligations.

But only the absolute bare minimum. I wouldn't make the same mistake as Yarrow.

I wasn't here to get noticed.

I wasn't here to be a star.

All I needed to do was survive four years without impressing any mages. All I needed to do was make myself out to be one of the least desirable potential partners in the entire student body.

Speaking of which, returning healer students—second-years and higher—came on the scene a week later. So did all the mages.

By then I knew my way around well enough. I knew not to venture near any of the mage housing or mage classroom buildings.

It was laughably easy to figure out which facilities were meant for mage use. The ones that were freshly painted, without a single roof shingle out of place. The ones that glimmered with frivolous decorative magic, with capricious high-up gargoyles and glowing tightropes that stretched arrogantly from roof to roof. The tightropes would never let you fall. At least not if you were a mage.

I certainly wouldn't be willing to try them out myself.

At first I had little trouble avoiding the influx of mage students. They strutted around like pretend soldiers in close-fitting militaristic uniforms and school-issued collars. It would've been funny if not for the fact that the healers on campus (me included) scurried out of their way as if we were legitimately intimidated.

We healers, regardless of gender, wore ankle-length skirts with deep folds pressed in the fabric. Our uniform was a simplified version of traditional healer robes. Prim and subservient.

Me, I just didn't want to stick out. I imitated my fellow healers. I tied my uniform properly. I bowed my head to the mage students, no matter how it grated on me. I shrank back to avoid eye contact.

The mage students, in turn, gazed past me as if I were a rotten potato.

So far, so good.

The first class I ditched was a session of Mage Studies: Introduction to Magiology. A course designed to teach us budding healers everything we needed to know about basic mage physiology. The care and keeping of mages.

The academy wanted us to understand the deep-rooted primal needs of our future healing clients. Or our precious future bondmates. I wanted to gag.

At any rate, I was already familiar with the basics. I'd done a lot of self-study back in the days when my only goal in life was to chase after Yarrow.

There were three reasons I skipped class at the first opportunity.

One, I really didn't want to be there. Simple enough!

Two, to test if I would get written up for it. There were seventy-five first-year healers, and all of us got lumped into the same lecture for Intro to Magiology. As long as I got my classwork done, perhaps no one would notice or care too much about the occasional absence.

Three, to perform reconnaissance. Scout out a good spot to go lurk in when cutting class in the future. I'm nothing if not a planner.

Sadly, my dorm was out of the question. The live-in steward kept a meticulous record of all comings and goings through the main door. I wasn't athletic enough to scale the grimy wall of the building unaided.

Even if I did possess sufficient upper body strength, what then? I'd end up climbing in my own window, lying dolefully in my own bed, and staring up at the sagging ceiling.

Instead I snuck over to the far east end of the island. I slipped past house after house. All at least four stories tall. Some partly on stilts. Most painted varying shades of peach and soft yellow and lavender and blue and grey. At this time of year, they had to be pretty much empty. Or so I hoped.

Mage students could opt into beachfront housing, and many did. But most of them clustered further down the shore, closer to the middle of the island. The beach here at the eastern end was broader and wilder, windswept like a miniature desert, interspersed with roped-off bird sanctuaries and enormous half-sunk stone ruins from ancient times.

A squadron of brown-black pelicans glided silently overhead. Real living pelicans. No sign of the magically crafted gulls that the academy used to spy on us no matter where we went on the island.

For the first time in days, it felt like I could stand up straight and breathe down to the bottoms of my lungs.

I'd been one of the most social kids in my neighborhood. I'd imagined being homesick, and I sure was. I hadn't imagined craving alone time.

But I found myself absolutely elated to realize there was no one else here except seabirds. I stood with my shoes in my hand and dug my toes into the cold sand.

Solitude ran down my throat like the sweetest of water. No healer students side-eying each other. No weary teachers looking at me like they wanted to shamble home and drink themselves into oblivion. No friendly locals dishing out the requisite island gossip about the ghosts of students past.

Above all, no mages.

Until I heard voices.

I was behind a grass-covered dune several times taller than me. Still much closer to the unoccupied rental houses than to the sea. The sand here was broad enough that you could've fit a decent-sized city train station right in the middle of it.

They sounded like three, four people. Boys. Older ones. Probably not first-years. Somewhere on the other side of the dune.

I couldn't see them. I couldn't hear what they were saying. Not in detail. But now I noticed magic gilding the air near those voices. I girded myself to back away.

Something shot through the air like a ball. I ducked, heart thudding.

A bird cried, startlingly close. I looked up.

The ball was a bird. A tern. A little white thing. Magic batted it back and forth in the air. It chirruped plaintively, almost incessantly now. The mages dissolved in laughter.

Okay, I thought. That was one very confused bird. But no harm done. They'd get bored soon enough. Wouldn't they?

Here was the perfect chance to slip away unnoticed.

"*SPIKE!*" hollered the voices.

I didn't see what happened. It was all much too fast. Instead I heard it: the thump of the tiny bird ramming the ground. The sickening silence.

It wasn't stone or concrete or asphalt. Sand was too soft to kill.

Soft, yes. Sand might feel soft if you walked in it barefoot. Not if you slammed into it headfirst from a tremendous height, accelerating as you went.

Okay, I thought. The magical game was over. They'd ruined their toy. They'd give up now, go find a less sadistic pastime.

Not that I wanted anything to do with mages, but mages were human, too. Mages could make mistakes. Maybe it had been an accident. Maybe they hadn't meant to hurl it down quite so hard. As long as this was just a one-time—

More gleeful yelling. They had another bird in the air now. A panicked black-feathered creature. A completely different species from the first.

I studied the scuffed shoes in my hand. A brutal calm overcame me.

I had decent aim at short distances. Surely I could nail a mage or two in the head if I tried.

I started to walk around the side of the dune.

A hand came down on my shoulder to stop me.

To this day, I still think I deserve a Board-certified Medal of Valor for not shrieking my head off.

The hand gripped me harder. With ferocious effort, I forced my scream back down my throat. I turned to glare at the culprit.

A mage held me in place. A very tall, plain girl.

Not plain as in bad-looking—plain as in utterly devoid of expression.

I knew she was a mage student because of the glow of the metaphysical magic core embedded deep in her torso. Because of her uniform. Because of the thick collar around her neck.

She had her uniform mostly unbuttoned. Like she'd forgotten to finish dressing. The breeze flapped at the open sides of her top. Beneath it, she wore a shabby white undershirt.

There was something peculiar about the shape of the magic branches that coiled around her core. Something that set my teeth on edge. Something foul and twisted. Something like a wall full of picture frames hung ever so slightly askew. Something like the squeak of a fork scraping mercilessly at a ceramic plate.

I got all that from a mere half-second glance at her messed-up magic. I had zero interest in further analysis. Momentary panic drained out of me into the sand beneath my feet. Hot irritation swelled up to replace it.

With her free hand, and still without the slightest flicker of emotion on her face, the mage put a finger to her lips. She hadn't said a word yet. I shrugged out of her grip.

I tried to, anyway. She was much stronger than she looked. She didn't seem to be making the least effort to hold me there.

I tried again. Still couldn't break free.

"*Excuse* me," I hissed.

"Don't do it," said the mage. Her voice was startlingly deep, somewhere on the lowest possible end of contralto, and as dull in tone as her face.

"Don't do what?"

The mage glanced at the shoes in my hand. I still had them half-lifted, ready to hurl. Maybe I ought to throw them at her. I had a point-blank shot at her nose.

If I were smart, I'd bow and scrape and simper my way on out of here. I didn't want to give any mage a reason to remember me. Especially not this one. That unnerving empty stare of hers seemed to suggest that she was carefully contemplating the best way to flay my face off and eat it.

But I wasn't smart. I was angry. I brandished my shoes.

"You see what they were doing over there?" At least I knew to keep my voice low. The mages guffawing on the far side of the dune wouldn't hear us.

She nodded.

"You don't think someone should stop them? Maybe you indulge in a bit of animal torture yourself, huh? Don't tell me this is some kind of mage student tradition."

She leaned in closer. I stiffened.

"You can't stop them," she told me.

"Don't tell me what I—"

"You're a healer," she said, right next to my ear. "Don't even try it."

My blood went rigid. I scrabbled futilely for a comeback. Belated fear bloomed deep in the pit of my belly.

From some mages around my age I could sense imperious condescension. Others radiated curiosity, as if we healer students were pets up for sale. Still others—the self-styled chivalrous among them—took on an attitude of paternalistic protectiveness.

From this looming black-eyed girl, I sensed nothing but factual detachment. An absolute dearth of interest. She wasn't just aloof. She was on another dimension altogether.

Yet she was also very, very close. I could see her breathing, if just barely. Her hand pressed down on my shoulder as if she were trying to make me shorter. I couldn't think of a single thing left to say.

She wasn't wrong, of course. Confronting those other mages wouldn't end well for me.

I recalled the sounds that little white bird had made, and the sounds it had stopped making.

That grotesque game over there—it was like a preview of life as a healer. Tossed around haplessly, a plaything for mages.

And then—

I'd been so choked up with helpless fury and furious helplessness that it took me some time to register a couple of things that should've been obvious.

Such as the fact that this girl had absurdly, incomprehensibly long hair: a thick black braid looped around her shoulders and waist like a sash, with plenty still left over to dangle down by her legs.

And the fact that the mages over on the other side of the dune were still hollering at each other, but now in tones of confusion rather than merriment.

And the fact that a sudden fog was filling the air, white and cold and as rapid as dry ice. The fog billowed up so densely that it began to obscure the mage girl's face.

Magic perception isn't tied to any specific sense organ, the way sight comes from your eyes or taste from your tongue. Everyone has some degree of magic perception. It's just that for a lot of people, it's so faint as to be downright indistinguishable.

As for those of us who do consciously perceive magic, our entire body can serve as the organ we use to discern it. Maybe that's why I got a chill when I saw the magic twining through the fog.

Just one single branch of her magic. Warped and jerky. Shaped like a limb that had been beaten till it shattered, then healed in all the wrong places. It crooked past me as the fog thickened and the yelling boys got more muffled.

For no reason in particular, I imagined that long spiraling thread of magic cinching tighter and tighter around me, stealing my breath.

In reality her magic didn't touch me. Not for a second. But the fog gushing out of it covered us from head to toe, until the dune beside us vanished. Until I could no longer make out my own sandy ankles.

"Don't go anywhere," the mage said, close enough to make me flinch.

Her hand left my shoulder. She walked past me. One step, two steps. And then she was gone. Devoured by her own fog.

I knew better than to bolt. I had no idea which way was which. The thick whispering of the ocean had receded. Now it seemed to come from all around me, a distant jeering crowd.

The fog filled my lungs. I hugged my uniform jacket closer. Not that it made much of a difference.

I heard irritated male voices, their words indistinct.

The tall girl murmured something in reply. She sounded exactly as cold and monotonous as she had when speaking in my ear.

A stifled silence.

Sheepish mumbles.

Male voices receding.

The fog thinned almost as quickly as it had come. I gulped naked air as if I'd been drowning.

The nearest sand dune came back into view. So did the stone ruins tumbling off into the sea far to the right. So did the distant washed-out line of the desolate blue horizon.

I peeked around the side of the dune, past tufts of tall bobbing grass.

The girl with the long braid stood gazing at the sand as if she'd been alone the whole time. No birds in sight except a few spindly sandpipers way down by the water's edge.

At first I thought the other mage students had completely vanished. Finally I spotted them. Already far down the beach, and rapidly getting farther.

The girl didn't move. She didn't glance up. I took a few tentative steps back.

Then I realized what she was staring down at.

Look, I didn't mean to walk over and join her. It just kind of happened. Clearly the magical fog had addled my brain.

Together we studied the corpse of a solitary white bird. It looked small enough to fit in my palm.

"You can't bury it with your eyes," I said.

The mage said nothing. After a moment, she knelt and started digging with her hands. Her dark braid slipped down to drag along the ground as she worked. She'd have a fun time trying to get the sand out later.

I cleared my throat. Still felt like I had fog in there, tickling my vocal cords.

"The other bird. The second one. Did it get away?"

The mage nodded.

I must have a bit of a self-destructive streak, because I kept talking.

"Great," I said. "One dead. One saved. For now, anyway. Maybe next time they'll move on to dismembering sea turtles."

"They won't do it again," the mage said flatly.

What, had they sworn her a pinky promise?

She dug into the sand around the dead bird to scoop it up without directly touching it. She moved it to the shallow hole she'd clawed with her fingers. She filled in the grave and smoothed it over.

Her unbuttoned uniform top hung slack around her. I pointed at the pins fastened above her pocket.

"You're a Rat," I said. In other words, a first-year student like me. The other mages had definitely sounded older. "I know how it works here. You can't make upperclassmen do a damn thing."

She rose slowly to her feet, brushed the sand from her palms. Wind coming off the ocean pushed black strands of hair around her face, almost into the corners of her mouth.

She gazed down at me from her full height without any emotion whatsoever. Just dark dead-looking eyes.

You are very small, those eyes said. You are very trivial.

That was when I had my epiphany.

"Your magic," I blurted.

"You know how it works here," she replied, as if mocking me.

"That's not fair," I said. "You—you're covering it up. Hiding it inside itself. Is that even—is that even a thing?"

"You know how it works here," the first-year mage said again, in the exact same way as before.

And I knew precisely what she meant.

Mage society had its hierarchies, its great families, its politicians, its celebrities. But one factor meant more to them—to our land of Osmanthus as a whole—than anything else.

Power. Sheer magical power. They quantified it rigorously. They classified all mages accordingly.

In theory, the greatest respect and honor was supposed to eventually flow to those with the greatest power. Regardless of birth name. Regardless of age. Regardless of personality.

Even if they were a lanky teenage girl with questionable posture, negative levels of charisma, zero facial expression, a poor-fitting mage uniform, and the darkest, dullest voice I'd ever heard in my life.

I couldn't count her magic branches. She had too many. She'd coiled them inside her like snakes, one behind another behind another behind another. Surely it hurt her to twist them so strangely. Yet she stayed rooted in place like a scarecrow. Like she felt nothing.

My throat spasmed. There was nothing left in my mouth to swallow.

I didn't need to count her branches anymore. I already knew down to my bones that this was the most powerful mage I'd ever seen in my life.

I tried to remember what I'd said to her. Things I definitely shouldn't have said, that's for sure.

I started to inch away. Like I planned on merrily hopping backwards across the entire length of sand. Past the empty pastel beach houses. All the way back to the stale-smelling lecture hall.

I should've just kept my butt planted there the entire time. Then I could've avoided this. Avoided her.

"Don't trip," said the mage with the braid.

Her face didn't move. In her weird wooden way, it felt like she was laughing at me all the same.

I flung my last scrap of dignity to the wind. I turned my back on her and fled.

2

No one liked my roommate. I'm not saying this to disparage her. It was a simple fact. I wasn't exactly drowning in newfound friends myself.

Her name was Saya, and she had mage fever.

Early on in orientation, we introduced ourselves to our healer hallmates. The guy a few doors down turned out to be a maniac for hot sauce—the spicier the better. The girls across from us were fraternal twins, studious and reserved.

Other neighbors spoke with hard-to-parse countryside accents. They hailed from the far eastern border of Osmanthus, from tiny towns I'd never heard of.

And what did everyone learn about Saya?

That she was here at school to hunt down her future bondmate.

Preferably one who was stupidly powerful, stupidly rich, and who would therefore offer Saya and her entire family a life secure in the lap of luxury.

This was by no means an uncommon attitude. There was a reason people had praised Yarrow for getting bonded to such a high-ranking mage at such a young age. Even though she'd ended up dropping out of school in the process.

The problem with Saya was that she lacked decorum. She didn't hide her ambition. Other healer students found her vocal hunger embarrassing. Despite the fact that on the inside, many of them nursed the same dream as her.

I got along with Saya well enough, actually. I couldn't relate to her one bit, nor she to me. But hey, she had a solid reason to be here at Guralta Academy, and she wasn't ashamed of it.

Good for her. Nothing wrong with different people having different goals.

So I let Saya plaster her wall with soft-focus portraits of famous duelists and other popular mages. I helped her take care of her hermit crabs. I told our hallmates to stuff it when they badmouthed her behind her back.

(I was under no illusion that they actually stopped badmouthing her. They just learned to stop doing it around me.)

Saya, in turn, tolerated my nightly tossing and turning.

This fitfulness had nothing to do with being away from home. I'd always been an erratic sleeper, to the point that I used to avoid staying over with friends.

Yet the nightmares got drastically worse right after I met that empty-eyed mage with the long braid.

Now I seemed to suffer violently every single time I closed my eyes to drift off. I'd wake up drenched in icy sweat.

Sometimes I went over to the windowsill to calm myself, huddled in blankets. Sometimes I caught Saya watching me from her bed with one eye open, saying nothing.

When I was little, I told my parents every single detail of my dreams. About being stabbed in the gut, crushed by dark machinery, flung off cliffs by shadowy hands. Over time I came to realize how much it pained them to hear this. Over time I stopped saying anything at all.

By the time they sent me off to the academy, my parents must've thought I was cured.

Doctors used to blabber about how the nightmares were a sign of sublimated stress. To me this sounded ridiculous. I'd never been an anxious child.

Older now, and trapped at Guralta Academy, I began to wonder if those doctors had been onto something. I jerked awake at terrible hours. Inwardly I blamed it on the mage with the black braid.

No—that was a foolish way to describe her.

The mage with too much magic. The mage with a monster inside her.

I still didn't know her name.

Running into her had spooked me enough that, at least for a time, I went back to attending all my classes. I kept my head down as I scampered from building to building. I rushed home to my dorm as soon as I finished up for the day.

The healer dorms were open to all genders. But not to mages.

With so much time spent taking refuge in our room, I got to know Saya better. Even as our classmates shunned her. She taught me the names of her hermit crabs. She quizzed me on Vorpal Studies. I helped with her Intro to Magiology homework.

One evening, Saya leapt up from her chair as soon as I came back from the healer baths.

"Don't change out here," she warned. "Change in the closet."

I still had a towel wrapped around me. "What?"

Saya had a fawn-colored bob and bulbous eyes. Even the faintest expression of alarm made it look as if those eyes were about to come popping right out of her face. She pointed at the window.

A black-headed gull flapped outside, startlingly close to the glass. A laughing gull. That's what they were called in the wild, at least.

This one gleamed of magic.

"Must be malfunctioning," I said. "Just close the curtains."

Saya shook her head furiously and launched into a series of elaborate hand gestures. After some repetition, I began to get the gist.

"You think some pervert in the administration is spying on us," I translated. "Trying to watch us change. Well, if they wanted to do that, they've probably got better ways than using the gulls."

I marched past her, towel cinched firmly around me. I pushed the window open one-handed and shoved the sliding screen aside.

I gave the magical gull a good smack. It tumbled away into the bushes far below.

This wasn't animal abuse, mind you. The spy gull was made from magic, without a single spark of life to it. The whole island swarmed with them.

I'd have resented their beady eyes mightily if I were a local, or a visitor who had nothing to do with the academy. But I guess people just got used to them. They'd become an inevitable part of the scenery, as natural as broken shells on the beach.

Afterward, I pulled the curtains and finished dressing.

"Doubt the birds can see through curtains," I said. "But if they can see through curtains, they can see through a door. If they can see through doors, it doesn't matter whether I change in a closet or stick my naked butt out the window. Thanks for your concern, though."

Saya seemed dissatisfied. "They've been acting strange lately."

"How?"

"They're watching us."

"Yeah. That's their job."

"Us in particular. I've never seen them hovering right outside anyone else's window."

I took out my diagnostics homework. Saya kept bringing up the birds. At last I resorted to distracting her by asking for mage gossip.

This worked far too well. In taking Saya's mind off the seagulls, I'd inadvertently sentenced myself to hours of chitchat. I made no secret of the fact that I was only half-listening.

Rumor had it, Saya told me, that senior mage students were trading around psychoactive magic.

Typical, I thought. Why'd they have to make everything magical? They had so many other options. They could try to grow their own mushrooms. Or go foraging for fermented marine flora. Or procure under-the-table alcohol from local stores. Or gulp down pharmaceuticals.

But no—for thrill-seeking young mages, only magic would do.

At this point, we were only a few weeks into our first semester. Somehow, Saya had already found time to compile a dossier on all the mage students she considered worthy of research.

That seemed to mean anyone who met at least one of the following three conditions:

(1) Ranked Class 7 or higher.

(2) In the school's originator program.

(3) From one of the great mage families.

The positive side of hearing Saya drone on about this was that it gave me an idea of who I ought to avoid.

"There's at least one Minashiro in our year," she said. "Class 9-4. Already slated to join the student council."

"Good for them." I didn't bother trying to sound sincere. A high-class mage from a famous family. Two out of three. That person must've earned a special place of honor on her list.

"There's also a Shien. She might be S-Class."

The same tier as Yarrow's bondmate. My gut clenched. I suspected I knew exactly who Saya was talking about, and I wished I didn't.

"A Shien," I echoed. I'd heard that family name recently. Not just from Saya. And not just in reference to the black-eyed mage on the beach, the one too lazy to button up her uniform.

Couldn't remember where I'd heard it. From my other dormmates? From one of the locals working at the school store?

"Her brothers went to Guralta, too," Saya added. "They graduated a while back. Five years ago. Eight years ago. Maybe more."

"Shien brothers ... alumni ... sounds familiar."

"It should. People still tell stories. Teachers. Students. Even locals." Saya turned to push books around on her already perfectly organized desk. "Better hope the Shien in our year isn't anything like her brothers."

"You aren't gunning for her, then," I said. "Not even if she's an S-Class?"

"And in the originator program, too."

"Three out of three. What a catch."

Saya shook her head. "Dozens of students dropped out when her older brothers were in school. *Because* her brothers were in school.

"Not just healers. Mages, too. They say the ones who had a chance to drop out were much luckier than the ones who got forced to stay."

Saya might be nosy, but she rarely spoke ill of any mage. I'd already been inclined to steer clear of the girl from the Shien clan.

The darkness in Saya's tone told me my instincts were right.

Stay away from that girl. Stay wary.

It had to be her, the one who'd made the fog. I'd glimpsed at least some of her inner magic, much as she tried to twist and hide it. I'd glimpsed enough that it made perfect sense for her to be S-Class: the highest tier of mage in Osmanthus.

On the plus side, I wouldn't have to worry about co-ed lessons—about being forced to work directly with mage students—for at least a few more months.

Or so I thought.

I soon learned how very wrong I was. Once May came around, the majority of us first-years would have to leave the island for a week-long training camp.

A full week of intensive mage-healer fieldwork. My worst nightmare.

If only I'd kept cutting classes. Sufficiently poor attendance would've disqualified me from the field trip. By the time I found out about it, there wasn't enough time left to make up the difference.

I contemplated other ways to get in trouble, and therefore relinquish my travel privileges. Blatantly cheat on schoolwork? Kiss a random mage?

Too risky. My parents couldn't afford for me to get outright expelled.

Start a fight? That required a co-conspirator. I wasn't about to go around randomly punching innocent bystanders. Saya wouldn't understand, much less cooperate.

Which was why I decided to fake illness. Food poisoning, perhaps. A believable story, considering the type of slop they fed us healers. But I'd have to make it disgustingly convincing.

A few days in advance, I did a test run. I pretended to have a terrible headache. This taught me that although the administration strictly controlled their supply of curative magic cuttings, they were rather lax about regular over-the-counter medication. Excellent.

The afternoon before the trip, the mage students held a pentathlon. Five showy tests of magical prowess. Saya went to watch, of course. So did just about everyone else.

That made it the perfect time to strike.

I scuttled my way over to the infirmary closest to the healer side of campus. It wasn't a healers-only facility, but I couldn't imagine any mage going out of their way to set foot there. Surely they'd consider it beneath them.

No nurses in attendance. They were probably cheering and clapping at the mage pentathlon, too.

Black scuff marks covered the infirmary floor, as if it were a test paper dinged for having all the wrong answers.

The windows stood open. A lukewarm breeze stirred transparent gray-white curtains.

The beds, too, had curtains. All drawn fully shut. All still and opaque, woven through with stifling privacy magic.

I did a quick spin once I entered. Making sure no one else was there, and no sneaky seagulls were watching.

Next to each sickbed stood a hoya plant, dark leaves dripping all the way down to the floor, pale pink-white flowers hanging in upside-down clusters like inverted umbrellas.

My parents kept a few similar plants at home. At night, the tiny felt-textured flowers would release an overwhelming perfume. Yet during the day their scent retreated, becoming virtually undetectable. Right now I smelled nothing.

I softly closed the door behind me.

Your basic fever-reducers and antacids were stashed in a locked cabinet at the back of the room. I picked the lock with a pair of paper clips.

This was not an impressive feat. The mechanism was about as basic as it gets. I definitely couldn't have cracked any of the other locked drawers, some of which glistened with a slick of protective magic.

I rooted carefully through jars of pills and sachets of powdered medicine. I didn't want to take an enormous quantity of drugs. Nothing that would risk permanent organ damage. I just didn't want the success of my faux illness to be solely reliant on my amateur acting skills.

I did have a back-up plan, of course. I hadn't been totally confident in my ability to pick the lock. And there was no guarantee that the cabinet's contents would be of any real use.

But that back-up plan would have to serve as my absolute last resort. Anything else would be preferable. Even a full course of fast-acting laxatives.

It was preternaturally quiet in the infirmary. So quiet that I jumped at the sound of my own hand pushing around pill bottles.

Yet I didn't notice anything changing behind me. I didn't notice anything creeping up on me. Not until a slight movement—a sly shadow—invaded my field of vision.

The first dark flicker of motion made me think of a cockroach. I held my ground.

Then something shot up and slammed the cabinet door shut, quick as a whip, nearly severing my fingers in the process. I yanked my arm back just in time. I whirled, a shout trapped high in my throat.

All the bed curtains were still closed. But as I watched, a long black rope of hair slithered back toward the furthest bed like a viper retreating to its nest.

I moved without thinking. I stalked after that fleeing rope of hair. I stood glowering by the bed at the very far end of the room.

I flung open the curtains.

A familiar-looking mage lay curled on her side in a slovenly tracksuit, dull eyes half-lidded, her thick black braid gradually shrinking down to a slightly less impossible length.

"*What*," I ground out.

She showed no sign of comprehension.

I shoved my fingers in her face. "You almost took off my hand!"

The mage went slightly cross-eyed, as if counting my digits one by one. Then she held out her own palm. "Glasses."

"Excuse me?"

She gestured at her bedside hoya plant. Which was well within her reach. Closer to her than to me, in fact.

A pair of black-rimmed glasses hung precariously from one of the meandering vines. I contemplated the mage's blank expectant face. I contemplated the glasses.

I reached over and picked them up by the lenses—using both hands, so I could get my fingerprints smeared over as much of the glass as physically possible. I deposited them in her waiting palm.

She sat up to don her glasses. She blinked. She removed them and, without comment, attempted to clean them with the hem of her track jacket. Her efforts only seemed to make the smearing worse.

She gave up and put them back on her face. Her eyes dropped to my right hand again.

"Looks intact," she said.

I was sorely tempted to curl my fingers into a fist and show her exactly how intact they were.

She's a member of the dreaded Shien clan, I reminded myself. A powerful mage from a powerful family. Don't do anything stupid.

"You were searching for something," said the Shien mage.

"Yeah, until you slammed the cabinet door on me."

"Locked it, too."

"What? When?"

She shrugged, as if to say *I work fast*.

"I was searching for something, all right," I said. "This is an infirmary. I'm sick as a dog. Might vomit all over you if I don't get some help, stat. You don't want that. So why don't you—"

She looked at me with such a dearth of either alarm or skepticism that I had no idea how to continue.

"Don't," she said as I spluttered.

I seized at this. Couldn't afford to be choosy. She hadn't offered me any other material to riff on.

"Don't what?" I demanded. "Don't retch at you? Can't make any promises. Don't interrupt your nap? Let me finish my search, then. I'll be out of your hair in a matter of minutes."

"Don't do anything stupid," she said, unmoved.

What a coincidence. That was exactly what I kept telling myself.

Wait—did this mage fancy herself a hero?

Was she trying to be charitable?

That had to be it. This mage saw me as one of those tormented birds out on the beach. Beaten down; in need of saving.

"Listen." I spoke in the most rational tone I could muster. "I'm not—I'm not digging around for pills because I'm trying to off myself, okay. I'm just trying to weasel my way out of training camp. That's all. Nothing to worry about."

Having made my excuses, I attempted to leave.

Her black braid snaked out and caught at my wrist, pulling me up short.

"I don't recommend skipping camp," she said.

I couldn't believe what I was hearing. "Look at you," I snapped. "You're skipping the mage pentathlon. That's just as big a deal. If not bigger."

"I was excused."

"And that's all I want, too," I said. "To be excused from the trip. What's it to you?"

I shook my forearm in an effort to free myself. Her braid coiled tighter in response. The breeze from the open windows faltered, then redoubled in strength. Sea birds cried piercingly somewhere far out of sight.

I fought not to focus on the magic branches curled around her core—intangible, seemingly dormant, but so very many of them.

"It's nothing to me, your attendance or absence," she said. "I don't know who you are."

"Of course you don't. So—"

"But I'm a Shien."

What was that supposed to mean? My mouth had gone infuriatingly dry.

"I already knew," I said. "Famous, aren't you?"

Her hair dragged at me like a leash, with the power of the single strand of magic braided through it. The skin beneath itched hotly, as if I were developing hives. Maybe I was allergic to her: to the brutality of overweening magical power.

I dug my heels in until she pulled so hard that I had no choice but to stumble forward, to stoop over her.

Still entrenched in her sickbed, implacable as a sea-hammered rock, the Shien mage looked up at me over the thick black rims of her glasses. "Not everyone goes to training camp."

"Exactly. They won't miss me. What's one less?"

She wouldn't let me break eye contact. "There's a tradition among mage students. A few always stay back on purpose. Mages are given the option of staying."

Whereas healers could only wriggle out of the trip by getting outright disqualified. Due to poor academic performance, for instance. It was considered a privilege to attend. The type of privilege you couldn't turn down of your own volition.

That said, the very weakest—the most unfit—were always eliminated. So why not me?

"Even mages don't all think it's a wonderful thing, then," I said. "Even some mages want to skip out."

"Those who stay behind have to do remedial work," she told me. "But overall they have more free periods. Less supervision."

Her voice was gravelly, as if I really had woken her up from a deep nap. There was a discomfiting rawness to its texture. It felt like something physical brushing me.

"The trip lasts a week. My brothers always stayed back." She paused. "Can you guess what they called it?"

Only now did panic finally finish clawing its way all the way up from my bowels to my brain.

What if a surveillance gull skirted by the window and saw us? Two students. A healer and a mage. A closed door. A bed with curtains. No chaperone.

"We can't—" Sheer urgency seemed to numb my lips, my tongue. It was like trying to speak in a dream. "We can't be alone like this."

"They called it hunting season," she said.

She showed no sign of releasing me.

Babbling wouldn't get me anywhere. I swallowed. I forced myself to speak slowly and distinctly.

"Are you going on the trip?" I asked.

The Shien mage didn't answer.

"You are," I said. "Then I'm staying."

She started to open her mouth. As if to give me more orders. Or to tell me what a fool I was.

I cut her off. "We'll get in huge trouble if anyone catches us meeting in private," I reminded her. "A first-year healer and a first-year mage. All alone behind a closed door. That's classic fraternization."

I realized as I spoke that, realistically speaking, I was the only one who would ever suffer any consequences. The world would end before Guralta Academy saw fit to expel an S-Class mage. And one in the originator program, no less. A mage backed by the full influence of the Shien clan.

"Let—let go," I said, almost helpless. My attempts at an argument had run out of steam. I had no plan for how to actually make her do it. "Let go of me."

To my astonishment, she did.

She let go immediately.

I stumbled back, clutching protectively at my wrist. Gone were any thoughts of pilfering laxatives.

Her braid slithered back into bed with her. Her fingers rose briefly to the collar around her neck, the same one worn by all mage students under a certain age. It looked as if she wanted to scratch red lines in the skin beneath.

The smart thing to do would be to cut my losses. Mumble an apology. Or simply say no more.

The smart thing to do would be to turn my back and leave. Get out of here as soon as possible. Before anyone caught us together.

I thought of standing barefoot in the sand, smothered by her fog. I'd fled her once, galloped off without looking back.

No shame in that. I could flee her again. No better way to demonstrate my intelligence, really. But I didn't want to. I didn't want to be the one running away twice in a row.

I squared my stance. Crossed my arms. Raised my chin. This time, I'd get the last word.

"I appreciate the warning," I said. "And I don't want to judge anyone solely by their family. That's no fair. The thing is, training camp might come with its own form of hunting season. I've heard whispers about the hazing.

"A big-name, high-class mage like you could go to any school in the country. Or you could skip the academy and call up a personal mentor to train you. There are very few co-ed institutions in Osmanthus. No need to go out of your way to pick one. No need to mingle with us riffraff."

"Guralta is prestigious enough for any mage."

"Maybe. Or maybe you showed up here to continue your brothers' work. Maybe you're trying to trick me into attending training camp. I can't judge either way. I don't know you."

"Wisteria Shien," she said.

It took me a moment to realize she was pronouncing a name. "Wisteria Shien," I repeated. "Wisteria Shien. Really? Not Shien Wisteria?"

"Wisteria Shien."

Given name first. Family name last. Her name order meant she was adopted. A common practice among the more renowned mage clans. They collected powerful children like trading cards.

"That's a lot of syllables," I said. "Wist-er-i-a. Like the plant? How flowery."

Wisteria Shien made a muffled noise.

"What?"

"Nothing," she said gravely. "And you?"

Unlike her, my family name came first. "Asa Clematis."

"You're a flower, too."

"But one whole syllable less."

"Only one."

"That's more than—uh, a twenty-five percent difference."

"You don't sound very confident."

"Do you judge people's correctness based on how confident they sound? Big mistake."

In the ensuing silence, I caught myself waiting for her to react again. She didn't oblige.

Her braid lay in a heap of coils beside her like a rope for rappelling down cliffs. She appeared content to keep looking at me—or through me—without expectation. Without amusement. Without any attempt at contorting her face to put me even a little bit at ease.

You don't understand how much those microscopic expressions matter until you encounter someone who flat-out refuses to play along. A minuscule widening or narrowing of the eyes. A second of tension near the brows or lips. A nod as small as a twitch. Everything that says *I'm listening, I hear you* or *please hear me, please understand.*

She had none of that. Her gaze didn't make me feel like a human being. I felt more like lifeless flames crackling languorously in a fireplace.

In a way, this made me a lot less self-conscious. She gazed into me with the unvarnished blankness of someone alone before the fire at the end of a long cold day, or in the midst of an endless solitary night.

I made a inadvertent sound in the back of my throat.

"Time to take my leave, Ms. Shien," I said.

"Please don't call me that."

"Time to take my leave, Cap'n W."

"That's more syllables than Wisteria."

"Sounds less like an old lady, though."

She didn't move a muscle, but her braid started to uncoil. The magic in it glinted menacingly.

I relented. "Fine. I'll think of something else."

That counted as getting the last word in. Right? Right?

I peeked over my shoulder as I left the infirmary. She'd already closed the curtains around her sickbed.

For the first time, it occurred to me to wonder what was wrong with her. Didn't appear to be a physical illness. Not one visible from the outside, at least.

I was surprised, in retrospect, that the administration would let such a promising first-year mage completely skip out on the much-hyped pentathlon.

There would be other such events throughout the year, of course. But this pentathlon was (according to Saya) a prime chance for both teachers and fellow students to size up the incoming crop of mages. To assess how they performed under pressure.

Anyway, I knew better than to attempt to crack my way back into the re-locked medicine cabinet. Wisteria Shien would stop me all over again.

I thus accepted my defeat with characteristic grace and maturity. I closed the infirmary door behind me with only the smallest of vengeful bangs. Time to activate the ol' backup plan.

3

THE NIGHT BEFORE the first day of training camp, more magical surveillance gulls flapped forebodingly outside our window.

Saya tried to report the gulls' misbehavior to the dorm steward. Wait, I told her. I wanted to see if I could figure it out on my own.

While Saya bustled around and packed her things for camp, I assessed our shared room with fresh eyes.

A few days ago, a spackled sheet of white paint the size of a dinner plate had fallen on my face. Just as I started to doze off. It wasn't the only part of the ceiling starting to peel, either.

We didn't live in luxury like the mage students. We did our own laundry. We cleaned our own dorms and classrooms.

No caviar in our cafeteria: we had mackerel soup for breakfast and grilled mackerel for lunch and stewed mackerel for dinner. You may think I'm exaggerating, and I am. But only a little.

I'd planned on resenting every second I spent at the academy. I still embraced this spirit of fervent resentment. I had to admit, however, that constantly burning with discontent was a bit more exhausting than I'd bargained for.

Much to my chagrin, I also found that I had an incurable streak of optimism. Or perhaps something different—optimism felt like the wrong word for it. I was gifted at mining a weird depth of enjoyment from prosaic aspects of day-to-day life.

Put simply, I wasn't miserable here. Far from it.

I didn't like having to worry about a mage lurking around every corner, but I did like watching airships pass over the island. I'd never seen so many airships in my life. There must've been a large airfield somewhere nearby, over on the mainland. Just about every single airship flying west across the sea seemed to pass Guralta Isle.

I waved at all of them, stopping only when a teacher informed me that they hardly ever carried regular passengers. Instead they were packed to the brim with cargo and the occasional diplomat. Osmanthus wasn't on the best terms with the people of distant continents. Yet trade vessels still flowed back and forth among the clouds, unstoppable.

I liked the strangeness of the broken driftwood furniture on the first floor of the dorm. It was a type of wood that didn't grow in the native forests of Osmanthus, that's for sure. It had almost the exact texture of well-moisturized human skin.

I liked the random stone ruins that jutted up here and there all over the island. I liked the colossal outdoor sundials and statues of flightless birds scattered about campus. I liked watching the geese and ducks and horses.

Yes, there were horses. A whole stable full of them. Ridden exclusively by the school's heavily decorated equestrian team, which only accepted those with previous experience, and which coincidentally had not a single healer on their roster.

Anyway, I told my parents all this each time I borrowed one of the dorm's transceiver shells. I forced myself to claim I liked it here. Figured I'd better reassure them, after how I'd picked a fight when they were just trying to say goodbye at the tram.

They worried about me not eating enough vegetables. They worried about riptides and ravenous marine fauna. They worried about typhoon season, which wouldn't be coming till much later in the year. They worried so much that I may have overdone it a bit in response, waxing on and on about all the best parts of island life.

I wasn't lying, though. I did like the corny nautical decor, mildew and all. I did like the plethora of bougainvillea tumbling from window boxes, in colors so brilliant they looked toxic. And the mosaic tile fountains. And how nearly all my classmates started collecting things like sea glass and fossilized shark teeth.

Mages aside, I had to find something to like about this place. Graduation was still at least four years away.

Like our classmates, Saya and I had acquired a few island finds of our own. We left them on our windowsill. These, perhaps, were what lured the gulls.

I tested holding up a sheet so the birds bobbing outside couldn't see the rest of the room. They still kept coming.

That settled it. Either it was me they wanted, or something special on the sill. The window itself was exactly the same as in neighboring rooms. Nor were we the only ones who put things there. I'd seen hallmates using theirs as a makeshift bookshelf.

The gulls were magical constructs, yes, but that didn't mean they were skillfully crafted. In all likelihood, quite the opposite.

Much of the magic on campus—on the island as a whole—was student work. The curly shells I used to talk to my parents, for instance, contained a magic skill called Transceiver. Several redundant copies of it, usually, grafted on by multiple different mage students. Most long since graduated.

No, mages weren't allowed in our dorm. But their artifacts—their practice magic—lingered everywhere. In the painted lampshades whose pattern changed to reflect the weather each morning. On the floor of the bathhouse, where a layer of magic was supposed to protect us from slipping. In the wonky melodium Saya had picked up from the Heap, a pile of discarded or abandoned mage projects that anyone could scavenge for free.

In reality, I think only us healers took advantage of the Heap. Mage students weren't particularly interested in dumpster diving.

Anyway, there was no market for much of this stuff outside the island. Normally, if you wanted to avoid slipping in the bath, you'd buy a mat for it. Not a magical one. Or you'd learn to watch your step.

Just because magic *could* be used for something didn't mean you could make a living off it. But the mages here cycled through all sorts of eccentric (and arguably useless) skills as part of their learning process.

I eyed, one by one, the objects arranged on our sill. An indigo rock from the ruins. A book of botanical art. A glass of cloudy yellow water in which a plant cutting struggled not to die.

In the dim twilight beyond the window—past the greedy-eyed flapping gulls—expansive footpaths wound around campus, magically lit up by garish installations of imitation coral.

The only other item on the windowsill was a magical trinket. A small model of a dark, spiky lighthouse.

If switched on, it glowed red whenever the sun went down. We'd been using it as a nightlight. There was a mechanism to increase the intensity of the light, although we always kept it at the lowest level. Right now its illumination wasn't even strong enough to paint the entire sill.

I picked the model up and waggled it at the gulls.

They went wild. For a frantic moment, I thought they might start body-slamming the glass. I'd never drawn the curtains so fast.

An accident? I wondered.

Perhaps the same mage student—be they current or graduated—had worked on both the lighthouse and the seagulls. Perhaps some sort of unintended resonance was occurring here.

Or perhaps they'd made the lighthouse a lure on purpose.

I could see the use in that. Call as many gulls as possible to a location of your choosing—and in the meantime, you could do anything you wanted elsewhere. Without the administration's sentries observing you.

That sort of decoy operation would be done for the very first time you got caught, of course. Considering that the lighthouse had just been sitting with all the other junk in the Heap, its creator must've deployed it judiciously enough to avoid detection.

I felt a frisson of admiration for the mind of the unknown mage.

Saya and I had been letting the tower shine its red light out our window every night, oblivious. At least we'd set it as dim as it could go, and closed the curtains while we slept.

Even so, the administration must've noticed a handful of their watchers acting strangely at certain times of day. Maybe the ones drawn to our window were still too few to be of tremendous concern.

Besides, the gulls were student work. Maybe all of them had a couple of inexplicable quirks.

I flipped the tower over in my hand. The initials *S. N.* were etched into the base. No accompanying date.

"Don't you need to pack?" Saya asked from behind me.

I didn't, because I wasn't planning on going anywhere. "Got some noodles to eat first," I said.

I pocketed the model tower. Saya didn't appear to notice.

"We just had dinner."

"I'm a hungry girl." I grabbed the aforementioned package of noodles off my desk and waved them at her. "I'll go have these outside, actually. Wouldn't want to gas you with the fumes."

Saya regarded me fixedly with those protuberant eyes of hers. "You said your spice tolerance wasn't that great."

"Oh, I was just being modest." I breezed out of the room before she could say anything more.

I was not being modest. Traditional spicy cabbage made my nose run and my eyes water.

These noodles, meanwhile, came with about ten dire warnings on the package. Not for consumption by children or pregnant people. Not for consumption by those with a delicate heart. That sort of thing.

I'd begged them off the spice maniac down the hall. Thinking he had a new comrade in arms, he'd also jubilantly lent me a few bottles of his hottest sauces. Plus disposable gloves, yogurt, bread, milk, and ice cream. Guess he didn't want me to die.

"Don't let the noodles touch your lips when you eat," he'd said. "And whatever you do, don't rub your eyes."

After adding hot water to the noodles, I ate them on a bench outside. Being outside, I didn't outright scream. But I came awfully close. Thank heaven I'd picked a spot with zero foot traffic.

Look—I won't reenact it for you. Suffice it to say that there was no taste I could decipher. Nothing but pain.

I was pretty sure, in fact, that it was by far the worst pain I'd ever felt in my life.

Each time I retched, the pain rebounded. The yogurt, which was supposed to offer some measure of solace, did absolutely nothing. It turned an ominous shade of red as I ate it. I used white bread like a sponge to sop excess spice from my mouth, then spit it out in the bushes. Disgusting.

Afterward, in the brief moments when I wasn't trapped in the bathroom, I cried incoherently to Saya about how my lips had doubled in size.

"You did this to yourself." Understandably, she couldn't muster up much sympathy.

I moaned something pitiful in response.

"Hubris," Saya retorted. "You really thought you could take it?"

"At least now you don't have to ask anyone else to look after your hermit crabs while you're gone," I said.

Or tried to. It didn't come out nearly that smoothly. But I think Saya got the gist.

Her eyes narrowed. "Don't claim you did this for my hermit crabs."

"I love animals," I said, garbled but triumphant.

There was no question of me going on the trip. Early the next morning, I was back to weeping frantically into my sleeves while engaging in intimate relations with the nearest toilet.

The dorm steward came to check on me every so often. No classmates showed up, not even those who would also be missing out training camp. I could hardly blame them.

Could some sophisticated magical concoction have cured me, or at least eased the symptoms? Perhaps. But even if they happened to have just the right thing readily available, I didn't think they'd waste it on someone who—to all appearances—had stupidly incapacitated herself for no reason. There were other healer students available to go in my place.

And that's exactly what happened. The dorm had grown far quieter by the time I staggered out of the bathroom, still burning all the way from throat to butt.

In the end, those noodles had probably dealt me more internal damage than any of the infirmary medications ever could have. Hah.

I took the rest of the morning to recover.

I had to wonder if this pain was anything like what mages felt. The more magic branches they had, the more twisted their branches got. More twisting meant more suffering.

All mages needed healing. The more powerful they were, the more they needed us. And the more, I suppose, they resented needing us. Just like how I resented any suggestion of being obligated to serve them.

I thought briefly of Wisteria Shien. Smudged glasses. Black eyes without any light in them. Magic branches woven like chain mail around and around her ethereal core.

She, for one, had shown no outward signs of pain from her magic. I was strongly inclined to believe that my ultra-spicy death noodles were far more excruciating than any minor mage-aches her power inflicted on her.

In any case, Wisteria Shien was none of my business. And by now she'd have left for the joint mage-healer training camp, along with all the rest of them. Good riddance.

Eventually I felt well enough to review my checklist for taking care of Saya's three hermit crabs. I took the model lighthouse off the windowsill again; I tucked it in one of my inner pockets. I sallied forth, hoarse and feeble, to meet my fellow training camp rejects.

4

NINE HEALER RATS got left out of the trip, myself included.

The nicknames for each grade were one of the few things mages deigned to share with us healers. First-year students were called Rats, second-years Shrimp, third-years Crabs, and fourth-years Sharks.

We all had to wear pins with our assigned creature. How horrific it would be if someone took a look at you and couldn't instantly tell where you fell in the academy hierarchy.

Mages often wore other pins as well. A cormorant if they were on the student council. A pelican if they were in the originator program. A blue heron for club captains.

We Rats, by the way, had a little chant to express our pride. I'd been forced to learn it during orientation. I'd striven ever since to scorch it from my brain. I strongly doubted that the first-year mages went around singing about what ratty Rats they were.

None of the other left-behind healers lived on the same floor as me.

I'd met them during orientation, but promptly forgot most of their names.

I'll admit that I didn't try too hard to ingratiate myself. I'd flunked out of the trip in an emergency act of self-sabotage. The rest had wanted to go: they'd simply missed the cut-off in terms of overall class performance. We missing nine were supposed to represent the bottom twelve percent of our grade.

I should note that there were overall more healers than mage students at Guralta Academy. This was not reflective of our proportions in the population. The idea was to give the elite mage students here a greater pool of resources. More to choose from.

Anyhow, whether my fellow healer rejects thought I was stupid or just plain out of my mind, I couldn't imagine them seeing me in a friendly light.

Then again, one of the last things Saya had said to me before she left was, "It would be a good idea to stick with the others."

I swear I tried.

The afternoon of the first day, we clustered in a sickeningly humid classroom for remedial busywork. At least it wasn't hot out. No need to tie back our sleeves yet.

One wall of the room was, for no obvious reason, covered in dirty mirrors with faded undertones of magic.

It felt like we were being watched. We probably were, considering that the teacher on duty strolled out the door as soon as he gave us our work.

There was, unsurprisingly, a lot of chitchat. Much of it led to the subject of mages.

I asked obliquely if anyone else had seen upperclassmen using magic on local wildlife.

Yes, they said: deer, brown rabbits, forest turtles, feral parrots. Not necessarily the kind of animals a mainlander would expect to see on a narrow island saturated with sea air.

But they lived here nonetheless. They cut across campus without any care for whether they were in healer territory or mage territory. Guess that made them much freer than the rest of us.

Whatever the case, it was a relief to hear that other instances of magic use with animals were generally more innocuous than the game of bird-tossing I'd seen on the beach. Making a deer hold perfectly still so they could take cute pictures with it, for instance. Not ideal. But not outright murderous, either.

"Might be good practice for wrangling vorpal beasts," someone suggested.

"Don't think it's quite the same thing," I said.

I was the first to finish the assignment, a series of tedious magic branch diagramming exercises. As I doodled in the margins, they spoke of the mage Rats who had gone on the trip, and those who had stayed.

This was how I learned that the Shien mage—Wisteria Shien—was still on campus.

The tip of my pencil snapped. I felt obscurely betrayed. Then came a kind of sour outrage.

No, she hadn't mentioned her plans. I'd just assumed she'd be going. I'd said it to her face. She hadn't disagreed with me. That was as good as telling me yes.

"The Shien's an S-Class," said one of my classmates.

"No, no," said another. "No way. She can't possibly be a real S-Class. No one's ever seen her use serious magic."

I blinked down at my broken pencil as I listened to the rumors. Purportedly she was a notorious failure. The shame of the Shien clan. A huge disappointment, considering how they'd gone out of their way to adopt her.

Something was definitely wrong with her. All the mage students said so.

I caught a glimpse of myself in the cloudy mirrors on the other side of the room. I reared back a bit, startled. I had a sullen set to my mouth. I looked like I wanted to contradict them.

About some of it, anyhow. Anyone whose magic perception wasn't completely borked could tell that she had more than her fair share of magic branches. Too many of them, really. They looked like stringy overfed parasites packed to fill every spare cavity in her body. Like the pale wound-up strands of a fatally root-bound plant.

Naturally, I said nothing. Wisteria Shien didn't need me defending her honor. Besides, my goal for the next week was to get along passably well with these other eight healer Rats. Strength in numbers and all that.

I thought I was off to a good start.

At the end of the school day, the other Rats peeled off one by one.

At first it seemed quite innocuous. One got called in for an academic consultation. One had to go interview for a campus job, although the rest of us agreed that he was very unlikely to get it, being a Rat and all.

Various others had cleaning shifts, or clubs to attend, or make-up work to do in the library.

By the time I started getting suspicious, there were only two of us left.

The other girl kept glancing over her shoulder and twitching in fear at the shadows of birds crossing overhead. I didn't ask her what was wrong. My stomach felt all out of sorts. And not merely because of its recent ordeal with my hallmate's noxious noodles.

We were in sight of our dorm when my companion squeaked out something unintelligible. She bolted like a horse.

I stood there for a moment without a single thought left in my brain.

I didn't know quite what was happening yet. I did understand on instinct that the other eight first-year healers had deliberately ditched me.

That in itself wasn't too much of an issue. Might be bravado talking, but I figured I could survive a week of being shunned. No, the real problem was—

"Asa Clematis," said a voice that I regrettably recognized.

I resisted the urge to turn around. I took a determined step toward the dorm building, which was sorely in need of a good power-washing.

A hand caught at the back of my uniform. I yelped, swatted it away, and in the process found myself face-to-face with Wisteria Shien.

This time, she had her top buttoned all the way up to the collar at her throat.

"Let's take a walk," she said in her usual bland manner.

"This is healer territory," I snapped.

"I haven't tried to enter your dorm," she said. "There's no rule against strolling the grounds."

She held out her arm. I stared at it. Surely she didn't expect me to take it.

She waited long enough that I could've sprinted to the door. I could've made it inside. Yet my feet didn't know how to get started.

Then she lowered her arm, seemingly unbothered, and motioned for me to follow her.

I didn't want to. Need I describe how much I didn't want to?

But I'd started to notice other figures on the fringes of my vision. None moving like normal people with things to do and places to be.

They stood perfectly still. Two or three by a bench. One under a humongous beech tree. One leaning on the balcony of an airy castle-like structure over in mage student territory.

Even from here I could tell that they were all mages. Not just from what I could see of their uniforms. From the hue of the magic that simmered in each of them.

Better to go with the wolf you know, I decided. I followed Wisteria Shien.

Not in silence, of course.

"So. Hunting season," I said.

I didn't wait long for a response. I was beginning to get the hang of this. I could tell she wouldn't offer me any satisfaction.

"And you're the ringleader," I went on. "Family tradition, right? When you warned me, you were warning me about yourself. Or were you trying to reverse-psychology me into staying? I'll have you know that my plans were set from the start. You had absolutely no effect on—"

"Do I seem like the ringleader type?"

"Well, no. Not when you put it like that."

She made a muted sound, one without any noticeable tinge of either affirmation or indignation. It was more like she'd simply run out of her daily allotment of words.

It was late afternoon. The golden hour. We crossed the gardens that separated the healer side of campus from the (much larger) side for mages. Peachy light drenched the titanic foliage of magically augmented plants.

I felt for the model lighthouse in my pocket. Wait a little longer, and it would start shining red. I could turn the light up, whip it out to blind every mage nearby.

And by putting the light at full strength, I might attract an entire flock of magical laughing gulls. I pictured myself pitching the model tower at Wisteria Shien's head. I'd stand back and watch black-headed gulls holler war cries as they plunged down to feast like vultures.

"You're smiling," she said.

"Smirking," I corrected. "Are we there yet?"

She pointed up ahead: straight at the largest sundial on campus. The other scattered mage students had drifted over to coalesce in a broken circle around it. They looked like cult members preparing for a ritual.

It was my first time viewing the sundial close up. Wisteria Shien's braid lashed the air like a tail as she led me there.

The base was enormous and round, the size of a decent swimming pool, covered in ancient runes and other obscure markings. Quite pretentious, given that I'm pretty sure it was a modern creation.

A vast metallic sphere floated in the air above, bound in place by layer upon transparent layer of magic. Too many to count. All pruned from different people. In rings around the sphere hovered rough-hewn megaliths in colors that made it look as if they'd been mined directly from the peak of a midsummer sky.

The shadows cast by the sphere and the stones indicated something, I suppose. Perhaps the number of weeks left till the next solstice, or the approximate time of day. Nothing nearly as useful as a cheap-ass watch.

"The game starts tonight. It lasts till the end of Rat training camp."

Wisteria Shien spoke both to me and to her audience of mages. She was in glasses again, eying a slip of paper she'd extracted from her pocket.

"You need a cheat sheet for this?" I asked.

"If you miss curfew, you lose."

"Go to bed early," I said. "Got it."

"If you go to a teacher for help, you lose. If a teacher finds out on their own, and tries to stop the game, you lose."

"That's a lot of ways for me to lose," I said. "How do you guys lose?"

"We lose if you win."

"If I make it to the end of the week, then. What happens to the loser?"

"Wist," said a sharp voice.

One of the mages had stepped forward. I glanced at her pins. A rat. A pelican.

"You don't need to answer all these questions," the nameless mage said to Wisteria Shien.

The reply: "It costs us nothing."

"Good," I declared. "I've got more. Who's that blond guy glaring like he wants to murder us?"

It appeared to take the great Wisteria Shien a good long second to remember him. "The pentathlon winner."

"He only won because you weren't there," said the other mage who'd approached us.

"Another question, *Wist*." I pointed at the third wheel. "Who's this? Your biggest fan?"

The girl I was pointing at looked as if she dearly wished she could drown me in the campus pond. "You should be grateful," she said, with deadly enunciation. "Normally you wouldn't receive any explanation. It isn't a true test if you go into it knowing how to win."

"What's there to be grateful for? I'm only getting the answer to something like one out of every five of my questions here."

I pivoted back toward Wisteria Shien, disregarding her sidekick. "You never said what happens if I lose."

"The game continues for the rest of the year."

"Or until the target drops out," interjected the sidekick.

"Who picked me?" I asked Wisteria Shien. "You, was it? I wasn't even supposed to stay back here during training camp. What'd I do to get on your bad side?"

The rocks in the air above shifted as if tired of waiting for her to speak.

"The other healers offered you up," she said.

Ah.

"A very civilized game," I pronounced. "Your famous brothers must be proud."

I wanted to laugh when I looked at the rest of them. There were at least a couple dozen in all. Given the sheer numbers—and the fact that the majority of mage Rats were away at training camp—most had to be second-years or higher. All these haughty, prissily buttoned mages taking time out of their busy day to menace little old me.

"Underage healers and mages aren't supposed to be alone together," I told Wisteria Shien. "Not like this. The sun's going down. Where's my chaperone?"

"You're alone," she said, impenetrable as ever. "We aren't."

"Catch!" someone yelled from among the encircling mages.

Had they thrown a literal rock at me? Oh, please.

I would've flinched—should've flinched—but reflexive pride made me snap to attention.

Against all odds, I caught the rock. I caught it too fast to see the traitorous thread of magic tied around it.

My palms stung. My throat was still raw, scoured by last night's fatal noodles. I felt every breath that clawed through it. I locked eyes with Wisteria Shien, or thought I did. The hard gold light from the west obscured her glasses.

She was—

Was she reaching for me?

Only then did I sense the magic bound to the rock in my hands. Only then did I detect it unfurling, unstoppable.

I was a helpless healer of mages. Without any magic of my own. With nothing but an empty hollow in the part of my torso where mages boasted a proper core. Once this magical trap activated, there wasn't a single thing I could do to block it.

5

I CAME TO BACK in my dorm, but not in my own bed. In the first-floor common room.

The first senses that returned to me were hearing and magic perception.

Muffled, unhurried footsteps. Casual voices from several walls away. A gloss of magic pressed into tall rectangles. This was a room with screenless windows, then. Instead of screens, they had a built-in charm to keep flies out.

I saw all this before opening my eyes. I saw magic all over the building, bits and bobs of it in ghostly shapes. Severed threads and branches, mostly static. None still connected to a radiant core buried deep in a human body.

That's how I knew I wasn't surrounded by mages.

As I woke fully, I made an effort to sit up. My body had gone heavy with dread. Someone had thrown a knit blanket over me, albeit rather carelessly. My ankles felt like ice.

I flexed my fingers. The windows were very dark, the many-limbed floor lamps dim and disapproving.

I'd never napped on this driftwood couch before. Needless to say, I wouldn't recommend it. The threadbare cushions offered little comfort, and the seat of the couch had an unsettling tilt.

There was no one else in the lounge until the dorm steward poked her head through the door. "Finally up? Get back to your room."

I struck a languorous pose. My joints creaked. It didn't come easy. "I'm in no rush."

The steward had worked here for decades and was, in fact, a very accomplished healer. Or so claimed our other teachers.

Now she looked down her long nose at me. "Don't try to be funny."

"How'd I get here?" My voice came out with a hint of a crack in it.

"Some mages said they found you snoring outside. Had to haul you in myself. You're lucky you weren't stinking of liquor."

The dorm steward left me. I slowly lowered my head into my hands.

Alone again. All alone with the sisal rug on the floor. With the gray-worn rocking chair upended in a corner. With the anxious ticking of my heart.

The wrought-iron clock on the wall said it was already well past nine in the evening. Curfew was at ten. At least I'd made it in the building, though not of my own volition. Better head up to my bedroom before the steward started throwing a fit.

I didn't see a single other student, despite having heard them chatting earlier. They must've darted back to their rooms like crabs fleeing to holes in the sand.

I felt like a walking bad omen. Under different circumstances, I might've enjoyed it.

In my room, I made sure the windows were shut, the curtains secured. I took a heavy breath. My throat twinged.

Then I started taking off my clothes.

I didn't know what I was looking for. I didn't want to be looking for anything. I didn't want to think about it. I held my imagination underwater and drowned it.

No new bruises. No hidden aches. Nothing unusual about my uniform, aside from a bunch of wrinkles acquired during my unplanned hours of slumber. The model lighthouse still hung in my inner pocket, now glowing a faint yet inauspicious hue of scarlet.

I held my underwear up to the light and scrutinized it as if trying to read the palm of a stranger. Nothing unusual there, either. I chucked it in my laundry basket.

A few minutes later, I took it out again. I studied it once more, this time more meticulously. Still nothing.

After a while, I pulled on an old T-shirt and sweatpants. I sat on my creaky bed. It was just me and Saya's three hermit crabs now. No one else to talk to. Not that I wanted to talk to anyone.

I should be relieved. Happy. Clapping my hands. By all appearances, nothing had happened to me.

The only physical aftereffects I could detect—and believe me, I tried—were some stiffness in my back, which I blamed on the driftwood couch. A scorched sensation in my esophagus, which I blamed on yesterday's noodles. Reddened and tender palms, which I blamed on the flying rock I'd caught.

A rock with a hunk of someone's magic grafted to it. It could've been any of them. One of the senior mages, most likely.

It didn't matter who it was. What mattered was what that magic had done to me.

Laughably little, if you thought about it. So it knocked me out for a while. So what? Such innovative bullying. I'd slept right through it.

After all that buildup. The menacing assembly of mages. The

foreboding shape of the sundial in the sky. The tension of the vanishing daylight—

What a letdown, right? How very anticlimactic.

I'd slept so much, in fact, that I couldn't sleep at all that night.

I lay there with my eyes open, listening to the hermit crabs busy at work in their tank. I'd known they were nocturnal creatures, but I hadn't realized quite how active they got in the dark.

If I ever found myself conscious this late, it was usually because I'd fought my way awake midway through a nightmare. I'd be too wrapped up in myself to hear the soft scratching of the hermit crabs. Or maybe it was just that my sudden bursts of panicked pacing always cowed them into silence. I guess if I saw a nearby giant jump to their feet in the middle of the night, shoulders heaving, I'd try to keep a low profile, too.

I'd survived one day so far. But only one day out of seven.

There was a message behind the seemingly inane magic of the goodnight rock. Whether or not they wanted to, any or all of those mages could have done anything to me while I slept.

It didn't matter that they hadn't actually done it. The message lay in the fact that they *could* have. They'd had hours to spare. The message lay in my struggle to sleep, to turn off the pouring faucet of my brain.

The message lay in my inability to stop picturing in vivid detail everything they *could* have chosen to do as I lay there on the ground before the base of the sundial.

For them, the goal of hunting season was to break me down. Make me run to a teacher for help. I could imagine so very many ways for them to accomplish that.

A healer teacher, of course. They'd be shocked if I tried to turn to a magister.

I didn't even know any of the mage faculty by name. I'd seen the Head Magister maybe twice in my life, both times during orientation.

Six days left.

Okay, sleep wasn't happening. I switched on my desk light (sorry, hermit crabs). Usually I'm not much of a note-taker, but I really needed to sort out my thoughts.

I stole one of Saya's pens and huddled in my chair with my knees to my chest.

There was some basis for optimism. For one thing, I suspected that the current version of hunting season had been greatly toned down in comparison to past years. At least in comparison to the era of the Shien brothers.

They'd even gone out of their way to tell me the rules. How magnanimous.

The mage students, I reasoned, would want the game to be sustainable. This meant they couldn't do anything so obvious or so horrific that the administration would be forced to put an immediate stop to it.

Such tactics would result in me losing, yes. But they would also make it difficult for future generations of mages to go on the hunt themselves.

Anyway, tormenting me wasn't their full-time job. They still had classes and schoolwork and extracurriculars. Even if the schedule might be a little lighter than usual this week.

They'd already demonstrated that they could and would use magic on me. I had a hunch, however, that magic wasn't necessarily the main threat. There were plenty of analog ways to get to someone instead. The Shien brothers had reportedly been very creative in that respect.

Besides, most student mages were still collared. The collars wouldn't actually stop them from abusing magic skills for nefarious purposes. Yet they served as a form of surveillance far more precise than the laughing gulls patrolling the island.

I couldn't pretend to understand the collars perfectly. From what I knew, they synced to a seismograph-like machine in the school records room. Each time a particular student used magic, the machine would scribble out a pattern corresponding to the exact skill they'd deployed.

That in itself wasn't necessarily incriminating. Think back to the mages who'd slammed that little white tern to death. All their collar records would indicate was that they'd been practicing some type of skill pertaining to wind or gravity manipulation. Or maybe just basic telekinesis. The records wouldn't show what they'd done with it.

Even so, the mere existence of the records might motivate my mage opponents to exercise some degree of caution. I sure hoped so, anyway.

Whatever happened, I'd be safest in the presence of teachers, and in healer-only spaces.

I did manage to steal a little bit of sleep in the end, close to dawn. It wasn't restful. I dreamt of being devoured by deep sea creatures. I woke up gasping for air so hard that it sent me spiraling into a coughing fit.

Hey, at least the mages here at the academy weren't monsters the size of a cruise ship.

I mentally thanked my spice-obsessed hallmate (I'd taken to calling him Pepper) for his generosity. I slipped a bottle of his strongest hot sauce in one of my inner pockets, opposite the lighthouse.

He'd let me take custody of it while he traveled for training camp. He'd warned me that it was at least twice as bad as the noodles. He'd warned me in no uncertain terms not to let even a microscopic amount of it touch bare skin.

Trust me, I wasn't planning on splattering it all over any mages that dared to approach me. I'd be the one getting expelled if they got seriously hurt. Or, heck, even if they didn't. They could send me home simply by feigning an injury.

It was just a tad comforting to feel the weight of the bottle resting there in my uniform, where no one else could see it. Not like I had any other allies.

I really didn't. I'm not exaggerating. I discovered this as soon as I went down for breakfast the following day.

The other eight first-years looked past me as if I didn't exist.

I'd more or less expected that. I did contemplate pressing the issue. It would've been fun to loudly greet them, sit myself down right in the middle of them, cheerfully follow them to other tables once they got up and left.

Then again, it was only the second day of hunting season. Figured I'd best conserve my energy.

I started to lift a spoonful of scrambled eggs to my mouth. A metallic glint caught my eye.

The other healers were very quiet. They looked away when I turned to stare at them. When I focused back on my plate, I felt them watching me again.

My heartbeat was very slow, very calm. I hadn't been particularly hungry in the first place. I sifted through the pile of eggs with the tip of my spoon.

Yep. Full of needles.

I didn't bother tasting anything. Just threw away the whole plate. I felt a little bad afterward—those needles might puncture the trash bag—but what else was I supposed to do?

It had been way too obvious, anyhow. The real danger probably lay elsewhere. In my glass of water, for instance, or my dessicated-looking fillet of mackerel.

The needles, I theorized, had been a decoy. A ploy to make me seize with relief upon the rest of my seemingly untampered-with food and drink.

Alternatively, the other healers might just be real amateurs at this sort of thing. I wouldn't risk it. I could get hydrated at a water fountain. I could afford to go hungry for a bit.

When I returned to my room, the door was unlocked.

I stood there for a moment and thought of the circle of mages. The faces there had not, for the most part, been brimming with hatred. If anything, they'd reminded me of spectators at a dueling match. Amped up on gleeful, careless adrenaline. Almost frighteningly devoid of real malice.

There had only been two exceptions: the blond guy who'd won the recent pentathlon, and Wisteria Shien's bristling sidekick. Those two might enjoy seeing me swallow sewing needles. Based on how they'd glowered at me, anyway.

Yet Wisteria Shien had been the one who stood up in front of all of them and woodenly read out the rules of the game.

I turned the knob of the door that had most definitely been locked when I left for breakfast. An itchy heat had begun to creep its way up the back of my neck.

I could deal with whatever they'd done to my stuff. Not like I had a lot of it to begin with. But if anyone had touched Saya's hermit crabs, I'd—

The hermit crabs: unharmed.

My school books: all gone.

I opened the window and stuck my head out to suck in fresh air.

Okay. Not the worst thing that could happen. If the texts weren't recoverable, the problem would be the cost. Couldn't make my parents buy them all over again.

I searched every corner just to make sure they weren't hiding anywhere. Just in case.

When I opened my desk drawer, it was filled to the brim with snails the size of well-fed mice.

The snails and I looked at each other. I think we made eye contact.

I slid the heavy drawer shut and cast my gaze out the window again.

No view of the sea from here. The sky was color-blocked by clouds in a way I'd never quite seen before. Rich blue above, pale withered blue below.

I opened the drawer again.

"Oh, c'mon," I said. Not that it was the snails' fault.

I began to feel sorry for whoever had gone to the trouble of putting them there. Some healer forced to do a mage's dirty work.

Who'd come up with this idea, anyway? A four-year-old? At least make it a bunch of poisonous spiders or snakes or scorpions. Or a fleet of tropical cockroaches.

I suppose they hadn't wanted to unleash anything that might risk infesting the rest of the dorm. Weak.

I started to reach in with my bare hands, then thought better of it. Back in the days when I'd tried to make pets out of garden slugs, my parents had warned me they were full of parasites. True or not, it wouldn't hurt to take precautions.

Luckily, Pepper had gifted me with what might as well have been a lifetime's supply of disposable gloves.

I walked into my first lecture of the day with dirt smudges on my uniform, no textbooks, and an enormous grin. I was also half an hour late, yet in an excellent mood.

I'd successfully transferred all the snails to the oversize garden on the border of healer territory. I'd tucked them among a bank of early poppies that looked large enough to devour human babies. My snails would fit right in there.

The teacher asked me to stay back afterward. Have a little chat.

"I've got another class to get to," I said.

"No, you don't."

Dang it.

The teacher's name was Mr. Rift. A healer, of course. Very tall; very gaunt and rickety. So unhealthy-looking that I'd heard people calling him a junkie behind his back.

I appreciated him more than the other teachers. He wasn't bonded to a mage, and he made zero effort to be likable. Nor did he pretend to be fond of his students. Mr. Rift got his job done and avoided overtime as if he were deathly allergic to it.

There, I thought, was a standard to aspire to.

He'd worked at Guralta Academy for a long, long time. Almost as long as the dorm steward. In our first lesson with him, he explained that he'd come here because it was the cheapest way to get a home by the sea.

Some teachers on our side of campus went around in healer robes. The full traditional kind. Not Mr. Rift: he wore button-up shirts in kaleidoscopic prints and pants that made his legs look like sticks.

After class, I followed him reluctantly to his office.

The office door seemed congenitally incapable of shutting all the way. An elaborate apparatus of buckets and towels balanced precariously by the warped window. The view from said window was largely blocked by the overgrown fronds of a hairy-trunked tree fern just outside.

"Nice room," I said. "Very chic."

Mr. Rift, ignoring my jibe, took a pitcher of barley tea out of a dented mini fridge. He poured us each a glass.

I sat myself down in a wobbly rattan chair. He tossed me a package of mass-produced oatmeal cookies. My hunger pangs peaked as soon as I saw them.

The cookies seemed extremely old, but I started chowing down anyway. I thanked Mr. Rift between swallows. See, I can be perfectly polite.

"Your books," he said.

"Forgot 'em. My bad."

"Don't talk while you're chewing."

"Sorry, mom."

"Asa, I have a story for you," Mr. Rift said. "I'll keep it short. Are you listening?"

"I'm always listening," I said sincerely.

He appeared unconvinced, but kept going anyway. "Some years ago, there was a healer student who got shut up in the caves below the cliffs."

"What caves? What cliffs?"

"On the western end of the island. They're wholly sealed off now." He steepled his fingers. "When the tide came in, that healer died. All the evidence suggested that they'd gotten trapped there on their own."

"Very tragic."

"Quite a few minors have died on this island," he said baldly. No sugarcoating from Mr. Rift. "Both before and during my time. Almost none of them were mages. Do you think anyone ever paid for it?"

I sat up straighter. The cheap rattan chair teetered beneath me. I looked him in the eye. "I'm not that stupid," I answered.

"The cave incident happened while two young Shien gentlemen were students here."

When neither of us spoke, I could hear a far-off yelling. Might've been one of the sports teams running through quick exercises during a free period. From elsewhere came the off-key bleats of some poor soul attempting to wring music out of a one-mage orchestra.

I knew what Mr. Rift was trying to say. I also knew he wouldn't interfere any more than he had to.

I waved a hand at the window. I meant to gesture at the sky, but it looked more like I was trying to say something about the menace of the lurking tree fern.

"The gulls watch over us," I said. "Won't the gulls alert the faculty if they see anything bad?"

"Don't count too much on those gulls," he advised. "They can't be everywhere at all times. And they can be fooled. They aren't sentient."

I couldn't complain to him about my fellow healers hazing me. I'd lose if I snitched. Besides, they were simply following instructions. All part of the same game.

My eight classmates had won the game in advance, in their own way. They'd won by process of elimination—by volunteering me to play the target. That must be why the mages spared them.

"There's another Shien at school right now."

As soon as the words came out of my mouth, I had no idea why I'd voiced them. This obviously wouldn't be new information to him. Surely that was the reason he'd name-dropped her older brothers: to warn me away from her.

Mr. Rift rubbed his long face. When he lifted his hands away, he looked—troubled. That was a first.

"You've met?" he asked.

"Unfortunately."

He peered at me as if unable to parse my meaning. Not the reaction I'd expected. "Did you get a look at her magic?"

"S-Class, isn't she?"

His brows lowered. "I thought you were more observant than that, Asa."

"I've been at healer school for barely over a month."

He made a shooing motion, as if to say *No excuses.* "We've been struggling to treat her," he said.

"We?"

"The healer faculty." Another silence. As if Mr. Rift were weighing whether to continue, or to simply give up and dismiss me from his office. "I've never seen a mage in so much pain. You couldn't tell from the shape of her branches?"

"They looked weird, yeah. But she didn't act at all like—"

He shook his head. "Never mind."

I started to protest, feeling oddly indignant. Mr. Rift silenced me by holding out another two packets of cookies.

"Tread carefully, Asa," he said. "Remember who runs the country."

Mages.

"Remember who this school was founded to nurture and educate."

Guralta Academy had been a mage-only institution for centuries before it ever went co-ed.

"And stop forgetting your books," he added.

I told him I wouldn't. An empty promise. I doubt Mr. Rift believed me. For my part, I was beginning to suspect I might never get them back in one piece.

6

In the morning, I'd been too busy evacuating the snails from my desk (and then rushing to class) to do any further cleanup. By the next time I checked up on the aftermath, my drawer was starting to emanate a most unusual smell.

I hadn't ever imagined snails as having much of a scent. But these extra-fleshy specimens certainly did. Or maybe it was just their leftover slime baking in the afternoon sunlight. I threw open the window and did my best to scrub out the stinking drawer.

I managed to sneak in a decent non-doctored meal by going to the cafeteria at an odd hour, a time when it was supposed to be closed.

I pleaded with the staff for scraps. Normally they would've refused. Since they let me get away with it, I had a hunch that they knew at least some of what was happening here. Same as Mr. Rift.

Likewise, I went to bathe at an hour when I was certain no other healers would be there. As a precaution, I kept my clothes and towel within sight the entire time. I felt quite triumphant after safely emerging from a quick soak. No need to sprint naked back to my room. An enormous success, given the circumstances.

I had not, however, kept my shoes with me.

When I went to leave the healer bathhouse, I found my shoes packed full of human shit.

I couldn't move. My brain still felt full of steam, too clouded up for any clear thoughts to breach its surface. I was in sleepwear now, my uniform bundled in my arms, damp towel tossed about my shoulders.

I found myself pondering the logistics of this situation, as if it were someone else's problem. Not the logistics of what the hell I was going to do about it. No, not that.

Instead my mind glommed onto the fact that a healer—a classmate—must've done this. Someone had personally gone to the trouble of collecting and transporting this fecal transplant for my one and only pair of school-issue shoes.

I couldn't conjure new uniform-worthy shoes out of thin air. I'd get written up if I started wearing sandals to class. I couldn't pitch these in an incinerator, much as I wanted to.

There was only one obvious next step.

Well. As part of my battle with the curdling remnants of snail slime, I'd already been planning to ask the dorm steward to lend me heavier-duty cleaning supplies.

I couldn't afford to waste time crying over it. I had more productive things to do than throw up.

I'll skip the revolting parts. Just know that I took care of it.

I walked barefoot back to my dorm. There was a strange swollen sensation of distance between my ears, as if I'd vaulted half out of my body.

I piloted myself from a distance. I made very good use of Pepper's disposable gloves. I scorched the insides of my shoes with so much bleach and goodness knows what else that I may as well have incinerated them, really.

I would've expected myself to be plotting revenge on my classmates. Strangely, I found I didn't care who'd done it. No more than I cared about who'd been in charge of sticking needles in my breakfast. It could've been any of them. Besides, they were just obeying some mage.

Wisteria Shien?

Would she bother working to source exotic jumbo snails? Would she micromanage the process of dumping feces in my footwear?

We'd only met a few times. I couldn't claim to know her in any real depth. But I couldn't imagine her caring enough to put in the effort to make this happen.

Long after I finished exorcising my shoes, my eyes still kept smarting from all the chemicals I'd begged off the dorm steward. I was lucky I hadn't accidentally gassed myself. I hadn't looked at any of the bottles too closely, or double-checked what to avoid mixing with what.

All I felt toward the other training camp rejects was a kind of vicious pity. They were the ones who got forced to ferry poop around. I ended up having to evict it, but which of us had lost more dignity? Which of us was the real sucker here?

I may have been prey in the mages' game, but at least I got to be a player. Any healers who'd gotten roped into harassing me weren't players at all. They were no better than props.

I hung my shoes out the window to dry. My flesh slowly reabsorbed the horrid coursing adrenaline that cried out *must purge, must eradicate*.

Only then did I start to feel the itchy sweat on my back, a filthy byproduct of all that scrubbing and scrubbing. Only then did a familiar enraged, sticky heat plod its way in blotches up the sides of my neck.

My memory again called up the expressionless face of Wisteria Shien.

She clearly had way more than nine magic branches, whatever the rumors about her being a disappointment to her adoptive family. Ten-plus branches: that made her the very definition of S-Class.

An S-Class and a Shien. Didn't that mean she unofficially outranked every other mage at school? If she gave orders, wouldn't they listen?

Her warnings to me in the infirmary had made it sound like she disapproved of hunting season. Yet here she was letting it happen anyway.

As it were an act of nature. An inevitability she could do nothing about. Like waiting till after those boys on the beach killed a bird before stopping them.

There was another possibility, of course. Despite her utter lack of shining charm and her dreadful conversational skills, she might very well be the ringleader. She'd denied it, but she could've been lying. It did seem to be something of a family legacy.

And she'd been the one to read out the rules of the game.

The more I thought about this, though, the less convincing it felt. There was no way Wisteria Shien had the energy to put together elaborate petty plots. She looked like she barely had the energy to get her butt out of bed.

Either way, by my reckoning, she was one of very few mages in the entire academy who ought to have enough influence to single-handedly stop hunting season. She was one of very few mages who had given me the impression of being less than eager to participate.

And what had she done to stop it? Seemingly nothing.

Part of me wanted to sit there and till the rich soil of my resentment till the moon came out. Sadly, it wouldn't be the best use of my time. Instead I went to ask the steward for help with getting my room lock changed.

"Lost your key?" she asked.

"Yup," I said. "Sorry."

Then she told me how much it would cost to replace the lock and issue new keys.

"Oh, wow." I dug my key out of my pocket. "Just found it. How lucky."

"Always happy to help," said the steward.

I consoled myself with the knowledge that the dormmates who'd been breaking into my room might very well be using a magical tool. Something a mage student had passed to them. In that case, swapping out the physical lock wouldn't do a whole lot to stop them.

At night, I got in the habit of wedging a chair under the doorknob. Couldn't think of any similar tricks for securing the room when I had to go out, though.

Eventually I settled for painting a bit of Pepper's deadliest hot sauce on the outside knob. I did it whenever I had to leave for more than a couple of minutes. Like for class. I used the bottle I'd taken to carrying around in my uniform wherever I went.

I continued carrying the model lighthouse everywhere, too. The black spikes made it look like it might come in handy for self-defense. Not that I had any idea how to win a fistfight.

The first time I opened the top-ranked hot sauce, it made a pop like a bottle of sparkling wine. I almost committed the nigh-fatal error of leaning forward to get a good sniff. I recalled Pepper's warnings just in time.

I used gloves when I applied the sauce, of course, and only dabbed on a little. Didn't want to use the bottle up too fast. I stashed extra gloves in my uniform for good measure.

Pepper had told me that the sauce could leave actual physical burns on bare skin. That you'd need emergency medical attention if even a speck of it got in your eyes.

I didn't think my hot sauce trap would stop anyone from breaking and entering. But maybe, as the burning kicked in, they'd find it more of a struggle to carry through their nefarious plans.

Anyway, the third day of training camp week was eerily uneventful. Which is not to say that no one did anything nasty. But none of it hit my panic button quite like the post-bath shock from a day earlier.

At least not until around six in the evening.

I'd been getting worrisomely lightheaded during classes. Still couldn't trust the cafeteria food, not so long as there were other people nearby.

As a countermeasure, I resorted to buying chips and energy bars from the school store. But I didn't have a whole lot of cash on me. Needed to start rationing it better. I was already on the verge of running out.

I'd been gone from my room for less than half an hour. All I did was jog down to the school store and back. Even so, I'd taken a second to reapply the spice trap on my way out. It was as fresh as could be.

I put a glove on my right hand to let myself back in. In my left arm I cradled all the junk food I'd bought.

The door was unlocked.

No surprise there. Hopefully this time someone was suffering for it. Touching their face with tainted fingers. Howling in agony in the privacy of their own room.

I dropped my food on my bed. I dropped my glove in the trash.

I'd left the window half-open for ventilation. An unsteady breeze riffled the edge of the curtain.

My desk no longer stank of snail scum. My lace-up school shoes—well, let's just say that I had inspected them thoroughly for any remaining trace of contamination, and found nothing.

Aspirational snapshots of renowned single mages still covered the entire wall over Saya's empty bed. The windowsill still bore its usual assortment of odds and ends. (I really needed to give the plant cuttings new water.)

No signs of sabotage lurked in the closet or beneath my watercolor-blue bedsheets. No fresh chunks of paint had fallen down from the cheaply spackled ceiling.

But something—

Something was missing.

My body seemed to comprehend it before my brain did. A rush of vertigo rooted me in place. The room felt creepily devoid of sound.

Then I got it.

The pale stone side table by Saya's desk.

The stone slab was cracked down the middle, but it had always been that way. The whole table was probably some mage student's detritus. We'd salvaged it from a mountain of abandoned furniture near the Heap.

The glass tank on top of the table stood wide open, its lid turned sideways.

I looked inside.

Trust me, I looked hard. Sometimes the three hermit crabs were easy to miss. Sometimes they buried themselves completely in sand. I picked up every single shell in the tank, just to make sure none of them had suddenly decided to trade up for a new house.

All empty.

A torn piece of paper stuck out from beneath the back of the tank. I tugged it free with quaking fingers. The words scribbled on it instructed me to show up at the eastern ruins by seven in the evening. Less than an hour from now.

My fist spasmed shut around the would-be ransom note.

I didn't bother locking my room. Didn't bother dousing the doorknob in hot sauce. I didn't know where I was going until I stood by the entrance to the first-floor common room.

I kept standing there in a daze for several long seconds. An ugly heat prickled my skin, my eyes—a sensation like bathing in the worst type of spice fumes. I started to slowly turn the handle.

Then I kicked the door in.

Five or six startled faces jerked to look at me. My left hand clenched the bottle of hot sauce in my uniform pocket.

"Fuck you all," I said, as if this were our usual evening greeting.

Not a single person made a single sound.

"They aren't mine." I heard my voice catch. Didn't care. "If anything happens to those stupid crabs, I will—*I will commit arson.* I'll burn this whole building down. I'll burn myself to death. I'll haunt every single one of you with my smoking, stinking—"

"Something wrong?"

The dorm steward hovered in the hallway.

"...Nothing," I said. "Just a little schoolgirl banter."

I looked back at my classmates. They made furtive eye contact with each other. Not with me.

Gophers, I thought. Stooges. Cowards.

Do whatever you want to my things. My books. My bed. To me myself. At least I had some rudimentary ways to fight back—my hot sauce, my rage. At least I understood what was happening.

Saya had told me that these were not the only hermit crabs she'd ever cared for. Years ago, when she wasn't looking, a neighborhood kid had taken her very first hermit crab. He'd torn it out of its shell, leaving it naked and injured. It died in a matter of days.

Hermit crabs had claws, sure. Given a chance, they could pinch for dear life. But they couldn't do much to stop a truly determined person from hurting them, from crushing them, from ripping their spindly legs off. In that sense, they were utterly helpless.

I shut the lounge door on the other healers. I told the dorm steward I'd be heading out for an evening walk.

I'd barely started moving, and my heart already drummed as if I were on drugs.

It almost felt like magic, like porting. One moment I was stalking out of the dorm. The forested path to get off campus passed by me in a blur of raw fury. Then I was striding down through the maze of vacation houses.

All I heard were my own hard footsteps, muted spring insects, and the still-distant rolling of the sea.

In the back of my head I saw Yarrow's frozen smile. Bet my classmates tried to smile the same way whenever mage students made fresh demands of them. But they were still amateurs at wearing a mask. They hadn't even been able to keep looking at me after I burst my way into the common room.

Wisteria Shien was different. She knew how to strip the expression from her face like stripping paint from a wall, leaving behind not the barest trace of color or flavor.

She wasn't on the side of the gophers. She was with the mages. The manipulators. The hunters.

The next time I saw her, I'd—

The thought hung unfinished. I'd reached the beach on the eastern end of the island.

I slipped off my much-abused shoes and socks. The sand was cool beneath my feet. Almost chilly.

There was still enough light to see end-of-day shadows. Even the smallest seashell shards cast a long, long sliver of shade. My own shadow cut a sharp blade all the way back to the grass-covered dunes. They crouched like defensive bulwarks before the final row of beachfront houses.

A distinct bank of heavy clouds hulked low over the horizon. Almost low enough to resemble an armada of boats.

I couldn't spot any other human beings on the beach. But that didn't necessarily mean it was empty. Stone ruins reared up where the sweep of sand rounded off to form a blunt point. The very tip of Guralta Isle. More toppled ruins jutted out from the heaving water beyond, pockmarked and pimpled with barnacles.

I clutched the ransom note in one hand, my shoes in the other. The note didn't demand any payment other than my presence.

Which I suppose meant *I* was the payment.

It told me exactly what to do. It told me they'd be watching.

I walked up to a leaning tower, a tumult of black and indigo and sky blue rock. A strange white lichen sprouted in crystalline patterns to cover the broken parts.

The ruins had no obvious entrance. Just a series of shorn columns and boulders. They muscled into each other near the place that once might have held some manner of door. I'd have to bend in half to shuffle through the tunnel-like gap.

The hermit crabs were inside, said the note.

Look. I could guess how this would play out.

So tell me, what else was I supposed to do? The dorm steward had let it slide, but technically we weren't really supposed to keep pets.

I'd have gone sprinting to tell Mr. Rift everything if I thought he could help save Saya's hermit crabs. The administration could certainly try to put a stop to the game as a whole. And I'm sure if they did—if the mage students discovered that I'd given up and confessed—we'd never see those hermit crabs again.

I followed the instructions on the note.

First I made some rude gestures for the benefit of whoever had been assigned to watch me.

Next I put my shoes back on. A safety measure. For all I knew, they could've seeded the entire path with rusty nails and broken glass.

Then I half-crawled through the misshapen tunnel into the heart of the ruins.

My brain kept bringing up what Mr. Rift had said about the cave system on the opposite end of the island. About the healer who'd died in there.

Was it low tide right now? High tide? I had no idea how to keep track of these things. How far up the ruins would high tide come surging?

It was surprisingly light inside, once I emerged from the narrow entrance. The walls rose high enough to feel like part of a shattered tower. But there was no roof up above, no end to the tower, nothing to hold me in but the infinite dimming sky.

A yellow bucket stood in the middle of the stone floor.

I rushed over to look inside, almost tripping on fallen debris as I went.

No cushioning sand in the bucket. Nothing but three quiet shells: one brownish grey, one with charismatic splotches of orange, and one a silvery color like the moon. Turban, Bubbles, and Pearl. Saya wasn't the most creative when it came to choosing names.

I picked them up and turned them over one by one. All were hidden as deep in their shells as they could go, with only the ends of their legs and claws showing. But they stirred minutely when I brushed them with a finger, careful not to get within pinching range.

All alive. The sheer relief felt downright dizzying. I too wanted to find a nice big shell to curl up in.

Crash!

I almost dropped the bucket.

A second before the booming crack of rock on rock, my magic perception had picked up a momentary flash like summer lightning. It all happened much too fast to think or react.

Once my throat stopped constricting itself, once I remembered how to breathe, I understood exactly what had happened. Didn't even need to go look at the aftermath.

I went anyway.

The entrance was blocked. A slab of rock far taller than me had fallen in just the right spot to seal it off.

Took 'em long enough.

I'd only been able to think of two reasons for the mages to lure me in here. One—to do unspeakable things. Two—to trap me inside.

Now here I was, thoroughly trapped. But it was definitely the preferable of those two options. Just so long as the tide didn't come up too high.

There were still a few hours left till curfew. I'd shown up before seven, just as instructed. I didn't have a watch on me, though. Nor did I trust my ability to estimate the passage of time.

Color began to leach out of the ruins as twilight intensified. No more pink light picking out absurdly elongated shadows. I didn't want to think about how dark it'd get in here once stars became visible.

I searched the walls diligently for weak spots, for hidden exits, for convenient rock-climbing crannies. There were no holes I could shimmy through. No surfaces jagged enough for me to ascend with confidence. Not while carrying the hermit crab bucket.

Even without the bucket, I wouldn't have been able to make it more than a few pathetic feet off the ground. Trust me—I tried.

Oh, I tried. I tried and tried. I tried until I knew it was pointless. Then I sat down next to the quiet bucket of hermit crabs. I cradled my raw hands.

I listened to the ocean beyond the ruins, the intermittent far-off cries of birds. I waited for true darkness to fill up the hollow space inside this abandoned facsimile of a tower.

I'd gotten what I came for. The hermit crabs were safe and whole.

All three of them. But I'd lose the game of hunting season if I missed curfew. And I was guaranteed to miss curfew if I couldn't find my way out of here.

The risks went beyond merely missing curfew, of course. Most islanders kept a good distance from the ruins. I could yell myself hoarse all night, and no one would hear me.

I'd get dehydrated. I'd be forced to go pee in a corner. How much time might pass before anyone thought to use magic to look for me?

I could imagine the other healer Rats dropping misleading hints about my state of mind, my whereabouts. Anything to throw the school off my trail. No doubt the mage students would find it deeply amusing.

I didn't have a grand plan to turn things around and win the game. Not from here.

You'd need magic for something like that. I'm a healer. And ever since Yarrow visited home with her new bondmate and that terrible rictus of a smile on her face, I'd never forgotten it.

I couldn't win. But I could avoid being stuck in the ruins overnight— or, worse, for days on end.

I reached in my uniform pocket. Not for the bottle of hot sauce. For the wicked-looking miniature lighthouse.

Right now the red light was faint enough that just a layer or two of fabric could completely snuff it out.

Twist the base of the lighthouse one way and the ringed spiky sections another way, and the brightness of the magic would double. And redouble. And redouble.

At full strength, it could paint the whole broken tower a stark emergency scarlet. From far away, you'd see a red light as fresh as blood spilling out through all the cracks, shining in a solid column high up into the sky. It'd look like the ruins had been reconstructed.

I was banking on the school's magical gulls noticing, swarming me from all directions, forming an enormous flock around the ruins, alarming the staff on duty.

But even if no one immediately picked up on the gulls' odd behavior, someone would notice the sudden light spilling from the silent ruins. A light powerful enough to pierce the night above. An eerie awakening.

Someone would see it, and someone would come. It was no better than begging a teacher to save me, of course. If I turned the lighthouse all the way up, I was bound to lose the game of the hunt.

Then again, I was also bound to lose if I missed curfew tonight. Might as well save myself another hour or two of sitting here on my butt in the thickening dark.

I adjusted my grip on the little lighthouse. The thorn-like spikes pressed dents in my palm. The dim red glow felt much colder and flatter than firelight.

All it would take was one firm twist.

My hands looked hazy.

At first I was inclined to chalk it up to exhaustion or hunger. I blinked.

But it wasn't just my hands. The eroded stone floor, the yellow bucket—everything was slowly becoming enveloped in a murky pallor. As if my vision were bathed in milk. As if clouds were sprouting from cracks in the ground.

The fog was shot through with magic.

I'd seen this exact magic before.

I dropped the fog-muffled model lighthouse back in my pocket. I crouched by the bucket of hermit crabs like an animal ready to fight to the death for its offspring. Cold mist seeped up inside my long skirt.

7

IN THE SPACE of a blink, Wisteria Shien stood next to me, hands in her pockets. Porting magic.

I had no idea how far she'd come. She could've ported from right outside the blocked entrance. Or from the street behind the first row of beach houses. Or even all the way from the mage side of campus. I didn't know what kind of porting skills mage students were allowed to use freely. I didn't know if she'd bent regulations to be here.

She was looking down into the bucket.

I picked it up and took a few hasty steps back, trying not to jostle the hermit crabs.

The fog swirled around us like a living creature pacing circles in a too-small cage. It had flooded up to my hips now.

"More fog," I said. "Is this the only trick you know?"

"It's good for camouflage."

"What're you planning on doing that needs to be camouflaged?"

We eyed each other like duelists about to launch into a no-holds-barred magesports match.

What was it her friend had called her? Oh, right.

"Wist," I pronounced sweetly. "Don't pretend you've come to help."

"Do you want to get out of here?"

The sentence structure was that of a question. Her voice made it sound like a statement.

I swished my arm sharply through the fog in front of me, warning her back. "I can get out on my own."

"By losing the game."

"Yes," I bit out. "By letting you win, you absolute nincompoop. What are you even doing here? Clearly the magisters don't give out enough homework."

"Practicing magic skills can be a form of homework."

My eyes just about cartwheeled out of my head. "Of course. So you got an assignment to pump the ruins full of mist. Port inside for no particular reason. Leer menacingly. You should've picked a night with more moonlight."

The fog muffled sound. Somehow, it also seemed to muffle my reflexes. As if there were a numbing quality to the chill damp touch creeping up my legs, creeping in the shadow of my skirt.

I didn't hear her move until she was already right in front of me, close enough to wrest the bucket from my grip. She didn't touch it. But her hands hovered as if ready to snatch it out of the air.

I stumbled back. My shoes scraped uneven ground. Couldn't see where I was stepping. The fog lapped higher and higher.

Wisteria Shien stepped closer.

I was seconds away from saying something I knew I would regret. *Don't touch me. Don't hurt me.* An indelible tinge of panic had set into my brain.

Because it was dark. Unnaturally quiet. Because she kept moving toward me at the same steady mechanical pace, no emotion in her body and no emotion on her face. The end of her black braid vanished somewhere deep in the sea of silvery fog.

My heel hit a rock.

I flailed—sputtered—almost lost hold of the bucket.

Part of me heard the hermit crabs sliding around in there and apologized to them profusely. They deserved none of this. Part of me still reeled from how close I'd come to tripping flat on my back, dropping everything, cracking my head open.

Most of me felt nothing but Wisteria Shien's bruising grip on the back of my arm.

"Ow," I said, once my body reconciled itself with the fact that we were no longer in danger of falling. "That hur—"

She let go. I poked gingerly at my sore tricep.

"Your hands," she said.

I clutched said hands—and the yellow bucket—closer to my chest. "What about them?"

She held her own hands out in front of her, palm up. Showing me what she wanted me to do.

My first instinct was to refuse point-blank. But I didn't. The words *how about no* stuck in my craw. I froze in place like a stage actor who'd missed their cue.

From the moment I first smelled the fresh cold mist, I'd been dead set against having anything to do with Wisteria Shien. Even if—especially if—she had indeed come to help me.

I didn't need the secret pity of a mage too lazy (or too cowardly) to openly oppose the hunt when other mages surrounded her. Maybe she saw in me a chance to salve her conscience.

Well, I wouldn't give her even the most microscopic of reasons to feel better about herself. I had more respect for the mages who reveled in hazing me than for a hypocrite who could only do good deeds under the cover of fog and night.

Truthfully, though, the lurch of my near-fall had shaken me up like a snow globe. I couldn't help thinking that Wisteria Shien might prove useful. But I could also see how risky it would be to try using someone whose motivations totally stumped me, whose face and body language were so utterly opaque.

I hung the hermit crab bucket from my left elbow. I turned my hands up, mirroring the pose she'd shown me.

Just as a test. Just to see what she'd do next.

Wisteria Shien looked down at my palms. They were raw and red, but not outright dripping with blood. I wasn't missing any fingernails. I could still push through the discomfort to grab and hold things.

"You tried to climb out," she said. It had the ring of a doctor pronouncing a diagnosis.

"Were you spying on me?"

She gave a short shake of her head. "My brothers did something similar. Long ago. Trapped me deep in a place where no one would come."

"And you mountaineered your way out?" I asked. "Sorry my fitness level isn't—"

She didn't move a muscle. So there was no time for me to dodge. A new tendril of magic shot out from behind her and wrapped around my hands as if to bind them together.

A shout rose in me. I tried to fight back as soon as I saw it happening—straining my wrists apart, jangling the bucket on my arm.

The magic felt like handcuffs. It also felt like being swaddled in warm water. I stilled as the redness and stinging drained from my palms, as patches of missing skin smoothed and faded and blended in.

When the magic dissolved, I could move again.

"First Aid," said Wisteria Shien.

"I don't want to owe you any favors."

I spoke without hesitation. Being an ungrateful brat is my specialty.

"First Aid is one of the skills I got assigned to practice this month."

"Ah. And I just happened to get in the way when you practiced it."

She nodded. Then: "I'm not participating in hunting season."

"You marched me into the middle of your creepy mage gathering and read me all the rules. But now you're claiming you had nothing to do with people pooping in my shoes."

"What?"

It was the first time I'd ever heard her tone shift like that.

"Don't give my shoes that look," I said. "Obviously I cleaned them. They're probably the cleanest damn shoes in the entire school now."

There was no wind inside the ruins. But the unnatural fog stirred fretfully between and around us.

Her voice dropped back into its usual flat register. "If I wanted to hurt someone, or get rid of someone, I wouldn't disguise it in the form of a game."

Curiously, I believed her.

"Is that a threat?" I inquired.

"I asked if you wanted to leave," she said. "I can get you out of here."

I started to inch back, then thought better of it. I held myself up very straight. I still had to tilt my head back to look her in the eye.

"Here's the thing I don't get," I said. "Why?"

Wisteria Shien attempted to answer. I took enormous pleasure in talking over her. "Do you endorse hunting season, or don't you? You're S-Class. You're a Shien. If you think it's so terrible, you can shut the whole thing down. You made those upperclassmen on the beach stop torturing birds. *You know how it works here.*"

Then—with some effort—I kept my mouth shut.

The fog rose slowly over our heads.

It thinned as it went. I could make out her face and the outline of her body, as if through a smudged window. Even after the mist completely surrounded us. Even after it puffed up to fill the entire stone structure. It nestled in the open air many stories above, a cloud speared in place by the broken tower's sheared-off bones.

Wisteria Shien motioned at the yellow bucket. "They shouldn't have involved living creatures."

"Hey," I said. "I'm a living creature, too."

So were the other healers, for that matter. Though it was hard to look past the fact that they'd offered me up—and kept offering me up—to save their own collective skin.

"But I agree," I added. "My roommate's pets have nothing to do with it. Can you make them off-limits? Do the other mages respect you, or don't they?"

Her hands were back in her pockets. Her uniform fit better than I remembered.

No glasses today, I realized. They'd have gotten frosted over from the fog. I was beginning to suspect those glasses of being fake, anyway. The kind that don't do a thing to change your vision.

"I have a lot of magic branches," she said.

"That's like bragging about the size of your—"

"Doesn't mean I can do any good with them. Doesn't mean I can use them safely."

"How reassuring," I muttered. "Just what I wanted to hear, with your fog all over me."

"It won't harm you."

"Plenty of mages hurt people by accident."

I stopped to sort out my thoughts.

"Okay," I said afterward. "I get it. You came into school seeming real intimidating. You could do a little swaggering when people didn't know you well. A little bluffing.

"Now they know you better. You had to drop out of the big mage pentathlon. Maybe it turns out that your standing inside the Shien clan isn't so great. Maybe you don't have what it takes to get all the other mages to go along with you. Even healer students hear that sort of rumor."

I raised the bucket. "But you like animals. You won't interfere openly, but you'll sneak in to perform a stealthy rescue. Sure, I'll take it. Hurry up and port us out of here."

"My porting skill only works on myself. And inanimate objects."

For a single strained moment, I was convinced she had to be joking. We eyed each other through the haze.

"You meant that literally," I said, by way of confirmation.

She nodded.

"So if I hold the hermit crabs and stand in the bucket—"

"I can port the bucket outside. You'll be left behind."

"With three hermit crabs and not even a bucket to hold them in. You're useless," I concluded, too bewildered for frustration.

Suddenly she turned, as if hearing something. I strained my own ears but could only detect the muted rhythm of the ocean.

She motioned for me to follow her. I watched her walk deeper into the fog, the end of her braid swaying by her ankles.

Soon the fog would swallow her. I couldn't honestly tell where she was going, or which direction was which. Couldn't even make out the implacable shape of the ancient stone walls.

Without quite meaning to, I found myself trotting after Wisteria Shien. I did my best not to shake up the hermit crabs.

She stopped.

I stopped—rather closer to her than I'd intended. But my lungs seized up for a different reason.

I peeked around her and saw the curve of the age-worn wall, the blocked-up entrance.

Except now it was only partially blocked, with a gap large enough to crawl through single file. As if she'd melted a hole in the rubble with acid.

White mist rose from the eaten edges of the rock like hot steam.

I wasn't an expert on the steps and stages of a mage's magical education. In fact, I preferred to know as little as I could get away with.

Unfortunately, I knew at a glance that this type of skill was difficult to acquire. Difficult to use. And incredibly dangerous. She'd casually evaporated solid rock while distracting me with small talk.

"Are you even allowed to do that?" I demanded. "This is—this is a historical site!"

"Someone else dropped the boulder there after you entered. I wasn't the first to defile it."

"Next time the magisters look at your collar record, they'll see that you used a skill for melting rocks."

"Not melting," she said. "Vaporizing."

"Even better," I sneered. "How do you plan to explain that?"

"It's an original. The pattern won't match any other skills on file. They won't know what it's for unless I tell them."

"They'll just let you get away with not telling them?"

She put a hand on her side. "When they ask me about it, I'll have an attack of terrible magical pain."

"I don't see this going well."

"It might work," she said. "Once. Perhaps not twice."

"Whatever excuses you feed them," I muttered, "don't mention anything about me."

Her eyes went back to the dark hole carved out by her magic. She seemed to be waiting for me to plunge into it.

I shook my head vehemently. "I'm not going first."

At my insistence, Wisteria Shien took the lead. We clambered through the makeshift tunnel.

Outside the enclosure of the ruins, her fog seemed more diffuse. But it remained dense enough to hide the waterline from view. I almost walked into the ocean by accident.

She nudged me to circle around behind the ruins. The fog followed us, coating the entire visible length of the beach. Those watching from afar would see nothing but a bottomless white murk.

"You look sick," I said.

I wasn't just mocking her. There was a feverish sheen to the side of her face.

Something about this jogged my memory.

"Mr. Rift mentioned you." I trudged along beside Wisteria Shien as I struggled to remember. I'd given up on keeping sand out of my shoes. "Right—he said he'd never seen a mage in so much pain."

"Pain is subjective," she replied in a voice almost piteously devoid of color. "All magic causes pain. That's the essence of being a mage."

"That's what healers are for," I said. "Supposedly. Me, I think it's your problem to deal with. *You* meaning mages in general. Don't outsource your own pain management to other people just because you can. Just because we've got no other choice."

"I couldn't agree more," said Wisteria Shien.

I couldn't tell if she was being sarcastic.

"Great." I turned from her. "This is nice and all. Love nighttime walks on the beach. But I'd better get these crabs back to their tank. Hopefully no one's trashed my room in the meantime."

She caught at the back of my top. "Not that way. It's being watched."

"What way, then?"

"The long way."

She gestured a path tracing the incoming tide, one that would take us far down the sand.

Lights glimmered on a pier in the distance. The temperature had dropped enough for me to wish I had a jacket, and the clingy fog didn't help one bit. The sky just above the horizon had turned a malevolent indigo blue.

"That'll take forever," I said.

"There's still an hour till curfew."

"You enjoy my company that much?"

"You were right about me liking animals."

That low monotone of hers threw me off. By the time the barb sank in, I'd missed my chance to stab back.

"Thanks for the escort," I said sourly. "So who trapped me in there?"

She made a sound that I opted to interpret as the verbal equivalent of a shrug.

"Yeah, yeah, you're not involved. Then who's the king of the hunt?"

"The winner of the pentathlon."

"Who?"

"You asked me about him at the sundial."

Now I remembered. Bleached blond hair and a death glare.

"Does this guy have a name?" I asked.

"Minashiro Tempus."

Minashiro. Another one of the great mage clans. Saya would know more about that than I did, but I wasn't completely ignorant. I'd heard of them before coming to the academy. Just like how I'd heard of the Shiens.

"If he's the leader, he's got more pull than you," I said. "Somehow. Even if you're the only S-Class. You afraid of him?"

"Not for myself," she said.

"What's that supposed to mean?"

No reply.

She kept looking my way as we walked. No clue why. Between the depth of the fog and the dearth of moonlight, there couldn't have been much to see.

I warned her to watch where she was going. To be fair, though, the beach wasn't exactly littered with obstacles. Here and there a limp strand of black seaweed. A solitary broken shell no larger than a thumbnail. Nothing that could've tripped her. And not a single other human being in sight.

"You keep your hair very short," she said.

Was this Wisteria Shien's idea of a scintillating conversation?

"You're one to talk," I retorted. "How much shampoo do you go through in a month?"

She lapsed into silence, as if performing earnest calculations.

"Never mind," I said hastily. "Don't overthink it. You already look like you're about to faint."

Once we'd reached a safe distance from the ruins at the end of the island, she steered me down a public access path to get away from the sand. We wound through the shadows of lifeless shuttered beach houses.

We emerged on one of the labyrinthine paved streets that twisted its way between yet more houses. Some of the mansions set further back swelled monstrously in size, as if straining for a view past the roofs of prime oceanfront real estate.

Wisteria Shien pointed me in the direction of campus and offered vague instructions on how to get back.

"Yeah?" I said, pretending I wasn't at risk of getting lost along the way. I'd never been to this particular neighborhood.

"I have—a friend."

"Congratulations?"

"In housing nearby."

Her voice was so low that I struggled to make out what she was saying. I tilted closer.

She'd gone as still as the ruins.

She'd left the fog behind on the beach. Without it roiling around us, it was easier to discern the numerous unused branches of magic she kept twisted up inside her, a seething light in her torso. Like something shameful shoved willy-nilly inside a cupboard.

I could see, in a way, what Mr. Rift had meant. Her magic looked painful. On a visceral level.

It was like how a visibly broken leg—with its knee bent backwards—would look painful. Like how a dislocated shoulder would look painful. Like how a snapped neck would look painful.

"Wist?"

The voice came from a side street. A girl's voice, tinged with something like horror.

I recognized her as she stepped forward.

A mage student. A fellow Rat. Wisteria Shien's sidekick.

She had a voluminous puff of hair behind a satiny headband, which contrived to make her look a good deal taller than me. Though not tall enough to match Wisteria Shien.

The streetlights here were alive: tall fleshy-lobed cacti with crooked lamps sprouting at random spots. Student work donated by the school, presumably. A mess of magic cuttings hung from the cactus spines like cobwebs. They came very close to brushing Wisteria Shien's uniformed shoulders.

The girl with the headband shot me and my bucket a look. Not a kind look. Then she turned her full attention on Wisteria Shien.

"Wist," she said. "What are you doing?"

"Playing with hermit crabs," Wisteria Shien said under her breath. She rested a hand on her side like a runner with a cramp.

"What?"

"Nothing."

The sidekick gave me another quick glance. I smiled and waved.

She dropped her voice. Not that it stopped me from eavesdropping. "You said you were going to stay out of it," she told Wisteria Shien.

"Did I?"

"It was definitely implied. Listen—you don't want to cross Tempus."

"Azalea." So that was the sidekick's name. Wisteria Shien remained more or less upright, but she'd come to a complete stop at the side of the road, hunched over in the light of that shining many-armed cactus.

She addressed the girl called Azalea without going to the effort of looking her in the face.

"Don't worry about me, Azalea."

Azalea didn't listen. She didn't seem like the type. As she pontificated about what a bad idea it was to defy this Tempus guy, I began to softly inch away. I, for one, had to get these hermit crabs back home before curfew.

"Don't worry about me," repeated Wisteria Shien. "Don't worry about me. Don't worry about me."

It was like the same toneless bell being struck over and over and over. I didn't look back. Fear grabbed me by the neck and steered me firmly away. Let the mages take care of each other.

I slipped. I slipped on absolutely nothing.

My arms windmilled. I nearly pitched the poor hermit crabs into a stranger's front yard. I nearly fell and shattered my tailbone, or perhaps the back of my skull.

I have no idea how I managed to recover my balance. Recover, that is, in the sense that I didn't outright kill myself.

I still ended up sitting on my butt in a patch of crabgrass, clinging to the hermit crab bucket for dear life. My screech had lanced through the neighborhood like the sound of a murder scene.

Worst of all, I hadn't made it nearly as far as I thought. I was close enough to the other two to share the light from the same overgrown cactus.

I reached out with my right hand and patted at the road that had so rudely betrayed me.

It was cold. Slick. Completely iced over.

Iced over?

The three of us stared at each other. Our breath puffed out, as distinct as Wisteria Shien's magical fog.

Azalea was the first to react. I saw the terror cover her face. Then, almost instantly, she rolled it up like a blind. Tucked it right out of sight.

"You need healing," she said to Wisteria Shien.

I raised my hand.

"Not from *you*," Azalea snapped. "You're a Rat."

"So are you," I said.

"You'll be useless as a healer!"

"Got any other healers on call? Got any porting magic?"

I waited a moment. It looked like I'd guessed the answer correctly. "No? Gotta run back to campus, then. Better run fast."

Her mouth twisted. But—and I had to respect her for this—Azalea didn't waste any time arguing. She dashed into the night like a deer, crossing lawns and gardens to dodge the black ice painting the treacherous road.

I set down the hermit crab bucket. I got carefully to my feet. Despite my shriek earlier, no one else had come.

Wisteria Shien didn't seem to see me anymore. Her gaze lingered in the breath-clouded air, unfocused. Her fingers dug into her side as if she sought to claw out some offending organ deep inside her, as if she wished to prise it free and hurl it down the street into darkness.

Magic enriched the space around her like static.

There was another reason mages needed regular healing, you see. For pain relief, yes.

But also to keep them from snapping—from going berserk.

Every cell in my body wanted me to go sprinting after Azalea. Each step toward Wisteria Shien felt like stepping off the edge of a skyscraper observation deck.

You aren't meant to be here, my body wailed. *You aren't meant to do this. Oh, this isn't good. This really isn't good. This isn't right.*

I clutched the spiky model tower in my pocket. I clutched it so hard that I may as well have reached over and stabbed myself with a fistful of cactus.

"Wist," I said. Careful. Even. Using the name her friend called her. I sounded like someone else speaking.

Now was not the time to needle her.

I could've taken the lighthouse out. I could've twisted it to maximum brightness, flooded the whole street with urgent scarlet light.

I could've called surveillance gulls from all over the island. I could've alerted the academy staff much faster than Azalea, panting as she sprinted a jagged path back to campus.

And I would still use the miniature lighthouse if I thought my life were in imminent danger. The only problem, of course, was that by the time I acknowledged the threat, it'd be much too late for any number of seagull flyovers to make a genuine difference.

If someone tells you about a shark in the water, you don't keep floating around merrily until you see the shark in person. You get the hell out of there.

"Wist," I said to the proverbial shark.

At last her eyes slid toward me. She gave no sign of understanding the words coming out of my mouth.

I kept talking anyway. Like murmuring to soothe a crazed animal. She probably wouldn't remember. I sure hoped she wouldn't remember this.

"You weren't kidding about being bad at controlling your magic," I said. "A little fog, a little porting, a little rock-dissolving. You used all of—what, three skills? That's all it takes for you to lose it?"

She sucked in a breath as if she'd been stabbed. Don't think it had anything to do with my chatter, though. I could see the wound-up magic branches writhing ferociously inside her, coming unraveled from the tight-clenched form she usually forced them to hold around her core.

She sank into a crouch. The cactus-lamp, bright as an angler fish, loomed out of the dark like some kind of malformed monster trying to swallow her up from behind.

The air around us got colder and colder, the ice on the road thicker and thicker. I didn't mind, really. Adrenaline burned in my chest.

Why didn't I whip out the model lighthouse? Why didn't I use it to summon help?

Well, now I would. I'd just waited an extra minute. I'd never seen a mage on the verge of going berserk before. I'd never seen Wisteria Shien on the verge of crumbling.

There was a wildness in her unseeing eyes, in the shaking of her back.

I'd never seen a mage so desperately helpless, so incapable of caring who stood there and looked down on them as they fell into pieces.

I'd never seen a mage so weak.

I watched this girl from the great Shien clan. This S-Class mage. Her long proud braid trailed in the dirt. I watched her struggle to hold herself together, and something in me wanted nothing more than to kick her.

Her arm shot out and seized at the pleated hem of my skirt. "Go," she said, with effort. "You have to go. You—"

I didn't kick her. But I didn't call for help, either.

I let go of the miniature tower. I extracted my hand from my pocket.

I knelt next to Wisteria Shien and told her, "You know, I've never actually healed a mage before."

She couldn't speak.

"Apparently I'm pretty gifted, though. At least when it comes to working out problems on paper."

The magic in the air was so thick now that I could feel it cupping my eyeballs, wedged in my teeth.

"Pardon," I said as I put theory into practice.

I slipped my hand up under the back of her uniform. I laid my palm flat against the clammy small of her back. Skin touching skin. It was the part of the body closest to a mage's magic core. As close as you could get without taking a scalpel and slicing them open.

8

THIS IS HOW you heal a mage.

In theory, anyway. Remember, this was my first time.

I hadn't chosen to be born a healer. If I had to heal a mage—to serve a mage, to soothe a mage—then, yes, I wanted it to be one who was doubled up in pain. Groveling at my feet. Ordering me to go away.

I might have to heal a lot of mages over the course of my life. If I couldn't find any other work after graduating—if I weren't allowed to take any other work—then I might not end up having much choice in the matter.

If nothing else, I wanted the very first time I touched a mage to be my choice.

Now here I was looking at an S-Class mage right on the verge of going berserk. Here was a situation where no sane healer would choose to stay.

I caught her by the shoulder to steady her as I pushed at the small of her back. Otherwise, I might've accidentally shoved her face-first into the scrubby grass and gravel at the base of the cactus street lamp.

I grabbed a fistful of her magic branches as if yanking at a fistful of hair. Not quite in a literal sense. Magic branches aren't a solid physical thing you can coil around your finger.

But we healers can still prod at them, manipulate them, smooth out the agonizing tangles. We can see them wince and shudder at our metaphysical touch.

Wisteria Shien's magic branches weren't the only part of her that shuddered. I felt a shiver go through her back. She twisted her fingers into the loose cloth of my sleeve.

She was pushing me away.

I reflexively peeled my hand off the skin of her back. It took surprising effort—felt like it'd been glued in place. She hadn't let go of my sleeve yet.

"Is it helping?" I asked.

I couldn't tell. Her magic was objectively less painful to look at than it had been before I started wrenching it about. But she was still doubled over. She showed no sign of being able to unbend herself.

She looked at me—past me?—with bloodshot eyes. "Don't."

"Don't what?"

Now it felt like she was pulling me closer.

"If you're so determined to go berserk," I said, "maybe wait till I've got a two or three-minute head start."

In my head I saw myself running. Slipping and sliding and rolling down ice-coated streets. Running until she exploded in wild magic like a grenade at my back.

"Try again," she said raspily.

I very nearly turned on her and ordered her to say *please*.

Her one hand tightened on my sleeve. Her other hand was braced on the gravel. Her magic branches looked—well, about as pleasant to drag around as a bunch of broken legs. The only difference, after my rough intervention, was that they appeared broken in somewhat fewer places now.

This girl was no match for my image of the elite Wisteria Shien, tall and dark and irritatingly mysterious. I could see why her friend called her Wist. A name snapped in half for a mage in danger of snapping, a mage already shot through with invisible cracks.

This girl was suffering.

And through it all she maintained a creepily perfect silence, her face as stiff as her voice, her breathing only detectable in the snow-colored clouds puffing from her nose and mouth whenever her chest heaved.

I put my hand up her uniform again, flat against her back. I heaved with all my strength at her magic, at the rampaging tendrils that pulsed around her core as if seeking to strangle her from the inside.

She let out a very tiny cry. I almost didn't hear it. I didn't think I'd hurt her more than she was already hurting, but—

She'd begun to slump sideways toward the spiked lobes of the cactus lamp. I wrenched her away from it. Which meant wrenching her toward me. Our heads collided with a vengeance.

I yelped, eyes welling, and clapped my hands to my temple. Wist made so little noise that for an instant I feared I'd knocked her out.

Then her braid curled in close to her like a tape measure retracting. She passed a hand over her face. When she lowered it, her features had settled back into their default dead look. As if that piteous cry I'd heard seconds earlier had been something from a ridiculous dream.

We let go of each other at the same time.

She touched the collar around her neck, then rose carefully to her feet. She moved as if it were her first time inhabiting her body. As if she were afraid of doing something to accidentally break it.

Our breath was transparent again, the air less bitterly cold. The ice paving the street sent up wan tendrils of steam as it melted and evaporated at preternatural speeds.

The healing work I'd performed on her was very forced and crude. Something akin to applying a tourniquet. Not at all a long-term solution.

I knew mage healing was never permanent. As long as you had even a single magic branch, you'd need periodic healing for the rest of your life. For your own comfort, of course, and also to ensure you didn't inadvertently become a danger to others.

I knew that. But her magic branches still looked impossibly tangled. Even now. Even after I'd yanked them this way and that with all my might. Was healing really supposed to be this difficult?

Was healing supposed to be this hopeless?

"You should go," said Wisteria Shien.

No—

Wist, I thought. Her name was Wist.

I scrambled upright, too. Just a little belatedly. "You could thank me."

She glanced sideways at me and started to do exactly that.

"Never mind," I said quickly.

"You wanted me to thank you."

"Doesn't count if you're only saying it because I told you to. Should've thought of it on your own. Oh well."

"...I can see why the other healers offered you up for the hunt," she said.

"Excuse me?"

"You'll miss curfew if you don't leave soon."

True. I stopped bristling. I turned to pelt away down the puddle-covered street.

"Wait!"

"What?" I demanded.

Wist pointed wordlessly at a yellow bucket on the ground. I'd almost forgotten the poor hermit crabs—the entire reason I'd ended up here in the first place.

I marched over and picked up the bucket. I wasn't the least bit flustered. I most certainly wasn't avoiding eye contact.

"You've got a job to do," I said to her. "Don't forget. You make sure the other mages know these hermit crabs are off limits. I'm the target."

My footsteps were loud on the wet ground. The cactus streetlight shone richly reflected on every surface that had been glazed in her now-vaporized ice.

I paused again and looked back. We were only about as far apart as the length of my dorm room. The end of Wist's overlong braid had wound itself around her left ankle like a prisoner's manacle. The sprawling cactus beside her cast down a strident overhead light that filled her eye sockets with shadow.

I raised my voice. Just enough to make sure she heard me. "Shouldn't your friend have brought help by now?"

"I can wait."

"You won't lose control again?"

"I've never actually gone berserk in my life."

"Sure seems like you came close."

"But you saved me," said Wist.

I didn't know how to reply to that.

"I'll be fine," she told me. Like I wanted or needed reassurance.

I didn't care. And it made no difference. My priority was making curfew. Whatever happened to her in the meantime was none of my business. Let her go into full berserk mode. Let her faint. Let her rot. Let her stand there like a dolt and listen to the ocean concealed by rows of houses.

So, yes, my bucket and I made curfew.

After returning, I kicked shut the door to my dorm room. I put Bubbles, Turban, and Pearl gently back in their tank and replaced the lid. I checked in the closet and under both beds and inside my desk to make sure no one had left me any presents.

I found nothing.

No dead fish or rodents. No disgusting messages painted on the wall with mysterious substances. Apparently the would-be hunters and their healer minions had exhausted their creativity earlier in the day. I let out a loud breath.

My brain refused to turn off that night. It was a relief to hear the hermit crabs moseying around in their tank, at least.

I like to think I'm a good person, and a smart one. Don't we all?

And it's not like I nursed an abiding hatred of all mages. I knew mages were people. They just happened to be the people who ruled over our glorious motherland, from mid-level bureaucrats all the way up to the Board of Magi.

I had my own life to live, if the world would let me. I wouldn't waste my time and energy hating mages. I wanted the option to waste my time on other things. I didn't want to be stuck healing mages—catering to their needs—from graduation all the way till retirement. Just because someone had decided I had a knack for healing.

No, I didn't blindly loathe the ground mages walked on. I wouldn't wish death on them simply for the sin of being born with magic. But considering all the power they wielded, magical and otherwise, I figured mages could handle a bit of hearty ire from one little no-name student healer. No harm done.

Maybe I wasn't the greatest person to ever live in Osmanthus. Maybe I didn't even qualify as being particularly good. Still, I didn't think I was an outright terrible human being.

If anything, after the pet abduction incident, the poop-shoe incident, and everything else they'd engineered in the name of the hunt this week—well, I felt perfectly justified in harboring extra rage toward every mage that crossed my sight.

But that didn't explain my reaction to Wisteria Shien.

I'd watched her on her knees. Her excessive magic branches jangling like a sack of broken glass inside her. The stifled tension in the backs of her shoulders. Breath turning to steam between open lips.

I'd watched her, and I'd wondered:

How can your face still show so little of what you feel?

Why aren't you writhing in pain?

Why aren't you crying?

Why won't you cry?

I'm waiting.

I didn't certainly want or expect to feel sorry for her. This was the price mages paid for their power. This was why they needed us healers, much as I wish they didn't.

I just didn't know what to make of the fact that my immediate response to glimpsing the vulnerable back of her neck was neither pity nor revulsion. Not even vindictive glee.

No. It was—dissatisfaction, I guess. A simmering dissatisfaction.

I didn't feel sorry for her, for how she'd ended up having a breakdown in the middle of the street.

I felt cheated because she wasn't broken down enough. Like looking at a half-drowned person and finding yourself consumed by the urge to hold them harder under water. Get the job done. Get it done right.

This school was doing something strange to me. Or maybe I was getting swept up in the bloodthirsty mood of the hunt. Or maybe Wist herself had a miraculous ability—intentional or otherwise—to bring out the worst in me. An instinctual gift.

9

I DIDN'T CARE MUCH for the school library.

It was a conglomerate of multiple linked buildings. The healer wing was—as you might expect—the most neglected. It always smelled of old stale clothes, like something forgotten in a storage box.

Whenever I went there, I wanted to bang the windows open. They formed impressive arches that let in plenty of dust-illuminating sunlight. But they weren't designed to admit fresh air. Not unless you broke them.

The mage wings of the library were much fancier, I'd heard. They had living scrolls that words and figures and data could stream across like water, the ever-busy water of Osmanthian commerce and power. Which could mean either magical or political power. In Osmanthus, they were more or less the same thing.

No one called healing a power, much less an art. It was simply something we were expected to do for mages. Because without us they couldn't endure the pain of tangling magic, and without us they'd all lose control and go berserk. Although I'm sure they would've preferred not to need anything from us healers.

The mage wings of the library also housed terrariums of the mind, marvelous spaces of knowledge shared with top mage universities throughout the country.

There were no strict written rules saying healer students couldn't go in there. But no one expected to see us in the mage areas. We knew better than to linger where we weren't needed.

Normally I would've avoided the library altogether, if only to avoid suffocating from its sheer mustiness. On the fourth day of hunting week, I reluctantly went between classes. By then I really had no other choice.

My school books were still missing. I'd kept searching for them, but they were probably already long gone. Drowned in the ocean, perhaps, or carted off for incineration or transmutation along with food waste and toiletry packaging and other assorted litter from daily life.

I needed to keep faking my way through classes until Saya came back from training camp. Once Saya returned, I'd try cutting a deal with her to share her books.

If I were extra lucky, maybe I could finagle my way into a part-time job and eventually earn enough cash to buy a new set of texts. That seemed like a long shot, though. Rats weren't usually allowed to work.

I just didn't want to let my parents know my books were missing. They weren't stupid. Regardless of how convincingly I acted the part, they wouldn't buy any fancy stories about somehow losing it all by mistake. They'd have a hunch about what was really happening.

Why make them worry more? They couldn't do anything.

Once I hunkered down in the library, I caught up with an approximation of my class reading quickly enough.

The wooden tables and windowsills were tattooed all over with past healer students' idle graffiti: names and initials, elaborate hearts, tentacled parodies of magic branch diagrams.

I absentmindedly added a few etchings of my own when no one was watching. It seemed like the thing to do.

I had no reason to linger here afterward. No reason at all. Yet somehow I found myself picking joylessly through older books. Healer memoirs and the like. Material that would do me little good when it came time to pretend I was keeping up with lessons.

I could still picture the layout of Wist's squirming magic branches. As if she were right there in front of me with her back turned, her shirt lifted, her magic core glowering ineffably inside her.

I could picture the pattern of tendrils—too many to count accurately—more clearly than I could picture her face.

And I kept seeing the shape of her magic, that snapshot recollection. Even when I didn't want to. Especially when I didn't want to.

I kept remembering how it felt to wrestle with her branches. Like untying a ball of string that actively wanted to stay knotted.

A mage couldn't will their magic to get more tangled. And they wouldn't do it, even if they could. There was no reason to; it would only increase their suffering.

It was simply the nature of magic branches to get messier over time. Like how it's the nature of dust to collect on shelves no matter how much you wipe them. Like how it's the nature of hair to fall out no matter how often or how little you wash it.

Maybe you're surprised that my first time ever touching a mage was Wisteria Shien. In the dark of night. Out on a random island street.

Well, you don't need actual experience with healing or using magic to be officially diagnosed as a healer or a mage. Just need an expert to look and see if you have a core or not.

Got a core and magic branches? Congratulations, you're a full-blown mage. Got a core and no magic branches? Feel free to call yourself a mage—a subliminal mage, anyway—but you won't ever use magic.

No core? You're a healer like me. Can you actually do any healing? That takes a little longer to figure out.

They did all sorts of follow-up tests when I was a kid. One time, an adult mage extended a magic branch through the air and asked me to try exerting any influence I could over it. Without making physical contact with the mage himself. Stretch my magic, he said. Smooth it. Push it around. Anything would do.

He yapped in surprise when I pinched his magic as hard as I could. He nearly knocked over his chair.

The remaining tests were all hypothetical in nature. A professional healer would treat a mage right in front of me. They'd ask me to explain what I saw happening, or to dictate what I'd do next.

With me being an eager know-it-all, sometimes I'd interrupt to tell them there was a better way to get it done. Tackle this branch first, or use that branch over there as a catalyst to untangle the rest.

They oohed and aahed. They took my parents aside to speak in private. I could tell it was for good reasons, exciting reasons. I was so proud of myself back then. What a self-important little idiot.

Not much has changed, you say? Very funny.

None of my reading—skimming, really—gave me a feel for whether what I had seen in Wist was normal. S-Class mages were extremely rare to begin with. As far as I knew, there hadn't been any at the academy for quite a few years before she showed up.

But were they all this needy when it came to healing? Had Yarrow's mage been in equally terrible shape before they bonded? And just how many magic branches did Wist actually have?

S-Class was the catch-all for any mage higher than Class 9. That is, anyone with ten or more magic branches. Which could in turn be imprinted with ten or more magic skills.

Wisteria Shien clearly had far, far more than just ten. She had way too many magic branches to try tabulating them at a glance. She had so many that they hid behind and beneath each other. Almost as if they embarrassed her.

The modern mage classification system had been revised several times in the past century. Any mage-related data from before that struck me as seeming awfully unreliable. You'd have to make a lot of assumptions if you wanted to compare the power levels of a modern S-Class with some notorious historical mage from ye olden days.

Like the Kraken. A foreign woman from long, long ago. The most powerful mage of all time, they said. Thousands of branches.

Or even more. There were so many tall tales about her that to this day, no one could agree on her exact number of branches.

If she'd really had so many, perhaps the exact number didn't matter. Would there be a meaningful, measurable difference in potential between someone with a thousand magic branches and someone with a thousand and one?

The very notion of it lay too far outside our norms. We didn't possess any agreed-upon method to evaluate delicate distinctions at such an absurdly high level.

Since the contemporary classification system came into widespread use, there had been only one recorded mage with three digits' worth of magic branches. Some guy from about half a century ago. He'd reportedly had a grand total of one hundred and eight.

But that now-dead mage hadn't been particularly adept at learning or using magic skills. And he'd only been able to deploy one skill at a time. Not very impressive, given his staggering quantity of branches.

I wondered if Wist had him beat.

I left the library when I realized I'd spent close to an hour flipping through tomes that had nothing to do with my actual schoolwork. It was a hasty, ungraceful exit. I blamed Wist for distracting me.

I blamed her again when I came to a reluctant halt in the shadow of the building.

The sky outside was splotched with stark white patches like the hide of a cow. Way up near the edge of the unfenced roof, against the background of that pastoral sky, a glimpse of magic had caught my eye. Or—to be more precise—it had snagged on the peripheral edges of my magic perception.

It was the same contorted magic that had been on my mind inside the library. And throughout most of the day, to be truthful.

I hesitated. Unfortunately, it wasn't like I had anywhere else to be. Nothing of importance to do. No one to see.

My only plans were to avoid swallowing needles (I had a perfect track record so far) and to stare with manic intensity at my dormmates until I could say with absolute confidence that they were losing sleep over their contributions to hunting season.

I didn't expect to inspire guilt. Creeping unease, however, ought to be doable.

The exterior of the library's healer wing reminded me of the dilapidated neighborhoods closer to the middle of the island. Places from which you could neither see nor hear the ocean.

Deeply ingrained dirt streaked a wall shadowed by lazy big-leafed grapevines. It was too early for them to be bearing any actual grapes, of course. They probably weren't meant to be plucked off and eaten, anyway.

No need to venture back inside. An outdoor staircase ran all the way up to the top. I'd learned on previous visits that if you skipped the right steps, the trip to the roof would become much shorter.

So—thanks to whichever past mage student had embedded their magic here—I didn't have to climb a full ten flights of stairs. I wasn't out of breath when I showed up on the library roof.

Invisible railing-like spikes of magic guarded the perimeter. Which meant there was no real risk of falling to the ground. But if you looked with your eyes alone, it would appear terribly unsafe.

It wasn't that popular a place to hang out. The surveillance gulls watched it closely. Mage students seemed to prefer congregating deeper in their side of campus.

As I walked out onto the roof, I saw a collection of lightweight sea-green sunshades, the type that need a constant breeze to keep them from collapsing. I saw bushes spotted with tiny white star-shaped flowers.

Over yonder, I saw the grand aviary that crowned the mage wing of the library. I saw taut magma-bright tightropes extending far off toward other mage facilities, and the curve of the magnificent floating sundial, and a hint of the massive stadium where they held major events like the mage pentathlon.

And I saw, curled up asleep in a hanging egg chair: Wisteria Shien.

She was back in her lazy tracksuit and glasses, her braid piled up beneath her head like a pillow.

I took a moment to study her. For the sake of thoroughness, I also studied my reaction.

There was a lot I could say, but no point in saying it to someone unconscious.

At least I wasn't overcome by the urge to shove her off the edge of the roof, chair and all. (The magic rails would catch her, anyway.)

Whatever violence had reared up in me when I witnessed her almost berserking, fighting not to cry out—clearly it had been a freak impulse. Temporary insanity.

Maybe her magic was so hideously tangled and twisted that, through no fault of my own, it called up something equally wrong and twisted in me. That might explain why I'd never reacted the same way to anyone else. She was practically in a class by herself.

Imagine being bound for life to someone who brought out the worst in you. It had been a long time since I'd thought of Yarrow so much, and with such a sweatily visceral sense of horror.

Please don't let me end up like Yarrow, I prayed again, for the thousandth time. Anything—anything—but that.

I stepped back toward the stairs, just as quiet as I'd come.

"Leaving?" said a sleep-hoarsened voice.

My mouth reacted before my brain. Well done, Clematis. "I thought mages from fancy families would've learned fancy manners."

"Manners?"

"Etiquette," I said. "You know. Like how if someone thinks you're asleep, you ought to just keep pretending."

"Don't remember that from finishing school," she mumbled.

I gave up on escaping. If I hustled back down the stairs now, it would feel like I'd lost an argument.

An argument over what? Beats me. But I hate losing.

"Do you ever actually attend class?" I asked. "Half the time I see you, you're sneaking a nap."

She pushed her glasses up the bridge of her nose. "You seeing me means you're not in class, either."

"Those are fake, aren't they."

"Hm?"

"Your fashion glasses." I pointed. "Why wear them? It's not as if you put a ton of effort into the rest of your appearance."

She glanced down at her rumpled tracksuit. "You don't like it?"

She spoke in the same level tone as always. Coming from anyone else, it would've sounded wry. Coming from her—frankly, I didn't know what to think.

"Does it matter what I like?" I said. A rhetorical question. "If *you* like your gym clothes so much, why don't you wear them all the time? Surely you don't care about matching your classmates. Or getting scolded for it."

Wist blinked slowly.

"True," she said. "I could do that."

"Bit lacking in imagination, aren't you?"

Her egg chair was poised very close to the edge of the roof. Close enough that I personally wouldn't have wanted to sit there if the breeze were any stiffer. The magic rails might break a deadly fall, but I bet the initial lurch off the edge would still come as a hideous shock.

I tucked my hands in the wide ends of my healer uniform sleeves.

"I owe you for letting me out of the ruins," I said.

At that she leaned forward, making the whole chair swing precariously. She looked rather like a bird popping its head out of a cage. The chair came to a halt only when she lowered her feet to the ground.

"You stopped me from going berserk," she said. "You didn't even try to take credit."

"Had to make curfew."

What I didn't say was that I could've gotten her much better and faster healing by calling the gulls with my model lighthouse. By alerting the professionals. But I'd chosen not to.

In my mind, at least, I hadn't done her any favors. Quite the opposite.

"Besides," I added, "I slunk away to save my own skin. Would've been a real pain if they learned we were alone together. Off campus. Late at night."

"We're alone together now," she remarked.

"It's the middle of the day. We're outdoors. And definitely more than three feet apart." I spread my arms wide to demonstrate that there was no way I could touch her from where I stood.

"It's still bending the regulations," she said.

I gestured over at the raised garden beds overflowing with purplish shrubbery. More specifically, at the black-headed gull that stood there on its flat webbed feet, watching us fixedly. Its whole body was iridescent with magic.

"I, for one, haven't memorized the school rulebook." I gave the gull a little wave. "I don't see our friend making a fuss over there. Until I hear him squawking, I'll assume we've done nothing wrong. No fraternization here.

"But," I continued, with my usual air of generosity, "if my presence makes you uncomfortable, I'm happy to remove myself."

I'd said my part, after all. I wasn't thrilled to admit it, but I did think I owed her one for getting me out of the ruins. It didn't matter if she disagreed, or if she couldn't understand it.

Someday—solely for my own satisfaction—I'd find a way to pay her back. Then I'd be happy to forget she existed. I'm sure the feeling was mutual.

"Wait," said Wist.

I'd turned to leave the roof. My body stopped in place when she spoke.

For a moment I thought she'd used magic on me. Then I realized there was no magic whatsoever, just the low cutting edge of her voice—the clearest I'd ever heard it. The sound of a high-class mage from a high-class family.

I'd halted purely on reflex. I wished I could punch myself.

By the time I'd recovered my wits, she was right next to me. Her abandoned chair let out a soft whine of a creak as it swayed emptily behind us.

She wasn't staring at my face. She wasn't staring at my extremely modest chest. Instead she stared at a spot somewhere around my ribcage. The lower left side of my loose uniform jacket.

None of the stuff in my pocket had anything to do with Wisteria Shien.

"I was leaving," I said.

"You have something magical in there."

"You have a magic branch woven through your hair," I countered.

"Yes," she said. "I'm a mage."

Again, I was much too slow to react. Her hands never reached for me. Her face never flickered.

Her braid leapt up like a rope of shadow. It dipped in and out of my pocket.

By the time I flinched, Wist had already stepped back again. The end of her braid dropped my model lighthouse in the waiting palm of her hand.

She rotated it gingerly, as if examining unexploded ordnance. "Where'd you get this?"

"My roommate took it from the Heap," I said. "Is that why you put magic in your hair? To be a pickpocket?"

"The Heap," she repeated.

"I had it on me in the ruins," I told her, indignation building. "I had it on me when you paraded me around by the sundial. It's a nightlight. A good-luck charm. And it's not mine to lose."

Ignoring me, she turned it over to scrutinize the bottom of the base.

"Give it back," I said.

She didn't answer.

"Give it—"

I lunged for the lighthouse. She held it up high out of my reach. I jumped, fingers outstretched.

Her braid pushed me away like a third arm. No—something stronger than a mere arm. Much stronger.

I glowered, breathless.

Could she tell that the lighthouse would lure surveillance gulls once it got dark out? Was she sharp enough to deduce that I could've summoned the gulls to the ruins to plead for help, could've summoned gulls to her side when she came within a hair's breadth of going berserk?

"I'm being hunted," I said. "Thought you weren't very supportive of hunting season."

Wist shook her head. No way to tell what it meant.

"You'd take this away from me?" I demanded. "For your information, this is the one tool I have that might save me from actual death if one of your pals takes it too far. I heard about the healer who died in the caves."

Her face still didn't change. But a tremor seemed to go through her braid as it held me back out of reach. A brief spasm. I could've imagined it.

"It was up for grabs in the Heap," I said. "Finders keepers."

"You've used this."

"Every night. Already told you—it's my nightlight. The world hasn't ended yet."

At last she tore her gaze away from the underside of the lighthouse. She looked past me as if asking the purple shrubbery—or the nosy gull that still squatted there—for a second opinion.

"Its light lures the gulls," she said.

Oh? Had she perceived that solely from the look of its cuttings, or from my curt verbal hints? I hadn't given her a whole lot to work with.

I swiped at the lighthouse again.

This time, she let me take it.

As my fingers closed around the spiky model tower, I stumbled. It was like the weight of my body forgot to extend all the way down into my feet.

I caught myself on my own. I most certainly didn't grab at Wisteria Shien. But even after recovering my balance, I had to clench the tower harder to remind myself that neither I nor the building nor the rest of the world was swaying. Dark spikes pricked at the inside of my fist.

"Sit down," Wist told me.

I shook my head.

"You look faint."

"So do you," I said automatically. "You look like a wreck."

"Are you volunteering to heal me again?"

"Not my job," I said.

I thought—hoped—she might leave the roof, now that she could no longer nap in peace. Now that there seemed to be nothing else left to say.

As soon as she vanished from sight, I'd curl up next to one of the flowerbeds. The dizziness would pass if I could just go prone for a few mindless minutes.

Instead I heard a light metallic scraping. Next came the distinct odor of fish.

I sat my butt down on the pale flagstones out of pure disbelief. It did feel much better than standing.

Wisteria Shien, S-Class mage, had extracted a slim tin of fish from her tracksuit pocket.

She finished popping the metal top, then set the open can down on the ground on front of me. As if attempting to lure a stray cat. The spy gull watched us with hungry eyes.

She took a miniature spoon out of her other pocket. She crouched by the tinned fish and offered her spoon to me handle-first, as if holding out a knife.

"The can was sealed," she said, like that explained everything. "You saw me open it."

I was not at a loss for words. I had never been less at a loss for words in my life.

I stuck the miniature lighthouse back in my jacket. I took a deep, deep breath in hopes of anchoring my consciousness back in my body—stopping it from fleeing the scene like a criminal. My vision seemed moderately less fuzzy around the edges.

"You walk around with cans of fish," I stated.

"Have it all," Wist said. "I'm not hungry."

"Are you really going to make me sit here and ask *why* you take naps on the library roof with canned fish in your pocket?"

"And a spoon," she added.

She thrust the spoon at me again. I contemplated slapping it out of her hand, but found myself rather lacking in energy. In the end, I accepted it.

"Can't spike a sealed can," she said.

"A mage could."

"If they have a suitable skill for it. Most don't. Most mages couldn't get anything in there without compromising the seal."

"And even if they pulled it off, you'd notice traces of magic," I conceded. "If you have good enough perception."

She'd guessed right about me being hungry. I'd done my best to ignore it. But I still couldn't trust the food served at normal times of day, or any food served anywhere near my conspiring classmates. Couldn't afford to constantly splurge on vending machines or the school store, either.

Pangs of anticipation pierced my jaw. I picked up the can and dug out a spoonful.

Oil-packed salmon. The side of the spoon sliced right through the soft white bones in the middle. At least it'd be filling. And I probably needed the calcium.

"So," I said after some chewing and swallowing. "People try to put stuff in your food, too?"

"Not at school."

"At home?"

"Only at home," said Wist. "Now it's a habit. Canned fish feels safest. Canned fish never makes me sick."

"I assume the Shiens have personal chefs." I scraped a chunk of salmon skin off the side of the can. Delicious—on an empty stomach, anyway. "What the heck do they serve you? Spoiled oysters?"

"The chefs are fine," she said. "The problem is my brothers."

She spoke in the same matter-of-fact way as always. Like she didn't think she was saying anything particularly revealing.

Maybe she wasn't. Unlike Saya, I could hardly claim to be an expert on mage families and their internal politics.

I busied myself with polishing off the can of salmon. Some water would've been nice, but I wasn't about to beg her for it.

"Thanks," I said afterward. "Fanciest canned fish I've ever had."

"I have more," she replied. "A lot more."

We engaged in a brief struggle over the dirty spoon and empty can. I opted to surrender after a token show of resistance. If she wanted to take care of clean-up, good for her. Didn't look like she had anything better to do with her day.

"Piece of advice," I said as I picked myself up off the flagstones. Felt much steadier on my feet now. "If I were in pain all the time, I wouldn't work so hard to keep a straight face. And I'd do a lot more complaining."

Wist contemplated the oily spoon and can in her hands. No sign that I ought to expect a reply.

Time to head for the stairs again.

Then: "If you were in pain all the time, maybe you wouldn't have the energy to complain."

The usual low, lifeless voice. I paused my step.

"If you did complain, eventually everyone around you would get tired of listening. And in the end nothing would be left but the same pain as always."

I took a stab at translating this. "So what you're saying is—why bother?"

"Why bother," she repeated. Not a question.

"If S-Class mages are so precious, the adults around you ought to do a better job of keeping you properly healed. Don't see why they wouldn't."

"I get healed daily," Wist said. "Sometimes twice a day."

I knew enough to recognize that this was abnormally frequent. "Then your healers suck at their job," I said.

Wist let out a sound that, coming from anyone else, I might've termed a snort.

Meanwhile, the black-headed gull flew off with a squawk. Hopefully because it had gotten tired of ogling the long-gone tinned salmon, and not to report my insults to the pro healers of Guralta Academy.

Sorry, Mr. Rift. Just calling it like it is.

I had my hand on the filthy railing of the outdoor staircase leading down from the roof. I had my right foot on the top step. Wisteria Shien, for some reason, had followed me like a dog on a leash.

I was about to question where she was going when I realized her gaze was now riveted to the side of my head.

"What?" I asked, unnerved.

"Your hair isn't completely black."

Not sure what I'd expected to hear, but it wasn't that.

"What?" I said again. Twice as dumbly.

"You have a white spot."

"Oh. This?" I patted my hair. It had grown just past bristle-length and was starting to feel somewhat soft. Might be time to shave my head again. "Did you think it was a bald patch? Well, it's not. Here."

Her hand landed next to mine. Exactly where I'd gestured for her to touch.

Past her light fingertips, deformed magic branches roiled in her body like a thousand trapped and tangled tapeworms. They pulsed inside her like the throbbing of a headache, or the throbbing of an overworked heart.

A dreamy spring breeze streamed past us. The sea-colored shades staked all over the roof fluttered and snapped and cast their curved swathes of shadow.

She was still touching that little white spot in my hair, the random patch like a birthmark. She was still touching the edge of my hand, my own hand frozen idiotically in place to the side of my own head. Right on the spot I'd tapped without a single intelligent thought in my brain, telling her how to feel up my hair when I should've been telling her to go away.

"Wist?" said a voice I thought I knew.

I leapt away from Wisteria Shien. I leapt away so hard that I very nearly flung myself down the stairs.

Dirty though it was, the railing saved me. I clung to it as I spun to see Wist's friend looking back and forth between us.

The sour-faced mage called—what was her name again? Asterisk? Azoth?

"Azalea," Wist said slowly, as if surfacing from a daydream.

10

There was a reason that, even at a co-ed school, the administration worked so hard to keep us apart.

Mage-healer bonding was much more permanent than marriage. If you figured out after the fact that you didn't suit each other—whoops, too bad. There was no mechanism for getting the equivalent of a divorce.

Yarrow, for instance, would be stuck with her frozen smile and her paunchy bondmate until either he or she kicked the bucket.

And Yarrow was a success story. Her grown-man bondmate had swooped in and plucked her out of obscurity.

What, then, would be considered a failed pairing?

Imagine a healer and a mage meeting at school. Two teenagers. Pretty faces; giddy laughter; love blooming in an instant. Let's say the mage was from a very prestigious clan. The healer? Not so much. Good-looking, but not all that skilled when it came to actually healing mages.

The mage's family would never let them be together. Not in a serious way. But there was one thing those two could do to ensure no one could ever separate them (except by taking a hit out on them, I suppose).

They could hide in an empty classroom. Or they could steal away into the bushes in some shadowed part of campus. Or they could sneak around near the pond by the stables. Or they could go swimming by the pier together.

And then, so long as no one came close enough to intervene at the last moment, they could bond.

It would be over soon enough. As far as I knew, bonding was a quick process, requiring only two willing participants. From the outside it would look quite chaste. But from the second they became bondmates, they would remain tied together for the rest of their lives.

Saya would term this a victory for the healer in question. They'd be permanently bound to a desirable mage and a powerful family. They'd never have to worry about going to university, or figuring out a career, or paying rent.

On the other hand, they might have to worry a bit about the possibility of getting assassinated by their bondmate's furious relatives.

Bonding a sufficiently skilled healer could actually increase a mage's power—make them grow new magic branches, or expand their ability to use multiple branch skills in parallel. It was the only thing in the world that could result in a mage jumping to a higher class, in fact.

So parents of mages cared a great deal about ensuring that their little darlings didn't bond some useless riffraff.

This, in turn, was why I'd entered the academy determined to come off as a human sack of useless riffraff. Neither impulsive student mages nor their more calculating relatives would want anything to do with Asa Clematis.

We lived in mixed-gender dorms. There were some guidelines meant to help prevent surprise pregnancies and various contagious diseases.

Yet overall, the school was much, much stricter when it came to any sort of mingling between healers and mages.

Seniors seemed to flaunt those rules more than underclassmen. I suppose they'd been at school long enough to know exactly how far they could take it. Or maybe they'd proven to the staff that they knew better than to bond a cute face on a whim.

Technically speaking, any manner of mage-healer fraternization ought to get both parties sent to a school tribunal. Someone had to file a claim about it first, though—be they a staff member, a fellow student, or even a concerned relative.

In the absence of a complaint, the faculty could exercise more discretion. In practice, some senior mages and healers might get away with openly going around as a couple. Others, meanwhile, might get suspended for an excess of eye contact.

Whatever the school code of conduct might say—and it said a lot of things—any type of mage-healer interaction could be labeled fraternization. Just so long as the administration disliked you. And the administration was always watching.

Rumor had it that the true purpose of the magical gulls was to detect and stop any attempts at illicit bonding between students. I halfway believed it. The whole island was chock-full of those black-headed gulls with their beady white-rimmed eyes. But they didn't react in the slightest when mages on the beach tortured non-magical birds to kill time.

The administration wouldn't care about those sorts of mage pranks unless it became bad enough to get in the news on the mainland. Only then would they crack down, I thought.

So I could see the gulls being mainly geared toward blocking student bonding. It made as much sense as anything.

But there were no surveillance gulls left on the library roof when the mage named Azalea found us.

We were outdoors. In broad sunlight. Two points in our favor. Then again, we'd been completely alone until Azalea showed up.

And—even if it was just Wist's fingertips resting tentatively on the side of my head—we'd been touching. It felt like we'd been touching for a very long time.

"You," Azalea said to me. "You again?"

I chose to comport myself as if I had nothing to hide.

"Asa Clematis," I answered. "Family name Asa, given name Clematis. And you? Don't think we've properly met."

"...Azalea Wren."

An adoptee like Wist, then. Assuming Azalea was her given name. I'd correctly pegged her for the type to answer out of reflexive politeness. Even if she wanted nothing to do with me.

It shouldn't have been such a surprise for a third party to appear on the roof with us.

Obviously she hadn't climbed the outdoor stairs. I'd been watching them the entire time.

But there were other ways to get here, especially if you were a mage. She could've come over from the rooftop garden and aviary in the mage wing of the library. She could've taken an indoor staircase. She could've tightroped all the way from buildings deeper in mage territory, the mage dorms or gymnasium or theater or art gallery.

Anyway, this girl was Wisteria Shien's friend. Normally it would seem logical for Wist to take the lead. Let them work it out mage-to-mage.

But Wist, after addressing Azalea by name, had proceeded to clamp her mouth shut. Very helpful.

"You're a good friend," I said to Azalea. "You ran to get help for Wist yesterday. Very kind. Very caring."

She narrowed her eyes at me. Maybe I shouldn't have said that. "You two were alone on the street last night, too."

"Scandalous," I admitted. "But we haven't done anything truly wrong. Don't report us. Would you screw over a friend?"

"*You* aren't my friend," Azalea said.

She cast Wist a reproachful look. One point in Azalea's favor: unlike some people, she knew how to make actual facial expressions. How to speak with more emotion than a dried-up prehistoric rock.

"I wasn't planning on reporting anyone," she added. "Should I?"

"No, no, no," I said swiftly. "Spare yourself the effort."

"I came here looking for you."

Wist stirred beside me, but still said nothing. I point at myself. Just to be sure. "Me? Really?"

"You," Azalea affirmed. "I have a message from Tempus."

"Who?"

"Minashiro Tempus."

"No, really, who?"

"I told you about him yesterday," said Wist.

I tipped my head back to search for clues in the faraway sky. Tempus. Tempus.

"The guy with the fake blond hair?"

Azalea made a stifled sound. The back of her hand covered her mouth.

"I mean, I only ever saw him once. I'm just saying, you'd think someone from one of the great mage families could afford a more natural-looking dye job. But maybe it's just how he wanted it."

Azalea had managed to put on an unamused expression by the time she lowered her hand. "Maybe."

"What's his message? I haven't told any teachers about the hunt. And I definitely haven't missed curfew."

"Your school books are in one of the dumpsters by the Heap."

My chest tightened. Hope is a treacherous feeling. "Minashiro Tempus wants me to go dumpster diving?"

"What you do is up to you."

Indeed. Well, I needed my books back.

On my way over to the dumpsters, I summoned a mental image of Azalea's magic. The ember-like core inside, and just one lonely branch coming out of it.

I'd seen her more than once by now, if only in passing. I'd noticed her magic each time. But I hadn't devoted much conscious thought to it.

Azalea Wren was Class 1. She could only ever possess and use one single magic skill at a time. That made her the weakest possible type of mage (other than subliminals, who had no branches at all, and who were really just mages in name only).

In a way, she was the exact opposite of Wisteria Shien.

To my knowledge, Guralta Academy normally set their admissions cut-off somewhere around Class 3. I had yet to spot other lower-class mages around campus. But there must be a reason the Wren clan had gone out of its way to adopt her. There must be a reason the academy had let her in.

The Heap of abandoned magical projects was housed in a kind of open warehouse. The dumpsters for non-magical trash waited further out back.

I stopped in my tracks when I was about to pass the Heap. I turned to my left, hands nestled primly in my sleeves. I looked up at Wist, and I made no effort to hide my incredulity.

"Why're you following me?"

She raised the empty salmon can she'd been carrying the entire time. Ever since I finished eating it. "I have business with the dumpsters, too."

I blinked at her. Specifically, at the front of her tracksuit.

Despite not being in uniform, she did have on the requisite pins. A rat pin, for instance—similar to my rat pin, although there were some differences if you looked closely. The mage rat pins had more of a regal air to them.

She wore one other pin, too. A pelican.

"You're in the originator program," I said.

Wist nodded.

I'd already heard that from Saya. It wasn't my first time glancing at her pins, either. But it hadn't really sunk in before. Had there ever been another S-Class originator in recorded history? Aside from the infamous Kraken, obviously.

"Azalea, too?" I guessed.

Another nod.

That made sense. The originator program was extremely small. I thought I remembered Saya going on about how right now there were only eight originators in the entire school. Just eight mages from all the grades put together.

If Azalea and Wist were both originators—perhaps the only two Rat originators—I could understand why they'd gotten close. Despite Wist's downright dire social skills. And I could also understand why Azalea would've been allowed into the academy. Despite only having one magic branch.

To tell the truth, I didn't know all that much about the nitty-gritty details of what set originators apart from other mages. I just knew the basics.

To summarize: originators were rare and valuable. Priceless, really.

In other words, this was just one more thing that made Wisteria Shien extra special. One more thing that made me want to kick her in the ankles. Cut her down to size.

For now, I pointed at the bank of outdoor trough sinks next to the dumpsters. "Don't forget to rinse your can first."

There were a lot of dumpsters to look through. At least they'd been treated with deodorizing magic. The scent they exuded was less offensive than the stagnant air in the healer wing of the library.

I didn't think I'd have to go too far in, either. The ostensible leader of the hunt wouldn't have sent me here merely for the sake of making me flounder around waist-deep in garbage.

If that were the end goal, he could've recruited my classmates to pelt me with trash from our dorm. No need to use my textbooks as bait.

I did entertain the notion that he might try to trap me inside. For instance, by placing the books far enough back that I'd have to vault my whole body into one of the dumpsters to reach them.

Maybe my entrance would trigger a magical trap. Maybe the dumpster would snap shut and lock itself. Maybe I'd end up stuck there screaming for someone to come let me out.

Guess I ought to be glad that Wist had tagged along. For whatever reason, she'd let me out of the ruins. She'd probably let me out of a closed dumpster. Although I strongly preferred not having to rely on outside help.

The dumpsters looked much gaudier than you might imagine: painted top to bottom with rainbow murals, and coated in shining magic cuttings meant to seal in their color. Normal city dumpsters weren't nearly this pretty.

It was yet another example of how casually they threw around magic here on the island. They had such a high concentration of mages-in-training available as free labor. No need to worry about the underlying cost, I guess.

Upperclassmen ran most of the school's waste management. They used garbage as the raw material for limited forms of transmutation and other types of magic practice.

It wasn't exactly on the level of industrial recycling, and not nearly efficient enough to be scalable beyond campus. At least not the way they handled it. But I'd never seen the dumpsters overflowing or leaking or swarmed by flies. So I suppose they got by well enough.

"Are these your books?"

I trotted over to see what Wist was looking at.

She stood before a dumpster painted with grandiose renditions of common vegetables. Long-stemmed spinach, lotus root, white radish, green-skinned pumpkin, enormous red carrots, purple potatoes.

This bore absolutely no relation to the contents of the dumpster, which appeared to consist mostly of discarded packaging and other paper-based products.

I stood on tiptoe to see inside.

My texts rested well within reach. Stacked neatly on top, even.

With their curling covers and stained edges, they looked deceptively cheap. This wasn't the result of thieves mishandling them, either. The paper had gone all wavy within hours of me first cracking them open.

But now there was one major difference.

Unfamiliar magic cuttings wound like wire around each book.

I turned to Wist. "Okay," I said. "What'll happen if I grab them?"

She'd been able to tell what the lighthouse could do just by looking at it. Hopefully she'd be able to parse these, too. I sure couldn't.

She took so long to answer that I started wondering if she'd fallen asleep on her feet.

"You'll get ported," she said.

"Where? Not to the caves, I hope."

"Farther than that. Off the island."

I clutched at the edge of the dumpster and leaned my head inside for a closer look. A papery wet-dog smell filled my nostrils to the brim.

"Can you tell who these cuttings came from? Anyone you know?"

"Not Tempus himself," she said.

"Who, then?"

"Perhaps a senior."

"One no longer collared," I guessed. "Well, doesn't matter too much whose cuttings they are. Doesn't change what I have to do in the end."

"You aren't planning on touching those books," Wist said.

"Do you have any idea how much these things cost? Of course I am."

"It's a trap."

"I can see that."

"Why would you...?"

Hah. I had her stumped.

She paused, then rephrased. "How do you plan on—"

"Like this."

I slapped one hand down on her shoulder and—at the exact same time—slapped the other down on my booby-trapped pile of textbooks.

11

MY BOOKS THUMPED to the ground at my feet. Dark loamy soil.

I stood in Wist's shadow, surrounded by shoulder-high leaves. Brilliant orange leaves, for almost as far as the eye could see. Spica.

I inhaled spica-filled air and promptly launched into a sneezing fit. Spica was a nice enough drink. But that didn't mean I was ready to take in the raw fragrance of an entire fiery field of it.

Wist, curse her, appeared unaffected. She raised a hand to her forehead to shield her eyes from the sun.

If she were anyone else, I'd have braced myself for outrage.

I was not the one who'd booby-trapped the books. I was, however, the one who'd decided to spring the trap. I was the one who'd made a calculated effort to drag her along with me.

"Sorry about that," I said experimentally. A cursory apology.

She looked about the spica field as if she were still getting her bearings. As if she were in no particular rush.

Not that I wanted her to rage at me, but I couldn't understand how she managed to stay so sedate. If I'd gotten ported here against my will, I'd be throwing a tantrum for the ages.

Maybe she kept her cool because she knew she had an easy way home. Because she was a mage, an S-Class mage with a porting skill of her own.

I was counting on that skill of hers, too.

I crouched to study my much-abused books. The magic cuttings were gone, all used up. Throwaways. They really had been created exclusively for the purpose of booting me far off campus.

Snap off a magic branch with a skill imprinted on it, and it becomes a cutting. Wait for the branch to grow back, and then you could snap it off again. Some cuttings were reusable; some were soon consumed.

The important part was that anyone could activate them. You didn't have to be the mage who'd originally pruned the cutting from your own magic. You didn't even have to be a mage at all. I was the opposite of a mage, and I'd set off the cuttings on my books with my touch.

On the bright side, those cuttings appeared to be gone now. They'd used themselves up like a firecracker popping. No chance of it happening again.

Now all I needed to do was get back to school before curfew. There were still plenty of hours left in the day, and I had a powerful mage beside me. No sweat.

That said, I had no idea where we were. On some farm, it appeared. On the mainland. There were no spica fields on Guralta Isle.

But I suspected we weren't too far beyond the island bridge. I couldn't imagine any student possessing a porting skill capable of shooting us halfway across the country. Not even a senior.

I gathered my books in my arms, then straightened up. "Ready to head back?"

Wist contemplated me wordlessly.

"What?"

She tipped her head to one side like a dog.

"Seriously, what?" I asked.

"We left the ruins yesterday," she said.

"What about it? Feeling nostalgic?"

"You already forgot?"

"Forgot *what*?"

"I can't port other human beings."

"............"

I listened distantly to the sound of my grand plan shattering.

The spica field echoed with the chirps of tiny hidden birds, with the swishing of spring wind combing its way through long leaves, and now with my shrieks of dismay.

I soon stopped spitting invective. Needed to keep my priorities straight.

I leapt at Wist and shamelessly clung to her sleeve. I managed it even with my books cradled under one arm. Not that this would have any power to prevent her from going poof if she decided to port home by herself. At best it might serve as a brief psychological deterrent.

"Wist," I said in my friendliest voice. "Wist, Wist, Wist. Wistie."

"Yes?"

Damn that poker face of hers. "Just establishing what great friends we are," I continued, undeterred.

"*Wist* is better than *Wistie*."

"I'll call you any name you like, Your Highness."

Clutching her arm, I felt her wince. Her face didn't move a muscle.

"What," I said, "you never wanted to be a princess?"

Wist shook her head vigorously. It was the most energetic I'd ever seen her.

If I were her, I'd leave Asa Clematis behind in an instant. I'd use magic to port myself straight back to campus, if I could make it that far in one jump. And I'd do it without a second thought.

I held her arm tighter. "Listen. I already owe you for the ruins."

"We talked about that."

"Let's talk some more. We get along so well, after all."

"You pulled me back from the brink of berserking," said Wist. "There's nothing to owe."

"No, no, no." I tugged at her until she stopped looking out at the rows and rows of orange leaves.

Springtime spica fields were said to be one of the most beautiful sights in all of Osmanthus (which was by no means a small country).

I didn't want her admiring the spica, though. Right now I wanted her to focus on me.

"The point here," I said, "is that I'm asking you not to ditch me. I'm asking you nicely. It'll be a worthwhile investment."

"Investment?"

"I'll owe you even more now," I told her. "If you help me get back to campus, I'll pay you back by the end of the day. I'll pay you back in full. You won't regret it."

Behind her glasses, her eyes traveled slowly from my face to my arm—forcibly entwined with hers—and then back again.

She stood almost entirely motionless, but the end of her braid twitched restively down by her legs. Once in a while it swung too far, struck a spica plant, and then leapt back to her side like a spooked animal.

"If it isn't clear—" I began.

"Are you...?" She kept breaking eye contact.

"Am I what?"

"Are you trying to offer me your...?"

"My...?"

"Your body?"

A very long moment passed before I reacted. A moment during which I stayed frozen in place, thunderstruck, and Wist gazed stoically away across the glorious waves of spica. As if in an act of mercy. As if spare me further embarrassment.

I dropped her arm. I took a robotic step back. I buried my face in my books. I gulped a few burning breaths. Then I reared my head up and went on the attack.

"I was trying to offer you my *mind*," I hissed. "I'll pay you back in knowledge. Knowledge!"

"Knowledge," Wist said blandly.

"The most valuable thing of all!"

We were in a standoff now, an audience of flame-colored spica arrayed behind each of us. We glared at each other.

I glared, rather. Wist looked the same as always: tired, hollow, and much too tall for my liking.

Then I began thinking more strategically.

"Was that supposed to be a hint?" I asked.

"A hint about what?"

"Are you saying you'd prefer to be paid back with my body? Is that what you want? You scoundrel."

"I—eh?"

I made a show of hugging myself. I looked up at Wist with piteous eyes.

"Can't believe you would prey on a poor destitute healer," I said mournfully. "Can't even afford to re-buy my textbooks. First I get harassed by my own classmates all week. Next comes the ultimate humiliation. Now I have to sell myself to—"

"No one. Is asking you. To sell yourself."

I wiped away an imaginary tear. Then I puffed myself up.

"I can read between the lines," I said in tones of the utmost bravery.

Wist removed her glasses. I suspected that what she really wanted to remove were her ears.

"I don't want your body." She stared intensely down at her glasses. The lenses were sorely in need of a good wipe.

I wilted. "You don't? Is there something wrong with me?"

"That's not—"

"I get it," I said. "You can't work up any interest in someone so much shorter and less—uh, voluptuous than you. That's a shame. But I still need a way to pay you back."

She put her glasses back on. "You keep putting words in my mouth."

"You keep letting me."

She fixed me with an inscrutable look. "Don't victim-blame."

"Wouldn't dream of it." I linked arms with her again.

I could feel victory on my fingertips.

"So. You'll take the long way back to campus with me. And you'll accept payment in knowledge. Perfect." I beamed. "I'm so glad we understand each other. I'm looking forward to sharing my wisdom."

I figured Wist would make at least a feeble attempt to continue the argument. But she didn't say a word. The end of her braid rose up like a rattlesnake. It absently flicked away a fly that had been zooming in hyperactive circles near my face.

I squinted at her. "Are you smiling?"

"Why would I smile?"

Good point. "Must've been a trick of the light."

Somehow I'd managed to secure her cooperation. I was lucky that she didn't seem too invested in campus life—she wouldn't mind missing out on a few more hours at school.

Did she belong to any sports teams or clubs? Very unlikely. Did she habitually cut class? No doubt about it.

Also: she was a pushover. That helped, too.

Ironic. And hard to explain. But she was. The faster and harder I talked, the more reluctant she grew to push back. I could tell.

Given how much raw power Wist possessed, I'd understand if she'd grown up spoiled and selfish. Used to getting her way in all things. I'd find it distasteful, but I'd understand.

I didn't understand how she'd ended up more inclined to yield, to keep her thoughts crumpled up inside her, to let a loudmouthed healer drag her around on a countryside farm.

She hardly knew me. I couldn't believe this was working.

We trudged our way out of the spica field, which was no small trek. We trudged our way down to the nearest road. It turned out to be a humble strip of gravel flanked by yet more farmland. Plus isolated patches of dark forest. And, between it all, freshly razed areas where the corpses of wild trees formed messy domes like giant eagle nests.

Several minutes went by before a single person came into sight.

I began to worry that I'd have to make Wist port to the nearest farmhouse or town on her own. Then I'd have to trust her to arrange for transportation. I'd have to wait for her to come all the way back to pick me up.

I don't like things happening without my input. I definitely wouldn't enjoy being stuck here. Me and the rustling spica and the packs of ravenous wild boars that probably lived in the gloomy-looking forest over yonder.

Thankfully, I managed to flag down a lady passing on a skimmer.

I was still in my school uniform, so I sweet-talked her with a version of the truth. We were Guralta students—model students, naturally— who'd gotten stranded after a minor porting accident.

The lady was going in the right direction. She agreed to take us to Baneberry, the mainland town closest to Guralta Isle.

For reasons I couldn't begin to fathom, Wist chose to loom ominously behind me the entire time I chatted up our benefactor. I grew seriously concerned that her brooding presence might spoil our chances of catching a ride.

I made sure to drop the name *Shien* a few times. It seemed to help.

I sensed Wist staring a hole in the side of my face after the lady dropped us off in Baneberry.

Whatever Wist thought, I was quite pleased with our progress. The sun was nowhere near setting, and all we had to do now was get to the tram.

"Got something to say?" I asked.

"Your grand plan was to hitchhike."

"Worked perfectly, didn't it?"

"How'd you know she would take us?"

Now it was my turn to be baffled. "I didn't. That's why I asked her. You've got to talk to people if you want them to help you. If that lady said no, we'd just have to go find someone else."

"It wouldn't have occurred to me," Wist said after a moment. "To simply find someone to ride with."

"Good for you, eh? Not all of us can solve all our problems with magic."

We were in the Baneberry shopping district, meandering our way over to the tram station nearest the bridge.

Our skimmer-riding savior had dropped us a few streets back. The roads further in only allowed bicycles and pedestrian traffic. Few buildings reached over two or three stories in height.

I eyed the sky, still blotchy with milk-white clouds. A new thought was beginning to brew at the back of my head.

"You in a rush to get back?" I asked.

"If I were," said Wist, "would I be here?"

True. She could still port herself to the heart of the island anytime she wanted to leave me in the dust.

"No afternoon classes?"

"I can miss a few classes."

"Hah. Sounds like me."

At the tram station, I stopped to study the timetable.

"The last one runs after sundown," I said, pointing. "That's hours and hours away."

"The next tram is in seven minutes."

I adjusted my grip on my books and turned to look up at Wist.

She leaned on a wall covered in huge colorful posters advertising local tourist activities. Jaunts to other barrier islands. Boating and fishing. Magical water-surface walking with a guide there to help. Fancy trains taking the scenic route down the full length of the southern coast.

Her face remained impassive. Her posture murmured of exhaustion.

Magical pain and physical pain were utterly separate. A physical massage might aid sore shoulders, but it wouldn't do a thing about soreness in your magic. Similarly, my kind of healing had no power to ease a backache.

That's why I didn't suggest that she try taking a seat on the nearest bench. Resting her body wouldn't make it any better for her.

Then again, I suppose if her magical pain were abnormally constant and abnormally severe, it very well might bleed over into her body. In the same way that mental stress could give you a headache, destroy your appetite, ruin your sleep.

"Want to take the next tram?" I asked.

"You want to stay?"

"That's one option," I said. "We could hang out in Baneberry a little longer. Take it as a gift from—what's his name again?"

"Tempus."

"Right. That guy. He laid the trap to send me here. Bet he never expected me to abduct you in the process."

"He didn't send us here. He sent us to a farm in the middle of nowhere."

"Close enough," I replied. "Anyway, he was thinking it'd be me all by myself. Must've figured I'd get stranded and miss curfew. Idiot."

We were already off the island. We'd failed to clear our trip with the teachers. That was a done deal.

Even if no humans reported us, the magical gulls would notice us coming back over the bridge. The tram was slow and full of windows. Not a vehicle for stealth.

The way I saw it, we were equally likely to get in trouble whether we rushed back right away or took our sweet time moseying home later.

As long as I made it back before curfew, Tempus would still end up losing this round of the game.

"I haven't been to Baneberry since my parents brought me over for orientation," I said. "Might as well enjoy the free trip. But if you're tired—"

"I have a token," Wist said.

"For the tram?"

"More general. I can charge things to a family account."

"Things," I echoed.

"Purchases," she said coolly. "Monetary transactions."

I studied the empty tram station. All those posters in tropical colors. They stood taller than Wist. Then I followed her gaze to the food stalls and shops down the street.

"You're offering to treat me?"

"You almost fainted from hunger on the roof."

"Hey, it wasn't that bad," I argued. Gotta defend my honor. "I was doing just fine. But thanks for the fish."

"You almost drooled when we passed the bakery back there."

"Slander," I said.

But I didn't fight her too hard. C'mon. If I could wrangle a solid meal and a mini-vacation in the middle of hunting season, far be it from me to pass it up.

Besides, I'd been secretly counting on Wist to pay for my tram ticket. I wasn't in any position to act prissy about taking her money.

Healers targeted in past years hadn't had it nearly so good. Especially the healers who'd found themselves hunted when her brothers were still enrolled.

In any case, the Shien clan was famed for its wealth. They could afford to cover my expenses for a scant couple of hours.

That was how we ended up in a cafe with hundreds of empty coffee cups hanging from hooks on all its walls. I devoured a buckwheat crepe with a runny egg in the middle. Quite filling. But I was only just getting started. Next I proceeded to attack an enormous nutty parfait interspersed with globs of black sesame paste as thick as tar.

Between bites, I questioned Wist. "You're fine with restaurant food? No way all of this came out of a can."

She nibbled at a tuna melt. "Depends who I'm eating with."

"You trust me more than your siblings?"

Her lack of response seemed like answer enough.

The waiter had given me a long slim spoon: the perfect tool for digging around in my tall parfait glass. I stuck it all the way down to the crunchy bits at the very bottom, then asked, "What's with the fog?"

"My fog?"

"Your fog. You learn that at school?"

"Not at Guralta."

I motioned at the pelican pin on her chest. "You're an originator. Did you invent your fog skill from scratch? If no one from the academy taught it to you, I mean."

Wist sat to my right, rather than across from me. Her eyes moved across the coffee cups hanging on the opposite wall as if she were trying to count them.

"Does it matter how I learned it?" she said eventually.

"No," I allowed. "But." I stopped to swallow a spoonful of black-sesame-swirled ice cream. The parfait would turn to soup if I dawdled. "Your collar. It takes a record every time you use magic. No one ever questions why you get it in your head to produce massive quantities of fog at random moments?"

"They question it. They question it all the time."

"You can't just use any magic you want, then. Not without an interrogation."

Wist bent her head in agreement. "We're discouraged from using skills that aren't currently on the curriculum. Or that we haven't otherwise gotten a waiver for."

"So they do scold you for going off-script. Yeah, what happened after you evaporated those rocks to get me out of the ruins? What'd they say about that?"

Her fingertips went to her collar. "When they first asked, my magic pained me too much to speak."

"And they believed it?"

"The next time, I had stomach cramps. They came back again to cross-examine me later. I said I couldn't remember which skill I'd been using. I said perhaps I'd been sleep-maging."

"That's just about the stupidest excuse you could've come up with," I told her.

She didn't try to contradict me. Because I was right. Mages prone to activating skills in their sleep posed a different kind of a danger from berserkers. But they could nevertheless be incredibly dangerous.

If the school magisters found evidence that Wist really did have sleep-maging tendencies, that alone might be enough to get her institutionalized.

"I assume they figured out you were lying."

"Not lying," she said. "Confused."

"Uh-huh. Must've been a big relief for them to realize that you weren't actually sleep-maging. That you were just fooling around with an unauthorized skill, after all. I see how you played it. Yeah, that sounds like a one-time trick."

"I can duck questions," said Wist. "I can make up excuses. Won't always work. But I get more leeway than most other mage Rats."

"Because you have a billion magic branches to spare?"

Wist ignored this. "Because I barely ever use magic outside class."

"Why do I keep seeing you use it, then?"

She spread her hands as if she too wanted to know the answer.

"Better not blame me," I said. "Not my fault I'm being persecuted. And no one asked you to intervene."

"...In the spica field, you clung to me and begged me not to leave."

"Did I? Huh. Sure feels like a long time ago, doesn't it?"

Whatever the reason, the more Wist used her magic between healing sessions, the worse it would ache. If even twice-daily healing wasn't enough to ease the burden, she'd never be able to wield her massive quantities of magic without cringing. Without hesitating.

I wasn't interviewing her just for the fun of it. My questions had a purpose.

But my thoughts weren't fully formed yet. First I needed to finish tackling my melting parfait.

After the cafe, we walked down to a marina full of cutesy boats painted in vivid primary colors. Most of their names seemed to be rather unfortunate puns.

Large ducks paddled by the docks, aggressively begging for scraps. I had to admire their dedication to getting fed. To them, we passing humans were essentially the equivalent of a slot machine.

I studied the ducks as I brooded. "What about magic cuttings?"

"What about them?"

I pantomimed putting my hands around my neck. "Your collar. How does it handle cuttings?"

"You're very curious about these collars."

"Why shouldn't I be?" I asked. "I'm at school to learn. And grow. And if you're about to comment on me ditching afternoon classes, don't. Doesn't mean I'm not hungry for knowledge."

I paused expectantly. A crow screeched from the rooftop of a restaurant overlooking the waterfront.

"Of course," I added, "if it's just that you're totally clueless about what the collar does with cuttings, no harm done. We can't all be budding scholars. Maybe you're not the sort people would describe as having an inquisitive mind."

"My mind," Wist said rigidly, "is as inquisitive as it needs to be. Cuttings get recorded at the point of pruning."

That meant the school staff could see when a collared mage student pruned a particular branch. Like the cuttings used to port us off the island.

Those cuttings could've been produced by anyone, though. A Guralta upperclassman, or someone long since graduated. Or a mage who had zero affiliation with the school.

Alumni obviously wore no collar. Select seniors got cleared to stop wearing theirs, too. If someone without a collar made the cuttings, the administration would've been completely blind to their existence.

Even if the administration did possess a record of the cuttings' creation, they'd have no idea when those cuttings actually got used (or if they ever got used at all).

Nor would they be able to tell who ended up using them.

"Are Rats allowed to make cuttings?" I asked.

"We're not forbidden."

"Are you any good at it?"

Her long braid twisted around on itself as if shying back from a memory of something foul. "I prefer not to."

"Because it hurts worse than using regular attached branch skills?" I guessed. "In your case, anyway."

I'd never heard anything about pruning being painful. But her magic was so inherently warped—and she had so much of it to get tangled—that there was no telling what might make it feel worse.

As we turned our backs on the breeze coming off the water, I spotted an airship passing high overhead.

I caught at Wist's elbow and pointed. She looked without comment.

"Wonder how close we got to the airfield," I mused. "Would've liked to see it. Tempus should've had the consideration to dump us somewhere more interesting."

"I'm not fond of airships," Wist said.

That was unexpected. "What? Why?"

Her stride lengthened, as if she thought walking faster would make me forget the whole thing. Fat chance. I half-jogged to keep up. "What'd airships ever do to you?"

"They look like cicadas," she said at last.

"They—what?"

I stopped. Wist stopped.

No more boats in sight. We were right by the entrance to an outdoor marketplace packed into a covered promenade. Past Wist, I could see hefty barrels of pickled vegetables and assorted grains. Sticky sesame-covered sweets. Grilled whole fish sold on skewers. Dangling strings of dark dried persimmon.

I was still stuffed from the cafe, but that didn't make it any less tempting. With some effort, I tore my gaze away from the food vendors.

"You've got a problem with cicadas?" I asked. Just making sure.

She had on her usual grim mask. I took this as a yes.

A malicious thrill went through me.

"You're afraid of bugs," I said. "Wisteria Shien is afraid of bugs. Boy, are you lucky you're not the one being hunted."

"'Afraid' is putting it too strongly."

I regaled her with the story of the slugs in my desk. I detected a hint of tension in the set of her mouth.

Back home, my parents were always growing a plethora of plants, both indoors and outdoors. That meant battling everything from whiteflies to tomato worms. I could've tormented Wist with plenty more tales of real-life infestations.

I didn't. But I did make sure to congratulate myself for my restraint.

We zigzagged from the harbor to the market to a small park that held the ruins of an ancient temple. All that remained were a series of disconnected pillars—shockingly large ones—and eroded lumps of stone that might once have been statues.

The pillars stood taller than the tallest trees in the park. Even then, there were a couple of trees that would've taken three of me to hug a full circle around their girth.

At the center lay a small pond, neat as a crater, with mossy islands stacked full of mud-brown turtles. Carp of every color swam past. Platinum white with patches of orange as bright as spica. Murky brown like the turtles. Pure gold.

Something flickered in my peripheral vision. When I looked up from the fish, I saw Wist's braid signaling to me like a semaphore flag.

She was way over at the far end of the pond, crouching on a low stone bridge. No guard rail. The water beyond the bridge looked shallower, stiller, choked with rocks and greenery. She pointed, both with her hand and the end of the braid.

I joined her on the bridge. I peered over her shoulder.

Tadpoles packed the water, little black blobs, shiny and constantly wriggling. They clustered furiously at the edges of half-submerged rocks, nibbling at what appeared to be a delicious meal of wet slime.

"Looks like a vat of black beans," I remarked.

"Do beans wriggle this much?"

"When you're in the middle of cooking them, sure." I squatted next to Wist. "These don't bother you?"

"Why would they?"

"You're leery of insects," I said. "I don't see much practical difference between these little guys and a pile of worms or maggots."

"I like fish," said Wist.

"So do a lot of people," I told her. "Tadpoles aren't fish."

"They aren't frogs, either."

This was the moment when I finally succumbed to temptation.

Her braid had coiled itself a couple times around her shoulders, but the end still dangled way down her back, twitching softly back and forth. At first I just watched it carve out an inaudible beat, steady as a metronome.

Then I reached out and grabbed it.

I'm sorry to report that Wist reacted very little, and very slowly. Made me wonder how she'd gotten so good at suppressing her reflexes.

She turned her head toward me. She was still crouched with her hands on her knees and her chin on her hands. Her eyes were the same color as the bottom of the pond, and just about as informative.

She'd touched me with her braid before. If anything, she seemed more comfortable pushing me around with her braid than with her own flesh, her arms and hands.

The blank look she gave me now made me feel, somehow, as if I'd done something much worse.

I coughed a shameful fake cough. I let go.

"Speaking of your braid," I said—although no one had spoken of anything—"you use it like an extra arm. You wave it around all the time. But I thought magic use pained you. I thought you were trying to be super minimalistic about it."

"It's a very minor skill," she said. "It's one of the oldest skills I have."

"Ever tried not swishing your braid around for a day or two? Might help with the pain."

"Of course."

"And?"

"I get antsy. And my magic branches still tangle and cramp."

"So it's a crutch," I said. "Could have worse crutches, I guess."

The swarming tadpoles wiggled on, oblivious to our conversation.

The park as a whole was just about empty. The only other people in sight were a shrunken old man and a high-pitched child playing with pigeons near the entrance. (Subliminal mages, both of them: they had magic cores, but no branches.)

I stood up to stretch my knees. I kept a respectable distance from Wist's braid.

"Question," I said. "Does this mean your collar record is totally packed with hair-kinesis magic? All day and all night?"

"Maybe not all night."

"The administration doesn't complain about it? With so much junk data, how can they even notice you using other skills?"

"The academy's been around for centuries."

"Huh. In other words, they've got plenty of practice."

I offered Wist a hand. She regarded it for several seconds longer than felt comfortable. "You want me to—?"

"Whatever you're thinking," I said in a rush, "it's clearly wrong." I put my hand behind my back. "I was inviting you to stand. Don't trip and fall in the water."

"Thought you were telling me to kiss it."

"I had my palm up!"

"Or to lick it," she amended. "Like giving your hand to a dog."

At this point Wist had risen to her full height, infuriatingly unhurried.

"You really have no idea how my mind works," I said.

"Likewise."

"Excuse me?"

"Nothing," she said innocently.

If you asked me why I thought she was feigning innocence, I wouldn't have been able to explain it. Objectively speaking, nothing about her demeanor or voice was any different from before, any less vacant of color.

Maybe I was the problem. She gave me nothing to work with, and my mind fought too hard to make sense of her nothingness. Like spying a cloud in the shape of an animal, or a face burnt into toast.

"Would be nice to see these as frogs," I said, looking back at the tadpoles. "Wonder how many will make it."

"That would be a lot of frogs."

"Do turtles eat tadpoles? Might explain all those turtles on the other side of the pond."

Wist drifted after me as I went to collect my books from a park bench. Beside them rested a paper sack of bakery bread Wist had bought on one of the narrow shopping streets, a place steamy with the scent of hot noodles.

I kept hearing distant shrieks. Couldn't tell if it was an exotic bird or the little kid cavorting by the park entrance. I turned toward Wist. She'd gathered up her sack of goodies; now she held it like a baby.

It took serious commitment to stay focused on her face. And not just because the bread in her arms smelled so ravishing. It was very hard not to let my attention drop little by little to the core in her torso, to the magic branches packing her body.

At a glance, I could state with confidence that she had more magic branches than there were tadpoles in the park pond. Which was saying a lot.

Standing next to a person with that much magic and not gawking at it felt like facing a deep dark hole—a gaping well—and telling yourself you absolutely couldn't look down at what lay within.

There had been moments today when my brain let the writhing presence of her magic turn into background noise. Just another bit of chaotic scenery, blending with the boisterous shouting of shop vendors, the hungry swooping of seabirds by the harbor.

But I also noticed each time someone visibly winced as she walked past. Not too many people. Perhaps one pedestrian out of every few dozen. Those who were blessed or cursed with extra-strong magic perception.

And I noticed, more and more, how continually she worked to fold up her magic inside of itself. To hide as much of it as she could get away with. Like how she made herself smaller by slouching. Like how stingily she parceled out her reactions, even when I tried my best to provoke her.

12

On the way to the tram, I figured it was about time to explain how I would pay Wist back.

First I indulged in a little equivocating. "Remember what I said about paying you back with my mind? What do you think that means?"

"Will you write me a poem?"

I tapped my forehead. "Told you it'd be knowledge, not art."

"My favorite present," said Wist.

"Are you being funny?"

"Are you laughing?"

"Take a look and decide for yourself." I had no pity chuckles to spare for Wisteria Shien.

"Anyway, I don't know how useful this idea will be to you specifically," I said. I wouldn't oversell it. "But if I were in your shoes, I'd find it interesting. That's why I think it'll be adequate repayment."

"Huh," Wist commented.

"I'll give you the details on the tram. Don't try to litigate it."

It was getting toward evening now. The light from the sky turned a color like aged honey. The five o'clock town bells rang through the market, the quaint marina, the sparsely populated parks.

Wist used her family token to get me on the tram. It pulled up a good twenty minutes before the next scheduled departure and then proceeded to sit there waiting, doors open.

The two of us were the first to board.

"When do you usually get healed?" I asked. "Not making you miss any important appointments, am I?"

"If you were, I would already have missed them."

"When do they heal you, anyway?"

"Every morning."

"Thought you said it was twice a day."

"Only if I ask for it. Only if I use a lot of magic in class."

My only memories of the tram were the intolerable squeaking it made when in motion, and that twist of guilt I'd felt after turning my back on my parents.

Without any other passengers, without any sign of going anywhere, it seemed like a completely different space. A glass-walled room where time had stopped. Where the peculiar heat of Wist's leg next to mine made me want to spring up out of my seat.

"Your healing," I said to distract myself. "Has it always been daily? Your whole life?"

"Not when I was small."

"They do say magical pain gets worse with age."

"I was on a weekly healing schedule for the first few years after the Shiens took me."

"What changed?"

She didn't answer.

I thought of Wist on her knees, wild ice coating a dark street. Yeah, I could guess.

She deposited her sack of bread in my lap without further comment.

"Already got my own books to hold," I said. "Carry it yourself."

"It's for you," she replied.

"Nice try. Feels like I ought to say no to that."

"Why?"

"I've been mooching off you all day," I said tartly.

"Half the day."

"Boy, that really clears my name."

I was about to keep going—about to say something extremely clever and cutting—when I saw her leaning her head on the wall. Eyes closed.

We were in the seats closest to the butt end of the tram. A hint of our reflections showed in the window glass across from us. Me with my arms around Wist's sack of bread, the long decorative sleeves of my uniform hanging down past my knees.

Wist's hands rested limp in her lap. Her braid wound itself around and between her wrists like a pair of manacles. Guess that was preferable to letting it drag on the floor.

The wall didn't appear especially comfortable. For a deranged moment, I considered offering her my shoulder.

Glimpsing our reflections made me come to my senses. Given her height, she'd have to bend her spine like a horseshoe to put her head on me. Once you took my boniness into account, the wall was clearly the superior option.

"Does resting like that help?" I asked. It wasn't as if the wall would do anything for her magic.

"Mm."

Which could've meant *Yes, No,* or *Shut up, you watery tuna.*

"Well," I said. "Thanks for the bread."

Maybe it was her magic. Or maybe she wasn't used to going out much. I'd better get to the point before she conked out.

"Your collar," I said.

Wist opened one eye.

"Could two different skills end up with the same recorded signature? Similar enough that no one could tell them apart."

"It's not impossible," she said after some thought.

"But you've never heard of it happening," I guessed. "So they're sort of like fingerprints."

Next came the crucial question.

"Can you tell what the signature of a skill would be before it gets inscribed? Or without ever going over to study its pattern in the records room? Like how a musician might be able to write out a song in proper notes and charts just from hearing it play over a melodium."

"Musicians can do that?"

"Not all of them. What about you? Imagine making a new skill. Could you predict the shape it'll take when it gets transcribed through your collar?"

I asked this because I personally had no idea. For one thing, I'd probably never be allowed to set foot in the records room myself.

Wist's braid adjusted its elaborate knot around her forearms. "I could tell," she said. It almost sounded like a question.

"Then the rest is up to your talent as an originator."

She eyed me sideways through her glasses. "The rest of what?"

A handful of other people had started boarding the tram. None looked like fellow students, and they mostly clustered at the far end of the compartment.

To be safe, I leaned in and lowered my voice.

"You're an originator." I waved a finger at her pelican pin for emphasis. "You can invent new magic skills from scratch."

"It isn't that simple."

"Depends on how proficient you are, no?"

I waited. To no avail. Seems like I'd have to spell this one out.

"There are skills you're supposed to have learned recently, right? Think of a skill that would be normal for you to practice outside of class.

"Or think of a skill that no one would find questionable, no matter when you used it. No matter how much it shows up in your collar record. Like that magic in your braid. They're already used to you flinging it around all the time.

"Here's an extreme example. Let's say you want to kill your roommate."

"I don't have a roommate," Wist murmured.

"Pretend you do. For the sake of argument. Pretend you're planning to murder them.

"If you could make a new murdering skill with the exact same signature as your hair-magic, there's your alibi. Just tell the investigators you were playing with your hair the whole time. That's how it'll look in your collar record."

She leaned her head back little by little and looked up at the ceiling of the tram. "If they brought in a forensics team—"

"That's just one example," I said, exasperated. "Never claimed it was watertight. I won't promise you a way to get away with actual murder.

"But there might come a time when you'll want to use magic without needing to explain yourself to the administration. Without having to deal with all those persistent follow-up questions. Can't hurt to have plausible deniability."

She touched her collar as if feeling it for cracks. "You're saying I should engineer new skills to match the exact signature of a previously recorded skill. On purpose."

"Right. If it were easy, I'm sure someone would've already done it. Or maybe they already have. And no one noticed."

A chime rang through the station. The tram lurched into motion, shrill as ever. I cupped my hands over my ears.

Wist leaned in and spoke through my fingers. "It has to line up perfectly with a pre-existing skill. That's the top priority."

"You got it."

"There's a strong chance that any new skill made that way would be completely useless."

"Can't know until you try," I said.

"No one else would think of trying."

"If it sounds nonsensical, maybe it is," I acknowledged. "But if it's an idea no one else would even think of, then as far as I'm concerned, it's worthy repayment.

"The rest depends on you. On whether or not you're good enough to invent a flawless twin skill. On whether or not you even see the need for it."

I lowered my hands from my ears. The tram's shrieking had eased a little. "Your call," I said.

Wist looked away.

The water between the mainland and the island was clogged with lush marshes: green stippled with hints of rarer blue and purple grasses.

As the tram crossed the long bridge, late-day light picked out tiny two-person fishing boats down below. Snow-white herons stood here and there in the marshy areas, wings folded in dignified solitude.

The type of mage collar Wist had around her neck—used only to preserve a record of the skills wielded by the wearer—was almost unheard of outside the academy.

The existence of that meticulous record was perhaps why Guralta students were given more freedom than other mages going through secondary school. They had permission to learn, erase, relearn, and practice a huge range of different skills.

Not that I'm an expert, but standard mage vocational institutes seemed to be about teaching them to master the use of particular fixed skills. Guralta, as the most distinguished type of secondary school, was more about teaching the art of general skill acquisition and mastery—and, for originators, skill development.

We took our time walking from the island station back to campus. We'd spent the afternoon marching all over Baneberry. I, for one, had begun to feel in it in my legs.

"Thank what's-his-name for me," I told Wist. "Timpani."

"Tempus?"

"Yeah. Nice free day trip, wasn't it? A good distraction from being hunted."

"Tempus isn't the one who paid for it."

"Thank your wallet for me, too," I amended. "Although he did get us our one-way tickets to empty farmland. Can't count that out."

I made Wist hold my books and bread while I stopped to yawn and stretch. "Today's only the fourth day of training camp."

"Over halfway through," she said.

"Three whole days of petty harassment left. And that's only if I don't lose." I blew noisy air out through my lips. "Honestly. You'd think elite mages from elite families would have better things to do than plot against little old me. Don't you have horses to ride? Duels to watch? Tea to drink? Political marriages to celebrate?"

"Don't ask me," said Wist. "Ask Tempus."

"I'll pass."

I didn't suggest going the long way. Nor did I suggest sneaking back onto campus via some little-used alternate route through the bushes.

If I were alone, I'd have been more discreet. I just figured no hunters would bother accosting me right under the nose of an S-Class mage student.

I realized my mistake when I spotted a tall, skeletal figure standing by the main school gate. He wore a shirt with an eye-riveting hibiscus print.

I immediately attempted to motion Wist off onto a side path.

Mr. Rift wordlessly crooked his finger at us.

Curses. Might as well get it over with.

The gate was another repurposed artifact from olden times, hewn from the same black-blue-indigo rock as the island ruins.

A mysterious silvery metal filled the cracks, buttressed the weak parts. The silver flowed like mercury, like a waterfall. Always shimmering with magic and motion. Bending to gravity, yet never running out.

There were rumors that in certain seasons, and at certain times of day, the liquid silver bits turned red as living blood.

As soon as we came within speaking distance, I brandished my books at Mr. Rift.

"Look what I got back," I said.

"You told me you kept forgetting them."

"Huh. Did I?"

I expected more snark in response. Instead he turned to Wist with a look of bemusement.

"Unexcused trip off the island," he told us. "It gives me no pleasure to say that I'm going to have to write up both of you."

"What're you talking about?" I pointed over my shoulder. "I just ran into her a little ways down the road."

Mr. Rift blew out a fatigued breath. "No need to twist yourself to come up with a cover story, Asa."

"Who says I'm—"

"I won't mention any possible fraternization between the two of you. I saw nothing of the sort."

"You sure didn't."

"You won't be called up in front of the school tribunal. But I can't ignore hard evidence of an unauthorized excursion."

"I'm serious. Who says either of us left the island?" I asked. "Separately or together. Try calling a witness."

He rolled his eyes. Very professional. "They don't sell that bread anywhere on Guralta Isle."

I glanced down at the branded paper sack resting atop my books. "Ah."

"Three weeks of detention," he said to me. "Starting after the end of training camp."

"Oh, c'mon—"

He didn't let me finish. "As for you, Shien—"

"She didn't mean to come with me," I interjected. "It was kind of an accident."

"An accident," intoned Mr. Rift.

"Basically, I kidnapped her."

"I wouldn't call kidnapping an accident, Asa." He looked at Wist again. "Well? Which is it?"

"I was happy to come," she said.

Luckily, her lack of inflection made it sound completely insincere.

"See?" I told him. "Clearly I brainwashed her."

Mr. Rift massaged his much-abused forehead. He was actually taller than Wist, now that I saw them together. He ought to have invested some of that height of his into width.

"I'll refer this matter to your advisor," he said to Wist.

"Thank you, sir. No need to mention...." She gestured my way without uttering my name.

A mage student calling a healer *sir*? Downright bizarre.

Mr. Rift nodded to her. Deferential, but not groveling.

The metallic silver fluid coursing down through the gate behind him gleamed golden and orange—the color of a spica field—with the last light of the aging sun.

His attention shifted to Wist's magic core. To the tortured branches surrounding it. "Do you need—?"

"Not today," she said. "Just rest."

I needed to get back and see what new havoc awaited in my dorm. By now, my only thought was of how soon I could extricate myself.

Rather, that should've been my only thought.

In my mind I saw it so clearly. As if it were something that had happened in real life, right in front of me.

I saw Mr. Rift putting his hand on her lower back, under her shirt. I saw her aberrant magic branches quivering with agony and anticipation. I saw her struggling to keep a straight face.

Let me be very clear. I hadn't observed the faintest hint of anything improper between them.

And there was nothing sinister or untoward about touching the bare skin of a mage's back in order to heal her.

I'd done it myself, after all. Less than a day ago.

Mr. Rift must've taken shifts treating Wist before. Surely he was one of the more skillful members of the healer faculty.

I envisioned other hands on her. The dorm steward. Random teachers.

My reaction didn't change. It was a tilted feeling very much like motion sickness. And a conviction—with zero practical experience to back it up—that I could do better. Mine was the hand that deserved to be there.

I didn't want to ponder the implications. Sometimes I had these weird egotistical flights of fancy. Sometimes I just couldn't get over myself.

That was what had landed me here at Guralta. If I'd been a humbler kid, less eager to impress, maybe I wouldn't have tried so hard back when they started testing me.

I didn't deserve anything in regards to Wisteria Shien, an S-Class mage I barely knew.

More to the point, I didn't want to deserve anything. Why would I? She'd saved me a few times, yes, but I'd cleared my debt with my intellect. Nothing remained to connect us. I had more in common with Saya's hermit crabs.

My only desire was for what every healer deserved, as far as I was concerned, but rarely ever got. A chance to decide my own path. Even if it were a path that had nothing to do with combing out matted magic.

I chased the images out of my head. I made my excuses to Mr. Rift and Wist. I slipped away from the two of them. Away from the resplendent school gate.

Not a bad day. Not a bad deal. I'd reclaimed my books. I'd eaten to fullness for the first time all week.

My right hand kept remembering the surprising coolness of her lower back. My palm went clammy as if trying to reenact the moment. I wiped it compulsively on my long sleeve.

To the rest of the world, she was everything. (Family strife aside.) An S-Class mage. An originator. A member of the Shien clan. Tall and—there's no polite way to put this—well-developed. Not that she seemed eager to flaunt it.

Put another way: she was supremely rich. Supremely powerful. And not unattractive, I suppose, if rather corpse-like in expression.

As an added bonus, she didn't appear to torture animals or healers for fun. A dream partner for an ambitious realist like Saya, if you could look past the stories about her siblings.

But not for me. None of that meant anything to Asa Clematis.

My dream partner was no partner. My dream mage was no mage at all. The greatest gift a mage could give me would be to leave me alone and let me get through school unmolested. Let me find a way to live my own life, far away from you lot.

Not that I'd ever said this to Wisteria Shien. Not in those exact words, anyhow.

Get out of my head, I told the version of her I kept seeing again and again. Get out of my head, I told her and my silent imaginary Mr. Rift, and all the other long arms reaching for her naked back.

Get out of my head!

She wouldn't listen.

13

Back in my room, I found one of my spare uniforms shredded. Cut to ribbons. They'd scattered the fabric about like confetti.

Look—I'd have been a fool not to anticipate something along these lines.

I'd hidden my other uniforms in Saya's pillowcase. I left a single set hanging in the closet as a decoy, to lessen the odds of them attempting a full sweep of the room.

That was the set they'd destroyed. As planned, the pillowcase stash remained intact. Of course, predictability didn't make it any less annoying. I hadn't owned a full week's supply of uniforms to begin with. Now I'd be forced to do laundry even more often. All the way until the end of the school year.

I hoped my doorknob hot sauce had burned the saboteurs again. I hoped they'd smeared it in their eyes. I ought to ask the steward if anyone had been rushed off to the infirmary.

Or maybe my fellow rejects weren't such slow learners. They might've started using gloves by now. Either way, I'd have give the knob a thorough cleaning before Saya came back.

I took the sack of bakery bread with me everywhere for the next two days. To class, to the healer baths—truly everywhere.

I didn't care how the faculty raised their eyebrows. The moment I left it alone, I knew I wouldn't be able to risk eating the rest. I'd have to throw out the whole lot.

It wasn't just plain sandwich fodder. There were fruit pastries, bean paste buns, bread stuffed with soft white cheese, chiffon cake, dense loaves packed full of chestnuts and dried figs. Stretched out over two days, it kept me unexpectedly well fed.

What else happened in the meantime?

Hunting season bled over into class. I'd arrive to find dead things and foul substances smeared on my chair, in my desk.

I ended up coming early and leaving late to do clean-up, eyes watering with nausea. Anything to keep the teachers from noticing.

From being forced to notice, rather. Had a couple close calls, especially with Mr. Rift. But he knew to respect the fact that I hadn't asked him for help.

Did I trust the mages and their flunkies to stick to the rules of the game? Not really. Why would I?

To begin with, I wasn't even a willing participant. I could meet every condition they'd set for me, and they might still make up some arbitrary reason to justify saying that I'd lost.

In fact, that struck me as being the most likely outcome. At the end of the week, just when I thought it was finally over, they'd try to crush me by making clear that the game would go on for the rest of the year. No matter what. Perhaps for the rest of my school career, unless I managed to offer up another human sacrifice in my place.

What, then, was my plan? Would I keep gritting my teeth through it? Keep telling my parents over the transceiver that everything was just fine and merry?

I couldn't help fantasizing about launching a counterattack. That's just the way my mind works.

But what would be the point of it? And what were my chances? I barely knew my purported enemy. I still struggled to remember his name.

Besides, he was a mage student. And not an eccentric one like Wisteria Shien. The odds were stacked so high against me that I knew better than to go out of my way to further provoke him.

Whoever he was. Timothy? Tohru? Titus?

For the time being, I put my head down and endured it.

Whether thanks to Wist or thanks to pure luck, no one went after Saya's hermit crabs again. At the moment, that was all I could really ask for.

Something would change by the time training camp ended and everyone else came rushing back. It might be for the better, or it might be for the worse. Either way, if I were going to make a stand, I'd make it on that future battlefield.

Right now I had a deadline in front of me. No matter how disgusting it got, no matter how they chipped away at my composure, round one would be over in a matter of days. I wouldn't give anyone the satisfaction of thinking they'd landed a hit on me.

Embarrassing though it was, I took to deliberately channeling Wist.

The uncomprehending eyes. The unmoving face. The weary, affectless voice. It was gratifying to see how instantly these mannerisms—or unnatural lack thereof—unnerved people.

She was almost too perfect a role model for stonewalling bullies. It made me wonder what had happened to hone her.

On the sixth night of training camp, the constant tension began to catch up with me.

I'd finished off the last stale scraps of Baneberry bread earlier in the evening. No stomach-mewling to keep me up. I wedged a chair under the doorknob before heading to bed.

I resigned myself to the usual cruel dreams.

Yet something kept me from tumbling over the brink.

It took me a while to identify the culprit as the air touching my cheek. Cold and damp, almost tangible.

I stumbled out of bed to go close the window.

The whole room was moist with spectral fog. I could see, but not well.

I hoped the hermit crabs weren't too perturbed. Couldn't hear them scratching around in their tank. Must be hiding in their shells or buried in the sand. Quiet and watchful, biding their time.

I did think about ignoring the fog. I was truly exhausted.

As proof of that, right now it was only a hair after eight in the evening.

I'd secured my room and collapsed into bed. I'd abandoned any notion of doing schoolwork. Saya would be back the day after tomorrow. If I wanted to keep my wits about me between now and then, I needed more rest.

Instead, roused by fog, I found myself digging one of my hidden uniforms out of Saya's pillowcase. I winced at the cold as I pulled it on. I made sure Pepper's hot sauce and the model lighthouse were safe in my pocket.

I still had the yellow bucket from the hermit crab abduction incident. I'd seriously contemplated repurposing it to set a water-filled trap over my door. The problem was that I couldn't work out how to stop the bucket from falling on me, too. So that idea remained shelved. And the empty bucket rested next to my bed.

Could always use it as an emergency bedpan or as a weapon to bash people. Better yet, both. Might come in handy if someone launched a full-blown siege on me.

As I watched the magical fog veil my room from floor to ceiling, I began to feel as if Wist were trying to smoke me out like a wasp.

Curfew was hours away. Nothing would stop me from strolling out the front door. Nothing except my knowledge that my dormmates wouldn't miss another chance to mess with my stuff.

Locking the door still made no difference. If they were getting in with a magical tool—could be something as simple as a cutting grafted to a paper clip—clearly it must be a reusable one. They'd broken in so many times already.

I reluctantly moved my chair out from under the doorknob. I double-checked that the door was indeed locked.

Then I turned and clambered out the open window.

I strove to move quietly. The screen squeaked when I shut it behind me. But simply fussing with the window wouldn't sound too unusual, if anyone were listening. I opened and closed it all the time.

I had a healthy respect for heights, and close to zero respect for my own athletic capabilities. I wasn't doing this on a lark. I was gambling that I could leave the building unobserved.

If no one heard me going down the hall, if no one spotted me passing the first-floor lounge on my way out, they'd have no reason not to think I remained barricaded in my room the entire time, snoozing the night away.

Thus far, they'd been careful not to launch any assaults on my property while I lay in wait to bear witness. Wise of them.

I'd already mapped the path down from the window in my head. Ages ago, actually. Never hurts to have an escape route.

For that matter, there was a standard emergency ladder stashed in our closet. The compact folding kind. The ladder would've made the trip to ground level much easier. But it would also be noisier, and far less likely to go unseen.

That's why I opted to risk my neck by free climbing. If not for the balcony protruding from the floor directly below, I'd probably have broken my skull open.

I made it down to the bushes short of breath but mostly intact. I'd managed not to kick anyone's windows in, or otherwise alert the remaining residents.

With any luck, no one would notice my absence.

More importantly: could I climb back up the same way afterward?

No way in hell, my friend. I planned to return before curfew and stroll back in the front entrance, bold as you please. Which was why I'd moved the chair away from my door. Would be pretty silly if I accidentally blocked myself from getting in my own room.

I looked forward to popping up out of nowhere and startling my dormmates, who (fingers crossed) would have no idea I'd left the building in the first place. I was all but rubbing my hands in anticipation.

When you're the only one on your side, you gotta take joy where you can.

The bushes guarding the perimeter of the dormitory were shot through with lush vines of pink jasmine. They smelled downright ambrosial.

Far off, a thread of fog wound subtly through the campus trees. Unremarkable, unless you were already looking for it.

The scent of nighttime jasmine trailed after me as I followed the fog off campus. It led me on a clever path through neighborhoods full of expensive vacation homes.

I dodged cactus streetlights. I tiptoed through the darkest patches of shadow in moonlit gardens.

The fog took me all the way down to one of the public beach access paths that cut between silent oceanfront houses. Then through a tall bank of grassy dunes.

As I set foot on the sand, it occurred to me—not for the first time—that this might be a trap.

The fog, however, was definitely Wisteria Shien's magic.

I have an astoundingly good memory for magic, if I do say so myself. I wouldn't mistake someone else's for hers. It was no more likely than mistaking the face of a random stranger for the face of my own mother.

In other words: if this were a trap, it was a trap laid with Wist's cooperation. Willing or otherwise.

Not that I had any deep knowledge of mage student dynamics, but somehow I couldn't imagine the others forcing her to do anything more involved than reciting rules off a piece of paper. If they'd succeeded, I kind of wanted to see it.

And if she'd laid a trap for me of her own accord—well, some weird part of me wanted to see that, too. I'd be sure to congratulate her. *You surprised me*, I'd say. *Didn't know you had it in you.*

A lone figure in dark clothing waited down by the edge of the water. The fog guiding me began to dissipate as I approached.

At first I assumed Wist was in her dingy gym tracksuit. Closer up, I realized my mistake.

She wore a coordinated pair of satiny black pajamas, loose enough to flap audibly in the nighttime breeze, and covered to an almost comical extent in dense, painterly embroidery.

"Don't tell me you bought these for yourself," I said.

Her braid spiraled around the length of her body as if trying to hide the pajamas. Too late for that. I kept gawking.

"There's a name for this style, isn't there?" I asked. "Something to do with the old monarchy. Royal embroidery?"

"Something like that," Wist said drearily.

"Doesn't it itch? All that stitching on the other side."

"You get used to it."

I remained unconvinced. I'd never seen true royal embroidery outside museums before. It was too dark to make out the colors, but they must've been deeply saturated. Clouds and arabesque patterns. Peony and plum blossoms. Birds with their wings spread. Delicate deer.

Massive quantities of silk thread; countless hours of manual labor. Maybe the Shien clan commissioned pajamas like these for all of their children.

In the process of ogling this display of unspeakable luxury, I noticed that Wist didn't have her usual pins on. Nor was she wearing a bra. (Don't ask how I could tell.)

Fair enough. She could've ported herself straight from her room if she wasn't in the mood for a lengthy walk below the moon.

Despite all that, she still wore her collar. Logically speaking, I suppose it made sense that mage students would have to keep their collars on at all times. Even if it made them uncomfortable. Even when sleeping. Even when bathing.

I dismissed the images that rose to mind at this last thought. They were unnecessarily detailed and most definitely uninvited.

"No glasses?" I asked.

"They cloud up too much. All the salt in the air."

"You better have called me here for a good reason. We may be outside, but this has got to count as fraternization."

"It's before curfew."

"Look at the moon," I said. "It's too moody. Highly suspicious. A perfect night for mischief."

Then I made myself shut up. Wist was the one who'd lured me out here. If she had something important to say, she could speak for herself.

Pieces of the moon glittered in the opaque water. The ocean looked like a vast and empty stage. It crashed its long lazy waves before us, leaving stranded patches of sea foam quivering gelatinously at our feet.

I followed Wist's gaze down the subtle slope of waterlogged sand.

Tiny clams poked out vertically, wiggling furiously to rebury themselves. Here and there, a drab-colored shore crab skittered sideways at alarming speeds, or paused briefly to grab something and eat. Probably one of those poor clams.

There are people who say that's natural. Nothing to feel bad about. I don't disagree. But there are also people who say it's natural for mages to rule over everyone else. Especially healers. Being natural doesn't make something good, or beautiful, or right.

"You seem let down," Wist said.

"You can tell?"

"Is it the pajamas?"

I snorted. "No. As I followed the fog here, I thought to myself that maybe you were setting an elaborate trap for me."

"Did you want me to betray you?"

I threw up my hands. "There's nothing to betray. Yeah, you helped stop me from losing the hunt. You gave me a can of salmon. You treated me to lunch and stuff."

"You're welcome," Wist said staidly.

"Whatever. It doesn't exactly make us blood sisters. But I'll admit to letting my guard down. Why else would I show up here just because you fogged up my room?

"It would've been interesting," I explained, "if it turned out you were the mastermind all along. A true Shien, same as those who came before you. The true engineer of the hunt. Not Te—Tenderloin?"

"Tempus," Wist said. A reflexive correction. Then, lower: "I told you before. If I wanted to hurt you—"

"I know, I know. You wouldn't fool around with amateur moves. Like making other healers pour cooking oil in my classroom desk."

I took a step closer. I wore my school shoes. Wist was barefoot, her toes clenching the dim sand. A half-full shopping bag sat slumped a few paces behind her.

"You'd go with the pro tactics," I said. "Whatever those are. Whatever makes a person really crack and give up. Where'd you learn them? Who taught you? Who broke you down?"

The moon shed little light on Wist, and not a smidgen of it entered her eyes. She regarded me for a very long time before answering. I held my tongue, and strove not to hold my breath.

"You're trying to provoke me," she said evenly.

I couldn't hide my grin. "Sorry." Possibly the least sincere apology ever uttered on this hallowed beach. "I'm not like this with other people."

That made her stare harder. "One—I don't believe you."

"What? Whyever not?"

"Two—don't blame your nature on me."

"I'm not this bad most of the time," I objected. "I'm not. I swear."

"You were the same around Mr. Rift."

"You were there."

"Now it's my fault," Wist said.

With my keen powers of observation, I detected a hint of incredulity.

"I'm telling you"—I almost clapped her on the shoulder, then thought better of it—"you bring out the obnoxiousness in me like no one else. You should be proud. It's a talent, really."

I half-expected her to lurch forward and strangle me. In a testament to her formidable self-control, she didn't budge a millimeter. Not even the tips of her fingers twitched.

"At first I wasn't going to use the fog to call you," she said, apropos of nothing, her voice perfectly level.

"What was your original plan?"

"Throwing acorns at your window."

"What are you, a squirrel?"

"Would've been less tiring than using magic."

"Thank goodness you didn't," I said. "What if you got the wrong room?"

I stopped, mystified, as my own words began to sink in. "Wait. How'd you know which room I'm in?"

Wist gazed out at the ocean. The wind plucked black tendrils of hair from her braid and whipped them about the sides of her face.

"No," I said. "Looking moody is not an answer."

"We have access to a lot of school info we aren't supposed to see."

"*We* meaning who, mage students in general?"

She nodded.

"That's all very well," I said, "but how're you going to explain your fog use to the collar monitors this time?"

"I always explain it the same way."

"And they believe you?"

"I tell them it's to humidify my room."

The tide washed up higher, nearly licking at the sides of her feet. I couldn't tell if she were joking. I decided I was better off not knowing.

"Seriously, why'd you make me come out here?" I asked. "If you get lonely, you can always talk to Azalea."

"In class we're doing a unit on shielding," she said. "Plus basic medical magic."

I named the skills that immediately leapt to mind: "First Aid? Barrier?"

"First Aid, yes. Barrier, no. They started us on Bulletproof."

"Isn't that super literal? Doesn't even work on knives."

Then again, more specific—that is, less useful and flexible—magic was supposed to be easier to get the hang of than more general skills like Barrier. That must be the reason they made first-years practice acquiring and executing a skill as impractical as Bulletproof.

Unless you were a certified prodigy, imprinting one of your branches with a new magical skill was just the beginning. Doing so meant you could attempt to use that skill. But there was no guarantee of being good at it. Especially not at first.

"I could explain using these class-related skills at any time of day or night," said Wist.

"Right. It's just practice."

"I came up with three new skills that mimic the exact signature of Bulletproof."

"Three!" I squawked.

A clumsy pause ensued.

"I promise," she said, "you won't be impressed."

"Try me," I insisted. "What did you name them?"

"These skills don't deserve a name."

"We'll see about that. What do they do? Get to the point."

Her shoulders had sagged a bit. She took in an audible breath.

"One is a skill to cut cupcakes precisely in half."

"It cuts things in half?" I asked. "That's cool. That's actually pretty overpowered."

"It only works on cupcakes," Wist said wearily. "Not apple turnovers. Not loaves of bread."

"Not people?"

"Just cupcakes."

"...Could see that being useful if I had a brother or sister. Might stave off some arguments. What's number two?"

"A skill to make mold spores visible in the air."

"Visible how?"

"They start glowing."

"What color?"

"Depends on the mold."

"On the one hand, I don't want to know how much mold floats around in my dorm," I said. "On the other hand, it might not be bad for parties. Get a little glitter in the air."

"Mm," she answered. No actual words: just a lone mournful syllable.

"What's the final skill you invented?"

"A porting skill."

"That sounds more promising."

"It lets me transport anything within my sight to the nearest egg."

"The nearest—huh?" I reviewed what Wist had said in my head. "Cupcakes? Eggs? Were you hungry when you came up with these?"

"It was an interesting exercise," she murmured, as if the conversation were about to be over. "But I couldn't produce anything of value."

"No, no. It's too early to say that for sure." I pressed my fist to the bottom of my chin. "I'd like a demonstration."

"Of all three?"

"You can skip the mold one."

She crouched to rummage in the bag on the ground behind her. She returned with a moderately squished cupcake balanced on her palm.

"Oh, good," I said. "You came prepared."

I studied the cupcake intently. It bore a crown of pale frosting. Pink, perhaps. Hard to tell its true color in the dark.

Nothing happened yet.

"I might need healing afterward," Wist warned.

"A small price to pay," I said. "I can heal you anytime." I motioned for her to get on with it.

Magic sliced through the vulnerable cupcake. A silent slash like summer heat lightning.

The cupcake itself looked unchanged. I reached for it.

Wist's hand flinched.

The cupcake tumbled off her palm and down into the sand. It landed in two separate pieces that, to her credit, did appear to have been divided very fairly.

Together we eyed the carcass at our feet. Petite clam-consuming ghost crabs scampered to and fro in the background.

"Think what you like," I declared, "but I'm going to eat that. I'll just avoid the sandy parts."

There were a lot of sandy parts to leave behind. Hopefully the crabs would be in the mood for dessert later.

I licked frosting off my fingertips. "Not bad. Maybe a little too much on the sweet side. How about the egg thing? Your new porting skill. Having some trouble picturing it."

Wist went to her shopping bag again. This time, she retrieved a brown chicken egg.

"Nearest egg," I muttered, trying to recall what she'd said about it. "Any kind of egg? What about insect eggs? Fish eggs?"

"It has to be a bird egg."

"Cooked or raw?"

"Either." She gave the one in her fingers a small shake. "This is hard-boiled."

"What if the thing you want to move is already right next to an egg? Like what if I were holding an egg, too?"

"If you're already close to an egg, it'll transport you to the next-nearest egg."

"Next-nearest egg," I mouthed. Not words I'd expected my lips to be forming tonight, or any night. "Seems complicated. Does it work on objects that are within your sight, but that you can't actually see with your eyes?"

"Like what?"

"My underwear."

Thinking before speaking isn't always my strong suit. I flapped my hands at Wist in a rushed plea for mercy. "Not my underwear," I said sheepishly. "Try pulling the stuff in my pocket."

Before I even blinked, she held not just her hard-boiled egg, but also my room key, my student ID, the miniature lighthouse, my borrowed bottle of weapons-grade hot sauce, tissues, and a few crumpled pairs of disposable gloves.

"You're too hard on yourself," I told her as I reached out to recover my belongings. "This is a great skill. Incredibly valuable. Just gotta make sure to carry around a few eggs at all times."

There was a certain frigidity to the set of her mouth.

A sudden impulse tickled me: the urge to stand there before her and do nothing. To watch her go increasingly rigid, her braid contracting on itself like an arm held taut to the point of trembling. To see how long it took her to look me in the eye and ask for help.

I didn't drag it out too much. I'm not a complete sicko. Besides, I wouldn't turn this kind of scientific curiosity on anyone who wasn't already an heir to the type of power and status that would never, ever be mine.

If anyone could afford to suffer a bit, surely it was Wisteria Shien.

Muted nighttime waves curled softly under the lopsided yellowish moon, bright and sharp-edged but less than perfectly full. I counted the sounds of a few more wave cycles.

I leaned in. I went on tiptoe to make sure she'd hear me.

"May I?" I asked, as if I were always this courteous.

I sounded like the ideal healer, soft and attentive.

Wist gave a jerky nod.

I touched the base of her back, beneath the loose silky pajamas. The thick scratchy underside of the extravagant embroidery grazed my knuckles.

I put my hand there, and then I went still.

The one thing they assured us of in healer class was that we couldn't possibly make things worse for a mage in pain. Healers were congenitally incapable of harming mages, they said. The worst possible outcome was simply being ineffectual. We could attempt to detangle their magic, but we couldn't scrunch it up beyond all repair in the process.

Everyone accepted this as a basic fact. To me it seemed bizarrely counterintuitive. Brush hair in the right direction, and you'd make it less tangled. Brush it backwards, and you could transform it into an impossible puffball of knots.

Our teachers and textbooks told us that the one thing we could do was brush in the proper direction. It was in our very name, after all. Healers. Born to soothe, to mend, to alleviate.

Every time anyone made a claim like that, I got tempted to test its veracity. To prove them wrong. But right now, it also gave me confidence that I couldn't hurt Wist any worse than she was already hurting.

"How can I help?" I asked. "Where should I start?"

She stirred. She looked at me uncomprehendingly, her face in shadow. We may as well have been speaking different languages.

Her braid had whisked itself out of my way when I moved closer. It avoided her back, winding around and around her neck as if to bolster the strength of the collar beneath.

I wanted to make her say it, say what she wanted from me. I might not have any idea what she was telling me. My only hands-on experience was with Wist herself, scant days ago. An act of desperation.

But I wanted to hear it from her own lips. In that severely dispassionate voice, forcibly flattened and scraped bare of all sentiment as it passed through her throat.

Then again, what did mages know about healing? Maybe she wouldn't be able to articulate her needs. I wouldn't be able to tell a masseuse what they ought to do with my leg muscles.

I still felt compelled to make her try.

"You're the only person I've ever healed," I said. "Tell me how to make it better."

"I've been treated by countless healers," Wist said finally. "Too many to remember. Don't overthink it."

I had to scoff at this. "I'm not having performance anxiety."

"Then why haven't you started?"

"Ah," I said. "That was almost imperious. Now you sound like a Shien."

"Asa." Still no anger in her voice. "Asa Clematis."

A jittery sensation ballooned in me, a kind of hyperactive longing to flee. When she spoke my name, I barely recognized it. It sounded like it belonged to someone else.

"There's a lot to untangle," she told me. "You'll never get through it all. Tug at the parts that irk you most."

I followed her suggestion. Even though doing so made me feel vaguely like I'd lost some obscure power struggle, one I didn't know how to name.

I looked for the knots in her magic branches that struck me as being most offensive, most blatant, most grating. I untwisted the twisty parts. I unspooled tightly wound-up threads as if running a long length of string between finger and thumb.

Unlike before, I could afford to take my time now. She wasn't about to go berserk at any moment. As my focus intensified, I stopped hearing the wind and the ocean.

But I never stopped smelling her. Her scent surrounded me like her fog, crept in as I breathed. A scent less sweet than the jasmine festooning the base of the healer dorms, and utterly unfamiliar. Yet with the same magnetic quality as that white-pink jasmine. Or night-blooming hoya plant. Something that demanded to be inhaled deeper.

I don't know if it was because her lavish pajamas were scented differently from her school-issue day clothes. Or because this time we stood close together, hardly a breath apart, instead of Wist huddled half-collapsed on the ground and me hovering above her.

My forehead bumped her shoulder blade. I had both hands to her back now, moving as if wrangling with the base of an invisible and unruly tail. I could prod her magic all night long and still not get to the bottom of those interwoven branches.

Wist said something. I didn't hear the words. But I heard her voice crack.

At some point, without my feeling it, she'd clenched at the end of one of my long dangling sleeves. Just like last time.

I only noticed once I released her back, and she in turn released me. There were visible creases pressed into the fisted-up fabric. Just how hard had she grabbed it?

"You went very deep." There was a wariness in how she held her body away from me. "Deeper than most healers know how to reach."

"Is that a bad thing?"

"No." She wet her lips. "No," she said again. A touch more firmly. "You're—you had no formal training before the academy?"

"I did self-study," I said. "But with the kind of books anyone could read. Nothing special."

She bent to take a water bottle out of her sandy shopping bag. She tipped her head back to drink from it as if I were personally responsible for depriving her.

"Healing is hard work," I said, and meant it. "I'm thirsty, too."

Wist lowered the bottle from her lips. She held it out to me. When I made no move to take it, she cocked her head for a moment. Then she wiped the rim with her pajamas. Royal embroidery and all.

The water was lukewarm.

When I finished drinking, I said, "The artisans who sewed those would cry if they saw what you'd done with them."

Wist ignored my warning. "I meant to ask," she said. "Why are you carrying around a bottle of hot sauce?"

Not to overly flatter myself and my little-tested healing abilities, but she did sound marginally less dead now.

I patted my uniform pocket. "How's your spice tolerance?"

"Not good enough for that. Have you tried it?"

"I ate noodles way weaker than this, and they made me sick enough to skip training camp."

"Is that a no?"

"Gee, what do you think?"

I took the bottle out and tried to make a show of spinning it on my hand. I ended up having to dive to keep from flinging it into the sand at Wist's feet. She didn't laugh. Which kind of made it worse.

"You saw nothing," I said. I secreted the hot sauce back in my uniform jacket. The white noise of the ocean washed away my humiliation. "The sauce is a weapon."

"A weapon."

"Of last resort. For self-defense. You really aren't supposed to let it touch bare skin."

"What does it do?"

"It won't melt you like acid," I replied. "I mean, it is edible. Technically. According to whoever makes the stuff. It won't leave a permanent chemical burn. But it'll be incredibly painful. And it won't wash off easily."

"Creative," Wist said.

"I know." I coughed delicately into my fist. "Hot sauce aside. You must be feeling a very deep debt of gratitude right about now."

"For your healing work?"

"Not that," I said, impatient. "I basically taught you these new skills of yours. These three astoundingly useful, valuable, life-changing skills. You could say it's all thanks to me."

Wist looked down at me.

"Yes," she agreed, in her most pristine monotone. "You could say that."

Post-healing, her braid had relaxed enough to dangle all the way to the sand at her feet. The paintbrush-like tip traced idle half-circles behind her. Same as how a kid might use their toe to drag restless lines back and forth. She'd have to shake it real hard to get even half the grains out.

"In fact," I continued, "I'm sure you're eager to express your thanks. In as tangible a form as you can."

"How was the bread from Baneberry?" Wist asked.

"Excellent." I'd give praise where praise was due. "Also, all gone now. Would you use these skills for me? If the situation ever warrants it? The magisters won't harangue you for it. They'll praise you for practicing Bulletproof."

She used the side of her foot to push modest mounds of sand over the sad remnants of her cupcake. The dregs of its dead body that had proven too tainted for me to pluck with my fingers and eat.

"Let me know if you have any cupcakes that need dividing." Her foot went on shaping those two tiny unmarked graves.

"That's just what I wanted to hear," I informed her.

Wist proceeded to offer me her hard-boiled egg, the one she'd brought to test her new porting skill.

I added it to the pile of junk in my pocket.

Sure, I thought. Tomorrow would be the last day of training camp, and the presumptive last day of hunting season. Whatever might happen, I'd probably need the protein.

14

Nothing happened. That was the creepy part.

Throughout the seventh day, no one tried anything.

I greeted my classmates with exaggerated loudness and cheer, as was my wont. They feigned deafness, as was theirs.

I discovered no new insults to my family written on my desk. No mystery animal blood smeared on the back of my jacket.

I didn't let my guard down. The lack of hostile overtures made my tension worse, in a way. The maestro of the orchestra must've decided he no longer needed these trifling preludes, all this harassment by proxy. I could only hope my fellow healers had lost at least as much sleep over their forced involvement as I had.

In my pocket I held Pepper's ultimate hot sauce (still over half full) and the miniature tower. No new hidden tricks.

Last night, before leaving Wist on the beach, I'd said: "If I wanted to call on you for a favor—call on you to use one of these extremely handy skills of yours—how would I do it? I never know where to find you."

She tapped the top layer of my uniform. Specifically, the lump of the lighthouse bulging in my pocket. "Use this."

"What's with you and this lighthouse?"

She kept mum. Fine.

"What'll you do if I use it?" I asked. "Follow the squawking of the gulls?"

"Something like that."

"Either way, it's a moot point. I can't use it during hunting season. Summoning the gulls is the same as alerting faculty. If faculty intervenes, it'll count as me forfeiting."

Wist lapsed into silence. Or perhaps it would be more accurate to say that she reverted to her usual state of wordless blank staring.

"I'll try to be nearby," she said after some time. "When I can."

"Did you just declare your intent to stalk me?"

"If you don't want me to—"

"Nah," I said. "Go wild. I'll take whatever protection perfectly-split cupcakes can offer me."

Later I complained about having to walk all the way back in the dark again. Especially considering that Wist could port herself back to her own bed in an instant.

Wist offered to go part of the way with me. A fine escort she'd make, the dark satin of her pajamas shimmering, gilt threads in the dense embroidery catching moonlight like the edges of a spiderweb.

I turned her down. "We're lucky the gulls haven't started circling yet," I'd said.

My last lesson of the following day took place in the classroom with a wall of tarnished mirrors.

Someone had opened all the windows. Sudden winds kept blowing stray papers off the desks of the unwary. Mourning doves cooed in the distance, the same set notes over and over.

I spotted a few magical gulls on patrol, gliding low in the sky. Useless things.

The teacher slacked off while we worked grimly through written problems. I pored over numbered and labeled magic branch diagrams, then scribbled down the order in which I'd untangle the branches. Didn't bother showing my work.

I left the room slowly, giving the other eight Rats time to scatter. This also gave them time to regroup and plot out how next to sabotage me. But—and I speak from experience here—I preferred that to following them everywhere, torturing them with my presence. And vice versa.

A mage student stood waiting for me outside the building. She wore a perfectly pressed uniform and a startlingly yellow headband.

I thought to myself again that her puff of hair was the only reason she looked taller than me.

"You," I said eloquently. "Who're you running errands for this time?"

"Who do you think?"

Wist did seem too inert to bother with ordering around her classmates. Not Wist, then. "Must be your boyfriend."

Azalea looked very much as if she wished she could kill me. "Tempus wouldn't want me. And I definitely wouldn't want him."

"Tempus," I said. "Yes. Minashiro Tempus. I remember. Did he tell you to take me somewhere?"

"Do you plan on coming along quietly?"

"What happens if I make a run for it?"

"You lose the hunt, I suppose."

I raised my hands in mock surrender. "Well, then. Lead the way."

Dinner was still several hours away. Clouds occluded the sun, making it seem rather later in the day.

We followed a footpath lined with colorful mock coral. We passed familiar sculptures of flightless birds, the ones that hulked in random parts of campus without any particular explanation.

I wasn't sure if they were supposed to be real living creatures, or something long extinct. The academy had yet to give me a solid grounding in biology.

"This Tempus of yours sure likes to delegate," I remarked.

"That's one way to put it," said Azalea.

"This Tempus of yours sure likes to make other people do his dirty work."

I took her lack of answer as agreement.

She led me through the border gardens, where ordinary flowers had stems like saplings, and a stray petal or leaf dropping from above might prove heavy enough to knock you unconscious. I wondered how my snails were doing.

Past here lay the mage side of campus.

"One thing I don't understand," I said. "Why does Minashiro Tempus get to be king over the rest of you? Is his family that much more powerful than the Shiens?"

"They're about the same." Azalea didn't look my way when she spoke. "The two clans are very friendly. He's closer to Wist's siblings than she is."

"But she can't pull rank over him? Or is it just that she refuses to?"

Azalea had begun walking faster. I kept pace, undeterred.

"Know what I find most off-putting about Wisteria Shien?" I asked. "She makes a big show of disdaining hunting season. But she doesn't actually take a stand against it. She doesn't actually make any effort to stop it.

"Feels hypocritical, to say the least. I'd respect her more if she admitted to being too lazy to fight Tempus. If she admitted to not caring what stupid games he plays, so long as no one gets outright killed. You can't stick a flag in the moral high ground and then put in zero effort to defend it."

Azalea stopped. We'd just passed the floating sundial. With the coating of clouds above, the shadows on the ground were too blurry and soft-edged to make any sense of what the sundial told us.

"If you think Wist is being lazy—if you think she doesn't care—"

"I do," I said immediately. "I just wish she'd admit to it. If anyone has the right to complain, it's me, no? I'm the one getting hunted."

"You know nothing," Azalea snarled.

"Can't know what I haven't been told." Easiest retort I'd ever fired. "So why hasn't the great S-Class mage put a stop to hunting season? Does she like seeing me get put in my place?"

Azalea didn't answer right away. Or ever.

I saw her tense and then catch herself, multiple times, as if forcing back whatever response had risen first to her lips.

I strolled alongside her. I didn't push it.

I hadn't been this deep into mage territory since orientation. They'd given us healer Rats a full campus tour. But the main point of it had been to warn us against setting foot in most of the mage buildings. And, no matter what, to never try walking the tightropes.

We wound through clusters of trees that seemed trapped in disparate seasons: some festooned in pink blossoms, others stripped naked. Many of the buildings here looked like castles reconstructed for tourists, with twisty open-air towers and a veritable zoo's worth of mischievous gargoyles.

The school store did sell a lot of scenic postcards. Very few of them saw fit to feature the healer side of campus.

"Since we're getting along so well now," I said to Azalea, "how about giving me a hint about what I'm here for?"

"Tempus will tell you."

"He didn't trust you with the details?"

Azalea didn't take the bait. Instead she pointed at an avant-garde structure. One made half of sky-mirroring glass, and half of traditional stone, complete with intricate gables.

The school's art gallery. Or museum. Whatever you prefer to call it.

She led me up to a fourth-story terrace on the glassy side of the building. It appeared to serve as an outdoor lounge of sorts, with swirly-legged black furniture arranged in an informal half-circle around a fire pit. The flames burned all the colors of an aurora.

Early May was not when I would personally have chosen to light a bonfire. That said, this one seemed to radiate a cold breeze. The kind of crispness and clarity that spring nights still sometimes brought to the island: a taste of chilly skin and bright stars.

Indoors, I glimpsed the outlines of model airships and sea ships. An ambitious diorama of Guralta Isle itself. And dark figures lingering inside the walls, gazing out at us. It was hard to discern much detail past the reflective glass.

Azalea had led me through empty back corridors and a plain side door to get here. I hadn't encountered any of the gallery space close up.

Aside from me and Azalea, there were only other two people out on the terrace. Both comfortably ensconced in separate couches near the fire.

Wisteria Shien and Minashiro Tempus.

Unless my eyes were deceiving me, they seemed to be having high tea.

Wist sat in her usual slumped way. It made my back hurt to look at her. No glasses.

They both wore the mage student uniform, fully buttoned. But Minashiro Tempus wore it with far better posture.

I'd only seen the guy once before. When Wist announced the start of hunting season by the sundial. He'd worn such a sour look on his face that I'd remembered him as being extremely unattractive.

Here in person, with a calmer facade, he wasn't downright hideous. Just not to my personal taste.

I gestured at the three-tier serving tray on the table between him and Wist. Grapes, tiny strawberries, froofy rice cakes and cupcakes.

"For me?" I inquired.

No one answered.

Azalea took up a position behind Wist's couch. The cold flames in the fire pit vacillated from color to color: yellow-green, purple-blue, pinkish-red.

"Time for closing ceremonies," Tempus said.

He had a very soft, cultured voice. Not the sort of voice you'd expect to hear coming from someone with such harshly bleached hair.

I counted his magic branches at the back of my head. Nine in total. Far more than most mages, even here at the academy.

Far less than Wist.

"Shouldn't we introduce ourselves?" I'd only ever heard his name from other people.

"No."

It was the kind of *No* you might use on an overeager dog.

I looked at Wist. I could see only the side of her face. I wanted to know her role in this.

A bored witness, called over by virtue of hailing from a similarly illustrious clan? A reluctant umpire? Or was she content to sit there and act as his deputy?

No one seemed interested in telling me. I jabbed a thumb at Wist. "What's she here for?"

"To spectate," said Tempus.

"Where's the rest of my audience?" I asked. "All I see are a couple lurkers indoors. Peeping through the glass."

Tempus took a sip of his tea. "Our seniors volunteered to keep the gulls and faculty busy elsewhere," he said. "Hunting season is a tradition for first-years."

"And a storied tradition it is." I gave a mocking bow.

He looked at me as if uncertain of whether he ought to take offense.

"I'm so honored to have been included," I continued, bright as can be. "Is this where you wrap things up by trying to murder me? I hear you're supposed to use the caves for that."

He put his teacup down. Hard.

Miraculously, it survived without breaking, but a few drops sloshed over onto the saucer. Pale brown. So Minashiro Tempus, a Class 9 mage, needed milk in his drink.

A mug of spica awaited in front of Wist. It appeared untouched.

If I thought I could make things better for myself by coming in all sweet and flattering, I would've given it a fair shot. After the past week, though, I was pretty sure that groveling before Tempus wouldn't make any difference. Nor would it help to butter him up.

In that case, might as well go for the opposite approach. Might as well have a little fun with it.

"Nervous?" I asked him.

He wiped his fingers with a scallop-edged napkin. Then he rose and—without uttering a word to either Wist or Azalea—strode to the edge of the terrace.

It wasn't far.

Like the library roof, the terrace had no physical railing. Tightropes the color of lava stretched in every imaginable direction, bridging the gap between the gallery and the nearest classroom buildings.

Tempus paused by a rope that appeared to extend further than all the rest, sloping upward to the pinnacle of a much higher tower. It ran through the air above a wide stone-paved path lined by old shaggy cedars and cypresses.

A few of the trees were wide enough at the base that my dorm room could've fit inside with plenty of space to spare. They might very well predate the academy.

"Going somewhere?" I said. I had a feeling I knew what he was about to tell me to do. "Go ahead. Walk on over. Be my guest. I'll be happy to finish your leftovers."

"Hunting season will end," Tempus declaimed in that creamy voice of his, "if you can cross this rope without falling."

"All the way to that spire on the other side?"

He nodded. "It's not impossible. No one will throw rocks. No one will sabotage you. You'll only lose if you fall."

"Incredible," I said. "What a deal. You do know that I don't have any circus training."

"We cross these ropes all the time," he said pleasantly. "Surely you can, too."

We meaning mages.

I didn't know exactly how the cuttings wound around these ropes were supposed to work. If I had to take a wild guess, I'd say that they'd refuse to let you fall—as long as you had a magic core.

Whatever the case, there was zero chance of this being a challenge I had any chance of actually winning.

I reached in my jacket pocket. I groped around until I hit the bottle of hot sauce.

If I held it still with one hand and grabbed the screw-top through the fabric with my other hand, I could wrest it open before anyone saw what I was fiddling with.

As I started to twist at the bottle, Wist turned her head.

A chocolate cupcake resting on the very top tier of the serving tray split smoothly into two perfect halves.

Tempus fixed her with an irritated look. The brief slash of magic must've caught his attention, even with his back turned. "What?"

Wist handed half of the cupcake to Azalea, who held it as if she weren't quite sure what to do with it.

Wist then brought the remaining half to her lips. She chewed. She chewed some more, with all the haste of a ruminant. She swallowed. She dabbed her mouth with a napkin.

Tempus's brows furrowed.

"Just trying to share," Wist told him. It was perhaps the most unemotional she'd ever sounded.

A gleeful premonition fluttered through my bloodstream. I twisted the sauce cap in the other direction. Closed it up tight again.

As satisfying as it would've been to dash deathly strong hot sauce in his face, it would also be certain to get me expelled.

Then my parents would be forced to pay full tuition. Fees scaled for the pocketbooks of mage families, not healers or subliminals. Fees to account for every remaining day, month, and year of academy schooling I missed out on. We might very well end up homeless.

Meanwhile, all Minashiro Tempus would have to worry about were a few days of seared skin and boiling eyes. He'd have a pretty good chance of not going blind. Probably. Although the warnings on the back of the bottle did sound rather dire.

He held out a pocket watch. "You have a minute to get started."

"Or I forfeit for dawdling?"

"You're already wasting time."

I went up to the edge of the terrace. Tempus waited nearby with his stuffy antique-looking watch.

Over by the fire pit, Wist leaned forward in her seat. Tall back still hunched. Elbows on her knees. The dancing of the flames hid her face from me.

Azalea took a reluctant bite of her cupcake half, having apparently failed to think of anything else she could do with it.

The cooing of mourning doves resounded from somewhere unseen. They'd been quite rowdy today. Please don't be lamenting my impending death, I thought.

"All right," I said to Minashiro Tempus. "Hope you're watching closely. I'll only do this once."

My palms went damp so fast that it felt like my pores were vomiting sweat. No amount of beginner's luck would save me here.

You don't need to be acrophobic to get light-headed at the sight of a mossy stone path several stories down, with no net to block your fall. At the thought of your head splashed open like an overripe melon. At the laconic swaying of the glittering line in the air that was supposed to carry you forward through sheer nothingness.

Some tightrope. It wasn't pulled taut at all. It sagged more than the hopeless waistband of my oldest pair of underwear.

I almost turned to Tempus to complain about it. But I didn't think any minor adjustments would be enough to keep this rope from dashing me to the ground like a piece of garbage.

I felt Wist's eyes on my back, black and unblinking and empty of hints. I prayed I could feel them, at least.

What was it Azalea had snapped at me?

You know nothing.

True enough. I'd gladly admit to it. I had no idea what Wist was thinking. I had no idea why she sat around a fire and shared jewel-toned fruit with Minashiro Tempus. Maybe she, too, wanted to hear the crack of my bones on the ground far below.

I was the one who stood here feeling the stakes—feeling them in the trembling of my ankles and fingers. I was the one who had to decide whether to forfeit, or take a step forward that seemed guaranteed to result in me falling.

Have I mentioned how much I hate pain? It's the only reason I've ever felt thankful not to have been born a mage.

I knew nothing of what truly moved Wisteria Shien. Yet I had a rising suspicion that something tight-coiled and malevolent lay in the nothing I knew. And it wasn't pointed at me.

I gambled on the Wist who'd stopped the boys who smashed a little bird to death. I gambled on the Wist who'd shown up in the ruins for Saya's hermit crabs.

I gambled on there being a deeper meaning in the cleaving of that chocolate cupcake.

I placed the bottom of one shoe on the shining rope. It bounced horribly. My gut twinged. My breath froze in my lungs.

My ears felt full of cotton. No more sound of mourning doves. No hoarse-barking crows. No black-headed gulls—the one time I actually wanted them to be around.

Tempus, gripping his pocket watch, had gone gray in the face. As if he were the one about to faint. The absolute gall of this guy.

In the end, raw indignation gave me the superhuman strength needed to pry my remaining foot off the edge of the terrace.

And then?

To no one's surprise—least of all my own—my left foot touched the tightrope for less than a millisecond before I started to fall.

I screamed as if a clawed hand had reached in to rip the sound straight out of my chest. Tempus screamed. A high female voice screamed. (Azalea?)

I screamed, and I plummeted.

Magic split the air like a guillotine.

I shrieked again, but I wasn't falling. I was tangled in tree branches, my long sleeves almost speared through with them.

Not thick, sturdy boughs: the slender branches at the very crown of a conifer. One growing beside the stone path. Much too far from the tightrope and the terrace for me to have reached it with my own strength.

I'd been ported.

There was something crunchy under my butt. Confused voices echoed from the terrace, but I couldn't process a word of them.

I tried to move away from whatever crackly thing I'd ended up sitting on. The tip of the tree swayed and groaned. I gripped fistfuls of flimsy branches and made a sound like a tea kettle.

In reality, it was only for a couple of seconds that I teetered there like a stranded cat.

Magic yanked at me again, this time depositing me on the black terrace couch next to Wist.

I immediately sprang up. I patted the back of my uniform. Specifically, the back of my long skirt. Some kind of wet sticky residue clung there.

I seized a fine-woven napkin from the table before the chilly fire pit. I wiped furiously at the problem area. Then I whirled on Wist.

"You dropped me on a bird nest," I said. "I killed those poor—I cracked the eggs with my butt!"

"Sorry." When she withdrew her hand from her pocket, she was holding a chicken egg. Sandy brown, and probably hard-boiled again. "Didn't realize this would only be the second-nearest one."

"Wist," Azalea said from behind the couch, her voice taut.

Tempus had put away his pocket watch.

"You fell," he said to me. "You lost."

"I didn't hit ground."

"Nor did you cross to the other side."

"Want to see me try again?"

"You fell," he enunciated. "As your prize, you get to enjoy a full year of hunting season."

"No."

That was Wist. She'd risen from the couch.

His face changed when his gaze moved to her. The civilized veneer dropped away. Now he looked more the way I remembered him. Contorted with crude fury, a coarse expression to match that brassy bleached hair.

"Your only task," he told Wist, "was to keep out of it. You were too self-righteous to do even that."

"You lost a while ago, Tempus."

One of his nine magic branches unfurled like a ghostly extension of his hand and whipped her across the face.

It didn't seem to leave a mark. She didn't try to block it. But the impact was hard enough to slap her head to the side. Hard enough to make me wince and scurry back from the seats arrayed around the fire.

Azalea did the opposite. She ran out in front of Wist, bristling. Soon they were all yelling at each other.

Azalea and Tempus were, at least. He belittled her for having only a single magic branch. She raged at him for hitting Wist. He called both of them parasites. *Cuckoo bitch*, he spat, and I nearly burst out laughing.

No one else seemed to see any humor in it. Guess he wasn't kidding. Guess this was the type of thing mages said to denigrate adoptees. Not that I wanted to understand it. I didn't care a whit about mage culture.

They were all too busy fighting to pay any attention to Asa Clematis. No one bothered to keep an eye on the healer observing from a safe distance.

No one—with the possible exception of Wist. She watched me sidelong as I took out my precious bottle of hot sauce and gently unscrewed it. My head throbbed. I did my best not to breathe the fumes.

I didn't care who called me a coward. Now would've been the perfect time to sneak down from the terrace. To turn my back and let the three of them fight it out.

Yet I didn't.

This thing that moved me was an utter stranger to me. Reckless. Self-destructive. Irresistible.

This was not an anger I knew.

Wist kept watching wordlessly as I crept up next to Tempus and dashed hot sauce at the side of his throat.

It splashed his jaw. It splashed his cheek. More importantly, a fat glob slipped right under his mage collar, anointing the inaccessible skin beneath.

I danced back as Tempus and his magic lurched for me. In all likelihood, he was about half a second away from smacking me straight off the terrace.

With luck, I'd hurtle into another tree. Alternatively, I'd end up like that white tern on the beach, flung down hard enough for mere sand to murder it.

Instead of stumbling off the edge, I stumbled straight into Wist.

Her magic had ported me back toward the egg in her hand.

Tempus was howling, incoherent.

I'd bet anything that he'd made the mistake of touching the sauce with his hands. He might even have touched his eyes with it, judging by their sudden and shocking redness. Or maybe the smell of it in the air by his face was just that excruciating.

He dove at the table, snatching cloth napkins to wipe himself, knocking the tiered tray of sweets and fruit on its side. Stray grapes rolled across the floor. He came very close to staggering headlong into the fire pit.

I glanced back at the glass wall, the covered gallery room behind us.

The figures I'd thought I'd seen there were gone now. As if they'd never been there in the first place. Or as if they'd fled in embarrassment.

Good decision. If I were a mage from a lesser family, I'd make a quiet exit from the scene, too. Tempus seemed like the type to hold a grudge against anyone who saw him like this. Liquid streaming from his eyes and nose, spittle and invective streaming from his mouth.

The next time I looked at him, he was dumping his own half-drunk milk tea down his collar. A hapless attempt to wash himself.

"You're a Class 9 mage," Wist said coldly. "Use First Aid."

He cursed her birth parents. He was half on the ground before her now, gripping the edge of the glass-topped table as if he were about to put his fists through it.

One of his magic branches slowly, jerkily wormed its way through his body. His hands. His neck. His eyes. The side of his face.

The spice hadn't outright sliced his skin open. There was no real injury to heal. Merely the illusion of one. But perhaps a basic medical skill like First Aid would suffice to blunt the burning.

It would surely be better than doing nothing.

My eyes had begun to sear, too. Better close up that bottle of hot sauce before I gassed all of us. I moved to put the cap back on—

I did still have the cap. Right there in my right hand.

My left hand was empty.

I turned to Wist. So did Tempus, as he staggered back to his feet. He wiped his mouth and nose with his wrist, then grabbed the last clean cloth napkin from the scattered table and wiped again.

The whites of his eyes were still dyed a solid red-pink. But the tears streamed less wantonly now.

I was the one who'd hot-sauced him. Did he appear to have any room in his sight for me? No. He glared at Wist, at the bottle that had leapt from my hand to hers when no one was looking.

"Yes," she said. "It was me."

She stooped to put her egg on the table before the fire. It rested in a nest of smushed miniature cupcakes and multicolored sweet rice cakes.

She didn't relinquish the bottle of hot sauce. Instead she looked back at Tempus.

She pushed up her sleeves one by one.

She turned the bottle upside down and poured it all over her fingers, her hands, her wrists, her forearms. As if crafting herself a pair of liquid gloves.

Azalea and I both made choking sounds. Azalea had her hands clapped to her mouth. Her eyes—opened as wide as they could go—grew waterier by the second.

Methodically, deliberately, Wist rubbed the gloppy red-brown sauce into her skin like mock lotion.

"Surely you can endure a little stinging," she said to Tempus. "This is nothing."

He attempted to answer. He abandoned the attempt before any real words had a chance to fully emerge. The threads of magic inside him quivered as if he were about to start hitting people again.

Bit by bit he drew himself up, smoothing his soiled uniform. In his floundering about, he'd crushed fallen strawberries with his feet and hands and knees.

Wist—hands dripping as if with blood—set down the empty bottle.

I had less than a day left to think of how I would explain this to Pepper. There was no way he'd expected me to use up the entire thing in his absence.

I also felt deeply sorry for whoever would be stuck with putting the terrace back to normal after all this went down. The mage students wouldn't be expected to take care of it themselves.

Unleashed from its bottle, Pepper's hot sauce was practically a biohazard. Hopefully the cleanup crew would be given appropriate gear.

Azalea, mouth still covered, backed away further. All the way to the shadowy glass wall. She coughed convulsively. Better not ever give her spicy food. My throat prickled, too, but she seemed to have it far worse.

Tempus kept staring at Wist as if Azalea and I had ceased to exist. Purple-green flames bobbed and swayed an uncanny dance in the fire pit.

"You're insane," he said. Strain had pushed his voice down a solid octave.

Wist wiggled her sauce-coated fingers in response, almost mockingly. Was I starting to rub off on her?

Tempus had a hand jammed in his right pocket.

Memory came to me like a revelation. The shade cast by the hovering sundial. Broken rings of floating blue-black stone. The booby-trapped rock someone had thrown at me. My stupid instinct to catch it.

I edged sideways, planning a path of retreat. Tempus wasn't even looking at me. I wouldn't make the same mistake twice.

Whatever happens, I thought, all you have to do is dodge.

He turned roughly as if to take his leave, as if to walk away seething across one of the many glowing tightropes. Wist lowered her red-painted hands, expressionless.

He reached the very edge of the terrace. The exact spot where he'd forced me to stand. Another step, and he'd be poised atop the tightrope I'd promptly fallen from.

Azalea kept coughing on and on in the background, stifled and urgent.

At the last moment, Tempus spun on his heel. He jerked something out of his pocket.

It all happened very fast.

My mind—without my consent—raced about ten thousand times

faster than the scene unfolding before me. Like an extremely short-term and inconvenient prophet, I saw what was coming.

He was aiming at Wist. He knew it. She knew it. I knew it. The emptiness in her face seemed to border on contempt.

Out of nowhere, a new certainty consumed me. Wist wasn't going to dodge. She wasn't going to flinch. Just like how she hadn't so much as flung up an arm in self-defense when his magic struck her in the face.

She'd willingly poured the hottest sauce in the world all over bare skin. And left it there to marinate. And pretended she felt nothing.

All these thoughts boiled up in the split-second it took Tempus to raise his arm.

Like a true idiot, I was already moving.

I lunged back toward Wist. I made it just in time to catch the thing he'd thrown at her. Something hard and rugged. Unexpectedly light. It had glittered with magic as it arced through the air.

Why did I do that? I asked myself as my fingers closed around it.

Also: *I really need to stop doing that.*

I'd caught it one-handed. Was I actually a genius at this? Maybe I should've considered taking sports more seriously.

Tempus shouted something incomprehensible. From the corner of my eye, I saw Wist reach for me, then snatch back her sodden hands. Which was a good thing. They might as well have been dipped in poison.

The missile I'd caught bore a magic cutting. The cutting leapt to my arm. Curled around my wrist like a bracelet, like a hungry worm. Sank in and vanished. My breath shortened and stuttered. The pangs of panic in my chest told me I was an unbelievable moron.

15

It was like those dreams I always had. Dreams of magic hurting me in every imaginable way.

First, my magic perception started to strengthen.

I could still see with my eyes. The thing I'd caught on impulse—the thing Tempus had hurled—was half an oyster shell. The kind anyone could pick up off the beach. Slate gray and ridged on one side, pearlescent on the other.

The cutting it carried had already migrated to me. No magic remained.

I could still hear with my ears. The sounds on the terrace surrounded me like garbled water, my mind content to let them flow around unprocessed.

I could still taste the latent spice in the air like thorns pricking the tender insides of my face.

But my magic perception heightened fast enough that it soon threatened to drown out every other sense. I had no control. It was a helpless, taut expansion, like having your pupils forcibly widened for an eye test.

Except that magic perception used far more than mere eyeballs. The discomfort strained at my entire body, top to bottom, back to front.

Wist was saying something. I turned to her.

A terrible mistake.

Her magic swarmed out like tentacles.

I tripped in my haste to get away, catching at the fireside chairs and couches as I went. The oyster shell dropped from my fingertips, clattered on the floor. Fallen fruit squished underfoot.

A long shadow thrashed at me, lassoed me around the shoulders, made me pull up short. Wist's braid. I jerked to get away. The braid was far more sinewy than my puny arms and legs.

A broken, frightened sound spilled like witless drool from my lips. Her torrent of magic branches soared up and then dove down at me, arrows pouring from the sky.

That was the problem with magic. It was a sword I couldn't reach out and hold by the hilt myself. A blade only mages could wield. A blade forever pointed at the rest of us peons, healers and subliminals alike. Being able to perceive the blade didn't make it any better. All it did was heighten your awareness of living life under the edge of a sword that could never be yours.

Her braid heaved me closer, so hard that I almost knocked into her. Her magic pierced me through, just the same as in my dreams, countless spear-like branches punching holes in me over and over and—

My body cringed uncontrollably. But I wasn't bleeding.

"It isn't real," said a voice in my ear.

Wist had put her tainted hands behind her back. She kept the searing sauce as far away from me as she could. Yet her mouth was very close to my hair. Her braid held me firmly in place.

"It'll wear off," she said quietly. "Your magic perception is under attack. Try to see past the warping."

Easy for her to say. I gripped at her braid with both hands as it strangled me. Her magic still appeared to slash me up like razors flung straight through my flesh. My bones and muscles convulsed with the urge to recoil from her, even though I lacked the strength to go anywhere.

"You were about to run straight off the edge of the terrace."

Okay. Fair. I fought to stop struggling.

From behind, Azalea seemed to be asking a question. Wist slowly straightened up.

Had I ever really seen her stand at her full height before? Maybe not.

"Tempus," she said.

For a moment I could've sworn her magic had punched him to the ground. I could've sworn she made the terrace shake with the force of her blow.

Might've just been my magic perception going haywire. The next time I looked, Tempus still stood there by his tightrope. Wary, petulant. The skin of his face and neck—the parts not covered by the mage collar—inflamed like a birthmark.

Wist stepped toward him. Step, step, step. Her hair dragged me along beside her. I doubted she had any awareness of how she'd ended up pulling me like a pet on a leash.

"If you wanted to be like my brothers," Wist said, "you shouldn't have settled for shutting her up in the ruins. She had plenty of air and space and light.

"If you wanted to be like my brothers, you should have ported her deep into the ocean. Not deep into a pretty spica field. You should have arranged for her to stumble in the ruins. Then arranged for rocks to fall on her legs and break them. Shatter them. You should've been willing to lurk close enough to hear her scream."

It felt like the first time I'd seen any light in her eyes.

His mouth had been hanging open. Belatedly, he compressed his lips. His eyes darted from Wist to me, and then back again.

"I don't—" he began.

Wist didn't let him finish.

"Tempus also had to meet certain conditions to win the hunt," she told me, dry as dust. "It wasn't simply a matter of you losing.

"Last time we all met back home—before the start of the school year—my brothers dared him to make a healer drop out before the end of training week. Drop out or disappear, they said."

"I don't understand." Tempus sounded plaintive. He gawked at the braid wound around and around my shoulders like chains to bind a criminal. "Why does it matter? Why are you doing this? You had every chance to—you specifically picked her!"

"What?" I said blindly.

He pivoted toward me with the eagerness of someone who'd finally found another sane soul to converse with.

"She promised not to mess with the hunt," he said in a rush. "Me and her brothers. She promised all of us. As long as she got to pick the target. It could've been any of you reject healers. Anyone not sent off to training camp. It was only you because she named you. She chose you."

I was too stunned to feel anything. Too stunned to formulate an answer.

I should never have doubted myself. I'd guessed it right at the very beginning.

Who picked me? I'd asked Wist under the sundial. *You, was it? What'd I'd do to get on your bad side?*

"Clematis lasted the full week. Clematis won the hunt." Wist was addressing Tempus again. "You lost. But you still violated our deal."

"You interfered!" he yelled.

"I didn't choose to get ported to Baneberry," she said. "Before today, the one time I helped Clematis was when you used the hermit crabs as bait. You should never have involved other—"

"They're just animals!"

The blazing fire went out. The aurora-colored fire at the center of the terrace. It guttered once and then vanished without warning, without a trace of ash, as if it had never burned there in the first place. Yet the unseasonable cold it had emanated still lingered.

If anything, the cold intensified.

I remained hypnotized by the illusion of Wist's magic stabbing me: in the heart, in the throat, in the legs, in the head. It's not real, I told myself. It's not real.

What was real: the absolute ice in her voice, in her gaze.

"You told my brothers I broke the rules," she said to Tempus.

In that moment, I understood that I had never before seen so much as a speck of anger infect her.

"They told me not to get in the way of your hunt." She spoke with the heavy deliberation of a judge. "I toed the line. I kept my mouth shut. I picked your victim. I let her struggle.

"I let you round up the other healers, order them to turn on her. I never told you to stop. But you still went mewling back to my brothers because you were too unimaginative and too cowardly to really go in there and break her."

Wist wasn't using magic on him. I understood that on an intellectual level, even if my drugged perception screamed otherwise. She wasn't using magic on any of us.

Nothing, physical or magical, forced Tempus to stay there and listen. He nevertheless seemed incapable of moving a single muscle fiber.

Same for me. I'd have been frozen here even if Wist hadn't tied me with her braid.

This was Wisteria Shien with her mask knocked only a fraction off kilter. This was the awful pressure—the presence—of an S-Class mage no longer trying to hide anything.

No. More than S-Class, surely. I just didn't know what else to call her.

I would've moved if I could. I would've shrunk from her, from Tempus, from all of them.

I would've tried to flee, and I would've failed. I would've toppled off the side of the terrace, like she'd warned me. Or—more likely—I'd have ended up vomiting on my knees.

"There were three people on the Shien estate who showed me any kindness," Wist said softly. The softness made it worse. "A bodyguard. A janitor. An accountant. All three were fired yesterday. After decades on the job. No pension. No severance. No honor. Chased off the grounds."

She tilted her head as if asking a question. "I'll never see them again," she said. "I have nothing left to protect."

Tempus's jaw quivered. He appeared empty of words.

A loud knocking came from behind us. From the glass wall way over on the other side of the terrace. Tempus jolted at the sound of it, jolted like he'd been shot.

Inside the gallery, a gaunt silhouette banged furiously on the nearest door.

Azalea rushed over to let him through.

Mr. Rift pushed back thinning hair. He stared at the ornate tea tray on the floor. The crushed cakes and trampled fruit. The splatters and blots of hot sauce, which happened to be the exact same color as old blood.

He started to speak, then burst out coughing. The spice fumes must've hit him.

He studied each of us in turn: Azalea, me, Tempus, Wist.

"You called for me," he said to Wist. His tone implied that he was beginning to doubt his own memory. "You require healing?"

Her braid released me, slithering deftly away. She showed Mr. Rift her still-dripping forearms. "Healing can wait. There was an accident."

He strode forward. "Is anyone—?"

"It's hot sauce," Wist answered. "No one got hurt."

I had to brace myself to keep standing on my own, without her holding me up. It felt like trying to compensate for the swaying of a train.

Violent hallucinations still ate away at my magic perception. Wist's magic branches surged from the floor like tree roots to skewer me. All the self-control in the world couldn't completely mask my wincing.

There were other mages nearby, not to mention a variety of pruned magic cuttings: in the fire pit, on the tightropes. Wist so dwarfed the rest of them that—even in my deluded state—only her magic seemed able to touch me.

"She—" Tempus cleared his throat. His voice still came out ragged, but somewhat closer to its original cultivated smoothness. "Shien used unauthorized skills."

"Minashiro, you know that's not my area of expertise," said Mr. Rift. "If you have concerns, ask your advisor to review the collar transcripts. What happened to your face?"

"That was the accident," Wist interjected. "Clematis brought us hot sauce. We were ... we were so excited to try it. Overexcited. Yes."

Mr. Rift surveyed the wreckage littering the terrace. "I can smell it," he said. "Very strong stuff. You were going to drizzle this on frosted cakes and fresh fruit?"

I decided to pipe in. "Great idea, right? You can see how well it turned out."

"You," he said.

"Me?"

I put on my most mild-mannered face. I stood as steady as I could. Not an easy task, given that to me it still looked as if I were being viciously impaled by magic branches from every possible direction.

"You shouldn't be here. You shouldn't be alone."

"I'm far from alone," I told him. "I'm with friends. It's like Wi—like Shien said. Me and three friends having a tea party. A hot sauce tea party."

"You're the only healer."

"Oh," I said airily. "I forgot. At least we're outdoors. And it's still daytime."

For a moment, I imagined I could see right inside Mr. Rift's head. I could see him begging me to shut up. Fantasizing about turning back around and forgetting he'd seen a thing. Reasoning that this situation—whatever it was—didn't necessarily fit the strictest definition of mage-healer fraternization.

I prayed that Mr. Rift would mention neither the word *fraternization* nor the possibility of tossing us all up in front of a disciplinary tribunal. Didn't want to give Tempus any bright new ideas about reporting me. He might end up incriminating himself in the process, but anyone could guess which of us would get punished worse.

"Asa."

"Yes?"

"I'm taking you back across the border," said Mr. Rift. "Wren, Shien, Minashiro—try to make a cursory attempt to clean up. I'll return as soon as I can."

"That's it?" Tempus demanded. "You can't simply—"

"Every single other faculty member is currently busy dealing with the ruckus by the caves," Mr. Rift said. "Save your anger for your seniors.

I only managed to slip away because Shien had specifically requested more healing.

"If you have any complaints you want to escalate, you'll need to wait for other staff to return. For now, you'll have to content yourself with my sincerest apologies."

He pointed me toward the door. I gingerly followed his lead.

Maybe it'd be easier to walk a straight line once I'd gotten some distance from Wist. I could only hope that the psychedelic effects on my magic perception would wear off in a matter of hours, instead of lasting for days.

Tempus muttered furiously as we left. I couldn't hear what, if anything, Wist said in reply.

I had to wonder what would happen once it was just those two and Azalea left on the terrace. Would they actually attempt to grudgingly wipe the food off the floor? Launch into an all-out brawl? Call a truce and escape the scene of the crime?

As we passed below the ancient trees beside the gallery building, Mr. Rift cast a critical eye over me. "Asa. Are you drunk?"

"No?" I said, struggling mightily to move normally.

Darts of phantom magic kept plummeting like falcons from the sky to pursue me. My magic perception—and, by extension, the skin on every sore inch of my body—felt stretched at the edges. Weirdly distended.

At least my voice sounded unaffected. "What, do I smell drunk?"

"You smell like hot sauce."

"Well, there you go."

"I didn't realize you were such a spice aficionado."

"I can hold my own," I said primly.

I was quite certain that Mr. Rift hadn't believed a word from any of us. But he was a man who knew how to pick his battles.

"What happened by the caves?" I asked.

"An elaborate prank," he replied. "Orchestrated by some of the older mage students. Very time-consuming. No, I'm not telling you the details. Wouldn't want to inspire you."

As we approached the border gardens, Mr. Rift turned and said: "Two more weeks of detention. For a total of five weeks."

"Are you kidding? I didn't even do anything!"

"I found you alone with mage students, on mage territory," he said wearily.

"Oh, so now merely existing in mage territory is a crime?"

"Would you like it to be six weeks?"

"Five sounds good," I said, perfectly meek.

16

THAT NIGHT, not long after darkness closed over the island, wet fog invaded my room again.

My magic perception had mostly reverted to normal. It still felt unnaturally dilated. But the imagined fragments of magic that swooped about me had grown easier to dismiss as mere ghosts. With luck, they'd fade away by morning.

The fog came in through the window after curfew. I didn't care quite so much about breaking curfew now that hunting season was ostensibly over. Then again, I already had five full weeks of detention starting tomorrow. Would really prefer to avoid letting my prison term get any longer.

I grumbled as I stripped sheets from my bed. I snatched up the empty yellow kidnapping bucket. I cleared the windowsill.

After a few minutes of preparation, I climbed out the bedroom window. Couldn't believe I was doing this for a second time.

The night was cool and misty, and not simply because of Wist's magical fog. Once again, I scuffled with the jasmine-tangled bushes at ground level, all spiky pink buds and white five-petaled flowers. I emerged from the tussle covered from head to toe in their scent.

My jacket felt weirdly light without the customary bottle of hot sauce, and my magic perception remained askew. Stinking of jasmine, I stumbled headfirst into Wist.

I'd thought she and her magic core were about two feet to the left. Should've relied on my eyes to guide me, not the lure-like light of her core.

Wist caught me by the shoulders and straightened me up. She had on another set of baggy silken pajamas garlanded with royal embroidery. The patterns seemed slightly different: morning glories and pine trees, bamboo and orchids, turtles and bumblebees.

"First order of business," I said in a whisper. I could be discreet when the occasion called for it. "I need an egg."

"Don't have any."

"Then get one," I ordered her.

A brown chicken egg appeared in her cupped hand. The shell was crusted here and there with pastel traces of what I assumed must be cupcake frosting.

I took the egg from Wist and put it in my yellow bucket, which dangled from a makeshift series of sheet-ropes.

Come to think of it, I could've just demanded that she teleport the egg-holding bucket back inside my room. As she'd proven just now, porting inanimate objects had never been a problem for her.

But I'd already gone to the trouble of crafting this stupid contraption. Might as well use it.

I jumped to grab at the other dangling end of the sheets. I'd used all the sheets from my own bed plus several spare sets, and in doing so had made the rope as long as I could. Almost long enough to do a full vertical lap of the building, from the bushes to my window and then back again.

I hauled on my rope, pulling and pulling, until the bucket swayed all the way back up to the windowsill. I'd left the screen open. Hopefully it was too early in the season for mosquitoes to colonize the room in my absence.

Wist looked—without judgment but, I imagined, somewhat quizzically—at the excess sheets knotted together and piled up among the heaps of wall-climbing jasmine.

"There," I said. "When we're done, you can send me back to my room. Back to that egg."

"I see."

"You really ought to learn a skill that lets you port other people more freely," I griped.

"You can eat the egg afterward," she said. "It's cooked."

We were still keeping our voices low. "Cute. Don't make me march all the way down to the beach again. Way too tired for that."

She took me to the oversize border garden instead. A much shorter trip. A slab of fog followed us, hovering overhead like a personal raincloud. A crude precaution against eyes in the sky. But we saw not a single other soul on the way there—neither people nor gulls.

The garden made its own illumination at night. It was much subtler than the fiery faux coral set up to light the campus footpaths. A quiet reflective glistening, something closer to moonlight.

The roses here had trunks like sequoia trees, and colossal thorns to match. Any vegetation more active in nature would be capable of causing mortal injury. I kept a wary eye out for carnivorous plants.

"Your perception," Wist said.

"Mostly better. That wasn't Tempus's magic on the oyster shell, was it? Seemed like someone else's cutting."

"A psychoactive cutting. The seniors have been circulating them."

"Why can't they just settle for doing shots or something?"

"Most psychoactive cuttings would be meant to affect much more than your magic perception. Tempus picked a mild one."

Right. Sure had felt mild when it looked as if her magic was goring me full of more holes than a cheese grater.

"Think he was trying to take it easy on us?"

She made a short noise in her throat. A solitary syllable of laughter, perhaps. "That's simply Tempus being Tempus. Everything he does is by half measures."

"You really in a position to look down on him?" I asked. "You picked me to be hunted. You nominated me. But you still couldn't seem to keep your nose out of it. I kind of see his point."

Behind her legs, her braid ticked back and forth like the inexorable pendulum of a clock. "Are you angry?"

"Take a guess."

"Would you like me to apologize?"

It seemed like a genuine question.

"Don't," I said. "What's the good of that? Anyway, I told you I'd be impressed if you turned out to be the mastermind all along."

"Did I?"

"No. You're definitely not mastermind material. But you specifically chose me as a sacrifice, then cozied up to me anyway. I respect the brazenness."

I had to sidle closer to get a good look at her face. Not that it revealed anything. "What I still don't get is—why me? Was it random? When did you even pick me?"

Beside her bloomed rhododendrons with flowers the size of traffic cones. Supportive magic sparkled in the underbrush, most likely to keep the entire disproportionate garden from collapsing in on itself.

Wist turned her head as if hoping to become one with the rhododendrons, to blend in and eventually vanish.

"I didn't know which healers would be left out of training camp," she said.

"You had to choose from among the rejects. That's why you warned me? When we met in the infirmary."

Wist nodded.

"Did you pick me to punish me? I ignored your warning on purpose. I went out of my way to skip training camp."

"I got the impression," she said gradually, "that you wouldn't crumble under pressure from the likes of Tempus."

"Guess that's a compliment," I said. "I'll take it."

"You forgive easily."

"Not at all. Just doing a basic risk-benefit analysis. You could be useful someday. If you feel the tiniest bit guilty over it. If you feel like you owe me."

"If I feel guilty—"

She cut herself off. I didn't press her to continue. I might be wildly off base, of course, but I suspected I knew what came next.

Directly or indirectly, she'd confessed most of it on the gallery terrace.

Her older brothers had allied with Tempus. Her brothers had egged him on. Her brothers had sworn her to inaction, to interfering as little as possible with the hunt. Her brothers had threatened the people—servants?—she cared for back home.

And now those people were gone.

If guilt wracked her, the bulk of it wouldn't be for me, an insolent healer she'd known for all of a month.

"I'm still full of questions," I warned. "Did you mean for Mr. Rift to show up and interrupt? That why you scheduled afternoon healing with him? You had it all planned in advance?"

"The timing could have been better."

"No one's perfect," I said glibly.

Wist wandered into the garden's bamboo grove, and I followed. This must be what ants felt like when they meandered among stems of grass. The bamboo stretched impossibly tall and thick. Hushed, green-tinted shadows enveloped us.

I spotted one of my hand-sized snails creeping juicily up the base of a younger stalk. I tugged at the back of Wist's pajamas to make her look.

The moment she saw it, she winked out of sight. I stood there empty-handed until I spotted her magic shining in the distance. She'd ported all the way out of the bamboo grove. Huffing, I scrambled to catch up.

"What's wrong with snails?" I asked, still breathless. "They can't attack you. They're slow and cute."

"Thought you were full of questions."

"Yeah, and that's one of them."

Wist pretended not to hear me.

"Fine," I said. "How pissed is Tempus? Do I have to keep watching out for him?"

"Hunting season is over."

"It's quite possible to harass someone without needing the formality of a corny name for it. Or half-baked rules to make it a half-baked game."

"He won't touch you," she said. "And he won't use your classmates to get to you. It's over. He knows I no longer have any reason to hold back."

Did I trust her?

On the terrace, when I first set foot on that all-too-bouncy tightrope, I'd trusted her with my life. Her and her nearest-egg magic. Did I trust her outside of that one desperate moment?

Not quite no, and not quite yes. I preferred to reserve judgment.

"Not just Tempus," Wist added. "None of us will bother you."

None of us. No mages.

"No more fog in your room, either."

Good. Saya would be back tomorrow.

"Co-ed lessons start in another couple of weeks," I pointed out.

"You won't have anything to worry about. But—"

"Here it comes," I said. "But what?"

She hooked her fingers inside her ever-present collar. It was hard to tell in the dark, but the skin of her hands and wrist looked rashy and irritated, even hours after their bath in lethal hot sauce.

For once, her braid had gone still. It hung down behind her, dragging on the mossy ground like a long and heavy chain.

Strands of a wide spiderweb spanned the gaps in nearby foliage. I decided not to mention it. Considering how she'd reacted to my poor snail, a similarly sized spider might make her port straight into the cradle of the nearest gargantuan tulip.

"You'll be asked to heal other mages for class," Wist said. "Magisters as well as students. I suggest you…" She'd begun rotating her collar as if she needed to turn it like a gear to crank the words out. "I suggest you hold back."

I repeated this in my head. Nope, not getting it. "Need a little more explanation than that. I'm new to this."

"If you heal others the way you healed me," she said carefully, "you'll attract a lot of attention. If that's what you want—"

"It's not," I said. "Definitely not. You think I should pull my punches? Good idea. I'll take it."

After a pause, I added: "So I'm really good at healing, then."

"For a beginner."

"Hah. Sure you don't need some now?"

"I'll last till morning. Mr. Rift took care of me earlier."

She walked me back to my dorm beneath a protective cloak of fog. We needed to be close by the building, so I wouldn't end up in another treetop when she attempted to port me to the nearest egg. Which would hopefully end up being the one stashed in my bucket.

I asked, out of morbid curiosity, if the hot sauce all over her hands and arms really hadn't bothered her that much. I could still see visible traces of the capsaicin burn.

"Magic hurts more," she said.

"Not all the time, though."

She didn't answer. I almost offered to heal her again. But I kept my mouth shut.

I wasn't a charity. And Wisteria Shien had zero need for my pity.

After landing on the windowsill next to my yellow bucket, after hauling myself safely inside, I took another peek out at the spot where she'd been standing.

Nothing remained but black hulking bushes and copious clouds of flowering jasmine. Fake coral shone a gaudy light on winding paths to places I didn't care about.

Wist was nowhere to be seen.

If fortune favored me, I might never need to speak with her or Azalea or Tempus again. If I followed her advice and made a poor impression when healing other mages, the faculty would be inclined to keep me far away from their precious favorites. Originators, legacy students, scions of top families, and the like.

If Wisteria Shien kept her word—if she kept her distance—she'd be doing me an enormous favor.

I ought to be glad for it. Grateful, even. I ought to sleep better than ever tonight.

And yet I still dreamed of magic mauling me. The same stupid stress dreams that had followed me everywhere since I was little.

I woke up three times between midnight and dawn. Gasping, grasping for something that wasn't there. Between it all, I still dreamed vividly of the horrors of a power that wasn't mine.

PART TWO

The Originator Exam

17

FOR THE NEXT three months, Wisteria Shien kept her promise.

I, in turn, made sure to follow her advice. When I got asked to heal mage students during class, I did it as sloppily as possible. Only Mr. Rift seemed to suspect me of messing up on purpose.

The first five weeks of that three-month period involved me serving out my detention sentence.

I was still stuck in detention when the rainy season started. I'd sit there doing my busywork while flocks of pet umbrellas flew by the classroom window.

The older mage students made them by ordering umbrellas in bulk and sawing the handles off. With the right cuttings applied, they'd float overhead and follow you wherever you went. If you forgot your pet at home, you could theoretically call it to come pick you up.

The umbrellas weren't very smart, though. They frequently got stuck in trees. They lacked the initiative to fix themselves when the wind blasted them inside out. There was a reason I'd never seen this sort of product for sale back in the city.

By the time I finished detention, the rainy season had mostly lifted. Afterward, it got warm enough that just about everyone went swimming on days off from class.

No one visibly marked certain stretches of the beach as being for mage students, and others as being for healers. Somehow, we all knew where to go anyway; we'd learned by osmosis.

Healer students mostly congregated on the eastern end of the island, by the largest ruins. The sand there was so much wider that it ended up being a huge pain to drag beach chairs and other such accoutrements all the way up to the water. I could see why the mages had left it to us.

Did I join my peers there? Rarely.

Once Saya and Pepper and everyone else returned from training camp, the other eight leftover Rats began acting like I was the one who'd wronged them.

They didn't talk shit about me. Not directly. But they worked so hard not to look at me, not to speak with me. They did nothing to discourage rumors that it was my own fault I got shunned.

I didn't care to waste my time dissecting whatever quirk of psychology made them act that way. Saya, Pepper, the twins across the hall, and the dorm steward were willing to acknowledge my existence, at least. That was enough to keep me from completely losing my mind. I don't ask for a lot.

Granted, Pepper was heartbroken when I delivered the news that I'd wasted an entire bottle of his spiciest hot sauce.

Yet about a week after the end of training camp, a brand new bottle showed up in the mailroom, extravagantly gift-wrapped. The package was addressed to Asa Clematis. It came with no message and no listed sender.

I promptly handed it over to Pepper, of course. I was beyond broke. It would've taken me another full semester to scrounge up enough spare change to buy him a replacement on my own.

I had a feeling I knew who'd sent the new bottle.

I didn't go out of my way to find her and thank her, though. Her family had money to spare, and she was the one who'd used up most of the original sauce. Replacing it was the least she could've done, frankly.

Co-ed classes for core subjects had started in late May, a few weeks after hunting season. For me, this made the long daily hours of detention far more bearable. I was about a billion times more motivated to study standard academic topics than anything to do with magiology or vorpal mysticism or mage healing.

The core classes for Rats were math and finance, continental history, culture, and biology. Plus physical education, for those not in any sports-related clubs.

I fantasized about turning out to be a surprise genius in, say, accounting. Then maybe I could justify becoming a banker, instead of dedicating the rest of my natural life to healing mages.

After some initial testing, the faculty sorted us into groups based on progress. Sadly, I ended up in the lower to mid-tier groups in every single core subject.

What was wrong with my mind? I grasped healing-related concepts intuitively, and much faster than those around me. But I didn't want anyone to commend me. I had to keep pretending not to get it.

Sometimes I just wanted to rip my healing textbooks to pieces. Useless grubby things.

Why couldn't I be naturally good at something that had more value to me and less value to mages?

Which is not to say that I wasn't willing to put in the work. I studied the core subjects like a maniac. At least for a little while. Until the futility of it all began to sink in.

If the government deemed me a solid healer—and by sponsoring me for Guralta Academy, they already had—I'd need to show world-changing levels of talent in order to be allowed to abandon healing in favor of anything else.

If music were my strength, for instance, I'd better be the type of prodigy so great as to earn myself a few fawning paragraphs in nonmusical history books.

I could demonstrate infinite passion for other fields. And I was ready to. Unfortunately, mere passion would never be enough to make society forget about my potential gifts as a healer.

Yarrow had warned me. Now I understood why. But she'd warned me too late.

I shared a few core classes with Wist, but none with Azalea or Tempus. They were probably more adept at academics than either of us. Much to my chagrin, even Saya ended up a level or two ahead of me in most subjects.

Wist, true to her word, stayed away from me. When she deigned to attend class—which didn't happen all that often—she spent most of her time with her head in her arms. Either blatantly sleeping, or pretending to sleep.

Right around the time when co-ed classes started, we healers got forced to attend a separate course on bonding. The teachers in charge were Mr. Rift, who looked as if he would rather be anywhere else, and a gung-ho young woman who usually taught statistics.

They explained how bonding might work as a business relationship, complete with contracts. The main objective of the class, however, seemed to be to scare us out of bonding carelessly. Whether or not love had anything to do with it, bonding was for life.

I raised my hand and asked if either of the teachers had personal experience with bonding.

It was a genuine question: neither of them wore bond threads. And what mage would let their bondmate spend the entire school year alone on an island? Unless they happened to be bonded with one of the magisters on the faculty, it didn't really make sense.

When I brought this up, Mr. Rift told me it was a private matter.

"Don't be a jerk," he said.

I raised my hand again soon after. I wanted to know if the mage students were being put through a similar course. If they too got to hear all the horror stories about bonding too young.

They actually made me step out of class for that one. Must've been something about the way I asked it.

It wasn't the only time I got kicked out in the middle of a lecture, either. During history class, I seized on a chance to ask what people called healers over in the island nation of Jace.

That one was kind of on purpose, I'll confess. Osmanthus had tense relations with all its neighbors, but historically speaking, Jace was one of our greatest enemies. Healers and mages lived very different lives there.

Or so the stories went. It was a little hard to believe in a place where mages didn't control everything.

It wasn't even that far away. Some of the airships that passed above us might be headed straight for Jace. The Jacian archipelago wasn't visible from our shores, but we shared the same ocean water.

Hell, if I'd been born there, my knack for healing might've made me a natural ruler.

From here in Osmanthus, it sounded ridiculous, of course. From here it seemed like a fairy tale. Or—if you were a mage—like a nightmare.

To sum it up: I had my disruptive moments every now and then.

When Mr. Rift called me to his office in early August, I figured it was to scold me for being a jerk again. (His words, not mine.)

With the rainy season long over, summer heat had reached its peak. So too had the deafening bellows of fat cicadas in every treetop.

The cicadas fell on their backs on verandas, on rooftops, on campus paths. They lay there bleating, too top-heavy to flip over until the footfalls of an innocent passer-by infused them with a fresh spike of adrenaline.

Then they'd rocket around drunkenly, screeching even louder. Every now and then, an opportunistic crow would snatch one up and flap away as its victim shrieked its final notes.

The cicadas were loudest. But it was also a season for killer hornets, for butterflies with stained-glass wings, for those fuzzy moths that look just like miniature hummingbirds, for blue-green dragonflies the size of my face.

There were multiple cockroach sightings on the first floor of our dorm. Occasionally I wondered how Wist was faring amid this explosion of insect life.

The vertebrate population had also undergone a drastic increase. There were more people on the island than I could've ever imagined back when I first arrived in April.

They filled all the oceanfront vacation homes. They went surfing and sailing and surface running and water tumbling.

Quite a large proportion of the vacationers appeared to be working mages. A far larger proportion, at any rate, than the piddling percentage of the overall Osmanthian population that could boast of a career in magic.

A lot of them must've been Guralta alumni and their families. Some brought along healers, bonded or otherwise.

I kept spotting visiting mages on campus. Meandering in the generous shade of the elder trees. Pointing out buildings and statues to their children.

They twirled genteel parasols on their shoulders and smiled fondly at passing students in mage collars. Their eyes skated straight past those of us wearing healer uniforms, in the same way that a city dweller might by habit look past squirrels or pigeons.

I passed yet another mage wedding as I crossed campus to get lectured by Mr. Rift. It was the third I'd seen this week alone. Mages marrying mages, for the most part.

Some seemed to have bondmates—but being bonded to a healer didn't mean you needed to marry them. Not much political benefit to it, compared to aligning yourself with another great mage clan. Plenty of people had a bondmate for the business of magic, and a proper spouse for the business of family.

Even with the windows open, Mr. Rift's office may as well have been a sauna. I borrowed a sheaf of scrap paper from his waste bin to fan myself.

There was a summer version of the mage student uniform, with short sleeves and lighter material. The healer uniform remained the same all year, unfortunately. The best we could do was quit wearing our jackets, and tie back our long dangling sleeves.

Mr. Rift served me cold barley tea again. The glass immediately started dribbling condensation all over his desk. I had to wipe my hand dry on my skirt after each sip.

"What'd I do this time?" I inquired.

No offense to Mr. Rift, but he seemed more exhausted with each passing day. Maybe he didn't take well to the heat. Or maybe my unasked-for comments in class were starting to fracture his last remaining sliver of sanity.

"Asa." He paused after saying my name, as if trying to squeeze out more time to think. "Do you know anything about the midsummer mage exams?"

"Midsummer? Then I assume they're over. The summer solstice was in June," I said.

"The exams are in August. I didn't make the schedule."

"Well, what about them?"

"The originator exam is very different from the rest."

"Mr. Rift, I don't see what this has to do with me."

"Strive to keep quiet and listen," he told me. "Just for a minute. I know it's difficult."

I gulped tea to stop myself from interrupting.

"The originator exam is personalized to each member of the program. It's much longer and more involved than the other mage exams."

I gulped tea furiously.

"I'm getting to it, Asa," Mr. Rift said tiredly. "Traditionally, each originator chooses a healer student to support them during the exam. They can pick any healer, regardless of school year. So usually they pick the absolute best. It's a tremendous honor to be selected."

I could no longer resist. "I really don't see why you're saying this to me, because—"

"Wisteria Shien wants to choose you."

The tea felt very cold in my belly.

"No," I blurted. "That can't be right. She promised—"

"She promised?"

I sat as still as a lump of rock in his creaky rattan chair. Sweat beaded on the back and sides of my neck. If I had a more delicate constitution, I'd have fainted dead away from the lack of cooling in here.

Somewhere outside, a chorus of cicadas howled their little heads off. I wanted to howl my little head off, too.

"If you really don't want to, I can try to decline on your behalf."

He sounded tentative. Too tentative for my liking.

"Can you?" I demanded. "Would it be that easy to get me out of it? What if she insists?"

"I can try," he repeated.

"If all you can do is try," I said, "then don't bother."

I tamped down the urge to chew my nails. I hadn't bitten my nails in years. I pressed the base of my palm to my mouth as I thought.

It was too hot to think. Right now it was too hot to do anything but sweat and bathe and sleep.

"When does this thing get finalized?" I asked at last.

"Next week."

"Can you get me a chance to talk to her about it first?"

"You'd like me to play chaperone?"

"You don't have to listen in," I said. "But yeah. Would appreciate it."

The next day, Mr. Rift asked us both to stay back after our co-ed history class.

He spoke to us separately. Kept it subtle. Other students streamed out the doors—mages through one door, healers through another, by mutual unspoken agreement. No one noticed that neither Wist nor I had moved from our seats.

It was a smallish lecture hall, with a few steeply tiered rows of desks. A frighteningly large fan spun in the domed ceiling. It looked big enough to suck us all up and slice us to bits. Big enough to launch the classroom off its foundation and send it swirling high into the sky.

It kept the room cool, though. And the veil of sound-dampening magic all around the fan blades kept us from hearing a thing.

Mr. Rift took a stack of notes out from below the lectern. He headed for a storage closet off to one side of the room.

"I'll be organizing," he said briskly. "Call me when you're done."

He left the closet door cracked for the sake of propriety.

I waved Wist on up to the highest row of desks at the back. The ceiling fan spun soundlessly above, vast and hungry.

Wist wore the short-sleeved summer mage top together with track pants. A peculiar compromise.

I couldn't even remember the last time I'd heard her voice. She wasn't one to speak up in class. She wasn't one to be conscious in class, for that matter. She ought to count herself very lucky that she wasn't prone to snoring.

She stopped at the desks one level below where I stood. For once, I was taller. I thrust my hands in my skirt pockets and glowered down at her.

"Traitor," I spat. "Liar."

Wist waited patiently for me to finish berating her.

"You swore to me that no mage would ever bother me again," I said, gaining steam. "You swore on—on the lives of your birth parents."

I may be slightly prone to embellishment.

"And it lasted for all of two months?" I demanded. "Three months? Is that all your promises are worth?"

"So it would seem," said Wist.

"You could've chosen any other healer in the entire school," I said. "Anyone! They would've been thrilled! You picked the one person who doesn't want anything to do with—"

"I'm sorry."

Her apology bore a downright impressive dearth of emotion.

"If you're sorry, then don't pluck me out of obscurity in the first place!"

I heaved an irate breath. Then another. Scream-whispering like this had to be bad for my throat.

"You must have a reason," I said, artificially calm. "Spill it."

"Tempus is planning something."

"Planning what?"

"Not sure. He's been talking to my brothers again."

I made a circular motion with my hands, urging her to hurry up and get to the crux of the matter.

"My exam will take place off-campus," Wist continued. "Off the island. I can't control what Tempus does in my absence."

I stared up at the fan as I mulled over the implications. It was rather hypnotic.

"You want to take me with you," I said, as if struggling to read out a poorly written script. "To protect me? From the machinations of big mean Tempus? That's a tad hard to swallow. We've barely spoken since spring, you and I."

"Tempus never forgets a grudge."

"There's one thing he and I have in common, then. Correct me if I'm wrong here," I said. "I'd bet the entirety of my empty bank account on the fact that you're the one he has a problem with. Not me. I'm nothing to him. And I'm happy to keep it that way."

"He has the impression that you aren't nothing to me."

I'm no mathematician, but this wasn't adding up. "Why?" I asked. "Because you volunteered me to be tortured for a week back in May?"

"Essentially, yes."

"That doesn't make any sense."

"I know your name. I know your face. He thinks I blocked the hunt, in its finest moment, for your sake."

"Right. After you served me up to him on a silver platter." I was—and I don't say this lightly—downright flabbergasted. "Just to clarify. Tempus noticed you acknowledge my existence once or twice. Genius that he is, he thinks this makes me hostage material."

"Correct."

"Why doesn't he just go after Azalea?"

"She's a mage," Wist answered.

I suppose that was explanation enough.

I tore my gaze from the fan and looked Wist in the face again. The seasons may have changed, but her expression remained the same. No clues. No anticipation. No expectation.

"What if I don't want to go?" I mimicked her pattern of speech, the slow deep crawl of it. I was pretty damn good at imitating her when I put my mind to it. "Will you force me?"

I waited.

"No," she said after a taut moment. "No one will force you."

"Then I'll go."

At first Wist said nothing.

Then: "What decided you?"

"You tried to warn me about hunting season," I explained. "I ignored you. Look how great that turned out for me."

"Mm."

"As long as I actually have a choice in the matter, I figure this time I'll listen to your warning. Don't make me regret it."

She didn't nod. She didn't blink. She didn't utter a word of response.

"It would be reassuring if you said something in reply," I told her. "Just as a courtesy. You know."

"Thought it might be better not to say anything at all."

"What? Why?"

"You've seen how well my promises age."

"Oh boy," I muttered.

I'll admit it was fun, though. Talking to her for the first time in months.

Which was a bizarre way to feel, given that Wist was a girl of few words and no smiles. I shouldn't have been nearly this comfortable.

Maybe her braid betrayed what her tone and expression would never give away. It wagged like the tail of a big dog, thumping softly into the legs of the desk behind her.

"Did you miss me?" I asked. "These past few months. Did you miss this?"

"What was there to miss?" she inquired, stone-faced.

Her braid kept wagging all the while. I held my stomach and wheezed until Mr. Rift poked his head out to make sure we weren't at each other's throats. My laughter must've sounded like murder.

18

I DIDN'T NEED to wait long to start regretting my choice.

The packing instructions ordered me to bring my gym clothes, and little else. No snacks. No water.

I complained bitterly to Saya as I went through the checklist. "I get that this is a wilderness survival course kinda thing, but I'm not the one being tested. Don't see why I gotta be deprived, too."

"If the Shien mage aces her exam, then you won't be deprived at all," Saya said reasonably.

She poked at the malfunctioning melodium she kept on her desk. A song like the croaking of a dying animal filled our room.

"You'll give the hermit crabs nightmares," I warned.

"Be careful," Saya said.

I looked up.

Her eyes were on the melodium. She silenced it, then pivoted in her chair.

"Yeah, I know." I resumed folding my track pants. "I'll be as careful as can be."

The cicadas outside were raucous even in the dark. Perhaps especially in the dark. Heaven forbid that any of us get a good night's sleep. I wondered if mage student housing came with soundproofing magic.

"This is like the opposite of training camp," I said. "You got busy packing for it. I lazed around."

"Almost as if you already knew you weren't going to attend."

"I'm a real prophet when I put my mind to it." I glanced up. "This thing—the originator exam—they're sending us to the same place as spring training camp. What's it like?"

"Mountainous."

"Mosquitoes?"

"Way more than here, probably."

This was the moment when my regret reached new heights. I threw Saya a plaintive look. "Give me something to look forward to."

"There's a cute farming town down in the valley nearby. Tasty souvenirs."

"Oh?"

"But I doubt they'll send you there. We did have a whole week for training camp. The exam will only be one or two nights, won't it?"

I groaned and flung myself down on my bed.

Right after Saya came back from training camp, I'd told her that the surveillance gulls were no longer an issue. They'd suddenly stopped haunting our window, I said.

Why? Who knows?

I also mentioned in passing that I no longer used the model tower as a nightlight. I made up a story about how its glow seemed to draw bugs.

I never explained the connection between the tower and the gulls.

At this point it was just a bit of trivia. I had no deep reason for keeping it to myself. Nothing except my recollection of how desperately Wist had seized it from me on the library roof. Something about that moment made me want to keep my mouth shut.

As spring changed to summer, Saya had added more plant trimmings to our windowsill. Mismatched glasses, murky water, plus the occasional hovering gnat.

Definitely no room left to climb out the window and escape down the side of the building. Not that I wanted to attempt anything like that ever again.

Saya was officially a member of the gardening club. Also the astronomy club, the fishing club, and just about every other co-ed organization in the entire school. I doubt she had an inherent interest in any of these activities. But I did have to admire her dogged commitment to getting to know more mages.

When I first mentioned Wist asking me to help with her midsummer exam, Saya had fallen silent. She shut the window—afraid of being overheard, perhaps—then asked me if I were okay.

If I'd learned one thing from rooming with Saya, it was that she was far more prone to sudden bouts of paranoia than anyone else I'd met at school, healer or mage. Maybe that made her smarter than the rest of us.

"I'm not worried about being alone with Wisteria Shien, if that's what you're asking," I answered. "We'll be closely monitored, anyway. No time for shenanigans."

"Shenanigans?"

"Hm? Did I say something?"

Saya took my clowning in stride. "Could be a very romantic situation," she mused. "Stranded in the woods. Under pressure to pass a test."

"Not all of us came to the academy to land a mage."

"That's what everyone claims, isn't it?" There was a mocking edge to her voice. "They're just here to learn. How noble. But a lot of healers do end up bonding mages they first met in school."

"Nothing wrong with that. Me, I've got no interest in any mages, period. And definitely no interest in bonding."

Saya twisted to look at me. She rested her chin on the back of her chair. "Someday it might be a choice between working twelve-hour days in a city clinic, or only having to treat your bondmate for the rest of your life.

"Someday it might be a question of what lets you keep your parents out of the poorhouse: a public healer's salary, or the wealth of a powerful bondmate."

"We're schoolgirls, Saya," I said. "Can't you wait a couple more years to start obsessing over all that stuff?"

"I come from a family of healers. We know how bad things can get for us."

"So I've heard."

"Here's the optimistic way of looking at it," she told me. "We're good enough healers to get into Guralta. Any of us could easily find a bondmate someday. As long as we're willing to lower our standards. It's practically guaranteed. Just can't afford to be picky.

"But right now we're still young. Right now there's still time to get a head start. If bonding is the answer, wouldn't you rather be bonded with someone who loves you? Or who at least respects you as a person. That kind of bondmate is a lot harder to find. Might as well start looking early. That's my philosophy."

It wasn't my first time hearing about Saya's philosophy, and it definitely wouldn't be the last. I went over to peer at her hermit crabs while she waxed eloquent from her desk.

Bonding might be the answer for some healers. I wouldn't deny that.

In its most ideal form, it might resolve all kinds of problems. Financial anxiety. Job security. A lack of direction in life. You'd get a place to live. Protection from other mages. Custom-made healer robes.

Even so. I didn't want bonding to be the answer for me. I wouldn't ridicule Saya for dreaming of it. Good for her. But I wouldn't dream of it for myself.

Bonding made me think of my neighbor Yarrow. Of how my years-long fixation on her had died as if shoved off a cliff into a bottomless sea.

All it took was seeing what bonding had done to her. My blood went clammy. My yearning inverted into revulsion. Into terror.

I looked at Yarrow, and all that remained for me to feel was a deep-seated fear that I was looking at my future self. She'd lost the ability to unabashedly occupy her own body and mind, to be alone in there with her feelings, to think and speak as she pleased.

Her bondmate was a houseguest in her own head. A guest who would never, ever leave. A guest who thought he belonged there. A guest who thought she belonged to him.

Worst of all, he was there because she'd invited him of her own free will. That was how bonding worked. It had to be willing, at least in the initial moment when you agreed to be bondmates. You'd be beholden to that one single moment until the moment you died.

I wasn't the same callow kid who'd melted when Yarrow smiled, who'd felt sunlight fill me to bursting whenever she stopped by my parents' garden. Nowadays I couldn't imagine ever having such pure and blinding feelings about anyone.

19

It was too early in the morning to see any chattering campus visitors, families of mage alumni with little children turning cartwheels. None of that.

As instructed, I came in gym clothes: knee-length shorts, a T-shirt with the school logo on it, a backpack over one shoulder.

We were supposed to meet by the spherical sundial. The one that floated high over its base like a wayward planet, ringed by weightless megaliths.

Wist sat in the shadow that fell from one of the megaliths. She rose as I approached. There was no one else in sight or sound except for the tireless cicadas. No other sundial on campus hung casually in the sky like this. I couldn't have come to the wrong place.

Yet in the moment Wist stood, I was convinced that I'd somehow gotten the wrong person. Despite the fact that no one else could possibly have so much magic packed inside them.

She too wore gym clothes. Running shorts over lean tights. No problem there. She had on her trusty fake glasses.

But her hair grazed her shoulders, plain and black. Her slouch seemed less pronounced, as if she'd lost a weight that had been pulling down on her all along, trying to shrink her.

"What?" I said witlessly.

"What?" she asked.

"Your hair—"

She tugged at a chunk of it. It really did only come down to the bottom of her mage collar. No endless sinuous braid to leave a silent wake in the air behind her.

"Had to strip all my branch skills," Wist said.

"For the exam? What's that got to do with chopping your hair off?"

"If I have the braid, I might keep trying to move it. To reconstruct the skill I move it with. The habit is too ingrained." She rubbed the ends of her hair between her forefinger and thumb. "The magisters told me to go in clean."

"Huh," I said. A classic display of intelligence. The shrilling of the cicadas swelled between my ears as if to drown to death any dangerous burgeoning thoughts.

"You prefer long hair?"

That jolted me out of it. "I don't have a thing for any length of hair. That would be weird."

"You're still staring."

"You surprised me. Just have to get used to it." I made a show of looking away. "How do we get there?"

She led me deeper into the mage side of campus. We wove between thick-legged statues of flightless birds. The crepe myrtles along the way were at the peak of their bloom, adorned with heavy panicles of hot pink and white and red and lilac.

"You're okay with all these cicadas?" I asked.

"They mostly stay up in the trees."

"Some like to dive-bomb people."

"I don't care for them," she said. "Doesn't mean I have a phobia."

"Sort of like how I feel about mages," I remarked.

We halted by an ostentatious array of fountains. The crepe myrtles here were tall enough to paint all the ground in dappled shade. Clear curtains of water poured past mosaic-tiled walls.

Upon closer inspection, each wall depicted a different scene. Wist indicated one rife with shades of green and jade. The heart of a forest, with not even a peek of sky showing in the upper corners.

"Oh." I spied magic cuttings baked into the mosaic. "It's a portal?"

"You sound disappointed."

"Thought we might be taking the train." Back on the mainland, we could've seen full green rice paddies, infinite rows of corn ready for harvest, terraced tea fields raking their way up and down the sides of high hills and low mountains. "Where's the fun in skipping the scenery?"

"It's an exam," said Wist. "I don't think fun is the point."

"Well, it should be."

I stepped forward to touch the portal. Wist caught at my elbow, yanked me back. Apparently we were still early. We were supposed to wait for the mage faculty to guide us through.

I swallowed a loud yawn. Watching Wist fidget would have to serve as my sole entertainment in the meantime. The loss of her braid had left her prone to twisting her fingers together as if weaving an invisible basket.

"You listened to me," she said abruptly.

"About what?"

"No one understands why I chose you."

Because whenever I got assigned to heal other mages—be they students or staff—I healed them as poorly as I could. This took a lot more work than doing it normally. I had to give the impression that I was sincerely trying my hardest, and still coming up short.

"They must think you picked me for my incredible good looks."

Silence.

"Uh, that was a joke."

I grabbed a pocket-sized towel from my backpack to dab at my neck. Didn't want to think about how sweaty it must get for mages wearing those collars all day and all night.

When I glanced up at Wist, the combination of glasses and shoulder-brushing hair socked me in the side of the head all over again. I just about melted into a puddle of pure folly.

I didn't know whether to blame the summer humidity, the brain-washing melody sung by countless desperate-to-mate cicadas, or my own pathetic lack of immunity to the length of her legs in those gym tights.

I was disgusted with myself for being so easily influenced. Nothing of significance had changed about Wisteria Shien. There was zero reason for me to see her differently.

Not now. Not all of a sudden. Not after months of shared classes, of not speaking to each other despite our proximity, of not thinking about her for a second more than I had to.

I hung back behind Wist once the magisters arrived. They weren't here to deal with me, after all.

I recognized some of their faces from brief encounters in co-ed classes and around campus. Hopefully I'd done nothing to make them recognize me.

They wore brilliant mage robes. A modern, professorial variant, with fewer layers and less floor-dragging length than the full traditional garment.

I hooked my hands on my backpack straps and kept my eyes on the tops of my grubby gym socks. I listened to the soothing white noise of the fountains. I moved where I was told.

The mosaic portal spat us out in a tiny town overlooking a farm-filled valley.

The houses were all in a uniform style. Walls of pale clay and dark timber. Roofs covered in interlocking tiles that from far off seemed to form a pattern reminiscent of chain mail.

We were somewhere on the mainland, in the less-populated area north of Osmanthus City. At least I think that's what they said. I never claimed to be any good at geography.

Guralta Academy owned a large swathe of property on this side of the valley. Or maybe they leased it from the government. I wasn't privy to the details.

Much of the school's funding came from the government. So too did its land. Like this empty shell of a town that they used for student events and mage alumni retreats. No one seemed to truly live here—not permanently. Except for a caretaker or two.

On the plus side, it felt far cooler than down on the island.

I sat on a bench outside, backpack in my lap, while the magisters talked to Wist. When I got bored, I dug out the model lighthouse I'd stashed away below my extra sets of clothes. I tossed it from hand to hand and pretended I knew how to juggle.

The little tower wouldn't call any magical gulls. Not here in the mountains. But given that the exam would run from nine in the morning today all the way to nine in the morning tomorrow, I liked the idea of keeping it around as a possible light source.

Let it be noted that I wasn't trying to smuggle it in, either. I'd already taken it out once, shown it to the magisters, and gotten their okay. My possession of this lighthouse wouldn't get Wist disqualified for cheating.

If she got disqualified for anything, it would be entirely her own doing.

Letting faculty take a good long look at the lighthouse might sound like a terrible mistake. Which was why I'd run it by Wist first, while we hung out and waited on campus. If she thought it was too risky, she could port the model lighthouse back to my room.

She could port objects, couldn't she?

Alas—when packing the lighthouse, I hadn't realized she'd be stripped of all her skills. I resigned myself to my fate: better get ready to quickly bury it under a nearby tree.

But Wist said it would be fine to ask. They wouldn't be able to deduce its true purpose without context clues, she told me. And its true purpose would have no relevance over in the mountains.

All the same, I'd been nervous when I took the model tower in my hands and held it out to the magisters.

Before I could mumble anything, Wist leaned past my shoulder.

"It's a nightlight," she said. She flipped over the tower to show them the signature on the bottom.

They studied the initials. They nodded. They told us we could keep it.

Wist had been busy with the magisters ever since, leaving me out here kicking at the lumpy cobbled road of the mountain town. Which was really a town just for show. A pretty facade.

After everyone emerged from the house where they'd been conferring, one of the magisters handed Wist a stuffed toy monkey. Its plush surface sparked with magic as if coated in static electricity.

Wist touched the monkey to my upper arm. Its little limbs clamped down.

I reached over to rip it off me.

Wist caught my hand. Shook her head.

"Ah," I said, quiet enough that only Wist could hear me. "This is how they make sure we don't passionately bond in the bushes?"

Might've been my imagination, but it felt like the monkey's grip on me got tighter. Wist released me. The toy monkey kept clinging to my shoulder.

"There are real monkeys out in the mountains," Wist said. "If you see one, don't make eye contact."

"Why not?"

"They'll take it as a threat."

"Any wild boars?" I asked.

"Probably."

"Bears?"

"No one mentioned bears," she answered, with the evenness of a lawyer.

"Great. You drag me out here to protect me from the ravages of mean old Tempus. Now I can get eaten by a bear instead."

"I can promise you that the exam doesn't involve bears."

I would've asked her what it did involve, then, but the magisters had begun hovering too close for comfort. I adjusted my backpack and kept my mouth shut.

They escorted us to the edge of town. At nine o'clock sharp, they left us standing there alone.

We stared out at various trails. One led down to a bamboo grove. One continued straight ahead into an old mage cemetery. One climbed steep up the side of the nearest mountain.

Soon after the magisters took their leave, Wist turned to me. "I've never seen you be so quiet."

"Was I really that quiet?"

"You didn't say a word to the magisters."

"They're your teachers," I said. "Not mine. Nothing good would come of them hearing me gibbering. They already think you're crazy for choosing me."

I swung my arms overhead, stretching. The plush monkey stuck to me like a monstrous furry tick. "What do you have to do for this exam?"

I expected her to whip out a piece of paper with instructions. Instead she showed me her left forearm.

"They wrote it right on your skin?" I said. This seemed somehow insulting.

"A memo might get lost in the woods."

"So the theory is that you won't lose your arm."

"Hopefully," Wist murmured.

"What if you sweat it off? Or go for a swim?"

"It won't come off till tomorrow." She tapped her wrist. There was magic in the ink.

She had two lists written on her in an odd mix of cursive and block letters. The shorter of the lists said simply:

To Reconstruct

- Bulletproof

- First Aid

The longer list began with *To Originate*, followed by a nonsensical jumble of bullet points. Something about fire, a key, a cabin, a sink, a peak.

"Hope you don't need help with parsing this," I said.

"I'll do the reconstruction first."

I wandered forward into the old cemetery while she worked.

The grave markers were gray stone, plain as fence poles, jammed together in clusters like incense sticks. As if they had to fight for their right to occupy any space whatsoever. Bulging tree roots carpeted every inch of unoccupied ground. Verdant moss topped the trees and rocks in the manner of a half-melted coating of snow.

The air was still sticky, but it felt nothing like summer. At least not compared to the island. What I could glimpse of the sky above appeared startlingly colorless, as if it lost all its blue without the wide ocean below to inspire it.

In the graveyard, I considered what I knew about originators.

Originators were a type of mage.

The rarest type. As indicated by the fact that out of fifty-something mage Rats, only Azalea and Wist were in the originator program.

Other mages—non-originators—could acquire magic skills in just one way: by being taught. Not via lecture or seminar or textbook. By standing inches apart from their teacher and waiting like a religious supplicant for the teacher to imprint one of their blank branches with the desired skill. It was a process like passing a flame from one candle to the next.

With sufficient training, any mage could share the flame. Upperclassmen could spread their skills to incoming students. In the same way, veteran mages helped propagate relevant skills in their respective fields. Manufacturing, architecture, the military, the arts—you name it.

Only originators could acquire a new skill through self-study, through imitation, through guesswork. Only originators could make up a new skill without being taught.

They'd made Wist get rid of her existing branch skills before the midsummer exam. Hair and all. The purpose of that, I suppose, was to test her ability to come up with pertinent new skills on the fly. With a time limit.

There had been eight tasks listed on her arm. With twenty-four hours to complete the exam, she could budget about three hours per item. Which would mean a lot of sitting-around time for her healer companion.

I looked about for a spot to nap and saw only graves. Forgotten people from a forgotten age.

"Done," said Wist.

My shoulders jumped.

I wouldn't call myself skittish. But Wist did have a way of popping up like a ghost.

"You recreated both skills?" I asked.

A translucent sheet of magic dropped between us and the headstones. "Bulletproof," Wist said.

I bent and picked up a stick. I lobbed it.

The stick passed straight through the pane of magic and bounced unceremoniously on the cemetery moss.

"Not stick-proof," she added.

"Clearly not. They didn't give you a way to test it?"

"Do you see any guns lying around?"

"I've never touched a gun before," I said. "Guess you just have to trust that you nailed it. What was the other one?"

A patch of warmth transferred from her hand to my shoulder. It sank deep into the muscle and then dissipated. The plush monkey hanging from my arm squirmed in place, as if ticklish.

"First Aid," Wist explained.

"Were you supposed to hurt me first? Don't think I had anything that needed curing."

"Did you want to be hurt?"

"Goodness, no. Go scrape your knee on one of the gravestones if you need to make sure your magic works."

"It works," Wist said. "I have a knack for replication."

"Will the magisters make you do a demonstration for them afterward?"

"Yes." She pointed at her neck. "The collar records each use, too. So they can confirm that I already executed these skills within the time limit."

"Hmm. Need healing yet?"

Wist hesitated.

"It's my sole pretext for being here," I reminded her. "Not like I have anything else to do."

She showed me her back.

The forest was quieter than I would've expected. Fewer cicadas than at closer to sea level. Or maybe they preferred to stay away from the crumbling mage cemetery. Or maybe something about the trees here muffled their wails.

I spoke as I worked. Mainly to distract myself from the sight of the collar covering the back of her neck. "Any of your relatives buried here?"

"Are there names on the gravestones?"

"Not that I can read." I plucked the strands of her magic as if playing a harp. "When was the last time you cut your hair?"

"I cut it this much every year."

"Really?"

"The magic calls it back."

"Couldn't you monetize that?" I said absently. "You have nice hair. Ever tried pushing the limit? Cut it daily. Grow it. Sell it. Bam, infinite income."

"Clema—"

"Or would that crash the market? What's the market for human hair like? Never thought much about—"

"Clematis."

Wist twisted. The hem of her shirt dropped. My hands left her back. She had a fist pressed to her mouth.

She said through her fist, muffled: "That's enough healing for now."

"Is it? I can go deeper."

"I'll get too relaxed," she said. "I'll collapse."

Perhaps she was joking. Perhaps not.

"All right," I conceded. "You're the boss here. Where to next?"

The map they'd given her was a regular paper type, folded up to fit in a pocket. I didn't see why they couldn't have scrawled her task list somewhere in the margins, instead of on her skin.

Wist theorized that they wanted to give her a fighting chance to complete the exam, no matter what. Even if the map got stolen by a gust of wind, or went tumbling over a waterfall.

"If we got lost in the mountains, I don't think finishing the exam would be a top priority," I said.

Wist touched her collar. "Can't get lost with one of these."

"We're being tracked? Wonderful."

"They'll find us. As long as we're together."

I patted my arm. "I'm sure they're tracking the monkey, too. Who knows? Maybe they'll come after me first."

Beyond the graveyard, with its rod-shaped stones crammed at violent angles, lay an even older-looking series of tombs.

I call them tombs, but they were no more than dark holes carved at irregular intervals in steep vertical rock, overgrown with finger-shaped ferns. They looked like the entrance to an animal den, or a very slender train tunnel.

"No way I'm going in there," I said.

Wist motioned me past the assembly of gaping tombs. They gave way to the most open land I'd seen all morning. Broad grass. Prehistoric burial mounds. A glimpse of the valley to our left.

Vines crawled all over the burial mounds, tight-woven as a basket, caging them in. Those vines reminded me of the magic inside her, its tangled rigidity.

"Grave wisteria," she uttered.

Here and there, a purple bloom hung down like a faded bunch of grapes. There should've been nothing left, though. The wisteria that I knew flowered exclusively in spring.

"A different variety?" I asked.

"Grave wisteria only grows in places like this. Not on trellises."

"Didn't expect you to actually know the answer."

"It's the ancestor of garden wisteria." She turned her head to the side, as if embarrassed. Not that it showed in her tone or expression. "This is probably the type I was named for."

She walked into the nearest barrow without looking back at me. I hadn't even realized there was an entrance.

The woody vines creaked apart to admit her, then snapped shut again afterward.

A brown grasshopper bounded past my feet. A few small deer stood silhouetted on a ridge far behind the wordless burial mounds. They lowered their heads to eat, taking slow dainty steps.

I glanced at the plush monkey on my arm and asked it how long I should wait.

The monkey had nothing to say in reply.

Then again, I possessed neither the muscle nor the magic needed to barge in after Wist. Nor did I have any desire to play at being an amateur archaeologist. The dead and their riches could rest in peace, thank you very much.

I stretched out in the grass and resigned myself to being trodden on by passing ants.

I succeeded in drowsing, though not long enough to have any nightmares.

I opened my eyes to see a backlit Wist crouching over me, hair tucked behind her ears. She'd hooked her glasses on the front of her shirt.

"Should've woken me with magic," I said. "Hear that's the nicest way to get up."

"I don't have a skill for that."

I rolled upright. "What happened in the burial mound?"

Wist held out her pinky. A candle-sized flame flickered to life just above the tip of her finger. She waved it back and forth a few times, fire dragging sideways through the air, then blew it out.

"I lit a torch," she said. "Among other things. Retrieved this key with my shadow."

The key in question hung from a ball chain necklace. Nothing about it looked particularly ancient.

"With your shadow?"

Her physical body didn't budge.

The left arm of her shadow, moving independently, slid through the grass and onto my ankle.

In one smooth motion it rose to my knee, my hip, my shoulder. It had none of the weight or heat of a fleshy hand. Yet something tickled where it touched me, a sensation like a many-legged bug creeping up under my clothes unseen.

Wist's shadow retreated. "It was the only way to take the key," she said. "A human touch wouldn't move it."

"Hope you put the torch out when you finished."

"Yes. Not trying to start a forest fire."

"That'd be a great way to fail your exam."

She hung the key around my neck. I shot her a quizzical look. "What's this the key to, anyway?"

"The place where we're supposed to spend the night."

"That's still a long way off, right?" I asked. "How long did I nap?"

"Maybe half an hour."

"You're making great time."

"Thanks," she said in a voice blanched of flavor.

"Already halfway though your tasks. Remake Bulletproof and First Aid. Conjure fire. Grab that key."

Wist was so far ahead of schedule, in fact, that I had absolutely no qualms about what I did next. I bounced to my feet. I looped my arm through hers.

She tensed. She started to call my name like a question.

I overrode her.

"Alone at last," I said brightly. "I wonder how close we can get before it sets the monkey off."

I snuggled up against her side. The monkey hung from my left arm without a peep.

"Are you trying to make me fail?" Wist asked, still frozen.

"Just trying to figure out how much freedom we have here. Or privacy. Whatever you want to call it."

I took mercy on her; I released her. But not before getting a good whiff of her gym shirt. Plain clean fabric with only the barest hint of her scent.

I swear it was something about seeing her hair loose and short that made me act stupid.

It made no sense. Objectively, this new shoulder-skimming cut was very similar to how Saya wore her hair. To Tempus, even. And I can guarantee you that neither of them would ever have this kind of effect on me.

I didn't even understand what I wanted to do with Wist. There was no way to put it into words without sounding like a psychopath. Touch her. Shove her. Push her off a cliff. Crack her like an egg.

Was it something unique to S-Class mages, the way her veneer of indifference summoned intrusive thoughts from an abyss I didn't know I had in me? Or was it something unique to her?

I held out my hands, palm up, as if beseeching for water. "Like I said, we're all alone."

I glanced briefly at the burial mounds, at their choking blanket of old vines. What had she called it? Grave wisteria.

"Us and a bunch of primordial dead mages," I amended. "Want to bond now?"

I braced myself for an alarm, a cry, a chittering of rage from the toy monkey riding my arm.

The monkey stayed silent.

For a paralyzed millisecond, I could've sworn Wist looked at me with naked confusion. It was there and gone so fast that I could've hallucinated the whole thing.

She took half a step back.

A thrill like no other pumped through me. She'd scarcely moved, and here I felt like I'd knocked her out cold in a boxing match.

I shrugged, lowered my hands.

"See?" I said piously. "There's no way anyone's listening to the words coming out of our mouths right now. We can say whatever we want.

"Just as long as we don't actually start bonding. Or making out. Doesn't look like the monkey would react to anything short of that."

Wist turned without a word, heading straight for a trail leading deeper into the mountains. I had to half-run to keep pace with her.

20

ABOUT TEN MINUTES into our hike, I offered to navigate. Wist—who must've assumed I was in earnest—tried to hand me the map.

I didn't take it. "You might not want to do that," I informed her.

"You offered."

"I was being polite."

If she hadn't already wanted to boot me into the nearest creek, she certainly did now.

"Look," I said. "I can read a map. But I can't promise I won't read it backwards."

Wist stopped, unfolded the map some more, and pointed. "This is the route to the cabin." Her finger traced a very roundabout path to get there.

"Why not cut across the water?"

"We have time to go the longer way."

"Safety first, huh?"

"There are three tasks at the cabin. I'd like to get them done before dark."

"Then knock the last task out before bed, or early tomorrow morning?"

"Do you have a preference?"

I raised my hand as if we were in class. "I vote for morning. Don't want to mess around with the forest at night. If you plan on going alone, of course, do whatever you want."

"You'd rather wait in the cabin?"

"Let me see what it's like before I decide that."

The trails were well-maintained, with worn stone steps set into the steepest slopes. Some parts even had a railing.

Water trickled through a lichen-painted tumble of rocks far, far below. Unfamiliar bird calls ricocheted sharply among the treetops.

The cicadas did sound different here, after all: more wheezy and mournful, less grating. The air, too, tasted nothing like the air on the island.

About the only thing that hadn't changed was Wist's willingness to forge ahead in silence. Soon enough, I was struggling for breath too much to attempt to provoke her into talking.

During a brief break, I asked her if she were supposed to use magic to obtain drinking water. Or if First Aid could be used to treat dehydration.

Wist reached inside her bag. She wordlessly handed me a regular steel bottle.

The alleged route to the cabin took us alongside a winding chasm with walls of basalt columns. Deep water filled the bottom. It was wide enough for boating. And unnervingly still, compared to the ocean. All along the gorge, we heard the sound of waterfalls rushing down unseen.

I waved off clouds of gnats. Deeper in the brush, neon yellow spiders crouched at the center of webs the size of hammocks.

The trail—though eroded and slick in places—remained unexpectedly clear.

At the end of the gorge, a lace-like cascade of slender white waterfalls finally came into view. Wist led us away from them, through crowds of thin-branched maple trees. They were the sort of maples with delicate baby leaves, leaves so decisive in hue that they made every other green in the world feel inadequate.

Wist stopped. I stopped beside her, plucking at my shirt to fan myself. Everything felt sticky.

"The cabin," she said.

I gazed out at a stretch of empty dirt. There were hints of a neglected garden. A few abandoned brooms. A rusting ladder on its side. Nothing that could be termed an actual building.

"Maybe you read the map wrong," I commented.

She showed me the list on her arm again. "I have to reveal it."

I took this opportunity to back up, stretch, drink the rest of Wist's water, and wipe the sweat from—well, from everywhere I could reach without putting on a strip show.

I'll tell you this much: the process of originating a new magic skill is deathly boring from the outside.

The most interesting thing Wist did was occasionally mutter to herself. Garbled syllables that fell short of full words.

Most of the time, however, she stared into space while flies circled her head. The magic inside her wavered like jellyfish tendrils, the vast majority of them currently skill-free. And therefore certifiably useless.

I almost missed the moment when she activated her newly imprinted branch. Magic blazed stronger inside her, brief and electric.

Then: a house stood in the clearing before us, the fringes of low maple boughs dusting its roof. It was sided in graying wood, unpainted, worn around the edges. Yet much less rustic than I'd expected.

"Looks comfy," I said. "I was picturing mud and logs. Or maybe a glorified tent."

I took the cabin key off my neck and tossed it to Wist, chain and all. She caught it one-handed. I shouldered my backpack and ambled up behind her as she bent to test the lock on the front door.

My brain whispered a warning. Nothing specific. An inarticulate hiss like the distant sound of waterfalls down in the misty gorge.

I caught at the back of Wist's shirt. I started to tell her to wait.

The key was already in the lock.

The door didn't move. Neither did Wist. Neither did I.

The rest of the world spun around us like a combination dial. Too fast to cry out.

When it stopped, Wist's hand still held the end of the key. My hand still clutched her gym shirt. The key was still stuck in the lock. Our surroundings were too dark to see anything beyond that. The air smelled musty and old.

"Those bastards." My voice squeaked. I coughed to cover it. "They set a trap," I said, striving for calmness. "Are mage exams always this nasty?"

"You saw it coming."

I could feel Wist right there in front of me, but she sounded faint. Far away.

"Only at the last second," I admitted. "Too late to make a difference."

"How'd you know?"

"A trace of magic in the lock. Very well hidden. Almost overlooked it."

I swung my backpack around in front of me, dug out the miniature lighthouse, and set it to medium. Red light spilled from my hand. It flooded the folds of Wist's shirt, the muscles of her calves, the door that stood facing her, the unknown room enclosing us.

Wist whipped around to eye the spiky black tower on my palm.

"Told you it'd be useful," I said.

"I can make light, too." Fire erupted in the air above her knuckles.

"This might be a sealed space. Don't waste oxygen."

"I don't think my fire wastes—"

"Anyway, you'll have to use other magic to get us out of here. Focus on that. Unless you were planning on blow-torching an escape tunnel."

Her flames vanished. Her shoulders looked a bit more slumped than usual. Hey, it wasn't my job to offer words of comfort. I set the model lighthouse on the ground and stepped back to better assess our predicament.

The cabin door remained upright, smack in the center of the room, totally unmoored from the stoop and walls that had originally anchored it in place. I could walk a full circle all around it.

I gave the door an experimental shove. It didn't fall over. Didn't so much as shudder. It nevertheless resembled a misplaced stage prop, something meant to be wheeled in and out of the spotlight at one's convenience.

I asked Wist to try opening the door, now that it was presumably unlocked. It swung open to reveal—no surprise—the other side of the very same room we were currently stuck in. We stepped across the threshold, one after another. No change.

Wist shut the door quietly, leaving the key in the lock.

I thought at first that we'd been trapped in a classical dungeon, stone walls and all. No visible entrance other than the now random-looking door in the middle of the floor. No windows. No light source other than the tower I'd brought, which resembled a lighthouse for pill bugs, and some moon-white mushrooms growing grumpily from the ceiling.

The dull red illumination didn't help matters. It lent a sinister tinge to every shadow.

Yet the pile of stuff stacked in one corner turned out to be exercise mats, not bodies. The knotted ropes hanging from the ceiling were the type they sometimes made us shimmy up in gym class.

I poked skeptically at racks of dumbbells and levitation balls. "Could be a regular storage space. Or do you think they're trying to send us a message?"

"Like what?"

"Stay fit?" I suggested.

I waited for Wist to point out that only one of us had struggled during the hike to the cabin, and it wasn't the one of us named Wisteria Shien.

She didn't mention it.

I turned slowly. She stood there with one arm holding the other. I contemplated the idea of being tactful, then dismissed it.

"Your brothers trapped you somewhere," I said. "A place like this?"

"Not quite."

"But it brings back memories."

She didn't respond.

I cracked my knuckles. Pretended to, rather. I couldn't make the sound, but I'd always thought it was a snazzy-looking gesture. "Whatever the case, you've got a new item on your to-do list. Gotta break us out of here. Porting should be the fastest way, no?"

"Porting skills take a long time to originate."

"How long is long?"

"Hours. Up to half a day."

"Damn. Might still be the best option, though."

She took the map out of her pocket, held it up by one corner without unfolding it. "The last task outside the cabin is to fetch something from the peak of the mountain. I'll need porting for that."

"And you don't have time to come up with more than one porting skill." I plucked the model tower off the floor so I could hold it like a flashlight.

I did understand her point. The more open-ended the porting skill, the longer she would need to perfect it. If she wanted to finish the test on time, she'd have to devise a skill with heavy constraints.

To escape this storage room, for instance, she might invent a skill capable of porting multiple human beings—her and me—to the nearest patch of grass or floor overhead.

Assuming, of course, that we were in fact underground. In an ordinary basement, one that just happened to lack any physical way to get in or out.

In theory, however, this room could be located in a magical liminal space. It could be floating in the clouds. There might be no aboveground area anywhere nearby for us to jump to.

If we made the wrong assumptions, a porting skill tailored to help us escape here might not work at all. It could end up being a giant waste of effort.

And even if it did get us out, it might prove useless for getting her to the top of the mountain afterward. By then there wouldn't be enough hours left in the test to originate a different porting skill, one better suited to summit-hopping.

I peeked over at the magic branches wrapped around Wist's core like fine threads around a bobbin.

"Has anyone ever actually counted your branches?" I asked. "All of them. The Osmanthian record is a hundred and eight branches on one person. Yours look like way more than that."

"Doesn't matter much if they're all blank."

"Are they?"

Her eyes fell to the plush monkey on my bicep. The lighthouse infused her hair, her face, her hands with an indelible red.

"I already proved the monkey can't hear us," I said. "Either that, or it doesn't care. Or it doesn't understand."

"The crux of the exam is acquiring skills." Wist's tamped-down voice and manner were remarkably well-suited to playing dumb. "I already finished five tasks. That's five branches imprinted with skills now."

Bulletproof to shield from a sudden assault. First Aid for light injuries. Fire created on command. Mildly tangible shadows to collect a key secured in a tomb. Unveiling the hidden cabin.

Only that last one seemed like it might come in handy now. I'd already noticed Wist attempting it, quietly activating the same skill again and again.

Nothing revealed itself in response. If it were that simple—if all she needed to do was find an unseen trapdoor—then we wouldn't still be twiddling our thumbs here.

"No," I said, since she refused to admit it. "You've got more than five skills on hand. A lot more, maybe. I don't think you stripped all your past skills in the first place."

"The magisters checked me for—"

I laughed humorlessly. "What, like checking for lice? You made a good show of it. You even cut all your hair off. But let's put it this way. They almost never have to check someone with more than ten branches.

"Two, three, five, six—if that's the entire number of branches they have to pick through, of course they can be sure no one's smuggling any old skills into the exam. They could take five to ten minutes per branch, and still be done in less than an hour.

"But you?" I gestured at her magic. It might've looked like I was taking a jab at her kidneys.

"If they attempted to go over every single one of your branches, it'd take days. Weeks. Longer than the exam itself. No one's got time for that. They did a spot-check and called it done, didn't they?"

She had so many branches that she could easily hide them between each other, shift them about so the examiners would get confused about which ones they'd already checked. It'd be like trying to keep track of individual strands when riffling through an entire head of hair.

"Even if I kept some older skills," said Wist, "the collar will take note if I use them."

"Pretend you reinvented them during the exam."

"I'd rather not raise suspicion."

"How about the skills with the same signature as Bulletproof? The ones you showed me before. Still have those?"

I thought she might insist on denial. But then the air lit up with a dizzying shower of gold sparks. Almost festive, in combination with the crimson light from my model tower.

I admired the view until I recalled the mushrooms on the ceiling. The black stains along the corners of the room. The fact that she'd mentioned devising a skill to illuminate floating mold spores.

I coughed so hard that tears came to my eyes.

"You were fine before you saw it," Wist remarked.

"Yeah, well, now I really want to get outta here. Before fungi start growing in my lungs."

The glorious golden swirl filled the whole room: shining pinpricks like a storm of dust motes. I swallowed a surge of nausea. I could've sworn that the stagnant odor enveloping us was getting steadily stronger.

I pulled the hem of my shirt up to cover my mouth. Wist glanced at my stomach, then looked very quickly at the opposite wall.

"Okay," I said weakly. Now I found myself consumed by the notion that everything stank of mildew, clothes and all. "I'm guessing you don't have any cupcakes on you."

"No."

"The nearest-egg trick should work, though."

"Remember when it dropped you in a bird nest?"

"There might be eggs in the cabin," I said. "Could be an easy way to port us there."

"This room might not be anywhere close to the cabin. Physically speaking."

She had a point. From here, we couldn't begin to take an accurate guess at the location of the nearest bird egg. We'd be porting blind.

It might work out perfectly. Or it might dump us on a slender maple branch stretching high into the air over the rocky gorge.

I ruffled my hair with both hands in an (admittedly futile) attempt to shake out falling mold spores. By now both of us, along with the air we inhaled, appeared to have been doused in glitter. I pleaded with Wist to turn off the mold-light before I convinced myself I was choking on it.

The sparks—thousands or millions of them—winked out of sight. Could've sworn I still felt them tickling my throat. They were still there, after all, just invisible. They'd been there all along.

I sneezed ferociously into my shirt.

"We didn't end up here by accident," I declared, after a hearty bout of sniffling. "This is part of the exam. *Your* exam. Think like the magisters. What exactly are they trying to test?"

Wist eyed the downward-pointing mushrooms clustered wanly overhead. "How I react when surprised."

"Seems a little too surface-level, doesn't it?"

She reached up as if to break off some of the mushrooms.

"Don't eat those," I told her.

"Wasn't going to."

Even on tiptoe, she couldn't stretch quite high enough to touch them.

"The way we got here...." she began.

"Everything spun around us."

"Not a standard port."

"It activated after you stuck the key in the lock," I said.

"I think—"

She stopped speaking and plucked her glasses from the neckline of her T-shirt. She fumbled a bit as she put them back on, blinking.

Should've done that earlier, I thought. Could've used them as a makeshift shield against the flurry of mold spores. Too late now, of course.

"I think—this room is meant to test the same area of competence as the hidden cabin."

"Yeah? What's that?"

"Engineering a skill specifically to counteract some other skill."

I got it. "You came up with a skill to nullify whatever magic was veiling the cabin. Then we could see it."

I tried to recall exactly what had happened right before we found ourselves down here.

"Everything spun," I said, eyes half-closed. As much to myself as to Wist. "It wasn't as instantaneous as a regular port. Or as smooth. Will that make it any easier to reverse?"

Wist had crouched to squint at the key in its lock. She looked like a parody of a spy.

"If you're just going to squat there while you wrack your brain about it, let me give you a touch-up," I told her. "No sudden movements."

I was getting too comfortable with slipping my hand up the back of her shirt. I felt the ridge of her lower spine, the annoyingly dry smooth skin.

We'd both hiked the same number of steps. Why was I the only one who felt gluey all over, my perspiration never fully drying?

Wist kept her head forward, her focus on the lock. But it was gratifying to see her grab at the door frame for balance. She did it when I twirled the tight-cinched loops of her magic branches in the opposite direction, unwinding fossilized coils. I couldn't possibly get to all of them, so I only picked at the most flagrantly tangled threads.

The door creaked. Wist's shoulders leaped in place. She let go of the frame and straightened up warily, like she'd pulled a muscle lifting weights.

"What makes someone good at healing?" she asked, without preamble.

"Wouldn't you know that better than me?"

"You're the healer."

"You're the client. You've been on the receiving end of all kinds of healers."

"You've improved," she said shortly.

"Is that a compliment?"

"Why wouldn't it be?"

"You aren't saying it like a compliment."

"This is my voice," said Wist. "I always sound the same." She touched a palm to the ends of her hair, right around her mage collar. "Your healing feels like cutting it all off. I feel that much lighter."

"And that's after only a few minutes." I flexed my hands at her. "I was just getting started. What if I had all day to keep working? You might feel like a whole new person."

She moved her gaze back to the door. A wordless rejection. Her loss, I suppose.

After months of schooling, I did have a sense for what made some healers more effective than others.

Healing, as a field, was moderately more meritocratic than magecraft. Most healers could improve through practice. But there no amount of studying would make a weak mage miraculously sprout a bunch of extra magic branches.

To heal a mage, you needed to envisage the shape their magic ought to take. How their branches ought to be arranged once fully untangled. Then you needed to figure out how to coax them there.

It was bizarrely precise work. Flail magic branches around furiously, as if having a food fight with spaghetti, and they might barely budge from their original position. Poke a single magic branch in a single innocuous-looking spot, and an entire knotted-up bundle of threads might unravel themselves all at once in response.

I won't pretend to be humble. I held back in class, as per Wist's advice. But I was good both at perceiving what to do, and at the actual act of manipulating branches. Very, very good at it.

At least compared to my peers. It was a little maddening to sit around in training sessions and watch everyone else struggle for an hour to stumble to a conclusion I'd reached in ten seconds.

Not that I let it show. I pretended to struggle right along with the rest of them.

Did this make me feel superior? Sure. My superiority was my secret to keep.

Did it make me happy? Not really. I wished I could transfer my healing gifts to someone who would appreciate having them. Saya. Pepper. The twins in the room across the hall. Anyone but me.

Why rejoice at being a talented healer when I didn't want the fate of a healer? My stomach turned over at the notion of being courted for bonding. My throat burned when I imagined decades of healing mages who didn't even think enough of me to look me in the eye.

But there was no easy way out of school. No magic trick to escape, like how Wist would eventually break us out of this dungeon full of gym equipment. I had to hang in there and bumble through the next four years. Or bankrupt my entire family. It was more like a prison sentence than a legitimate choice.

21

We ended up being stuck for several hours in the moldy mushroom dungeon. The whole time, Wist worked on reverse-engineering us a way out.

Since I wasn't a mage, there was nothing I could do to help speed things up. Instead I occupied myself by stacking levitation balls at the back of the room. The highest I got was a perfectly balanced pile of six, which came up above my shoulders. Not bad.

When Wist was finally ready, she took the key out of the freestanding door and waved me over. She put a hand on my shoulder to make sure I didn't get left behind by accident. Then she inserted the key back in the lock. A sliver of her magic entered with it. The world whirled around us in the opposite direction from last time.

Never had I been so glad to once again breathe outside air. As I inhaled, I wondered how many invisible mold spores had piled up in my lungs.

It smelled gloriously fresh out by the re-emergent cabin. After the motionless stink of the basement—or whatever that space had been—the dank undertones of disintegrating leaf matter and living earth came to me as a welcome accent.

Wist's tasks inside the cabin seemed fairly straightforward. Clean an old sink. Unlock a locked box.

I stuck around to witness the sink-cleaning part. If only for the novelty of seeing a mage gaze grimly down into a steel basin covered in layer after layer of calcified white and brown buildup.

"Your instructions say to clean it," I observed. "They don't say you have to clean it with magic."

I hunted through a nearby cabinet until I found sponges, a scrub brush, vinegar, baking soda, and dish soap. I deposited the supplies in Wist's line of sight. Just in case.

In the process of exploring the rest of the kitchen, I also discovered a prodigious quantity of canned fish, beans, and corn. These, it seemed, would have to be our food for the day.

Wist visibly perked up when I read off the labels. I wasn't too thrilled myself. We healers already got fed way too much mackerel back on the island. Although any amount of fish would of course be preferable to wasting away in the woods from sheer pickiness.

I took another turn about the cabin while Wist had her staring contest with the sink.

The aesthetic—if you could call it that—was markedly different from the school's island facilities. Threadbare quilts covered corduroy furniture rife with suspicious burn marks. Paintings on the wood-plank walls depicted green-blue mountains rather than the blue-green sea.

I'd always been puzzled by how so much art on the island showed the ocean. How uncreative. If you wanted to see the real thing, all you had to do was take a short walk down to the beach.

When I was on the island, I had no difficulty imagining the surrounding sea. The city and the mountains and the plains between them were what became harder to picture. I could summon memories of busy downtown train stations, but the images seemed like something from a fantastical dream.

I returned to the kitchen to find that Wist had invented a new skill for scouring. Her magic made the sink stains and scaling flake off like dry mud. The surface beneath emerged spotless, but she still had to clean all the dusty residue by hand.

Can't say I minded watching her scrub. She had real muscles, though you'd never guess it from her usual attitude. Much as she loafed around in other core classes, she far outstripped me in PE.

All the mages did, for that matter. The academy micromanaged their diet and condition. Tried to, anyhow. I couldn't imagine that the diet part was going too well with Wist, unless they already knew to account for her predilection for all things canned.

Magical fitness and physical fitness had undeniable links. Which was the one good thing about being a healer at Guralta, rather than a mage. No one really cared how many pull-ups I could do in a row. I just had to go through the motions of participating.

After proclaiming the scouring of the sink complete, we went to the bedroom to locate a locked treasure box. Opening it would be Wist's final task in the cabin.

There was one bedroom. Not a large one. The first thing I saw: a wide swathe of ripped wallpaper. Second: a meager window with wire mesh embedded in the glass. Third—

"Guess I'm sleeping on the floor," I said.

Two single-size beds awaited us. One happened to be laid out directly on the rust-colored rug. A few flat pads and a blanket.

"I'll take the floor," Wist answered.

"They obviously meant it for me."

"Do you care who they meant it for?"

"Usually I'd say no." I patted the docile plush monkey. It was still glued to the same spot on my arm. Better not give me any trouble when I went to take a bath.

"But," I continued, "I can sleep fine on a floor bed. No worse than on a mattress. It's no skin off my back.

"You're the one who suffers from magic pains. You're the one doing all the work today. Take the good bed."

At that point, I considered the issue settled.

Wist delved through a closet to find the box she was supposed to unlock. I went back downstairs and made us bowls of different canned foods all jumbled together. Wouldn't call it cooking, but it got eaten all the same.

By evening, Wist had magically popped open the sealed box. Inside awaited a single brass button and a note instructing her not to lose it. Proof of her success, or something like that.

Meanwhile, I'd pried the monkey off my arm long enough to get a much-needed shower. (It clung to Wist's ankle in the interim.)

When I came back upstairs, clean at last, Wist appeared to be in the process of constructing a second makeshift floor bed. It was too dark to see anything outside the window now.

I paused in the doorway.

"Hear me out," I said.

"Go ahead."

"On the one hand, this is the second floor. On the other hand, we're about as deep in the woods as it gets."

Wist attempted to smooth lumps out of her limp layer cake of sheets and quilts. In doing so, she made it worse. "What are you trying to say?"

"I saw a spider the size of my foot in the bathroom."

Her hands went still.

"I got along fine with it," I clarified. "We made peace. My point is, if you're squeamish, you might be better off up on the raised bed. I won't take offense. If anyone thinks floor beds are inferior, they're flat-out wrong. I don't care how it looks."

I waited for Wist to reply.

At this rate, she'd run out of time.

"I mention all this because there's a giant centipede on the wall behind you," I said finally.

For a few beats, she refused to believe me. And we both knew it.

I saw the exact moment when she acknowledged where I was looking. To my immense disappointment, she didn't scream. She didn't make a sound. Her magic flared instead, as if her magic were her voice.

The centipede by the window burst into flames.

A furious battle ensued. Me using blankets to beat at the fire, desperate not to burn the house down. The arms-length centipede writhing as it fought to rocket to safety, flames and all.

Even by the time I flung it out the window—together with a bundle of sheets—it still hadn't stopped moving. Nor was the fatal fire fully extinguished.

I seized the model tower to light my path, then dashed out of the cabin. Heaven forbid we start a wildfire.

Some minutes later, I shuffled back inside dragging dirty sheets behind me, my shower wasted. Luckily for us, the centipede hadn't bitten anyone. Wist and I silently checked under the dresser and bed frame. No other wriggly friends in sight.

"You don't want to get bitten by one of those," I said eventually, "but they aren't aggressive. And they eat cockroaches. Next time you see one, try thinking of it as a standoffish pet. An extra-leggy cat."

Wist gave a decisive shake of her head.

"You sure you want to sleep down here?"

She went back to fixing her improvised floor bed. How stubborn. You'd never catch me digging my heels in for no reason.

22

I SWITCHED OFF the red glow of the lighthouse when it came time to sleep. Wist, true to form, made no attempt to chit-chat.

Only then, in the cover of night, did it occur to me that today marked just the second time we'd ever been alone indoors. No human chaperone. (The toy monkey was always with us.)

Unless you counted the ruins. In which case today was the second day we'd ever been totally alone in a space with a roof. First: the infirmary all those months ago. Then the mystery storage room earlier in the afternoon. And now this centipede-infested cabin.

It would've been far too stifling to sleep with the window closed. With it open, the massive choir of cicadas and frogs and crickets drowned out Wist's breathing. I could almost pretend I was alone.

Hearing so many nighttime frogs made me remember the throngs of springtime Baneberry tadpoles. How many had survived to date? I drifted off to distorted memories of their squirming.

In retrospect, it was kind of depressing. All that seething motion and life. Most of it now gone. Most of it destined to fatten neighborhood birds and fish.

In the dream that followed, I was locked in a pale room like a coffin. Grave wisteria grew about my ankles. Magic needles the length of porcupine quills pricked me to the point where I should have died. But I didn't.

I woke up so hard and fast that I almost gave Wist a bloody nose.

I sat dazed in the dark. I got the impression that she'd been leaning over to check on me, and had dodged just in time.

When I looked down, I found myself clutching the plush monkey with both hands. Like I wanted to strangle it.

"You're too close," I told Wist.

My voice creaked. My mouth had not a speck of moisture left. It almost hurt to speak, to force air out past the dryness.

Not that I let that stop me.

"You'll make the monkey angry," I said.

Wist drew back. Not far. She sat cross-legged on the carpet near my pillow, as if settling in for the long haul. "You were crying out in your sleep."

"Did I wake you?"

Wist put her hands in front of her in a way that might have meant *no*, and might have meant *yes*.

Only the faintest of silvery light leaked in through the old window. I couldn't make out her face, but given how little her expression usually revealed, it didn't feel much different from talking to her in broad daylight.

At last I managed to simulate swallowing. Made me want to go brush my teeth again. "Bet you feel sorry for my roommate."

"You often have nightmares?"

"Often? Hah. Every night."

Wist seemed about to say something.

"No," I added swiftly. "It's not what you're thinking."

"I wasn't," she said in that bland way of hers. "I rarely do much thinking."

"Very funny. Yet strangely convincing."

My brain had finally started to come to its senses. "There isn't any special reason I have all these bad dreams. I'm extremely prone to them, that's all. No more, no less. An unfortunate quirk. Like being prone to getting pimples."

I hadn't checked the time, but it must be quite late now. The frogs outside sounded much more muted than before.

I heaved a sigh. "What I'm trying to say is that only one of us here has childhood trauma. Sorry to disappoint."

"Why would that disappoint me?"

"It seemed like a bonding moment," I said reluctantly.

"A what?"

"Not THAT kind of bonding! You know what I mean."

Even up here, in the cooler mountain climate, it still bordered on being too hot to sleep at night.

Perhaps anticipating this, Wist hadn't brought her overembellished princess pajamas. Instead she wore something plain and light, with bare legs and straps the width of my pinky finger.

She was mostly covered in shadow. But I could see just enough for my mind—with or without my permission—to imagine the rest.

I looked fixedly at her naked shoulder. It was the first safe spot I'd found to moor my gaze. The room felt oppressively humid. As if even propping the window open hadn't been enough to stop our mingled breath from crowding out all the rest of the unblemished air.

She'd joked about not thinking.

At least I assumed it was a joke. She might very well have been dead serious. I couldn't rag on her too much for it. I was having some trouble thinking myself.

It was her fault for being too close.

Then again, all she'd done was sit next to my floor bed. She wasn't even touching the bedding.

"Are you—"

I didn't even know what I was trying to ask.

"—gonna keep your hair like that?" I blurted.

The forest frogs and crickets momentarily went silent, as if struck dumb by secondhand embarrassment.

"Keep it short, you mean?"

"Yeah. You could ... you could save a lot on shampoo. Not that your family needs to skimp."

"I'm used to having the braid," Wist said. "I'll grow it back."

"That'll take years and years if you do it naturally."

"Might happen very fast," she said obliquely.

This conversation was about to hit a dead end. If it hadn't already. I made a sound like a half-killed yawn. "Better try to sleep again. My bad for disturbing the peace."

Wist reached out and put a hand on the toy monkey. My back stiffened.

"You're holding it very tight," she said, eyes on the monkey's face. What was visible of it past my interlocked fingers, anyway.

I'd been strangling the monkey since the moment I jolted awake. Wist must've begun feeling sorry for its plight. I forced my hands apart.

"You once asked why I put magic in my braid."

"Did I?"

"You didn't understand why I would move it around so much. Even when magic use makes the aching worse."

I let go of the monkey. Wist laid it gently down on my pillow.

"I don't remember," I said. No point in hiding it. "How long ago was this?"

"Baneberry."

"Oh. Months ago."

"I dodged the question."

"And you've regretted it ever since?" I asked.

"Not exactly."

I didn't get why she was bringing up such an old conversation. Under the cover of night. In this space where the humidity levels made it feel more like being in a fish tank than in a proper room.

I scooted back down in bed and plopped my head on my pillow, next to the magic-infused plush monkey.

Wist didn't leave.

"When I was younger, I didn't want to use magic at all. If I could avoid it."

"This your version of a bedtime story?"

She made a noncommittal sound in her throat.

It occurred to me, out of nowhere, that maybe Wist was trying to distract me from the nightmares. Or maybe she feared that I'd rip the monkey's head off in my sleep if I didn't learn to relax a little. Or maybe she was simply the type to get more talkative when the lack of light made it hard to see the look on her face.

"My tutors warned my parents that the more I avoided magic, the more difficult it would get for me to use it."

"I've heard of that," I said. "It's more of an issue for multi-branch mages. Or ones extra prone to pain."

As part of my reading for class, I'd skimmed case studies of mages who became so avoidant that they could never use their magic without having panic attacks.

Some lived the rest of their lives without ever wielding a single skill again. They'd go in for regular healing, sure. Other than that, they might as well not have been mages at all.

It's a common part of growing up, isn't it? Get mauled by a dog as a child, and perhaps you prefer to keep a safe distance from other people's dogs when you're older. Get poked in the gum too hard at the dentist, and perhaps you do everything in your power to avoid future visits.

For mages, magic wasn't an appointment they could skip, a hot stove they could learn not to touch with bare hands, a food they could refuse to eat raw. It was an integral part of them.

Only healers could help with the pain. And because of that, the only thing mages could do to keep their own suffering to a minimum was to use magic as little as possible. For some maladaptive sorts, this meant refusing to use magic at all.

Personally, my sympathy lay with those mages termed dysfunctional. Those who declined to participate. Those who—maddeningly, in the eyes of the government—hated the subsequent pain much more than they enjoyed exploiting their own inner power.

There weren't a lot of them. But if more mages were like that, if more mages were unapologetic slackers, then life might get a bit freer for healers here in Osmanthus. Just a bit.

"They insisted that I use at least a little magic every day," Wist continued. "Didn't have to be anything meaningful."

"So you got in the habit of swishing your braid around," I said. "Exposure therapy."

My conjecture was correct. She told me how it had taken her months to develop fine motor control. Along the way, her hair had shattered antique vases from the family collection. It had lashed one of her adoptive sisters hard enough to leave yellow-green bruises.

"Did she do anything to deserve it?"

Wist considered this. "The vases were innocent. My sister was not."

I laughed. "You're more spiteful than I thought."

Eventually I reminded her that she'd wanted an early start tomorrow. (Or, by this point at night, was it already today?) She still had one task left to finish before the exam ended at nine in the morning.

I didn't scare myself awake again that night. Which is not to say I slept well. The shape of her shoulder clung to my sight even after I closed my eyes. The way something bright can brand itself on your vision. That made no sense, though—she'd been a murky form veiled in shade. There was no reason for her to linger.

We rose before dawn. It didn't feel the least bit like morning. I scratched the crust from my eyes. Then I reminded Wist of an important fact.

"You know you can leave me behind," I said. "I can entertain myself for a while. And the cabin seems safe."

The magisters would come pick us up here at the nine o'clock deadline. I wasn't the one being tested. Besides, I'd already accomplished my duty. I'd healed Wist right after we staggered awake.

There was no rule saying she had to keep me with her, either. Yesterday she'd gone in the grave barrow alone. She could do it again: she could complete the final task on her own.

"Might need more healing," said Wist.

"So soon?"

"There might be another trap along the way."

"You were the one who got us out of the basement." Obviously I'd give her full credit for that one. "All I did was lounge around wasting precious air."

"It helps to hear a different perspective." After a moment, she added: "If you prefer not to come—"

I dissolved in a yawn. "Forget it. Whisk me away. I'd just be sitting here counting cans, anyway."

"You wouldn't go back to sleep?"

"Oh. Good idea."

But I did go with her in the end.

The last task was to ascend to a specific peak and retrieve proof of having been there. An object stipulated by the magisters.

The good news: it was an old, low mountain. Not the kind with a stony pinnacle jutting up high in the clouds.

In fact, all the mountains around here were thoroughly covered in greenery from base to tip. One might argue that they were more like giant hills than the type of mountain you'd climb to set a continental record.

At the moment we were on private land, owned by some combination of the school and the national government.

People would flock to the public parts of the mountains, of course. For the moderate exertion of well-shaded hikes. To see the mountainside unfurl with new greenery in spring, and inherit the colors of an angry sunset in fall.

Here, however, we seemed to have been spared from running into strangers.

We left most of our bags in the bedroom. Outside the cabin, in a fresh set of gym clothes, Wist did a few half-hearted stretches. The enchanted monkey once again hung onto my arm for dear life. Somehow it seemed cooler out in the open than back in the house.

The map made it look like there were trails all the way to the peak. Technically we could've walked there. Didn't need magic to move your legs. But it wouldn't be possible to get back to the cabin on time afterward, even if we knew the path by heart. Even at a full run.

Wist claimed to have developed a porting skill while I slept. One that—unlike her previous general porting skill—could work on both of us.

If it were that easy, I thought, she could've skipped the explanation. She could've jumped us straight to the peak without further ado.

I crossed my arms. "What's the catch?"

"I can only port to places I can see."

"So you'll have to do a ton of smaller ports. Better hurry up and get started."

"To take you along," Wist said, "I have to carry you."

"Is that a metaphor?"

She held her arms out in front of her, as if holding an invisible stack of firewood. Then she moved her arms behind her and leaned forward, as if hauling the firewood on her back.

"Your choice."

"You spend half the night on origination, and this is what you come up with?" I demanded.

"Had to make the skill narrower to finish it in time."

"Then you should've made it so the only person you can take along is me."

"That's already one of the conditions."

I thumped the plush on my arm. "I can't believe you're telling me to become this monkey."

"Front or back?" Wist asked, unmoved.

"Or you could toss me over your shoulder. Efficiency over dignity, right?"

"Didn't think of that."

I scoffed. "There's a lot you weren't thinking of, buddy."

I contemplated my options. No matter how much our height difference, and how much Wist outperformed me in PE—despite her visible lack of effort—I couldn't imagine her being able to hold me up in front of her for long.

A couple minutes, sure. I wouldn't bet against her. But for however long it took to port to the peak in baby-step increments? While constantly using magic?

I was tempted to make her try. Just to see how quickly it backfired. To feel her arms shake. To laugh at her.

If I had to cling to her neck like I was being rescued, though, I'd rather do it from behind.

"Make yourself shorter," I ordered. "I can't jump all the way up there."

Wist bent her knees to oblige.

Which was how I ended up getting carried piggyback. Wist's arms wedged under my knees. My hands clawing her shoulders. Trying not to sniff her hair like a pervert.

"Weather feels cooler up here," I said.

"Does it?"

"I was being funny."

"If you say so," Wist murmured.

Then one of her branches ported us to the head of the trail: the start of our journey up the mountain.

It wasn't the slickest port I'd ever experienced. It felt like my organs made the leap a millisecond before the rest of me.

I was about to open my mouth and snidely criticize her technique. I never got a chance—she worked too fast. Before I could squeeze out a word of complaint, she did it again. And again, and again.

Most of the time, she ported us as far up the trail as she could see. On relatively straight stretches, that could be quite a distance. On switchbacks, she'd stop and try to a maneuver to a point where she could get a glimpse of the top. In most places, the trees and brush were much too dense to afford a clear view.

The peak wasn't high enough to make anyone short of breath. If my lungs heaved, it was because the rapid jerky porting had rendered me thoroughly seasick.

Wist slid me off her back. I took a dazed seat on a boulder.

A few seconds passed before I remembered that I didn't need to keep holding my arms up like they were still laced tight around her neck.

I had no eyes for the scenery.

I grumbled nonstop until the urge to vomit reluctantly subsided. Wist stayed by my boulder all the while. We must've been making good time.

Slowly I realized that sunrise had come as we traveled to the top of the mountain. To our left, the sky was still sleeping. To our right, the emergent sun dared us to stare at it.

Wist offered me a hand. I stood up without taking it.

"Stand still while I heal you," I told her.

I'd lost count of how many times she'd used her porting skill in the process of getting us up here. She could've been feeling equally sick—in her magic, rather than in her flesh. Not that it showed on her face.

Only after I finished untangling a few dozen of Wist's branches did I look up and really take in our surroundings. I removed my hand from her back. I scrubbed my palm on my shorts.

The so-called peak was a small flattened area of dusty dirt and jutting rock. Barely large enough for one or two families to sit down and have a comfortable picnic. No guardrail.

The tops of the nearest trees came up to around our ankles. The dark green mountainside slumped down below us, all the way down to the wide tilled valley I'd seen yesterday morning. Then more faded mountains on the far side, walling the valley in.

All that hiking and porting, and yet from here it didn't look steep at all.

The air felt almost bearable. For a summer morning, anyhow. The glare of the rising sun threatened rising heat.

There was one obvious spot to stand if you really wanted to soak up the view. The place where you'd set up an easel if you were an artist. I followed Wist over there and found her looking down at a cluster of worn stone figures.

The doll-size statues had little shape to them. Round heads but no defined facial features. Bodies like a melting snowman. They wore sun-faded bonnets and button-up jackets.

"Looks kind of like your uniform," I said to Wist. Although right now she had on a top with the school logo plastered all over it.

She knelt and plucked the middle button off the middle statue.

"Stealing?" I asked.

"They told me to take it. Proof that we reached the top."

So now all we had to do was get back to the cabin, and the exam would be over. It had been a packed twenty-four hours.

"While we're here sunbathing," I said, "I've got a question."

Wist straightened up. The baby mage statues only came up to around her knees. Not a healer among them, I noted.

"Why are you still part of the Shien clan?"

She just looked at me.

To be fair, that was the exact reaction I'd expected.

"You weren't born among them. Correct me if I'm wrong, but I get the impression that they treat you like shit. Most of them, anyway. You said something back in hunting season about how your brothers fired everyone you cared about."

"You're not wrong," she said. Her face was a blank.

"You're not literally bonded to that family. You don't have to die to escape. You're not an indentured servant, either. I could understand feeling stuck with them when you're six years old, or nine years old, but what about now?"

"What about it." She didn't phrase it like a question.

"Is there anything left to stop you from walking out on them?" I asked. "Or is it just more comfortable, being a Shien? They aren't financially abusing you, that's for sure. Are you better off staying with them than leaving? Brothers and all."

I'd been to the theater. I'd seen tales of feuding mage families, marriages to seal alliances, the scandal of transferring from one family registry to another, the merits of inbreeding.

An S-Class mage would never truly be at risk of going homeless. The government wouldn't permit it. Clans on unfriendly terms with the Shiens would surely be happy to take her in. Even if she insisted on going solo, government agencies would support her. They'd find work for her after she graduated.

Unlike us plebes, an S-Class mage couldn't possibly flunk out of Osmanthian society. Even if they somehow wanted to. An S-Class mage would never be allowed to fail.

"What does it matter?" Wist finally asked.

"It's your life," I said. "That's for you to decide, isn't it? How much does your life matter?"

She wedged two fingers inside her collar as if seeking more air. "Didn't think you would be interested in what happens in mage families."

"Generally speaking—no," I admitted. "You're different. You dragged me out here. Least you can do is pay me for it."

"With knowledge," Wist said dryly. "Not with my body."

"See, you get it now."

She released her collar. Her hand dropped. The newborn sun, roasting us from the east, tried its best to paint color into the implacable black of her hair and eyes.

"I could petition for emancipation," she said.

"What, like a divorce from the clan?"

"There's a legal process for it. Technically."

"Don't think they'll let you go that easily?"

She shook her head.

"What've you got to lose by trying? Assuming you even want to leave," I added. "If you don't, you're sitting pretty."

She half-turned to glance back at the row of squat mage effigies. "My mind is always clearest right after being healed."

"You're welcome."

"There's a brief window where everything makes sense. Independence seems logical. I can imagine a future more than a few hours away. Then it starts to cloud over."

She touched the side of her head. "People talk about magical pain as being unbearable. But it has to be bearable. Existing means bearing it. At least some of the time. The problem is the fog that comes with the pain. The fog chokes out my thoughts.

"Days or weeks pass, and it's like I was swimming at the bottom of a lake. No light. No sound. Almost no memory of what I did, or what was done to me. Days or weeks can pass without a single conscious thought."

I considered what she was trying to say. "That won't change whether or not you're with the Shiens. So you don't think emancipation would make much of a difference?"

"When the pain resurges, when my head gets clouded, I can't put together a coherent plan for leaving. I can't. But more than that—"

For a moment Wist blinked down at me as if she'd just snapped awake from a reverie. Then, more slowly, she continued.

"Threatening to leave the Shiens is my last piece of leverage," she said. "Someday I might need to use it."

Mages who didn't get healed enough would eventually snap and go berserk. There was a clear connection between mage pain and the risk of berserking, even if no one had ever succeeded in reducing it to a foolproof formula.

Perhaps Wist's mental fog lay somewhere along the same spectrum. An early warning sign that she was bound to go berserk without periodic intervention. A low-level predecessor to the state of being berserk, even.

Textbooks discussed mage berserking as if it were an on-off switch. No real transition. No middle ground to speak of. But Wist had gone to the edge—right before my eyes—without fully berserking. That couldn't have been the first time she came to the brink of it, either.

Depending on who you asked, berserk mages acted like monsters, or like their worst inner selves, or like they'd been taken over by a completely different personality. Usually one much wilder and crueler. More bloodthirsty. The tangling in their magic made them do it; the tangling jerked them around like puppets.

I thought of Wist being hounded by the ever-present aching in her branches, her head full of mist.

If she were almost constantly in a state of twilight, her brain and body seized by some kind of precursor to full berserking, did it make her act unlike her true self? Or hew closer to her animal instincts? Or was the fogged-up Wist the real Wist simply through a form of squatters' rights—by not leaving her time or room to have ever become anyone else?

It didn't have to be that way.

Call it arrogance, overconfidence born of ignorance—call it whatever you want. You're not wrong. Even now, after just a few extra months of school, I could already see far deeper into her snarled magic than I'd been able to see back in spring. I could clear the fog for much longer than she was used to, I thought.

But she kept stopping me after less than ten minutes of healing. She didn't seem to want to let me try.

"It explains a lot," I said. "You talking about your head getting clouded up. You're not all there, are you?"

"That sounds like an insult."

"Well, it's true," I retorted. "You can hold a conversation, but it's like talking to a prisoner through a closed door. To someone covered in chains. You're bound up in the web of your own magic."

Her left hand kept fiddling with the button she'd swiped from one of the worn-down mage statues. She didn't say anything back.

Still, I didn't think it was unsolvable. Or maybe *solve* was the wrong word. Her branches would always be numerous, and they would always be with her, and it would always feel like they were covered in thorns.

But someone—at least one person somewhere out there in the world—had to be capable of giving her truer relief, of clearing the fog out for longer. A healer, or a whole team of healers.

With the potential power she had, why wouldn't the Shiens surround her with all the top healers in the nation? They'd adopted her because of that power, hadn't they? Why wouldn't they want her to be in the best possible condition to cultivate it?

Even Mr. Rift hadn't questioned the intractability of the deepest knots in Wist's magic. Consciously or not, she appeared content to leave everyone around her with the impression that she was stuck this way. Incurably and inextricably bound to a certain level of suffering.

Like her pain was an inevitable payment she had to make in exchange for her massive number of branches. She may not have asked to be born with that gift, but she owed a lifetime's worth of interest on it anyway.

Was she the one who'd convinced herself it had to be this way? Was it the fog in her brain speaking, or her magic itself?

Or had someone indoctrinated her—and the rest of the Shiens—into believing that healing could do no more for her? That there was no point in ever hoping for better? That whatever agony remained between healing sessions would be hers to keep and bear forever?

All these questions flew through me in an instant, swift as a flock of birds passing overhead.

I hadn't meant to reach for her magic. Not from the front. It was a gesture without intention. As I wracked my head over Wist, some part of my body decided that this was just the right thing to do. As simple and intuitive as clutching her neck when she carried me.

My fingertips touched her stomach through her shirt. She didn't flinch away, but she grabbed my arm. Hard. The way you might grab someone who'd put a knife in your belly.

I stared blankly down at my own hand making a shape like a cage near the light of Wist's core.

What was I trying to do?

Before I could even begin to figure myself out, the toy monkey screamed in my ear.

I shrieked, too.

I tore myself away from Wist like a startled cat leaping six feet in the air. I covered my ears. The monkey's voice pierced clean through my hands. I tried covering the monkey's plush face instead. Didn't make much difference.

Wist was saying something, but I couldn't hear her.

Then the monkey stopped abruptly, so abruptly that it was like it had never made a sound in the first place. Still couldn't hear much.

My hands—both of them—found their way to my frenzied heart.

"Dear heaven." I'd shot past the point of cursing and come all the way back around to sounding like a grandmother. "Do you think—"

"A warning sound," said Wist. "Only meant for us."

"You don't think it alerted the magisters?"

"Not from what I can tell."

I sat down heavily on a nearby rock. If there hadn't been a nearby rock, I'd have put my butt right on the dusty ground.

"Can't believe *that's* what set it off," I said. "I wasn't even doing anything!"

Wist smoothed the front of her Guralta-brand shirt.

My actions had been a tad irregular, sure. I didn't normally go around feeling up people's abs. I'd never tried to heal someone from the front.

But why would the monkey find fault with two seconds of innocent contact? It hadn't let out a peep of complaint when I intentionally tried to provoke it yesterday. When I rode Wist's back like a burr. When I manipulated her magic to heal her. When I sleepily ogled what I could see of her between nightmares.

It wasn't possible to bond without explicitly confirming each other's intentions. You couldn't just trip on a rock and bond by accident.

Maybe the monkey was supposed to be able to read my intentions. Maybe it had read—no, misread—me as I moved without thinking. Maybe my lack of a clear motive for reaching out to her had given it room enough to worry.

I'd been preoccupied, mulling over the tangled pattern of her magic. Mulling over the tangled pattern of Wist herself.

I raised my head. My ears had finally stopped ringing. "Guess I owe you an apology."

A long pause followed.

"For what?"

I pointed at the monkey on my shoulder. "What do you think? For jeopardizing your exam."

"Seems fine now."

"You're awfully easygoing."

Wist sat next to me. I scooted away, just to play it safe.

She moved closer again. I wouldn't have risked it myself, but clearly she wasn't all that worried. At least the monkey was on my left side, rather then being conspicuously squished between us.

"Thank you for coming," she said.

"Thank yourself. You made me come."

"I know you wish you didn't have to. I know you'd rather be somewhere far away from school property. Far away from mages."

Oh, this was weird.

"No need for gratitude. You're the one who got through all your tasks," I told her. "I was just there as a supply pack. A human water bottle."

"You did more than that," she said. And again: "Thank you."

Something in me did a strange little flip.

It was one of those very, very rare times when she didn't sound utterly dead inside. It sounded like she meant what she said.

I had no idea how to respond to that.

I didn't look at Wist. I looked at the farthest line of aging mountains in the distance. Low beaten-down shapes. A faded gray-blue on the horizon, almost completely camouflaged by the sky.

Part Three

The Clematis Gambit

23

I CAME AWAY from the originator exam with the illusion that I'd learned a thing or two about Wisteria Shien.

It soon became clear how very wrong I was. For a couple of days after the exam, though, I floated around wrapped in an inchoate sense of superiority.

On the morning the test ended, we'd ported—again in many small jumps—back to the cabin. When the magisters arrived, Wist presented them with the two brass buttons she'd been ordered to collect. A polished one from the lockbox in the bedroom, and a tarnished one from the peak.

With the exam being officially over, the magisters magically whisked us back to the empty mountainside town (thus sparing us the return hike). They refused to tell Wist whether or not she'd passed. They still had to do another review of her collar records back on campus. Yet the mood seemed bright.

That changed as soon as we returned to Guralta, walking out through the mosaic fountain portal. The wailing of the island cicadas smacked me like a sonic attack. I squinted haplessly into the sunlight.

Then Azalea popped up and ran over to Wist.

The timing was too good: she must've been lurking nearby, awaiting our return. Not hard to do, I suppose, if she knew Wist's deadline. Her own personalized originator exam must've been held on a different date. And likely had completely different requirements.

I didn't catch anything Azalea said. I only started paying more attention when I realized that Wist had stopped in her tracks. I turned and strained to hear them speak, but the rushing of the fountain gave their voices cover.

I trotted back over to them. Wist flicked a look at me as if she'd forgotten I was there. Azalea promptly clammed up.

"Guess I'm not wanted here," I said. "I'll take my leave."

I'd meant it as something of a joke. It seemed to come true, though, the moment the words passed my lips. It was so true that no one really needed to say anything more.

I raised my chin and escorted myself from the premises. I left them to their mage secrets.

I wasn't entirely surprised when Wist went back to ignoring me in our shared classes. She was keeping her original promise. She would do nothing to draw unwanted attention to me. Few people even realized that she'd picked me to accompany her for her midsummer exam.

What did surprise me was that the next time I saw her—a day or two after we awkwardly parted ways at the fountain—her braid had already grown back. All the way to its original length. Long enough to risk dragging on the floor unless she looped it a few times around her arm or waist or shoulders.

So she'd missed it enough to force it to lengthen with magic. Or maybe she'd saved the original braid, the one she'd chopped off before the exam. Maybe she'd stored it in her bedroom like a severed lizard tail, then magically reattached it. Maybe she'd transmuted raw material from the school dumpsters into high-quality hair extensions.

For an originator, the possibilities were theoretically almost endless.

More and more often, we healer Rats got asked to do hands-on work with mage students of the same cohort. The mages were rude about it, at best. Healing was practice for us, not for them. They saw their very presence as being an enormous gift to us.

We usually drew lots to pick a partner. About a week after the exam, I got assigned to Wist.

We were in the lecture hall with the menacing fan that filled the whole ceiling. I pushed my seat back to go find her. Probably way up in the back row of seats, as usual.

I spotted her as soon as I turned. Not far behind me, actually. She had her hand raised.

Puzzled, I waved. She didn't so much as blink in my direction.

Mr. Rift and a magister came over to see what Wist wanted.

"I want a different healer," she said plainly.

For a moment there was nothing but the silence of the magically muted ceiling fan spinning high above our heads. Then came an astonished muttering from the rest of the class, mages and healers alike.

The mage students might complain about who they got randomly matched with in these practice sessions. But I'd never seen anyone request a change of partner. Not once.

The mages didn't have to do anything except tolerate a few attempts to heal them, after all. Even the most ineffectual healer couldn't outright harm them. The worst that might happen was that the mage might feel like their time had been wasted. And they'd have to sit through this class regardless of who they got paired with.

The magister in charge barked an order for everyone else to pipe down. Mr. Rift stooped to exchange a few quiet words with Wist, who by now had lowered her hand. From a couple rows closer to the front, Saya turned to give me a penetrating look.

I lowered my butt back into my seat and stared down at the empty lectern.

In each school year, there were more healers than mages. They engineered the student body like that on purpose. So mages would always feel like they had a choice. All Wist had done was exercise her ability to choose.

I just didn't understand why.

It took repeated warnings from the teachers for the murmuring to finally subside. No way Wist could pretend she'd pulled this as part of some scheme to keep her classmates from taking notice of me. Quite the opposite—I hadn't been gawked at by so many mages since hunting season.

I wasn't hurt, exactly. What was there to be hurt by?

I was just confused. It was as if short-haired Wist had been an impostor. A different person altogether.

I kept stewing after class ended. I kept stewing later that night, as I dodged Saya's questions.

Finally it occurred to me that this was the first time at Guralta that I'd been genuinely humiliated. Not just in others' eyes, but in my own sour gut.

Hunting season had been full of petty wretchedness, full of attempts to shame and degrade me with surface-level filth. Yet nothing they did then had been able to penetrate down to my pride.

Wist was the first mage I'd healed with my own hands. The only mage I'd ever made an actual effort to heal well. She herself had said that my abilities way outclassed everyone else. When I tried, anyway.

I didn't aspire to be a great healer. I'd have gladly traded healing for any other talent—for an aptitude with numbers, a rapport with animals, a solid head for business. But I'd believed her when she praised me.

It wasn't the *ooh*s and the snickering in the classroom that got to me. It was Wist—who never raised her hand, who never spoke up—going out of her way specifically to assert that I wasn't good enough.

I'm telling the truth when I say that I still didn't care what any of the other Rats thought of me, be they healers or mages. I hoped to never see them ever again once I graduated. Which would be three and a half long, long years from now.

Somewhere along the line, though, I'd fallen into the trap of caring what Wisteria Shien thought. Not a lot, mind you. The tiniest speck of caring imaginable. Just a smidge.

And look where that had gotten me: alone and hot with embarrassment. Trapped together with the formless beginnings of a savage fury that had no conceivable outlet.

I fought hard to ignore it.

The following week, a stranger called to me as I crossed campus.

Great, I thought. Just my luck.

I desperately wanted to pretend I hadn't heard anything. Unfortunately, my magic perception had already told me this man was a mage. If I power-walked away without a word, he might very well report me to the academy for insubordination.

I stopped. I plastered a polite look on my face. It felt all wrong.

He was a Class 6 mage. Younger than most of the teachers. How much younger? Hard to tell. He wore light, draping clothing that looked like it might've been pieced together from the flailed hide of a deconstructed linen suit.

He sat on a bench in the shade of a beech tree. We were deep in the healer side of campus. Part of me wondered if he'd gotten lost.

When I looked back at him, the man beckoned me over. I reluctantly approached. There was still a solid half-hour left until my next class. Unfortunately.

I realized four things upon drawing closer.

One: a nondescript cane rested on the bench next to him.

Two: he wore a Guralta graduate ring.

Three: he held a delicate folding fan in his lap, the kind made from artisan paper.

Four: his thin-framed glasses were embedded with such a plethora of glaring magic that it felt almost impossible to look him in the eye.

If he needed vision correction, the lenses alone would do it. That meant the magic cuttings grafted all over his glasses must've had some other purpose.

Those glasses were the one thing about him that looked extremely expensive. An accessory befitting a Guralta alumnus.

Maybe this guy had called me over by mistake. Maybe he'd discover his error and dismiss me as soon as he glimpsed me close up: a healer student in a rumpled uniform, ruthlessly chopped hair, a face unused to simpering, a rat pin fastened to my flat chest.

"Can I help you, sir?" I asked, still hopeful that he might hit me with an immediate *No*.

The mage waved his pleated fan, utterly unhurried. Must be nice, having a breeze on your face on a day like this.

My eyes kept drifting enviously to the dark birds strutting about the bulging tree roots off to his right. A couple of mangy-looking grackles. They could parade around all they wanted without getting bothered by passing mages.

"I'm looking for Rift Landon's office." The man sounded almost apologetic. "Could you take me there? Only if you have time, of course."

"Um," I said. "Who?"

"Rift Landon. A healer. One of the teachers here. I believe—"

"Ohhhhhhh." Now I got it. "You mean Mr. Rift." I'd never heard his given name before.

"So you do know him."

"Well, yeah." I reflected briefly on my word choice. "Er, yes. Sir."

He snapped his fan shut one-handed and slipped it smoothly in his pocket. Then he took his cane off the bench beside him and rose to his feet.

Stooping slightly, he was of a height that could only be described as medium. Impressively average. About the same height as my father, if I had to take a guess.

"Lead the way." Something about his smile and tone suggested that he was the one doing me a favor, rather than the other way around.

I grudgingly obliged. At least it would be over soon. We were already very close. So close that I could all but glimpse the tree fern outside Mr. Rift's window.

There were fuzzy-trunked tree ferns all over the island. When I first came, I'd thought that they were a type of palm tree. Not everything here was what it appeared to be.

I had to slow down to keep from getting too far ahead of the nameless mage. He heavily favored his left leg. At the same time, I had an inkling that he could've moved much faster if he wanted to, cane and all. Eager though I was to rush to escape his presence, the same didn't seem to be true for him.

"It's right there," I said, after escorting the mage to the building entrance. "All the way down the hallway. Left side. You'll see a label on Mr. Rift's door. Dunno if he's in now, though."

He thanked me effusively for my guidance, to the point that I began to wonder if I could detect a hint of sarcasm. No matter. I bowed clumsily and turned to leave.

"Oh, one more question," said the mage.

I had no choice but to turn back. I kept my scowl on the inside. I gave him an expectant look.

"Do you know Wisteria Shien?"

"No," I said immediately. And I do mean immediately. An instinctive reflex, like catching a ball hurled point-blank at my face. "Who?"

"A first-year student here," he answered. "Just like you."

"A healer?"

"A mage."

"Never heard of them," I declared.

The mage dug in his pocket. For a moment I wondered if he were going to whip out his paper fan again. Instead he took out what appeared to be an old coin.

"If you ever encounter Wisteria, would you give her this?"

He smiled at me. But it clearly wasn't meant to be a free-answer question. It was multiple-choice, and every possible response was just some variation of *Yes, sir*.

I held out my hand. He dropped the coin in my palm. I didn't recognize the design.

"Don't worry," he assured me. "It's a replica."

"I might never run across this Wisteria," I said. "Even if I do, I might not know it's her."

"Nothing to be concerned about, although I appreciate your conscientiousness."

"You're welcome?"

"I like making bets, you see. The uncertainty is part of the fun. Wouldn't it be terribly boring if everything in life were predetermined?"

The air hung too still around us, thick curtains of summer noise and heat and humid moisture. The door to the building full of healer classrooms and faculty offices stood closed and voiceless. It had several deep dents in the bottom, like someone blinded by rage had kicked it hard enough to break their own foot.

I curled my fingers shut around the coin. It really was just a plain old coin. I'd have noticed any hints of magic on it.

I sensed that this time, the mage with the cane would be content to let me go. I could scurry away without another word.

"Sir," I said.

"Yes?"

He sounded very gentle. Friendlier than all the magisters working here at the academy, that's for sure. But there was far too much magic on his glasses to see his eyes.

"May I ask your name?"

His smile broadened. I already regretted asking.

"Shien Nerium," he said. Without a moment's hesitation.

24

I PASSED THROUGH the rest of the day's classes in a daze. None of them were with Wist.

I didn't know what to think about any of this. I fiddled testily with the coin in my pocket.

A sudden summer storm blew past the island in early evening. The type that would make huge lightning bolts crack down over the ocean, if you were in a place where you could watch the water. Back in my dorm, I only saw diffuse flashes followed rapidly by the stony grinding of thunder.

The rain came so fast. Healer students caught outside screeched like birds as they pelted for shelter. But the whole thing ended in maybe half an hour.

Saya and I had been assigned to clean the first-floor lounge today. We got started some minutes after the storm gave way to silence.

If we were any other pair, our dormmates would've crowded in to chat and hang out. Not in our case. They studiously avoided us, leaving the entire lounge empty. Which made it a lot easier to perform our cleaning duties, to be honest.

I wiped the window-glass while Saya dusted the crannies of the driftwood couch. Better her than me: caressing that wood felt far too much like caressing skin.

Sundown should've been at least an hour or two away, but the storm had brought in a ceiling of leaden clouds, thick as night. As the sky cleared, it turned a shocking yellow. Forgotten western light slanted in sideways to illuminate all the spots we still needed to scrub.

"Hey, Saya," I said.

Somewhere behind me, she made a sound to indicate that she was listening.

"You know a lot about the famous mage clans."

"More than you, yes."

"The Shien at school with us—"

"The one who rejected you the other day?" Saya inquired.

I moved on to the next windowpane. "I wouldn't quite put it that way."

"How would you put it?"

"She, uh, declined my healing services."

"In front of the whole class."

"You shouldn't heal someone who doesn't want it from you," I said virtuously. "It's just business. No hard feelings."

"You really don't know why?" Saya asked. "I was curious."

"I assume I wasn't up to her standards. Only the best healers for Wisteria Shien."

Saya moved to the wall and began adjusting framed black-and-white etchings of various fish. Not part of our cleaning checklist, but the subtle skewing must've bothered her.

"You're not the worst in our year," she pointed out.

"Wow, thanks. Now I feel great about myself."

"You'd rank a lot higher if you put in the effort."

I pretended not to hear her. Saya—more so than other people—seemed to grasp that my efforts led me in the opposite direction. To sabotage my own schoolwork. To blend in with the lower end of the healer student rankings.

"Enough about me," I said. "We were talking about the Shien clan. Aren't there a bunch of older brothers and sisters?"

"Believe so."

"Are all the rest of them named after plants, too?"

Saya studied the ceiling. "Shien Nerium. Shien Ficus. Shien Miyu—"

"Right. Of course you know. We ought to hold a mage trivia contest. You'd win big."

"There are three others I didn't name."

"I got the gist."

Going by their name order, it sounded as though the older siblings were Shiens by blood. Unlike Wist.

I wiped the edges of the last window. Then I did it again.

"I met Shien Nerium on campus today," I said casually.

A soft clatter.

When I looked over, Saya held one of the framed fish etchings in her hands as if she'd ripped it clean off the wall by accident. She hung it back up without a word.

"You spoke to him?" she asked afterward.

"He spoke to me. Asked for directions. Gave me a coin."

"He paid you?"

I put down my cleaning cloth so I could show Saya the old coin.

"Not in real money," I said. "You recognize this? He called it a replica."

Saya was consistently top of our class in history. Although it was entirely possible that you didn't need that level of knowledge to know what kind of coin Shien Nerium had made me take from him. It was entirely possible that I'd failed to recognize it as a result of my unusual ignorance.

Saya held the coin out in the light from the window, still dyed a freakish post-storm shade of citrus. "Would be worth a lot if it were real," she commented.

"How old is the design?"

"Centuries. If not more. Imperial-era."

I knew the general outline of that time period. The old monarchy got absorbed by an amoeba-like empire from another continent. The country we now called Osmanthus—with its Board of Magi and all the other trappings of the mageocracy—birthed itself in the process of fighting for independence.

So this was a coin of the vanished Blessed Empire. The coin of a lost enemy, with a figure of a conquering lady posed on it.

The coin was too small and the figure too distant for the woman's face to have any real detail. I could make out ancient-looking clothing and a whole lot of hair swirling around, but that was about it.

"The Kraken?" I guessed.

"The Kraken," Saya agreed.

The greatest mage in history. Or in myth, you might say, if you were a stickler for hard evidence. The hero of the fallen Empire. Not that she'd stuck around to help them when they fell.

Saya handed the coin back. I pocketed it. I got to work on rubbing dust from the all the long crooked limbs of the many-branching lamp in the corner.

In the end, we ran through the dorm steward's checklist one last time to make sure we hadn't missed anything. I asked Saya to mark the windows finished. She gazed down at the sheet without reacting.

"Saya?" I prompted.

She raised her head. "Be careful of Shien Nerium," she said.

On the whole, Saya came off as far more human than the likes of Wist. But with those overlarge eyes of hers, she could muster up a deeply unnerving stare when she put her mind to it.

"He's the one who tormented healers back in school?"

"Not the only one. And not just healers, from what I hear. Mage students, too. Even faculty."

"Well, he has no idea who I am," I said. "He has no reason to care, either. Didn't even ask my name. Maybe he just stopped by the island for a day or two, anyway. He must have a job or something, right?"

Saya shrugged. So she didn't know the details of Shien Nerium's career.

"He must have family duties," I amended. "If nothing else. Must have better things to do than lurk creepily around campus."

Saya looked unconvinced.

"I'm sure I'll never see him again."

I hoped I spoke the truth.

That night, I twitched awake amid dreams of blood spurting from places that really aren't meant to spurt blood. Took a while to assure myself that there wasn't dark liquid seeping up the stained walls, smirking at gravity.

I glanced across the room at Saya. A motionless lump. She'd gotten new earplugs around the start of summer. They seemed to work remarkably well.

The model lighthouse sat on the windowsill, dark and silent. I kept it switched off by default nowadays, so its red glow wouldn't draw curious gulls. Quite a few of the plant cuttings beside it had graduated from glasses of water to proper pots.

The spikes marching up the sides of the miniature tower looked sharp enough to cut. But those thorns were just for show. You'd have to try really hard to actually hurt someone with them.

I took the tower in hand and turned it over. I squinted to read the initials on the bottom. They were only just visible, picked out in the silvery light from the window.

S. N.

Saya and I had rescued this model lighthouse from the Heap of abandoned student projects.

On the library roof, Wist had seized it from my pocket and demanded to know where I'd gotten it from. Whether I'd used it.

Before the originator exam, she'd shown these initials to the magisters. That alone had convinced them to let us keep the lighthouse.

Wist had never said too much about her brothers. Except—

Her brothers were the reason she preferred to eat from sealed cans of food. Like a cat. Her brothers had encouraged Tempus to make hunting season his own. They'd framed it as a game he could win or lose in their eyes.

She'd called Tempus's version of hunting season weak and pathetic, compared to what her brothers could come up with.

She'd spoken as if she knew from experience.

It was then—at some ungodly hour of the night when even the hermit crabs knew to keep quiet, peering down at Shien Nerium's initials—that I made my decision.

I didn't know what the coin meant. All I knew was that it couldn't mean anything good.

He was Wist's brother, not mine. Their family was none of my business. But that didn't mean I had to blindly do as he said.

Wist seemed newly determined to shut out my existence, anyhow, to the point of refusing to pair up with me for so much as a scant fifteen minutes in class. Didn't see how I could force her to take anything from me, be it a coin or a rotten tomato. Short of throwing it straight at her head.

I wouldn't bother. I'd keep the coin to myself. Shien Nerium's message to her—or whatever it was supposed to be—would end with me.

Not for Wist's sake, of course. I resented the idea of being forced to play messenger for a pair of ultra-wealthy mages. The aristocrats of our modern age. If Shien Nerium had something to say to his adopted sister, he could very well go find her and tell her himself.

25

For a Friday in mid-August, the weather turned out to be remarkably livable. I heard people talking about it in the dorm and before classes, strategizing about how soon they could make it off the island to cavort in Baneberry. Or planning to hit the waves as soon as they were done for the day.

With so many tourists at the beach now, it had gotten easier for healer students to frolic in the surf without feeling like they were intruding on mage student territory. In the current breakdown of the oceanfront population, visiting mages and their entourages far outnumbered those from Guralta Academy.

Subliminals and healers and mixed families showed up, too. Non-mages weren't forbidden from renting property on the island, after all. They were simply much less likely to have the money, and to know it was an option in the first place.

Take me as an example. I'd heard of Guralta Academy since long before coming here. I understood that it was located on a place called Guralta Isle. I hadn't realized that said place included miles of sandy beaches and—during peak season—many times more visitors than locals or students.

Either way, I doubt my parents could've afforded to foot the bill for a Guralta vacation. Even cheaper routes, like booking a hotel room near Baneberry and taking day trips across the bridge, would've been something of a stretch.

Now imagine an afternoon that felt appropriately summer-hot yet not muggy. With just the right amount of wind to quickly dry any traces of sweat, and coast-to-coast blue skies so empty of clouds that it seemed almost oppressive. I was as eager as anyone to scamper off and enjoy myself while the miracle lasted.

But I didn't.

Mr. Rift had assigned us a project that culminated in crafting models of magic branch configurations. Like with pipe cleaners.

I found the whole thing absurd, and I told him so. There was no way physical objects could accurately depict the true relationships between magic branches.

"Even the most sophisticated maps of the continent contain some necessary distortions," he replied. "Maps of the world, even more so. Does this mean we shouldn't bother making maps at all?"

"Ink and paper are physical," I said. "Geography is the physical land beneath our feet. That's still using one physical object to represent another.

"The distortions involved in making pipe cleaners stand for magic branches are much worse than flattening mountains into two dimensions. Or rolling a globe out into a rectangle like pie crust."

Mr. Rift paused as if asking a higher power to grant him patience.

"Asa," he said.

"Yes? Have you been enlightened?"

"You aren't wrong. But please bear in mind that this is a standard part of the curriculum. It's been part of the curriculum for years."

"So?"

"I won't tell you to rejoice," he continued, "but many students enjoy a chance to do something different from their usual classwork. Something more tactile."

"Good for them," I said. "I think it's useless."

"Would you prefer a group project?"

"Don't even joke about that."

"For your information, Asa, I might have considered letting you propose an alternate assignment."

"Really? I'll—"

"I might have considered it if you weren't in the bottom third of my class."

Darn it. Foiled by my own scheming.

"I complain about you to my parents, you know. All the time."

Mr. Rift called my bluff. "And what do they say in return?"

I reluctantly spoke the truth: "I haven't mentioned any other teachers by name. Mr. Rift must be doing something right, is what they say."

"How kind of them."

"That's my parents. Kind and clueless."

If I had to do this stupid pipe-cleaner-wrangling assignment, I wanted to get it over with as soon as possible.

Although the actual due date was a full week away, I chose to stay behind in the workshop that glorious Friday afternoon.

Unsurprisingly, I was the only student who lingered. Everyone else blasted off to go swim or shop or sunbathe or party or do sports practice or tend to other club-related duties.

In my defense, I didn't have any social obligations. I didn't belong to any school clubs yet. Nor did I have any money to spend on entertainment. My parents might try to send me a bit of allowance for my birthday next month, but it wasn't like I could use that to open a tab at local shops.

Once or twice, I'd taken out Shien Nerium's replica coin and contemplated selling it for cash. There had to be at least one shady pawn shop or antique dealer somewhere on the island. Maybe I could trick them into thinking the coin was real.

Just kidding. Kind of.

Anyway, that was why I hung back while everyone else pranced off to splash each other in the surf.

I fiddled grimly with pipe cleaners. Mr. Rift sat at the teacher's desk and grimly did paperwork. A fine pair we made, on this spectacular summer day.

The workshop had long high tables and stools instead of individual desks. It had cabinets full of construction paper, wire, blocks of clay, super-strong glue, and other such supplies.

All in all, it was about as sophisticated as an art classroom for little kids. Mage healing didn't exactly require high-end laboratory equipment.

I grumbled under my breath as I wrangled fistfuls of garishly colored pipe cleaners into shape.

Another thing I hated about this project was the fact that the classic magic branch configurations all had ridiculously pompous-sounding names. Usually derived from the now-dead researchers who had first identified each pattern. No way to keep all the necessary vocab straight except through stone-cold memorization.

When my complaints increased in volume, Mr. Rift looked up from his desk. "No one is forcing you to do this right now, Asa."

"I am."

He didn't chuckle. "Consider the fact that this type of project could help other students gain a better understanding of magic branch dynamics. Even if you find it unhelpful yourself."

"Consider it considered," I said.

"Different people learn in different ways. Don't be snotty."

The project itself was a pain, but I derived some entertainment from curling purple pipe cleaners around my wrists and fingers like fuzzy jewelry.

Mr. Rift warned me not to waste supplies. He threatened me with detention when he caught me trying to sculpt yet more pipe cleaners into the outline of a racehorse.

The sweet breeze from the open window reached agonizing peaks of freshness and beauty as I worked. It made me want to toss all these furry sticks in the air and go zooming in wild circles outside.

I'd almost finished by the time Mr. Rift's chair scraped the floor.

He was still behind the desk at the head of the room—now with his hands braced on it, standing. "I need to step out," he said abruptly. "Leave the door unlocked when you're done."

I craned my neck to see who or what he was glaring at. We were at opposite ends of the room, though. His view out the window must've been very different from mine.

After Mr. Rift left, I went over to his desk. I stood there and looked in the direction he'd been looking. All I saw was sun-dappled campus grass and clover. Splendid coral-lined paths. The titanic gardens in the distance.

I powered through the rest of my pipe cleaner artwork at record speed. I labeled each structure and transferred them carefully to the shelves along the back wall. Together with my half-done horse. Then I bid good riddance to the workshop.

Curiosity had me hoping to catch Mr. Rift outside the building. Alas, no such luck.

I'd stretch my legs a bit before dinner, then. It would probably end up being something like cold mackerel curry. Better build up my fortitude before diving in.

Someone said my name as I passed the border gardens.

Had my long-lost snails learned to speak? For all I knew, by now they might be the size of small dogs. I peered up at the gravity-defying foliage. It was really much too large and heavy to hold itself up on its own.

The voice told me to turn around. I looked over my shoulder, back at the healer side of campus.

Weathered wooden picnic tables stood scattered under a stand of shadowy trees. There was something off about their placement, like everyone had abandoned them in the middle of a rowdy outdoor party, never to return. I couldn't remember ever spying these tables in use before.

Boy, were they in use now. One of them, anyway. Someone had tossed down a white tablecloth adorned with a twee pattern of sea creatures and sailboats. It clashed with the many-colored floral paisley of Mr. Rift's shirt.

Mr. Rift sat around the table with Shien Nerium. Plus some other guy—a tad younger than Nerium, and also a mage—who I'd never seen in my life.

Mr. Rift and Shien Nerium had blue bowls of ice cream in front of them. The third guy hunched over an arrangement of acorns placed directly on the tablecloth. He appeared to be playing some manner of private game, squinting and leaning like a billiards champ before flicking one acorn into another.

"Asa Clematis," said Shien Nerium.

He was the one who'd been calling me. Must've gotten my name from Mr. Rift.

"Hi," I said.

Mr. Rift appeared even more doleful than usual. His face would get stuck like that if he weren't careful.

I waited for someone to enlighten me as to why they'd brought me over.

A large bag reminiscent of an instrument case leaned up against a nearby tree. I pictured Shien Nerium—or the mysterious mage beside him—packing it full of napkins, extra tablecloths, dishes, and spoons. Perhaps it had a cold compartment for ice cream.

Speaking of which, I observed no signs of melting. The blue ceramic bowls bore a frigid glaze of magic. Shien Nerium used a silver spoon to take an ant-sized bite.

I couldn't say how long they'd been lounging here, but without those bowls, the ice cream would likely have dissolved to soup.

I, for one, had no such protection. So much for today being the nicest afternoon we'd had in ages. Dawdling here while these grown men had a leisurely picnic was making me sweat.

"Uh. Guess I'll go now?"

"No, no," said Nerium. "You came at just the right time."

"For...?"

He had that folded-up paper fan with him again. He tapped himself on the chin with it, smiling. "Patience."

The unfamiliar mage beside him kept pushing around acorns. Mr. Rift regarded me with an expression verging on mute horror. He didn't appear to have touched his impeccably preserved ice cream. Cicadas thrummed in the trees overhead.

"You did contact her, no?" Shien Nerium said to his neighbor. He got a short nod in response. The *her* didn't seem to be referring to me. But if not me, then—

Shien Nerium took off his glasses.

It was my first time seeing his naked eyes. They'd previously been obscured by the jangling of magic all over the frame and lenses. So many different cuttings that I couldn't even begin to guess at their purpose.

Unless it was all one big game of misdirection. Perhaps he'd grafted on a bunch of pointless cuttings solely to dazzle and distract anyone with half-decent magic perception.

He was stout in stature and had a hairline that looked about two decades older than the rest of him. Not someone you'd assume to be from one of the great mage families. And the eyes behind the glasses were every bit as ordinary as the rest of him. A plain, amiable brown.

"Here," said Shien Nerium.

He held his glasses out to me.

Mr. Rift snapped to attention. "I don't think—"

"It won't hurt," Nerium added, seeing my hesitation. "Do me a favor, Asa Clematis. Take them."

Mr. Rift extended a hand. "I'd be happy to hold them for you."

I'd never heard that voice come out of him before. It wasn't his teacher voice, that's for sure. He was the oldest one here, and the only actual staff member, yet had no real authority. Not over these visiting mages.

Nerium looked him up and down. "But that would be so much less interesting," he said gently.

He turned to me again.

The faster I got this over with, the faster I could escape.

I took the glasses.

In my defense, I fully expected it to hurt. A static shock, perhaps, or a stinging like jellyfish. Or maybe the goal was to activate some other kind of prank. Indelible ink splashed all over my hands. Fart sounds as loud as a siren.

Any personal item with that much magic invested in it would surely also include a couple of anti-theft measures. Other people's cuttings didn't come cheap, even if you were a mage yourself. Perhaps especially if you were a mage. Mages from the right family would have the money to pay price in full without a second thought.

Shien Nerium had been telling the truth, in a way. Nothing hurt me.

What happened instead: the moment I touched the frames of his glasses, my legs crumpled beneath me like they were no more than long balloons filled with air.

I sat in the moss-eaten dirt, and I couldn't feel it. I couldn't feel the glasses in my hands. I was very lucky, I thought distantly, that I hadn't lost control of my bladder together with the rest of my body.

The sound of the cicadas receded, as if the sudden and brutal dizziness left no room to let them in. Yet for some reason I could still hear that one unnamed guy at the table clicking his acorns together without a care in the world.

My lungs got stuck in a shallow gasping cycle, like my face was just barely sticking out above the surface of a choppy sea. I needed more air. I couldn't force my breath to restart properly, to pull all the way in, to inflate my chest. That was what began to hurt. That was what made my hapless fingers clench the dirt.

Virtually no time had passed. It was just that each second after my collapse felt stretched as unnecessarily long as it could go without snapping.

Mr. Rift and Shien Nerium were yammering at each other, rapid words I couldn't make sense of. Some vindictive part of me wanted to squeeze my fist around those high-end glasses, get my fingerprints all over them. They'd fallen down into my lap. I wished I could bend them in half. But I already knew I lacked the strength.

A familiar trace of magic grazed the fringes of my perception. A quick blotchy impression like those blobs of color you see when ducking into a dark room after pickling your vision in sunlight. A formless ghost.

Someone bent down and took the glasses off my lap.

I instantly felt human again. Like my own body had abruptly decided to throw down arms and cease its rebellion.

The turnabout was rather disorienting in its own right. I sucked in greedy gulps of air, almost blinded by how they finally filled me.

Then I looked up at Wist's legs, clad in her signature dark maroon tracksuit. At the thick black braid hanging down her back. The end of the braid coiled around her ankle to avoid wallowing in the mix of mulch and soil where I sat.

Relief tingled in my throat like a hot drink. I'd never been so glad to see her. And I hated it.

She still held her brother's glasses. How come the anti-theft magic hadn't knocked her down on the ground right next to me?

"Kind of you to port over so quickly," Nerium said to her. "Those cuttings never did have much of an effect on you, did they?"

Wist tossed the glasses at him.

He caught them. Unfolded them. Examined them with a critical eye. After a moment, he took out a cloth and started polishing the lenses.

Wist looked over her shoulder at me. I froze like a bug exposed by the removal of a sheltering rock.

She started to offer me her hand, then pulled back. Her braid uncurled from around her leg and reached for me as if telling me to grab it like a rope and pull myself up.

I recalled her asking to change partners in class. Before I'd gotten anywhere near her. She'd done it with the same unreadable look on her face that she had on right now.

I have a very, very good memory for certain things. Once I saw a particular mage's magic close up, it stuck in my head much more clearly than their name or their face. That was how I recalled most of the mage students I'd encountered in co-ed training sessions—by the look of their core and their branches.

I have an equally pristine memory for slights against me.

Some I might choose to disregard. Like how my dormmates had done their shambolic best to make me miserable during hunting season. They'd been pawns acting to please Minashiro Tempus, who in turn had been acting to please Wist's fabled brothers. One of whom was now delicately cleaning his glasses about three feet away from me.

With hunting season long over, my dormmates were more than happy to leave me be. They did so with a thoroughness that bordered on shunning. I wouldn't have much to gain by retaliating. But that didn't mean I'd ever forget their willingness to kidnap Saya's hermit crabs.

And I wouldn't seize at Wist for help just because she now acted like nothing noteworthy had happened since her exam.

I wiped my hands on the heavy pleats of my long uniform skirt. I got up clumsily, but I got up on my own.

I contemplated walking away without another word.

Instead I stepped forward to stand next to Wist, rather than behind her. The least I could do was show a little solidarity with Mr. Rift, the only other healer here. He appeared to be trapped at the opposite side of the picnic table, with no obvious escape route.

Shien Nerium put his glasses back on, once again cloaking his eyes behind dense bright masses of magic.

"Wisteria," he said in tones of reproach. "You've been avoiding me all week."

For all the drama of her entrance, Wist seemed disinclined to say another word.

The mage seated next to Nerium flicked an acorn at her. It nailed her in the torso, then dropped to the ground at her feet. He flicked another at the exact same spot, as if showing off his aim. Bulls-eye.

"Ficus, say a proper greeting to your little sister," Nerium ordered.

Another Shien brother, then.

The stranger lifted his head.

With the pretty, sullen features of a born model, he looked absolutely nothing like either Nerium or Wist. Much closer to the stereotypical image of a high-class mage.

He didn't spare a glance for me, thankfully. He looked straight at Wist.

"Your favorite bodyguard cried like a bitch when we fired her," said Shien Ficus.

Wist didn't move. I couldn't even say for sure if she were breathing.

"Hard to imagine, isn't it? Just thought you should know." He flicked another fat acorn with casual flair.

This one smacked Wist in the cheekbone, inches from her eye.

I flinched. Wist didn't.

"Where are your glasses, Wisteria?" Nerium asked, as if Shien Ficus hadn't said a word.

"Don't need them to see," she said roughly.

Nerium put on a wounded look. At least I think he did. A bit hard to tell, with the mask of magic occluding his eyes. "They were a gift from your brother. Isn't that reason enough to wear them more often?"

To my dismay, he raised his paper fan to his mouth and turned to me as if I were a trusted confidant. "Surely you've seen her glasses? They aren't merely for fashion. You know that way she has of staring at people? Those dead-fish eyes."

She was doing those dead-fish eyes right now, albeit at the ice cream and the acorns, rather than any one person at the table.

"The glasses make it ever so slightly less unsettling," Nerium said. "That's why I always tell her to keep wearing them. For the sake of those around her."

He shut the fan again with a crisp flick of his wrist. "Wisteria has always been poorly socialized. We were terribly worried about how she'd fare alone at school. I'm so glad to see she's learned to mingle with those of other backgrounds."

I won't lie—it took me a full second to realize he was talking about me.

Shien Ficus stopped playing with his acorns. "Other backgrounds?" he said.

"Ah," murmured Nerium. "True. Wisteria's birth parents were quite destitute. Perhaps that's what draws her to the likes of you"—he gave me another nod—"and Azalea Wren. I see, I see."

I couldn't keep it in any longer.

"Sorry," I said. "Uh—sorry, sir. Nice family reunion you're having here. Beautiful stuff. Really don't think it's right for me and Mr. Rift to keep intruding. If you don't mind, we'll just—"

His smile vanished. I took an inadvertent step back.

"Give it to her, then," he said.

"I don't have—"

"Why did you reach for your pocket?"

Damn it. Yes, I was an idiot. Shouldn't have kept his coin with me. Should've pitched it in the trash the day I got it.

"Your friend has a surprise for you," Nerium said to Wist.

"We aren't friends," I blurted.

He gave me a speculative look. "Oh? My apologies. I hadn't realized you were even closer."

"That's obviously not what I meant."

He tapped the end of his fan to his lips. "It's not nearly so obvious as you seem to think, Asa Clematis."

Wist was looking at me in a way that made me feel like perhaps her brother had a point after all, with his whole thing about wanting to make her wear glasses. It'd work better if hers brimmed with as much magic as his.

She opened her mouth, forming the first syllable of my name. Then she seemed to think better of it. "Did he give you something?"

Maybe this was what it would take to get me out of here.

I dug the coin from my pocket. I held it out on my palm so Wist could take it. Take it and free me from all this Shien clan crossfire.

Her eyes dropped to my hand.

The moment Wist saw her brother's coin, magic crackled in the air with a sound like the heart of a bonfire.

A second later, cicadas rained from every single tree around the picnic table.

I yelped and leapt about and waved my arms overhead for protection. The ground underfoot started to feel extra thick and crunchy. Then I noticed—seemingly a touch later than everyone else—that the cicadas weren't dive-bombing us. They'd fallen down silent and dead. Every single one of them.

No point in trying to swat them away, then. From the corner of my eye I saw Shien Nerium calmly pluck one out of his ice cream bowl. It was longer and wider around than his thumb.

Shien Ficus rose to shake cicadas from his hair like a wet dog. Mr. Rift sat unmoving with his hands laid flat on the tablecloth, looking as if he wanted to set fire to the entire picnic area.

I glanced warily at Wist.

She had her head bowed. She gripped her left arm with her right hand as if she were trying to manually juice every last bit of blood and plasma from the pulp of her muscle.

Shien Ficus straightened up. He bounced a particularly fat dead cicada in his palm like a sports ball.

"Gross," he said under his breath as he tossed and caught it, an idle warm-up.

Without warning, he swiveled and pitched his cicada straight at Wist.

It ricocheted off the air an inch from her nose and went flying somewhere far, far away, a dead brown stray bullet.

The picnic table cracked down the middle with a sound I felt in my bones. The two halves slumped together, forming a deep V-shaped trench into which slid the ice cream bowls and scattered acorns and yet more fallen cicadas.

Mr. Rift caught my eye. I began inching toward Wist. Her magic branches swirled inside her as if they were trying to strangle each other. She hadn't gone fully berserk yet. But this kind of furniture-destroying wild magic was an extremely bad sign.

Shien Nerium held up a hand to stop me.

"Property damage?" he said to Wist. He shook his head sadly. "I'm heartbroken, Wisteria. I was sure you were better than this."

He turned to Mr. Rift. "Rest assured, we'll cover the cost of any needed repairs."

"That won't be necessary." Mr. Rift's flat tone somehow reminded me of what I was accustomed to hearing from Wist. "Guralta Academy is a school of magecraft, of magiology. We're more than prepared to accommodate for the occasional accident."

"That's good to hear."

"More importantly," Mr. Rift continued, "an accident of this nature indicates that your sister needs healing. You'll have to excuse us."

"I'm just so disappointed," Nerium said mournfully. "We taught her impeccable self-control back home. What happened?"

"She's over a decade younger than you, Shien. She has time to keep learning."

Mr. Rift stepped back from the broken table. A clear sign of his desire to leave.

I was close enough to Wist that I could reach for her and seize at the ends of her magic.

With the Shien brothers watching us, I didn't know if I should. She was still digging her fingers into her arm. Her braid hung paralyzed in the air behind her. Nothing about her posture invited any form of human contact whatsoever. Maybe it'd be better to wait for Mr. Rift to get us out of here.

"One last thing."

Shien Nerium looked at me when he spoke. Perhaps because I—unlike Wist—had made the mistake of looking back.

"Ficus and I will be hosting a reception this weekend. A cozy little gathering to kick off our vacation. Wisteria will be there, of course. I hope you'll come too."

I opened my mouth to say: *Yeah, no thanks.*

Wist pinched the flesh near my elbow before the words had a chance to come out.

Startled, I stole a look at her. It hadn't hurt at all. Her fingers felt unsteady. But it was enough to make me shut my trap.

"I look forward to seeing you there," Nerium told me.

He tapped his fan on the edge of the tilted tabletop. "Ficus, help me clean this."

Mr. Rift ushered me and Wist away without offering to pitch in. Thank goodness.

I tried not to tread on dead cicadas in the process of hustling away from there, but it proved almost impossible. All three of us crushed them as we went, crisp nuggets of juicy insect meat. In the immortal words of Shien Ficus: gross.

We hadn't quite walked out of sight of the Shien brothers when Wist veered over to the nearest bush. She dropped to her knees and vomited at its roots.

She was astonishingly quiet. If I'd kept my back turned, I wouldn't have had any clue what was happening.

26

Mr. Rift took us to the infirmary closest to the healer side of campus. Empty and locked. He made us tag along after him while he went to fetch the key.

"Does anyone even work here?" I asked. Mr. Rift shrugged.

The fancy infirmary near the gym facilities got a lot more business from mages. But if my fellow healer Rats felt sick, they wouldn't bother trekking over. They'd seek help from the dorm steward, who had a stash of standard medication, and who might direct them to hole up in a spare room if they needed rest.

Wist, for her part, went straight for the bed at the very back of the room, all the way up against the wall. The same place I'd seen her curled up the last time I came here. Back then, I hadn't even known her name.

It was a peculiar feeling to look again at the gauzy fog-colored window curtains, the hoya plants trailing their long inquisitive vines by each bed. Only a few were in bloom.

No one had swept the floor in a while. Below each hoya pot lay a scattering of minuscule dried-up flowers and dead yellow leaves.

In case you're wondering, Mr. Rift did give me a chance to go my own way. Nothing obligated me to be here.

I opted to stick with him and Wist regardless. I didn't think too deeply about why. Curiosity has always been one of my deadliest vices.

Once we stepped into the infirmary, Mr. Rift asked Wist who she wanted to heal her. I felt her tug at my sleeve.

Mr. Rift nodded.

"Hey," I said to him. "You're the professional here. Shouldn't you be the one to take care of her?"

"She's requesting your services." He indicated Wist's hand on my sleeve. "The best healer for any mage is the healer they prefer. The healer they're willing to have touching their magic."

Something about that struck me as glib. Before I could question it, Mr. Rift added, "This isn't a class with dozens of people watching, Asa. I don't see any particular need for you to hold back."

Of course Mr. Rift would realize how carefully I calibrated my performance in public. To dazzle no one. To be forgotten. To become the healer no mage in their right mind would want touching their magic.

He turned his back and went over to fuss with the medicine cabinet at the opposite side of the room.

Technically, Mr. Rift couldn't walk out and leave. At least not according to school's anti-fraternization regulations. Now that he'd brought us here—just the two of us—he'd be forced to stay to the end. Our trusty adult chaperone.

The hefty curtains around Wist's sickbed stood half-open. She'd retreated to this familiar spot like a wounded animal slinking back to its den.

I pulled up a seat.

She'd rinsed her mouth at an outdoor water fountain after throwing up. Once we reached the infirmary, she'd declined Mr. Rift's offer of something else to drink. Now she lay sideways, facing me, as if deliberately making it difficult to reach her back.

"You sure you want healing?" I asked.

"You don't have to."

"I know I don't. I'm volunteering out of the goodness of my heart. As a safety measure, if nothing else."

"I'm not about to go berserk," said Wist.

"Tell that to the cicadas."

"That wasn't wild magic."

I recreated the moment in my mind. Cicada corpses carpet-bombing us—all of us, Wist included—from the towering trees.

"Excuse me?" I said, as blankly as Wist herself. "You're claiming you just happened to possess a preexisting skill for slaughtering massive amounts of cicadas? Plus another one for smashing picnic tables?"

"The skill isn't supposed to kill them," Wist said wearily. "Normally I use it to stun cicadas. Keep them still. One at a time."

"Never thought you were in favor of mages taking their stress out on animals."

"I don't use it for fun."

"Then help me understand." I spread my hands. "In what situation do you so desperately need to use magic—magic!—to paralyze a cicada? Paint me a picture here. Seems like hauling out an entire warship to spear a single tuna."

"Sometimes cicadas will fall on the path," said Wist. "On a balcony. A terrace. Outdoor stairs."

"That's part of summer, isn't it? So?"

"What do you do?" she asked.

"What do I do?" I parroted, bewildered.

"What do you do?"

"I step around them and go on my way."

"But sometimes they buzz at you," Wist said. "They see hints of your movement. They start having fits. They flip onto their backs or flip back over onto their front. They rocket off the ground. Sometimes your shadow touches them, and they panic so hard they shoot right into you."

"So you freeze them in place with magic." I paused to digest this. "What would you do if you weren't a mage?"

"Turn around and take a different path."

She seemed serious. I gave up on questioning it.

"I get why you have a skill that could be twisted to whack cicadas senseless. Sure. Doesn't explain the broken table."

"It's a work in progress."

"The table?" I asked. "I mean, yeah. It is now."

"The skill," said Wist. "Remember my skill of division? The one that only works on cupcakes."

"The one you made to spoof Bulletproof." I kept my voice low, in case Mr. Rift was trying to eavesdrop. "What about it?"

"I've been working on an expanded version. One that can split more things in half."

I leaned forward in my chair. "All right," I said. "I understand that you weren't erupting in wild magic. Those were legitimate skills you already possessed.

"I understand why Mr. Rift isn't standing over here urging us to get on with it. It's not the worse possible type of emergency. You're still a few long, long steps away from going berserk. I'll give you that."

I looked Wist hard in the eye. Those black expressionless eyes that her own brother had called unsettling. By now I'd gotten used to them.

"I get all that," I emphasized. "Doesn't change the fact that there was no reason for you to use those two skills right then and there. Doesn't change the fact that you lost control."

Wist didn't shrink from me. But I daresay she came close.

"Yes," she said. "That's my problem. But I'm not berserk. I haven't lost hold of myself. No one's in danger now."

"What're you trying to tell me?"

She dropped her gaze. "You don't have to sit there and heal me."

"Damn right I don't," I retorted. "We've been over this. Didn't want me touching you in class either, did you? You were done with me the instant you passed your exam."

"I—"

I got up. "I'll ask Mr. Rift to tap in. You shouldn't have grabbed my sleeve like that. You shouldn't have pretended to pick me."

Her braid darted into the air between us as if to corral me. It stopped just short of actually touching me. After a long sheepish moment, it slunk back into bed with her.

"What," I said, without the inflection of a question. Asa Clematis was not amused.

"I wanted to apologize." Wist had never been one to talk loudly, but now her voice had dried to a trickle.

"For dropping me as soon as your exam ended?"

"For letting my brothers find you."

"Did you tell them about me?"

It would make sense, come to think of it, if Shien Nerium had already known who I was when he first approached me. When he forced me to take custody of the coin that had shocked Wist into slaughtering five trees' worth of cicadas.

Wist looked at me as if she couldn't understand what I was saying.

"The morning we got back from the exam," she said, "Azalea told me they'd arrived on the island."

"And?"

Wist sat up in bed. Her magic branches grated together inside her. It looked as painful as bones meeting without cartilage, gears grinding without oil.

"My fog is one of my oldest skills." She faced the dark teardrop-shaped leaves of the rambling bedside hoya plant. "The second or third skill I ever originated.

"I started making the fog to hide from my siblings. Mostly from my brothers. Mostly from Ficus and Nerium."

"Did it work?"

"It helped a little. Better than nothing. It helped until Nerium got his glasses."

"What do those glasses do, anyway?" I'd been wondering.

"The cuttings on them amplify his magic perception. To inhuman levels. Like he's a magical microscope. And a telescope. And a bloodhound. All in one person."

At last Wist darted another look at me. "I warned Tempus not to tell my brothers anything about me." Her voice hardened a fraction. "Or anything about you. This time, I think, he was motivated to listen. My brothers didn't hear any fresh news of you from Tempus."

She dug her fingers into the base of her braid, cradling the back of her neck.

"It was bad enough that they showed up right after the exam," she said. "I thought maybe—if you didn't heal me, if we didn't set foot near each other, if we never spoke—I thought there was a chance Nerium might not notice anything.

"But he found you anyway. It must've been the glasses. He spotted traces of me on you."

"Even days after the exam?"

"Even then."

I watched the paintbrush-like tuft at the end of her braid twitch back and forth on the infirmary bedsheets.

"You know," I said slowly, "I wasn't hoping for you to start acting all chummy after the exam. You understand very well that I don't want attention. I figured you'd go back to treating me like any other healer. Fine.

"But flat-out refusing to pair up in class is a whole different kind of special treatment. That's gonna draw just as much speculation as being friendly. That really, truly pissed me off. In case you couldn't tell."

"Didn't want you coming too close," said Wist. "Didn't want to risk leaving any more traces of my magic on—"

"Yeah, great job," I snarled. "A commendable effort. Worked real well, didn't it? Your brothers found me anyway. Now hurry up and roll over."

I paused. "Unless you have some other reason for not wanting me to heal you."

She rolled onto her stomach, wordless.

I tried to imagine what it'd take to make her lose her cool now. Dropping a live cicada on her spine, perhaps. Or—whipping out Shien Nerium's coin again might do the trick.

Instead I pushed up her jacket for better access to her lower back. It seemed too hot out for her to still be wearing the same long-sleeved tracksuit all day. Maybe it was nevertheless more comfortable than the summer edition of the official mage student uniform.

Wist's fallen cicadas and table-splitting may not have been wild magic. But wild magic—unbound by the framework of skills imprinted on branches—was only part of what made berserking mages such a enormous threat.

A mage on the brink of snapping could just as easily wreak havoc with their standard skill set.

And Wist, despite her half-assed attempt to strip bare for her recent exam, still seemed to carry around a far deeper pool of skills than most mages.

Heck, most mages could count their entire skill set on one hand. Or two at most. Their limited number of branches in turn severely limited the number of magic skills they could hold at any given moment.

At any rate, berserking was the name for a particular state of mind and magic. A violent loss of personality that could only be neutralized with the most advanced forms of magical healing.

A mage becoming angry and abusive, a mage lashing out in public, a mage misusing their skills—none of that necessarily fit the definition of going berserk. It was a very precise term. Almost medical in nature.

If they so chose, a powerful mage could do incredible harm purely of their own accord, without losing their mind for a second. Thankfully for the rest of us, few would make that choice.

Mages could commit murder with or without magic, without or without berserking. Mages could do terrible things of their own free will, just like anyone else.

I took my time healing Wist. The only sounds from inside the room were her meek breathing and Mr. Rift shuffling around over by the cabinets.

I understood now, after close to half a year of formal schooling as a healer, another reason why Wist might never have received adequate healing. At least not to the point of untangling her as thoroughly as other mages.

So much of our training seemed geared toward making healers think in certain regimented ways. Like constructing magic branch dioramas out of pipe cleaners.

It would take the school's entire supply of pipe cleaners and an entire year of work to even begin to attempt designing such a model for Wist. And it'd still be all wrong.

Our training was perfect for gaining competency in healing mages with up to nine magic branches. Mages in all the standard classes. Might not be quite so useful for S-Class mages. But in fairness, most healers could go their entire lives without meeting a single S-Class.

Meanwhile, Wist bore so little resemblance to the S-Class examples in our textbooks that I didn't really see the sense of lumping her in with them.

For normal mages, healers had to sort out the knots in the equivalent of up to nine strands of spaghetti. For S-Class mages, there might be a few extra strands on top of that. Still not enough to cover a full plate.

Wist's magic, on the other hand, was an entire serving platter bearing a huge mountain of spaghetti strands. No, not even that—an enormous vat seething with noodles, too deep to guess at how far down the bottom went. From that perspective, I could understand why other healers hadn't made a whole lot of headway on her magical pain.

I could also admit that maybe my optimism about being able to heal Wist more deeply than others—if I just got the time and space to try it—might stem from sheer inexperience.

It was easy to say such things when you had no idea what you were talking about. Like eating at a restaurant and immediately deciding you could cook way better than the chef. Or like listening to a piano tuner hard at work and telling yourself that you—with zero experience—could fiddle around with the strings and hammers to produce a far better sound.

At the same time, I definitely saw things in tangled-up magic that others seemed to miss. I saw how prodding one knot in Wist's branches would lead to a completely different knot unraveling. I couldn't put into words what made me reach that conclusion. I couldn't have used it as an answer on a written test. But it worked.

I was frighteningly good at this, wasn't I? A tweak here, a tweak there, and large swathes of her magic branches slid apart as if greased with butter.

That said, there were plenty of healers in Osmanthus. A microscopic percentage of the population as a whole, but more than enough to treat all the nation's mages. I still didn't think that being freakishly good at healing obligated me to devote my life to it.

Here and now, though, I found myself willing to use my talent for Wist.

When I reached a good stopping point, I released her magic branches. They slithered away like slender eels darting back into the safety of a grotto.

I tugged her top down to cover the small of her back. "It's the worst part of summer," I said. "Aren't you hot in this?"

Wist turned on her side to look at me. "The island gets plenty of wind."

"Not indoors."

She raised her eyes to the ceiling fans. Which, I might add, were currently turned off.

If she did get overheated, maybe she wouldn't even notice. Physical discomfort seemed to be among the least of Wisteria Shien's concerns.

I went over to the nearest window and pushed open its thin gray-tinged curtains. A couple of tall date palms clustered outside. They appeared almost ready for harvest, dangling startling orange clusters of fruit that looked more like some sort of clinging parasite than an organic part of the same tree.

Wist slowly sat up. She propped up pillows by the headboard to lean on. The very end of her long braid clasped itself over her left shoulder like a watchful hand.

I returned to my chair by her bed. "I've got questions."

Wist waited in silence.

"Those glasses you wear sometimes—they were a present from your brother?"

"I had to wear them more at home," she said.

"But you don't need them to see."

"When he first gave them to me, they came with the same anti-theft cuttings as his own glasses."

"So no one could touch them but you?"

Wist made a small noise that might've been meant to convey amusement.

"So no one could touch them but him," she said. "For the first few months, they made me feel what you felt earlier. What brought you to your knees."

"And you just—put up with it?"

"That's how long it took me to figure out how to remove the cuttings."

I truly didn't understand what Wist was saying. I'm not being disingenuous here. When the cuttings on Nerium's glasses struck me, I hadn't known how to breathe. Much less stand.

Wist might be an natural-born expert at enduring magical agony, but that was all on the inside. A whole different realm from physical incapacitation. How could she possibly have carried on normal conversations at home and walked from room to room and brushed her teeth under the influence of those cuttings?

Her own magic was already a bad enough burden. Why had she willingly accepted the gift of her brother's sabotage on top of that? What had driven her to stagger through the weakness and shortness of breath for months at a time?

Maybe back then there had still been people at home with her she wanted to shield. Maybe she'd had some other reason to let it happen.

I'm not saying she did anything wrong. I'm not saying she could've acted any other way. I don't know the full story.

I just couldn't fathom it. My imagination locked up—abandoned the attempt. My chest tightened like a heart attack at the thought of that anti-theft magic, at the prospect of experiencing it for more than a few scant burning seconds.

"The coin," I said. Perhaps not the wisest choice of topics. But it was the first that leapt to mind. I could still feel Shien Nerium's coin right there in my pocket.

"I'm sorry."

I stared at her. "*You're* sorry?"

"I overreacted."

Hand in my pocket, I turned the stupid coin in my fingers. Over and over. Getting the metal stink on my skin.

"Can't tell you if I agree with that," I said at last. "I don't know the context."

"It was a game he and Ficus used to play."

"A game," I repeated.

"I flipped the coin. They decided the consequences."

"Wow. What a game," I said. "Really deep ruleset."

"There's nothing dangerous about the coin itself."

"I'll keep it as a memento, then. Or we could get rid of it together. Make it into a whole ceremony." I mimed throwing Nerium's coin out the window. "Fling it in the sea."

From the corner of my eye I saw the coils of Wist's braid winding gradually tighter around her body. The steady constriction of a python coming in for the kill.

"I'm used to my brothers," she said. "I was—startled—to see the coin in your hands. Nothing more. It won't happen again."

"For the record," I told her, "they didn't actually do anything to me. You know I'd be complaining if they had."

"No," Wist agreed. "But they could have. They still can."

She reached for my hand. She peeled open my closed fingers. She looked down at the figure of the Kraken on the coin. Our fair nation's ancient enemy. This time, no dead insects showered from the ceiling.

Wist tapped the coin on my palm. "This time, they did nothing except send me a message. They know who you are now. They've marked you."

"I'm no one," I protested.

I didn't mean it in a self-deprecating way. To a grown-ass mage from one of the great families, Asa Clematis might as well have been the name of an inedible forest mushroom.

"They saw my residue on you. Nerium can perceive the difference between repeated closeness and a quick one-time pairing for class. I'm—"

"No more apologies." I stuffed my hand back in my pocket. "How long are they going to be on the island?"

"Till the end of September."

"Over a month? That's longer than hunting season." I blew out a breath. "I'll try to lie low. Sounds like Azalea already knows to watch her back?"

"It won't be like hunting season," said Wist. "And they aren't staying on campus."

"Hope that means it'll be easy enough to avoid them. Would be even easier if we weren't stuck going to their party this weekend."

"You don't have to attend."

"You pinched me when I was about to say no."

"I'll cover for you if you prefer not to show up."

"But you recommend going," I said. "As the more peaceful option. Don't you? Like how you tried to recommend that I go to training camp. You were sitting in the same bed back then, too."

The coils of her braid relaxed a fraction. So did I. It had gotten to a point where I'd begun wondering if she might inadvertently crack her own ribs.

"First we just have to endure another month," I said to Wist. "That's doable. But don't stop there. Let's think bigger."

"Bigger?"

"Think in the long term," I explained. "See, usually I'm all about holding grudges."

"I hadn't guessed."

"Hah. Aren't you sweet. So I love holding grudges. But I'll make an exception for your brothers."

"I know it's not that easy for you—I'm just talking about myself here. Me, I plan on doing my darnedest to forget their faces after this month passes. I'll forget their names. Forget I ever met them. Those assholes are nothing to me. Grown men lashing out at schoolgirls? Pathetic."

"In fact," I added, "I'll do Tempiss—"

"Tempus."

"Same difference. I'll do Tempus a favor and try to remember his name instead of theirs. He at least has the excuse of being young and impressionable."

I raised three fingers. "After this next month is over, our goal should be to get to graduation without ever seeing another Shien on the island. Three and a half more years. Question is, what's got to be done to make that happen?"

For an extraordinarily prolonged moment, Wist said nothing.

She opened her mouth to utter a syllable that fell short of becoming a full-fledged word. Closed her mouth. Glanced at the open window as if looking out for assassins.

At last she leaned toward me and asked in a very quiet voice: "Are you suggesting that we murder them?"

"Heavens above, do I sound that much like a mob boss?"

We blinked at each other.

"Although," I said, "Mr. Rift did mention that your brothers sealed a healer in the western caves, back in the day. One could argue that there is a precedent. One could argue that they deserve it."

I shrugged. "Hey, I'm not making that argument. Just saying. It could exist. I could see the potential for it. But no. Let's not do anything stupid."

Wist sank back into her pile of pillows. "Sometimes it's hard to tell what you're thinking."

I squawked so loud at this that Mr. Rift rushed over to make sure we weren't at each other's throats. In the throes of indignation, I very nearly toppled clean out of my chair.

Wist accusing *me* of being difficult to read? I strove to convey my outrage to Mr. Rift, but somehow I don't think he fully got it. Meanwhile, Wist watched me flail with what may or may not have been a ghostly hint of a smile. Believe me, that girl knew exactly what she was doing.

27

When I returned to the healer dorms that evening, the steward passed me an envelope formed from decorative pleats of interlocking colored paper. I opened it to find a party invitation in the traditional style, inscribed like a poem on a single vertical sheet.

On Saturday afternoon—the very next day—I followed the address on the invitation to the Shien brothers' beachfront villa. (First Wist made me stop to meet her at one of the cactus street lamps a block away. So at least I didn't have to arrive alone.)

It was my first time seeing Wist in the summer mage uniform, with its lighter-toned fabric and nautical styling. She wore her solid-rimmed glasses, too. Perhaps to satisfy Nerium's demands. And long dangling earrings, with a whole tassel of strands that hung like thin silver chains past the bottom of the mage collar around her neck.

Cuttings hung with them. One line of light on each side, the width of a bright hair. Just enough magic to lessen the weight on her ears.

"Didn't know you had piercings," I commented.

Her braid twisted itself uncomfortably behind her. "An old gift from Ficus."

The holes in her ears or the jewelry that hung from them?

I didn't ask.

"Man," I said. "Anyone ever give you a gift you actually wanted?"

Wist glanced up at the sky. A true summer blue, almost periwinkle in parts, dotted here and there with a lazy spackling of translucent clouds.

"If you have to think about it that much, that's a no," I advised her.

I too was in uniform. No different from any other season, except with the hanging ends of my sleeves bound up behind me. All healer students did that in summer, baring our arms to above the elbow.

There was no point, after all, in attempting to blend in. No matter what I wore, no one would mistake me for a mage.

I'll admit to being a little tense when we first walked up to the property. Wist's obvious stiffness didn't help. I was grateful, for once, to spot the black-headed gulls running surveillance overhead.

Don't ask me what I expected to happen at this shindig. Mentally speaking, I'd braced myself to be cast on a bonfire as a human sacrifice.

Instead, in the first few moments after we slipped inside the mansion, I went almost completely unnoticed. Any eyes that grazed us went immediately to Wist.

Presumably everyone knew the elder two Shien brothers. And if they knew the Shien brothers, they must have heard of Wisteria Shien.

Intentionally or otherwise, she did cut a striking figure. Once we crossed the threshold, she drew herself up so straight that she seemed to have grown a solid five inches.

Most of the people here were adults. Most of them were mages. But not all. Knee-high children ran underfoot, a mix of mages and subliminals.

I suppose most mages did choose to keep all their blood children. Even those born without any usable magical power. They just wouldn't get top billing. And they definitely wouldn't ascend to head of the family.

What was the last time I'd been to any sort of event like this? A neighborhood barbecue back in the city, maybe. Or an autumn festival in one of our local parks last year.

Normally I'd keep myself busy by chatting with strangers. The old people resting in quiet corners looked like a prime target. Alternatively, I'd chase around the most energetic kids, or find someone's pet to play with. I'd never been shy.

Here, however, I stuck to hovering in Wist's shadow. I had no idea how elite mage families would react to some random healer student throwing balls at their children. Or loping around growling in the role of a pretend monster.

I began to relax when it became apparent that our hosts had better things to do than torment us. Shien Nerium, deep in conversation with other mages, barely found time to smile and wave.

As for Shien Ficus, I only spotted his golden head from behind. He was talking to Tempus, one of the few other Guralta students in attendance.

I paused to study them from across the high-ceilinged room.

The long cut and orange tinge of Tempus's bleached hair made it seem rather as if he'd tried and failed to pull off the same look as Shien Ficus.

They were right around the same height, too.

Tempus leaned in much closer than he needed to. It wasn't that rowdy in here. People spoke and laughed at a cultured pitch, properly modulated for the setting—the harmony pierced only by the occasional raw shrieks of passing children.

"That idiot," I muttered, watching Tempus watch Ficus. "Now I get it."

Wist put a hand on my back. She nudged me out of the path of a man coming through with a serving tray. "Hm?"

"Tempus." I elbowed her until she looked in the right direction. "He's practically slobbering. Has he always been that mad for your brother?"

"Ah. Well. A lot of people are." Wist spoke in noncommittal tones. As if she felt a bit sorry for Tempus, almost.

I snorted. "The power of a pretty face."

Out back awaited a ridiculously blue infinity pool, one already full of lithe swimmers. From certain angles, it looked as if the pool waters extended all the way to the sea. An extravagant optical illusion.

And a totally unnecessary one, from my perspective. Why travel to an island if you were just going to float mindlessly in a sanitized pool?

If I were the ocean, I'd be thoroughly offended. Fish pee and sharp shells underfoot and the threat of stinging jellyfish: that's the price you're supposed to pay for the taste of the air, the somnolent sound of the waves.

Needless to say, neither Wist nor I had brought swimsuits. Without knowing what lay in store for us, it didn't seem too smart to risk getting caught dripping and barefoot.

Wist refused to touch any of the party food. As children in swimsuits reached up to gobble from the serving tables, I turned to her and asked if it were safe to eat. The crab legs looked awfully tempting.

"Should be fine," said Wist.

"You're not hungry at all?"

She extracted a slim can of tuna from her pocket and spun it between her fingers with unexpected finesse. "If I am, I have this."

I watched her put the can back from whence it had come. I slid a half-step closer and dropped my voice. "You never explained what your brothers used to do to your meals."

"If I went into detail, you'd lose your appetite."

"I'm in the den of the enemy," I said. "I don't have a whole lot of appetite to begin with."

The slender hanging ends of her earrings were right at eye level for me, pooling on her collarbone. The silvery chains winked and stirred and caught the light even when she held herself quite still.

"The poison wasn't so bad," Wist said with an air of contemplation.

"Excuse me?"

"Sometimes they put—stuff—in my food that doesn't bear mentioning in polite company."

"I'm not polite company," I told her. "But sure. Okay. Given your druthers, you preferred poison. Like what? Cyanide?"

The earrings rippled when she shook her head. "Toxic substances from around the manor. Pesticide. Cleaning fluid. Industrial glue and paint. Some types of medication. They made a game of it."

"Sounds like they made a game of everything."

"They'd mix it in my stew or my sauce or my soup. Make me eat or drink it. Then see if I could invent a skill to protect myself before the symptoms got too bad to keep going."

She spoke as if it were something that had happened to an entirely different person. At best a distant acquaintance. She spoke as if explaining the rules of an obscure regional sport.

"Not much of a game," I said at last.

"I preferred it to dirt," Wist replied. "I preferred it to mold and rotting meat and—"

She stopped. I made no more mention of the party food.

We retreated to a deck overlooking the pool out back. Few other people had ventured this high up.

From here we could see the grass-peppered dunes and untrodden sand that lay between the pool and the sea. Today the ocean bore distinct patches of different colors, jade green and muddy brown and deep sapphire. I couldn't remember why that happened. The shape of the currents, perhaps, or changing depths.

Coming to this gathering in daylight did feel somehow safer than having to show up late at night. The problem was that it left a very long time between now and our ten o'clock curfew.

I suggested staying for half an hour and then slipping away. There were plenty of other guests, what with all the mage vacationers and their respective retinues. No one would miss us. No one would miss a student healer named Asa Clematis, at any rate.

Wist said we'd know when it was permissible to leave. Now was not that time yet. Sneak away early, and her brothers would find a way to retaliate.

I privately suspected that they needed no pretext to retaliate. She could expect the same treatment no matter how she behaved, no matter what she did or didn't do to appease them. But I kept my mouth shut. I deferred to Wist. The Shiens were her family; she was the expert here.

This villa, it turned out, was no ordinary rental. The entire property belonged to the Shien clan, land and all.

I asked Wist if vacationing at Guralta Isle was a Shien tradition. She said she'd heard of relatives visiting the island back when Nerium and Ficus were still in school. But most of that took place before her time. Nerium had graduated the year they adopted her.

A few older mages down in the pool spied us up on the balcony. They called out to Wist.

I'd figured this would be coming sooner or later. I motioned her onward.

Wist looked over her shoulder as if expecting me to follow.

"No way," I said. "Don't need them asking who I am. I can entertain myself for a bit."

She went on her way down the stairs to the pool. Alone, I wandered back inside.

There was plenty to gawk at now that I'd overcome my initial paranoia about being chopped up and devoured by a secret cult of mage cannibals. Glittery aquarium fish swum about in glass-plated ceilings and floors, rife with seaweed as frilly and colorful as any terrestrial garden of summer flowers.

A few people handed me dirty plates as I passed. I'd thought the Guralta student uniform would be fairly recognizable. But maybe that only applied to mages. Maybe this outfit made me look like part of the event staff on duty.

I went looking for an inconspicuous place to offload my stack of dirty dishes. Soon I thought I'd found the kitchen. Instead it turned out to be a genteel open bar framed by decorative wooden lattices.

I set the plates on the far end of the counter when no one was looking, then turned my back on them. In lieu of anything better to do, I poured myself some mango juice. I leaned over to read the sepia label on a bottle of spica liquor. I'd been telling the truth about not being hungry.

Traces of old-fashioned piano music drifted over from a nearby room. It kept stopping and starting, as if someone who hadn't played in decades was fooling around at the bench.

I couldn't decide if the melody fit the scene or not. The brilliant fish trapped underfoot seemed to feel similarly. They darted back and forth with no heed for the piano's halting rhythm—and, I fancied, a distinct air of ambivalence.

"Clematis?"

I won't claim that I recognized her voice as soon as I heard it.

But a painful premonition pierced me anyway. A instinctive hope bound up with horror. I prayed to be granted some tiny fraction of Wist's granite implacability. Every little bit would help.

I swear it worked. By the time I turned to look at Yarrow, I could feel no expression left on my face at all.

28

I HADN'T SEEN Yarrow in years. I knew that much by heart. But in the moment I was too frazzled to count the years, to understand exactly how long it had been.

She was still young. Young enough to remain a senior at the academy, if she hadn't left early.

Young enough to not yet be considered a full adult, at least under certain sections of Osmanthian law.

The anonymous pianist stumbled and tripped and replayed the same phrase over and over, somewhere out of sight. Through the wall, a man and a woman laughed deep in their bellies.

Even now, in flat slippers, Yarrow had a couple inches on me. She wore a sundress: modest, calf-length, with a soft pattern of yellow flowers and a diaphanous long-sleeved blouse on beneath it. She had her hair tucked behind her small round ears and a dark blue bond thread hanging loose around her neck.

I hadn't spotted her bondmate yet. Then again, it was a very large house.

My glass of mango juice felt cold and slippery. I set it shakily down on the counter. No one appeared to pay us any heed.

"Sorry." I gestured impotently at my uniform. "You tried to warn me."

Her face wasn't nearly as frozen as I remembered. She blinked at me as if she had no idea what I was talking about. Then she covered her mouth with her hand and laughed—as quiet and breathy as my own anxious whispering. But her laughter had always sounded like that.

When she lowered her hand, there was no frigid smile. No wide terrorized eyes.

I'd ragged on Tempus when I saw him with Shien Ficus. Truth is, though, it takes one to know one. I could be every bit as vulnerable to the hypnotic power of a beautiful face. Yet what churned in me when I gazed back at Yarrow was still a kind of sick fear. I recognized this girl, this woman. This healer. But I didn't *know* her.

Nor had I known her—not really—back when I was a kid who kept running headlong into her waist to demand hugs. Who made her brush my hair, in the times when I had hair long enough for brushing.

She turned to the counter and began making herself a drink.

"I was worried about you, Clematis," she said, slow and gentle. She dropped ice cubes one by one into her glass. "I think I gave you the wrong impression."

"Is it okay for you to be here?" I asked.

"I hope so. We received invitations."

"Your bondmate's clan." I spoke sotto voce. "Do they—what kind of relationship do they have with the Shiens?"

"Mutual rivals," said Yarrow. Her mouth curved. "No need to look like that. It isn't a blood feud."

"What did you come for? Reconnaissance?"

She took an inquisitive sip. The taste seemed to please her. "To enjoy a pleasant afternoon," she said. "To look at stars in the evening."

Our eyes met. Yarrow touched her bond thread as if to make sure it were still there. The mango juice turned to liquid queasiness in the pit of my stomach.

Her look of peace fractured. But only for the barest of seconds.

I struggled to swallow. I kept my voice low. "The last time I saw you—"

"So here's where you were."

Someone clapped me on the back. Another voice I couldn't recognize.

Not, in this case, because I couldn't tell who it was.

Because I'd never heard her talk like that before. Not once.

Wist sounded—

Wist sounded perfectly normal.

She came up beside me and slung an arm over my shoulder. As if we were the kind of buddies who did this all the time. No big deal.

I whipped my head sideways to gawk at her. She tossed Yarrow a relaxed smile of greeting. Adjusted her glasses. Touched my glass of mango juice with a questioning look.

I nodded numbly.

Wist picked up my mango juice and drank nearly half of it with a few fluid bobs of her throat. Afterward she set down the glass again. Let out a small sigh. Dabbed her lips with a napkin.

"From the Gwindel family?" she said to Yarrow. Casual and friendly.

Yarrow made a movement that I suppose might qualify as a curtsy. "I hope we're not imposing."

"Not at all," Wist assured her. "My brothers are always happy to broaden their circle."

The only part of her manner that felt remotely familiar was the metronome-like way her braid swished back and forth in the air behind her.

"We grew up in the same neighborhood," Yarrow said to Wist, dipping her head at me.

I was frankly much too flabbergasted to contribute anything of intelligence to the conversation. But I nevertheless felt compelled to flap my lips.

"Yarrow went to Guralta, too," I said, as if this meant something.

A thoughtful look came over Wist's face. "We might have met before. At one of the year-end banquets, perhaps?"

"Certainly," said Yarrow. "I—"

She stilled like an animal hearing a sound too high-pitched for our human ears. She rubbed her bond thread between her fingers. She glanced down and absentmindedly smoothed the front of her sundress.

She smiled sweetly at us, as if she hadn't been in the middle of saying anything at all, and excused herself.

"Bondmate must've called her," Wist muttered under her breath as we watched her leave.

I glanced up, startled all over again. Wist's arm released my shoulders.

Mere seconds ago, she'd sounded just as sociable as Shien Nerium. Now all expression had vanished from her voice, her face.

"Didn't know you could do that," I said helplessly.

She leaned her weight on a stool by the counter. "I try not to."

"I can tell."

"A couple times a year is my limit."

"Why's that?"

She pitched forward without warning, dropping her forehead on my shoulder. Her long earrings glittered against the fabric of my school uniform.

I stood motionless. To be honest, my first instinct had been to leap out of the way. It took a whole lot of willpower to make myself stay there and catch her.

"It's exhausting," she said, muffled.

I patted Wist clumsily on the back. Her braid circled around behind me as if it were about to pull me in closer. My breath felt strangely high and quick in my chest.

My internal scales had gone akilter; they didn't know how to measure anything anymore. I'd come face-to-face with Yarrow, who I used to love so much—a child's love, sure, but one giddy enough to keep me up half the night. I'd stood right across from her and felt so little that the very absence of it ached.

Only now, with Wist leaning on me, did something akin to the old yearning start to unfurl. It felt like the senseless urge to press on a bruise.

The amateur piano music from a couple rooms over had ceased. The would-be player must've grown weary and given up. A tingle of paranoia ascended my spine.

There were too many people here. Too many mages. None of them cared about me, surely. But they might care about keeping an eye on Wisteria Shien.

After some time, I convinced Wist to venture out on the sand. We were still in sight of the villa. And we weren't the only partygoers to wander out here, although the rest appeared to be couples. Our hosts could hardly accuse us of skipping out early.

Tiny sanderlings and larger sandpipers scurried about in the dark wet swathes where the surf met the shore. We couldn't stray too far from the house looming prettily behind the dune grasses.

I settled for walking circles around the birds' tiny footprints, soon washed away into nothing. The usual colorful fingernail-sized clams dug themselves down into the sand. I crouched, momentarily inspired by the urge to dig for mole crabs.

It wasn't the prospect of dirty hands that stopped me—it was the thought of how Wist might react. A nice plump mole crab would be just about the size and shape of a wingless cicada.

I straightened my knees, dusting my palms off on my long Guralta skirts. The pleats were already sprinkled with sand, anyway.

"Surprised me when you downed my juice," I said. "Thought you were dead set on boycotting all your brothers' food and drink."

"Something came over me." Wist spoke as if she herself failed to understand what had made her hand take the glass.

She shook her head a bit. "Notice anything unusual at the party?"

"Like what?"

"The atmosphere."

"I don't have much experience socializing with high-society mages. Not sure I could tell you what's unusual and what's not. Atmospherically speaking."

"A lot of people seem unusually ... happy."

I laughed in the back of my throat. "I'd be pretty damn happy, too, if I were part of the ruling class."

"Consider your friend, then."

"My friend?"

"The healer from the Gwindel clan."

"You mean Yarrow?"

"Nothing about her struck you as strange?"

I opened my mouth to deny it. No words emerged. When I last spoke to Yarrow, years ago, she'd been just as graceful. She'd also been all but begging for the kind of help that neither I nor anyone could give her. She'd been locked inside her own skin and head with her bondmate, where no one else could penetrate.

Yarrow at the party had not been the same as before she bonded. But she'd come off as relaxed and comfortable, her smile unforced.

"You're implying something," I said to Wist. "What?"

She tipped her head at the pool and the villa. "A lot of them are on psychoactive magic. The younger set, anyway."

"Something to perk them up?" I guessed. This party would be a far bloodier tableau if they were using that awful hallucinogenic cutting Tempus had hurled at me on the last day of hunting season.

"Something like that."

"Thought you guys frowned on mind-altering magic."

"The older generations do. Most use is illegal."

That got my attention. "What if a—uh, concerned passerby reported psychoactive cuttings running rampant here? Could we get your brothers busted? Fined? Kicked off the island? Sent to jail for a night?"

"Doubt anything would come of it," said Wist. "The Shien name has a lot of pull. And they know where to draw the line."

"Damn."

I considered, then dismissed, the idea of proposing a stroll to the nearest wooden fishing pier. It didn't look that far down the beach from here. But a round trip might end up taking longer than it seemed.

I asked Wist what she knew about Yarrow's bondmate. The only S-Class mage from the Gwindel clan.

He was close to forty now, Wist told me. A respected chancellor to an older relative who held a seat on the Board of Magi. Give the younger Gwindel another few decades, and he might very well ascend to a Board seat himself.

I had nothing personal against the Gwindels. Nor did I think Yarrow would ever have chosen me instead, even in a world without mages or healers. I was fine with that. I was over it.

At the same time, if we lived in that hypothetical world without mages or healers, I was absolutely positive that Yarrow would never have chosen her current bondmate, either.

Nothing against him. But he was over twice her age, a conceited man with a beer belly.

Not that I'd ever exchanged words with him. Not that I'd ever seen him up close. Those few far-off glimpses I'd gotten were more than enough. A comfortable superiority coated him like grease caking machinery.

Now here she was, shaped by years of being his bondmate. The path smoothed by a sprinkle of soothing under-the-table psychoactive cuttings. Just enough to take off the edge.

Now, perhaps, she preferred this life of being bonded to a future Board member. Even though her old self would surely have wanted anything else.

I turned to Wist and caught her eying up the pier. Further beyond it lay more beach, and more beach, and finally the ruins at the end of the island. But that was too far to see from here.

The moment I stopped paying attention to the sand, something grabbed me by the ankle.

I squeaked. I stumbled into Wist. I sounded like a dog getting stepped on.

Wist staggered, but managed to hold her ground. I was too busy shaking my right leg to pay her much heed. I seized her shoulders for balance and furiously kicked to break free.

I didn't make much headway. My foot felt bolted in place. The thing around my ankle was neither a skein of seaweed nor a mutant mole crab nor any other sort of creature from the depths of the ocean.

It was sand in the shape of a human hand. Damp and opalescent with magic. Compressed to the hardness of sandstone, yet gripping me like flesh. The worst part was the sheer air-warping heat. I was absolutely convinced I'd get second-degree burns from these hot sandy fingers on me, if I hadn't already.

"Wist—" No idea what I planned to say next, but I said it anyway. "Wist—"

She stood rock-still. More hands clawed at her ankles and legs, anchoring her in place. Far more than on mine.

"I'm coming." She spoke as if addressing the hands themselves.

The one that had been holding me vanished in a crumble of steaming wet clumps. I immediately raised my right ankle for a closer look, heedless of how I had to hop around on my left foot to keep from falling.

The skin hadn't melted off, at any rate. I observed an almost disappointing lack of visible injuries.

The hands clutching at Wist dissolved more reluctantly. They released her only when she turned to face the villa, the darkening ocean at her back.

"Ficus," she said, as if to explain the grasping magic.

"He could've picked a less dramatic way to call you back inside."

"He could have," Wist agreed, "but he wouldn't."

Her brothers' business was with her, it seemed, not with me. Not yet, anyway.

Wist disappeared somewhere in the mansion to have an audience with Shien Ficus and Shien Nerium. I plunked myself down in a pool chair up on the deck and rubbed my ankle resentfully. If Wist was the one they wanted, why waste magical energy picking on me?

After a few minutes, I realized that the Shien siblings must not be the only mages gathering in some other unseen room. The population of the infinity pool had dropped exponentially.

I spotted even fewer adult mages indoors—though babbling mage children still scrambled around, now with healer or subliminal guests watching over them.

Which was why, when Tempus's bleached head caught my eye, I strolled on over to needle him.

Nothing I could say here would serve as adequate payback for hunting season. But it might amuse me. On an occasion such as this, trapped in a den of magical strangers, the prospect of a little personal amusement seemed just about priceless.

Tempus hovered by a banquet table, intent on composing a plate of hors d'oeuvres that he appeared to have no interest in actually eating.

"All the other mages went off somewhere," I observed. "They didn't want you?"

He paused over his artistic arrangement of scallops and shrimp. He turned slowly. He regarded me as if I'd crawled out of a garbage pail like a rat on my way to greet him.

"They're just showing Wisteria off," he said.

"You weren't invited?"

"I wasn't interested."

I found myself startled anew by the aggressive softness of his voice. It was like his visceral disgust at having to trade words with me stood locked in battle with his well-bred impulse to present an elegant facade. His smooth speech forcibly concealed rough fault lines in the manner of caulk pouring into cracks.

"Funny," I said. "Wouldn't have thought you'd pass up a chance to hang all over Shien Ficus."

Tempus, having only just finished constructing a delicate pyramid of seafood, nearly dropped the whole thing. He put his plate down—more loudly than he needed to—and shoved his hands in his uniform pockets. To hide their unsteadiness, I'd bet.

"And you?" he asked, with commendable composure. "Shouldn't you be sucking blood from Wisteria's hip?"

It took me a moment to parse his meaning. "Like a tick?" I guessed. "No, I'm afraid we've both been abandoned."

"I haven't—"

"Must be a lot of competition for Shien Ficus," I said. A stab in the dark, but it seemed to hit flesh. "And he's well out of school. A bit old for you, isn't he?"

Tempus was beginning to take on an expression very similar to the one he'd worn when he tried to make me cross a campus tightrope. If only I had another bottle of Pepper's ultimate hot sauce to shake at him.

I nailed him with my best unpleasant smile. Then I tossed off a breezy farewell and darted away to the safety of another room.

I wasn't worried about any immediate repercussions. Tempus would consider himself too dignified to chase me down in front of witnesses. At a Shien-hosted beach party, no less.

In the middle of my flight, I ran once more into Yarrow.

She was in a room with a piano. Possibly the same room where other mystery guests had been tickling the keys and carousing while we spoke earlier, over by the latticework bar.

Now Yarrow addressed a small cluster of healers and subliminals. They appeared oddly deferential.

I wanted to eavesdrop, but couldn't justify getting close enough. Instead I contented myself with exploring the fringes of the room.

Generous skylights made the space feel like a solarium. There was a fireplace tucked in one of the walls, cold and ashen.

At first glance this struck me as strange. But even people living right on the beach might enjoy a hearty fire in winter.

My waiting paid off. As I pretended to examine the spines of books stashed in a library-length shelf, Yarrow's little circle started peeling apart. A few more minutes, and I looked up to see her sitting alone at the piano bench.

I turned, hands in my pockets. "You used to play."

Yarrow gave a half-shake of her head. "Barely."

"Forgot it all?"

"My family had a miniature upright piano. Remember? Nothing so large as this."

"So try playing it," I said.

Yarrow declined.

With her seated at the piano and me standing, I was taller for once. Obviously. But it felt very strange. It would be easier to talk to her if I pretended she were a brand new acquaintance.

I cleared my throat. "You're here for vacation?"

A patient nod.

"How long will you and the Gwindels stay on the island?"

"Until around the end of September, I think."

Same as the Shien brothers. How did upper-class mages find so much free time to lounge around by the sea? Didn't they have jobs?

Not normal commuter jobs, I suppose. Investments, trust funds, family businesses. Or cushy government positions with enough leave for them to faff around at the shore without a care in the world.

"What's so special about the end of September?" I grumbled.

"Your birthday," said Yarrow.

I'm not proud to admit this, but I was momentarily dumbfounded.

"My birthday," I said, recovering. "Of course. The most important event of the year. No, let me guess. Mr. Gwindel wants to watch the Guralta Cup?"

"A lot of mages travel to the island to see it in person."

The Guralta Cup was some kind of mage contest or tournament. Exclusively for upperclassmen, if I remembered correctly. Hadn't realized it was popular enough for adult mages from all around the country to come watch.

"There are shells back in the dorm," I said abruptly. No point in dancing around this. "Shells with Transceiver on them."

"I remember."

"Is there any way I can reach you? Just while you're here on the island. I won't waste your time."

"Reach me for what?" Yarrow inquired.

She kept her face pleasant and neutral. Though the mere sight of her didn't strike at my heart in the same way as it used to, it was still rather nerve-wracking to stand there and make demands of her.

"For business," I said.

"Business."

"Mutually beneficial business," I insisted. "You said the Gwindels have a rivalry with the Shiens. Might want to talk a bit more about that someday."

She pressed one of the white piano keys, so slowly and tenderly that it scarcely made a sound. I still jumped a little. The room felt very large and expensive, and Asa Clematis felt very small.

Yarrow wore a slight smile. "Bold of you to make such a proposal here and now."

"I'm just a student," I said. "An unaffiliated healer. I'm no one important."

She reached up and tapped her hairpin. A slender thing. Minimalistic design, black lacquer finish. Plus a surface-level coating of magic.

Then she told me how I could speak with her through the transceiver shells in the healer dorm.

I excused myself soon after. This new Yarrow made me nervous. In an entirely different way from the Yarrow I'd known as a child back home in the city.

29

IT WAS EVENING—though still sunny—by the time Wist reappeared. Summer days stretched a long way. They felt even longer when you were skulking about in a rococo beach house owned by the Shien clan.

In Wist's absence, I acquainted myself with the artwork on the walls. An incongruent mixture of dead Shien portraits and dramatic sea monsters.

I watched the staff whisk away old food, much of it untouched, and lay out new platters. I dodged the smallest mage children, some barely old enough to be mobile. They'd developed a game of barreling into people's legs like cannonballs.

Even after older mages started filtering back onto the first floor, I didn't have a clue where they'd all been gathered. A secret basement? They reappeared in small knots, twos and threes, avidly gossiping. Their chatter washed past me like birdsong.

As I strained to overhear them, a familiar magic crunched at the back of my awareness. It was a sensation like the sound of crushing a dry autumn leaf.

I turned, puzzled. No one else reacted.

I followed the faint crackle of magic to what appeared to be a secondary kitchen, all bright lights and black marble and sparkling pastries. It had been put to use, I deduced, as a staging area exclusively for desserts.

No one stopped me from slipping inside. A few staff members fussed with something at the opposite end of the room, their backs turned. Subliminals, all of them. The air bore such a rich buttery scent that you could've bagged it and sold it as a treat in its own right.

The black marble counters weren't a pure black like Wist's hair. They were shot through with gray and white, a pattern reminiscent of streaks of fat in raw meat.

Wist stood with her hands braced on one of those counters, head bent over an arrangement of watercolor-tone cupcakes. They looked more like decorative flowers than something you were supposed to bite into and destroy.

I stepped closer. Her magic crinkled. Nothing happened.

Upon closer inspection, I realized she was using her old cupcake-cleaving skill. She split them in perfect halves, without leaving any visible seams in the frosting. No one would know the cupcakes had been cut until they tried to pick one up.

On the one hand, you could argue that she was doing the caterers a favor. These cupcakes were rather too extravagant to be eaten as-is.

On the other hand, there was the fixed tension in her shoulders. The way she severed them rhythmically, one at a time. This whole scene had the air of a murderer repeatedly plunging their knife back into a long-dead body.

"Wist?" I spoke quietly, not wanting to startle her. Or draw other people closer.

She stopped magically stabbing the tender cupcakes. She tilted her head to regard me.

"Don't take this the wrong way," I said, "but it smells like you drank the whole bar."

"Yes," Wist pronounced. She put her hand on my head. As if she'd mistaken me for an animal demanding pets.

"Yes ... to what?"

"I was on parade," she said. "They needed me drunk. To better demonstrate that famous self-control. Look how well we taught her, he told them."

She stopped to pat my hair, then added, "Nerium, I mean." As if it weren't already obvious from context.

The dessert staff were all the way across the room from us. But this didn't seem like a conversation to hold in sight of strangers.

I took Wist's arm to pull her elsewhere. Past the pool and back down to the beach. Or to the garden out front, facing the street.

She stayed rooted by the counter, immovable. It felt like tugging on a tree trunk.

She reached up, heedless of how I yanked at her. She pressed at her forehead as if testing her skull for soft spots.

"At least have some water," I said. "I can—"

Now that same testing hand touched the side of my neck. We contemplated each other with a kind of mutual bewilderment. Wist's fingertips were almost cool enough to induce shivers. The whole room felt unnaturally chilly, in fact. Perhaps they kept it that way on purpose, so as to better preserve the delicate sweets.

Wist looked at me as if I were the next cupcake in line to be split.

"...Water sounds nice," she said after an excruciating wait.

If I'd been drinking, I'd have done a spit-take.

I started to duck away from the tingling of her fingers on my neck.

Then I thought better of it. I caught at her bare wrist instead. This time she followed me without complaint, loose and pliant, as though she'd never resisted in the first place.

After a brief detour to find canned water, I got her outside.

The garden in front of the house was filled with spiky tooth-edged succulents that looked more like hostile sculptures than living plants. I took her out back instead, to a landing midway down the long stairs that descended from the pool area to the sand.

The lingering heat outside felt downright pleasant after the shivery air of the staging kitchen. From here we could look up at the pool's weir wall and moat-like catch basin, hidden structures that together cast the illusion of endless azure water. We could hear bright splashing and muddled voices, but not individual words.

Occasional figures—seemingly unrelated to the party up in the villa—passed by on the beach below. They hauled fishing rods or walked big floofy dogs, much larger than the dainty bird-boned specimens I was used to seeing back in the city.

I asked Wist if her brothers were finally done with us. They'd already used her to put on a show for their mage guests, according to Tempus. What more did they need?

"Nerium requested for us to stay longer."

"What for?"

"He wants to speak with you after the party."

"I gotta be back at the dorm by ten."

"There are a lot of young families here. It won't run late."

If we weren't allowed to escape yet, she really did need to hydrate.

I held up the sealed can of plain water I'd pilfered from a fridge. Wist eyed it as if she didn't know what to do next. I popped the top open and shoved it into her hands.

As she drank, I spotted dried curls of old bird poop anointing the prettily painted railing around the wooden landing. Even the Shiens overlooked a few uncouth details here and there, it seemed.

Wist put her can down on the flat railing. (She narrowly missed grinding it in said bird poop.)

"Maybe I should have taken both legs," she said. She tapped her fingernails on the side of the can.

I kept my mouth shut. She wasn't done yet.

"Maybe I should've taken his arms. Maybe I should've taken his life."

I pictured Shien Nerium. His cane. His unconventional gait.

"His left leg's a prosthetic," I guessed.

"Yes."

"Because of you? Something you did?"

"Because of me."

"But that's not why he started torturing you."

"No. It started as soon as they adopted me."

My eyes stayed on the sea. Low, tired waves crawling up the brown sand. Just doing the bare minimum.

"No one can judge you for having violent thoughts," I said.

"If I acted on them, I'd become exactly what Nerium already thinks I am."

"What's that? A mage with enough latent power to absolutely crush him to bits?"

"Something monstrous," Wist said.

"What's wrong with being a monster?"

She didn't try to answer.

I fingered the imperial coin in my pocket. Unable to either force it on Wist or toss it back in Shien Nerium's face, I'd kept carrying it around with me.

"The Kraken got named for a monster," I told her, "and she's the greatest mage who ever lived. Be like the Kraken. Embrace it."

"Did the Kraken embrace it?"

"Who knows? History is all hearsay anyway."

"That sounds vaguely deep," Wist said. "But."

"But?"

"You're only a few points away from failing history class."

I bristled. "Don't bring my grades into this. I'd retain more if the curriculum were less biased."

With the salty sea breeze sweeping away the stench of alcohol, I'd almost forgotten that Wist was sopping drunk. Not that it had done much to affect her demeanor.

I did wonder about the legality of her brothers making her consume so much. But perhaps drinking laws were different for mages—as were so many other parts of the legal code.

"Clematis."

"What?"

"I want to touch the back of your head," Wist told me.

"Um. I see." No idea how to interpret that one. "Sure?"

The ocean air dulled her glasses. The metallic strands of her earrings glimmered like tinsel, undaunted.

I thought she might pat me like a dog again.

Instead she slid her fingers through the stubby hair at the nape of my neck.

I went still in the way that you might go still with a giant wasp swooping past your head.

Somehow, when I glanced up, I'd figured she would be much closer. She wasn't, not at all. Her hand moved as if seeking something to grab harder. But my hair was too short to pull at.

Indignation boiled up from my belly to my chest to my throat. Wist was dead wrong if she expected me to lean in, to seize the front of her uniform, to go on tiptoe to close the gap. She was dead wrong if she thought I wouldn't pull a face of disgust at the overly sweet drunken scent on her.

I started to shove her away. My hands froze on her shoulders.

A black-headed gull perched on the railing, glistening with magic. Watching us avidly.

"This is private property," I hissed at it. "Shoo!"

It was bold as a city pigeon. It didn't flap off until I reached out to swat at it. Even then, it only retreated to a stretch of railing five or six feet away from us.

I took an exaggerated step back from Wist. I held up my hands.

"Look." I spoke for the bird's benefit. "Nothing happened."

It appeared unconvinced.

Stymied, I dropped my voice. "I know I'm the nearest warm body and all," I whispered to Wist, "but what happened to that legendary self-control of yours? Finish your water! Clear your head!"

She obediently drank the rest of her can. Then she murmured something I didn't catch. I would've pressed her on it, but the surveillance gull kept observing us with those distinctive unblinking eyes, rimmed in subtle dark red and two bright slashes of white.

We fled inside to evade the laughing gull and its brethren. We'd been off-campus and outdoors, within earshot of the busy infinity pool. I'd pushed her away. That had to count for something.

Besides, there were far sketchier things going on at this party. Smug clouds of contentment and glittering smiles: the product of illicit psychoactive magic. Or so Wist claimed.

30

To my surprise, the guests really did start to dissipate around sunset. They would be back later for stargazing in another couple of hours, around the time when I needed to leave to make curfew.

Gloved staff wheeled elaborate telescopic devices out onto the upper-level decks and the patio by the pool. As the lilting rhythms of polite conversation drained out of the villa, an impressively peevish-looking Tempus popped up to summon me to a more private set of rooms.

He made a point of not inviting Wist. She followed anyway.

We passed through the piano parlor, its glassy ceiling now dark. Beyond lay a hallway lined with slender vases that protruded from the walls like water spouts, fountaining out long tufts of dried flowers and decorative grass.

At the end of it all, we found ourselves in a sprawling den.

Shien Ficus stood across from an elaborate life-size painting of a crowd scene. The canvas filled an entire wall.

He beckoned to Tempus, who immediately trotted on over.

Then Shien Ficus raised one hand and tossed something with an easy flick of his wrist. A dart sank into the pupil of a painted woman's right eye.

Tempus dashed forward for a closer look. Upon returning to Ficus, he bent to scribble on a notepad. As if he'd been recruited to keep score.

Ficus reached for his next dart. He kept them in an elaborate carrying case that looked equally suitable for storing surgical instruments.

I could already see it happening: Shien Ficus would throw each dart as soon as he felt ready. Regardless of whether or not Tempus had leapt out of the way. And I'd bet anything that Ficus wasn't using the safer soft-tipped type of dart, either.

"Tea? Spica? Coffee?"

I looked to my left. Shien Nerium sat at the corner of an expansive leather couch.

The side table held a folded-up fan and several crystal glasses half-full of amber liquid. No ice.

That could've been the color of tea or spica, sure, but it wasn't the first thing that came to mind.

I demurred.

Honestly, I was still distracted by the decor. Not the painting-turned-dartboard, no. Nearly every other wall was mounted with enormous taxidermied sea turtles. They varied in hue from shiny topaz brown to a yellow-white like true ivory. They varied in size, too, but even the smallest had to be at least as long as Wist was tall.

"Antiques." Shien Nerium sounded rueful. "I hope you understand."

"Indeed." I mean, what else was there to say?

The whole time, Wist was right there, just a step or two behind me.

No one acknowledged her presence. Not Tempus or Ficus, now deeply immersed in their bizarre game of darts. And not Shien Nerium, resting on the couch with a genial smile and his artificial left leg stretched straight out in front of him.

I assumed his left leg was the artificial one, that is. His clothing provided too much coverage to tell from the outside.

"I fear you might have gotten the wrong impression of us," said Shien Nerium.

"Nothing to fear," I said at once. " I'm nobody, right?"

He took a sip of his so-called tea. After setting it down, he picked up his folding fan and flicked it open and shut, open and shut. This one had paper the color of charcoal, painted with an elaborate design in tones of dull gold.

"There's a reason I would like you to understand us." He looked up at me through his glasses, opaque with magic. "Won't you humor me?"

I risked a glance back at Wist. Her face was set. She hadn't started pinching me yet.

Guess that meant my response was up to me. Shooting him down and walking away didn't appear to be a legitimate option, though.

"I'm all ears," I told him.

The sharp thump of a dart at the back of the room punctuated my answer. Tempus let out a cry like a wounded kitten.

I might be something of a prophet, after all.

"Imagine," said Shien Nerium, "imagine you knew someone who was clearly destined to be the most powerful living mage in Osmanthus. Perhaps in the entire world."

"Golly gee," I muttered. "Wonder who that could be?"

"Imagine you knew them, and they were a child. Children can be frightening, can't they?"

"What a weird question."

"You've never been startled by a child's cruelty?"

"Children are just people. The only difference is their age."

I'd stopped modulating my choice of words. If Wist prodded me in the back, I'd take that as a sign to try harder.

For now, it didn't seem worth the effort. Whatever his flaws, her brother wasn't too easily offended. At least not in comparison to the likes of touchy Tempus.

"Age makes all the difference in the world," Nerium countered. "They're impressionable, malleable, amoral creatures. Children only know right from wrong because they get indoctrinated with it from birth. And even that level of indoctrination doesn't keep everyone from living spotless, sinless lives—now does it?"

"You can say that again."

He touched his fan to the side of his face. "If you met a child with that much power—a power quite dangerous, I'm sure you'll agree, for any one person to have—what would be the most important thing to teach them?"

I eyed the dead turtles on the walls. "Dunno. How not to be a psychopath?"

"Discipline," Nerium said. "Restraint. The most important thing to teach an overpowered child is a self-control equal to the power inside them. In Wisteria's case, that means frankly inhuman levels of self-control. For her own sake, as well as for the sake of everyone around her."

Something tugged lightly at the back of my uniform, at the dangling excess fabric of my sleeves bound with a sash behind me.

At first I thought Wist might be trying to tell me something. But all she did was keep holding the very end of my sleeve. We stood quite still.

"Oh, and one more thing. Can you guess?"

Nerium still spoke as if Wist were invisible. Not because he couldn't see her. Not because she'd used any sort of magic. Because he hadn't meant to invite her into the room, into the conversation. No need for him to kick her out, I suppose, when he could so meticulously ignore her existence.

"I'm not so good with philosophy," I confessed.

"Humility," he said.

"Humility?"

"If you disagree about how important these lessons are, imagine stripping Wisteria of her self-control and humility."

He smiled with just the sides of his mouth. He patted his left thigh. "She needed it drummed into her. Ironed into her. Seared into her. Made an inextricable part of her. No one is ever going to succeed in stripping that girl of her self-control and humility. And for that, I'm willing to take credit. Much as I might usually avoid the spotlight."

I looked over my shoulder at Wist again. No visible reaction. Even her braid hung calm and relaxed down behind her, swaying only a little from side to side.

But of course. None of this was news to her. She was used to it.

Nerium had plenty of material left in his set. "My parents weren't prepared for what needed to be done after they took her in," he confided. "My brothers and sisters—well, they were scattered in age, but all basically children themselves. I was eighteen when we adopted her. The only one of us near adulthood. And the only one of any age who immediately saw and understood what needed to be done with her."

"Very impressive, sir," I said.

There was a warning tension in my skull.

Wist still held my sleeve without complaint. Ficus kept playing darts, aiming for the defenseless orifices of bustling figures painted in intricate traditional garb. Part of me hoped for him to nail Tempus again. Preferably right in the back of his straw-bleached head.

Screw it. If Wist didn't like what she was about to hear, she could lunge forward and cover my mouth.

She could try to, at any rate. Good luck with that.

I raised my hand as if addressing a teacher. "Question," I said. "A couple questions, actually."

Shien Nerium gestured with his fan for me to continue. So generous.

"Don't you guys base most everything on power? The higher-class the mage, the better." I didn't pause to hear his answer. That much was a given.

"So I ask you this." I cleared my throat. "Weren't you just trying to make her as small as possible in order to defend your own position? Weren't you just angling to protect your own spot as heir to the family? Aren't you the one who benefits most from Wist not having any ambition?"

The magic-clogged glasses studied me for what felt like a very, very long time.

Wist stirred behind me.

"How hurtful," Nerium murmured.

He didn't sound particularly hurt.

"It wasn't easy," he said. "Yet I saw it as my sacred duty. I persevered, despite everything." Again he touched his own leg.

"We've done the world a favor by keeping her humble. Imagine if she grew up spoiled. Her every wish granted. Everyone around her simpering and currying favor." Ever so briefly, his mouth twisted. "Terrifying."

Wist didn't attempt to speak. But I felt her much closer now. Almost close enough to rest her chin on my head.

Rage on my own behalf—now that I knew how to deal with. It was an old and comfortable friend.

Rage on behalf of someone else—that was altogether different. It still retained the power to strike me out of nowhere. To pummel the breath out of me. To paralyze me with its strength.

"Perhaps I need a better analogy," said Shien Nerium. "One might compare having Wist in the family to owning a very large and dangerous dog. It would be perfectly reasonable for most people not to trust that dog.

"If you could trust such a dog, your trust would stem from its training. Handled properly, it would be thoroughly trained not to hurt its masters. It couldn't even conceive of harming them. It would more readily hurt itself first."

I looked pointedly at his left leg. At the cane leaning up against the side table. "Seems like that worked out real well for you."

"All lessons need to be learned somehow."

"While we're being honest with each other," I said, "who's to prove you haven't been milking your leg for sympathy?"

I wished fervently for him to stop smiling. To no avail.

"I don't suppose you've heard the details," Nerium said mildly. "I'll leave out the gruesome parts. Suffice it to say that Wisteria came to the very brink of berserking."

"Figured as much. You don't need to—"

"She didn't obliterate my leg. The bones and flesh remained. If the very same injury had come as the result of, say, a train accident—then my leg could very well have healed to something resembling its original state. Don't underestimate Osmanthian medical magic."

He caressed his left knee.

"Wisteria didn't merely wound me. Her magic lingered in my leg. Cuttings buried like shrapnel, defying extraction. Cuttings to stymie any attempts at treatment. Cuttings to ensure constant, unbearable, incurable pain. The sort of magic best characterized as a genuine curse."

Nerium looked at me over the tops of his glasses. Boring brown eyes; eyes that bore no identifiable malice.

"I didn't need to lose my leg." His voice had gone all distant and fond. "I chose amputation."

"But—"

"It was the only sure way to free myself from the curse. Wisteria couldn't figure out how to undo her own work, wrought half-consciously while on the verge of berserking. Other originators might have been able to offer a solution eventually. But there was no guarantee they'd succeed. And no guarantee that it wouldn't take years.

"It was a terrible curse," Nerium said quietly. "If removing my leg hadn't been an option, I would have killed myself from the pain of it. I planned my death out in great detail. I hope you never have to do the same."

"From the pain of it," repeated a voice behind me, cold and grating.

There was no way Wist didn't notice me flinch.

Shien Nerium pushed his glasses higher up the bridge of his nose, concealing his eyes again.

"From what I remember," said Wist, "I tried to pour all my magical pain into you. To mirror in you what I felt day-to-day. How surprised I was to find that you couldn't take it. To find that you would willingly chop off your leg to be rid of it. No one ever offered to chop off my magic."

Nerium traced the top of his thigh with the end of his folded-up fan. The spot, I would guess, where his prosthetic met a stump of flesh.

"Magical pain and physical pain are two different beasts. As different in nature as physical and mental pain." His voice was soft and fluent where Wist's was harsh and forcibly flattened. "I know of no formula for accurately converting one to the other.

"You didn't make me feel what you felt, Wisteria. You gave me physical pain, immeasurable levels of it. You didn't wish for me to be the same as you. You wished for me to dwell in my own inimitable realm of suffering."

He set his fan aside. He sipped thoughtfully from his crystal tumbler.

"I didn't kill myself. But in some ways I do feel that I died. The pain obliterated what I thought of as my inner self. Blotted me out like a thumb crushing a sugar ant.

"After the amputation, I found myself keenly aware of what I'd lost. At the same time, I felt like a phoenix, miraculously revived from ash and ruin. I had been no one and nothing in comparison to the size of that pain."

"An inspiring story," I said.

"I do hope so."

He clasped his hands together, as if to mark the end of story time, and looked up at Wist again. He was not smiling.

"Wisteria, if you can't resist the temptation to interrupt, I suggest you remove yourself from the source of temptation."

Something wordless passed between them. Not telepathy. Something even my magic perception couldn't pick up on. A taut understanding between siblings, or enemies.

"I'll go make sure Ficus isn't killing Tempus," Wist said without humor.

"An excellent idea," Nerium told her.

It was just the other side of the room. But when Wist left, I longed to dash after her. Even at the risk of getting stabbed by steel-tipped darts.

"Can't stay long," I said swiftly. "Gotta be tucked in bed at my dorm by ten. School rules."

Shien Nerium gestured at a cuckoo clock hanging on the wall between two bloated stuffed turtles. "We have at least half an hour to speak at our leisure. Nothing to worry about, Asa Clematis. I respect the academy rules above all else."

Why did he have to make it sound so ominous? I wracked my brain for some other pretext to slip away.

He patted the seat of the leather couch.

"Sit," he said, "and hear me out."

I obeyed. But I left an entire open couch cushion between us. Nerium regarded the empty space with amusement. The thudding of darts punctured our silence.

On the bright side, I hadn't heard any subsequent screaming from Tempus. Not for a little while, anyhow.

"My understanding," said Shien Nerium, "is that you would prefer not to be at Guralta Academy."

I wondered where he'd gotten this from. Mr. Rift? Tempus? Wist herself? A healer classmate? I didn't make an enormous secret of it.

"Maybe," I answered cautiously. "No point in crying over it now. It's a done deal. I'm already here."

"A bit distasteful, isn't it? Exploitative, one might say."

I schooled my face into a mask of bland neutrality. "Not sure what you're talking about, sir."

"The government covers all your expenses until graduation. Very generous. But if you leave before then—voluntarily or otherwise—you'll be heavily penalized."

I couldn't see where he was going with this. Unless he meant it as a veiled threat. Unless this was his way of warning me that he planned on having me tossed out of school. Which did seem entirely plausible. But at the moment, it didn't quite ring true.

"Sir," I said, "I'm afraid I don't—"

"What if you could afford to leave?"

"Excuse me?"

"What if," he continued, infinitely patient, "someone could pay all the fines for leaving? As a gift, you see. No strings attached. Leaving you free to go wherever you like, do whatever you want. No debt. No burden on your family."

Over by the game of darts, Wist appeared to be keeping an eye on us. But there was no way she could've heard the exact words coming out of Nerium's mouth.

My hands rested in curled fists on my knees. My heart beat at a pace completely out of sync with my motionless body.

"That'd be nice," I said slowly, "in a fairy tale."

"How about in real life?"

"In real life, how could anyone trust an offer with no strings attached?"

Nerium smiled. "I hope this doesn't sound condescending. An amount of money that seems like an enormous sum to you might not be such an enormous sum to others. Would you ever buy a friend lunch, if you had the spare cash, without expecting anything back in return?"

"If I had the spare cash," I said. "Which I don't."

"To me, paying your quitting fees would be as light a matter as buying a friend a casual sandwich."

"No offense," I told him, "but I don't think the academy will accept counterfeit currency."

He laughed. "Not all the Shien clan money is in replica coins. I can assure you of that much."

He plucked his fan off the table and spread it open, revealing the painted design. Gold-rimmed flowers and abstract swirls.

"You seem like a very practical-minded young lady. Much more so than most of your peers."

Couldn't really disagree with that. I spoke up anyway, though. Just on principle. "No need to put down my classmates."

"Of course not. My apologies." He turned his fan over, as if there were secrets written on the back. "As a show of good faith, I would be happy to draw up a proper contract. And to pay your family in full, all in advance."

It was easier to speak when I looked down at my hands. "That's a very favorable deal for me."

"I'm glad to hear that," Shien Nerium said modestly.

This conversation felt like clinging to the side of a mountain without ropes. Like inching my way across two-inch footholds at the edge of a cliff. I had little hope of not slipping up.

"And if I decline?" I asked, reckless. "Is that where it all reverses? Where the prospect of money falling from the sky transforms into threats against my parents? If it's so easy for you to bribe me to leave, it must be just as easy to—"

"Tell me, is that what you think of us? Do we canter around committing murder and extortion as, oh, a little palate refresher between meals? Do we bathe in the blood of peasants?"

He seemed genuinely interested in my answer.

There were moments when I found it easy to forget that this harmless-looking man had allegedly—back in his school days—murdered a fellow student by sealing them in the island caves. That he'd doctored Wist's soup and eggs with lavish helpings of bleach and weed killer, over and over, demonstrating the dedication of a scientist running a years-long experiment.

He and Ficus had invented plenty of other games, too. Wist didn't seem inclined to volunteer many details.

He called children cruel and amoral because he himself was cruel and amoral. He thought the world and people around him must inevitably reflect his own nature. Such narcissism.

"I think," I said—with every last scrap of diplomacy left in me—"it doesn't really matter what I think. My parents are subliminals. I have no heritage. I'm just a healer in training. And I'd rather not be a healer at all."

"Then my offer must hold some appeal for you."

I sat with my thoughts before saying anything more. An awkward silence was the least of my worries here.

I'd brought up my family because I wanted to know as soon as possible if he considered them a legitimate target. That would save me the anxiety of making a choice. That would leave me without any choice at all.

Yet for whatever reason, he didn't seem ready to pivot to threatening them. Maybe he wanted to see how far he could get by playing nice with me.

Maybe, for all that he'd managed to torment Wist back in the Shien family home, he lacked the pull to single-handedly get away with crushing the lives of unrelated civilians.

I heard myself when I swallowed. I hated the sound of it.

"I have to decline," I said.

Shien Nerium waited as if expecting me to elaborate further. I didn't.

"So you want more," he murmured. "A dazzling head for business. I can work with that. Why don't I pay your parents double the amount they would owe to the government once you drop out? That's a very healthy profit."

"I'm honored," I said stiffly. "But it's not—I can't accept any amount of money. I'm sorry."

The next time Nerium spoke, the pleasure had left his voice.

"What puzzles me is the fact that you haven't even asked why. Surely you're wondering what made me bring you this offer. Surely your uncertainty about my motivation is what makes you hesitate."

I'd left a sizable gap when I took my seat, perched warily on the edge of the couch. Shien Nerium hadn't moved so much as a millimeter in my direction. But the space between us—large enough for two or three of Wist to fit comfortably—suddenly felt much too small.

I hadn't asked about his reason for bribing me because I didn't care to hear him lie to explain it.

In any case, the reason was obvious. He hadn't plucked me from obscurity out of a spirit of charity. He came after me because he thought I meant something to Wist.

He was imagining something there that didn't exist. We'd gone months after hunting season without saying a word to each other. Perfectly comfortable months.

Yet Wist had so little in the way of close friends. Perhaps that stark absence made minor developments seem more significant. Her choice of which healer to partner up with for her originator exam, for instance.

I considered my current predicament. Seated on an expensive couch with Shien Nerium, listening to him try to casually bribe me into dropping out of school.

This very situation might explain a lot. It might explain why Wist remained aloof from virtually everyone else at the academy, mages and healers alike. Azalea and Tempus were the only classmates I'd seen her exchange words with on a regular basis.

Fewer connections meant fewer points of vulnerability. Fewer points of access. Fewer people for her brothers to discover and lock on to.

I wouldn't be anyone's tool.

Shien Nerium's folding fan snapped shut. My shoulders twitched at the sound of it.

"Let me be the one to ask, then," he said. "Are there teachers you care for? Do you like them enough to stay at school for them? Rift seems very fond of you. Both you and Wisteria, actually.

"If you're wondering how I could tell, it's because he was careful to speak of you in only the most neutral of terms." A slight grin. "He would never risk praising his favorite students to me and Ficus."

"Mr. Rift is a pain in the butt," I said.

"So you wish to stay for Wisteria?"

"I'll stay for myself," I snapped. "It's very simple, sir. You know why

I didn't want to attend Guralta in the first place? Because I got almost zero choice in the matter.

"Nothing makes me less interested in doing something than getting pushed real hard to do it. That's just as true for you forcing me out of school as it is for the government forcing me in."

"That's a disturbingly shallow reason to turn down a life-changing amount of money."

"We can't all be deep thinkers all the time." I was on a roll now. "Anyway, it would be life-changing for *me*. For you and your clan? Pocket money. Change thrown at a street busker."

"I'll decide what changes my life. I'll stay at the academy even if I resent every second of it. With all due respect, sir, I would resent the weight of your money much more."

31

WAS IT THE MOST comfortable conversation of my life? No. But it didn't end with me getting hurled off a cliff as a gift to the old gods of the sea. The Shien brothers let us walk out of their villa afterward. Figured I'd take that as a victory.

Wist must've sobered up some by the time we started heading back to the academy. She didn't say much as we walked, though. She was lucky she didn't have to stop and vomit in the shrubbery.

We reached the edge of campus, a spot where it would've made sense to split off in opposite directions: Wist aiming for mage territory, and me trekking alone to my healer dorm. Only then did she try to speak.

"Make it quick," I warned her.

She clammed up again. I threw up my hands. After a round of hushed bickering, she convinced me to come meet her early the next morning.

She didn't mention why. No need to spell it out. We'd left the scene of the party. But her brothers had yet to leave the island.

Even once I was on my own, silence refused to envelop me. Choirs of insects rasped and practiced their scales in the darkness. Human hoots and shouts bounced around campus, too. Summer nights were always noisy.

I glanced up at what stars I could see past the towering campus trees. Mages would be gathering back at the Shien villa right about now, ready for stargazing and more drinks and dessert.

What went through Shien Nerium's head when he looked through his telescopes?

I kept wondering. And as I brushed my teeth that night, I considered what it might mean to leave the academy. For it to be a real possibility.

Wouldn't be missing out on much, would I?

Island life wasn't bad. But classes were a drag. I distrusted most of my dormmates, and the feeling was mutual.

Admittedly, there were a couple exceptions. Saya and I got along well enough, considering how different we were. The twins in the room opposite ours treated me cordially. Pepper (from down the hall) remained convinced that I was a fellow spice lover. He never missed a chance to make me taste-test new samples.

He meant no harm by it. He seemed thrilled to have a hot sauce buddy. I still couldn't bring myself to break the truth to him.

The day after the party was a Sunday. No big exams coming up. No reason for anyone to skulk around the library at sunrise.

The building was closed, in fact. But the familiar outdoor stairs still wound up to the roof, blocked only by a pitiful padlocked gate that barely came up to my waist. I examined it carefully for magic cuttings.

All clear.

I hopped the gate.

A subtle fog filled the roof, cool on my skin. Wist must've been worried about people watching us from the ground.

A needless paranoia. No one except a few teachers would be up and about around this time. Not here, anyway. Early-rising sports clubs would do their morning workouts down by the sea or at the gym.

A chaos of birdsong pulsed from the aviary that topped the mage wing of the library over yonder. I wouldn't call it beautiful. Many of the birds had not been blessed with any particular melodic talent. Some squeaked like furniture on a resistant floor. Some screeched like monkeys.

Here on the roof of the healer wing, the daytime sunshades were all folded up. The fog partly obscured the network of gleaming mage tightropes in the distance. I checked the hanging egg chairs, but found them empty.

The next time I looked up, I realized Wist had been there from the start.

There was a regular pedestrian bridge spanning the gap between rooftops. But there were also a number of tightropes.

Wist stood right in the middle of one, still as a pigeon, hands in her pockets. She had her back to me. She faced the cacophony of morning birds.

Her black braid hung perfectly straight. An unusual sight. It dangled well past the luminous rope on which her feet perched. The tuft at the end of her braid traced slow figures in the air, as if practicing strokes for calligraphy.

She wore her mage student uniform again today.

The last time I'd been up here with Wist had been in the middle of hunting season.

Which was now long over. But part of me felt hunted anew. By the original instigators, of whom Tempus had been a wan imitation. An older generation of hunters.

I could guess at why Wist might've wanted to talk to me after the party. Yet my guesses were just that—wild suppositions. I found myself struck anew not only by how hard it was to read Wist, but also by how hard it was to place her.

Whose side was Wisteria Shien on? Did she belong to any side at all?

She was a mage student who associated little with other mages (Azalea being the only real exception). She was a member of the Shien clan, gifted with their token and all the free-flowing money it bestowed on her, but not of their blood. Her Shien siblings saw her as an uppity impostor. A threat to be stamped out.

She had magic in spades. Which in turn meant she had power, and not merely the magical sort. She had the ability to battle for a stronger place—among the Shiens, or at least among her fellow students.

But all she tried to do was avoid occupying too much space, avoid picking fights, avoid belonging anywhere. Belonging somewhere—staking her claim—would mean needing to defend it. Instead she dodged.

Then again, her very source of status also seemed to be what held her back. The ever-deepening crenellations of her magic. The insistent way it tangled up inside her like tripwires. The constant cramping haze of pain. Cobwebs filling her mind, veiling her eyes, dragging at her arms and legs.

Healing her did feel a bit like defusing a bomb, one that would immediately start reassembling itself the instant you stopped to dust your hands off.

I swallowed to clear the early-morning thickness from my mouth. I called out to Wist. She hopped on over to my side of the roof, quick as a crow. Mages really did have no fear of falling from those tightropes.

"You dressed up," I said.

She looked down at herself. "This is my uniform."

"Do you steam it yourself? Or do you have a magical device to—actually, never mind." I wasn't *that* curious.

"You turned Nerium down," Wist said.

"You heard us?"

"Why didn't you take his offer?"

I looked up at the morning sky. No answers there.

"You tell me," I said eventually. "Do you trust your big brother? Would you cut a deal with him?"

"In this case, yes."

"Hard to believe."

"That amount of money is nothing to him. He would gladly have paid you in full."

I could detect nothing different about her manner except a faint air of restlessness. It roiled the diffuse fog surrounding us. But she didn't let any impatience show on her face.

"Sounds like you would've preferred for me to take his bribe," I observed.

"It isn't too late to change your mind."

"So your goal is to get me to take the money and run. Good riddance, eh?" I could hear myself speaking faster and faster. "Want to toss me out that badly? Well, guess what: I don't want mages telling me what to do. Is that so hard to understand?

"And don't you dare testify about how safe it would be to take a favor from your brother. I don't buy it for a second."

I saw Wist glance back across the bridge and tightropes. As if she could escape over to the high domed aviary and the rooftop gardens around it.

I recalled the moment last night when she and Nerium had exchanged looks. She'd backed off without another word of argument.

I spoke the thought aloud as it occurred to me. "You knew what he was angling for, what he had to offer me. You knew, or guessed, why he made us stay back at the party."

I moved in front of her, forcing her to face me. "You weren't surprised for a second."

Wist inclined her head.

I glared. "Would've appreciated some forewarning."

"I didn't want to sway you."

"Wow! How patronizing!"

I stalked a testy circle. Wist watched me from the corner of her eye.

"This is just like hunting season," I said. "You helped me here and there, but you didn't stand up and condemn it till the very end."

She didn't say a word to defend herself. I rolled my eyes. "Yeah, I know you had your reasons. I know who you were protecting."

As I passed behind her, I swiped spitefully at her hair. It tried to dodge me, but I managed to get my grubby little fists on it anyway. I held it bundled like a jump rope. The thread of magic in her braid shone silver.

It twitched here and there, as if testing my grip. It twitched as subtly as the pulse you can feel in your wrist.

Wist herself tolerated my hair-groping without budging. She didn't need to move a muscle to infuriate me.

"Do you want me to vanish or not?" I demanded.

"Better than the alternative."

"Tell me about this alternative."

"If he can't bribe you to leave, he'll punish you for staying. Hunting season would come back with a vengeance. This time involving seniors."

"Now forget the consequences," I said, "Forget what seems safest. All the worst-case scenarios you're thinking of—pretend none of them will ever happen.

"Would you still want me to accept your brother's offer? Would you still want me to leave school?"

Her gaze traced the tether of her hair down to the coils massed in my hands. Then she looked me in the eye.

"Yes," Wist said.

"Why?"

I gave her a long time to answer.

Nothing.

"Oh, c'mon."

I hurled her piled-up braid back at her. It wrapped itself in fretful circles around her waist.

"Surely you can come up with *something*," I told her. "Not gonna stand here and insult myself. But even I can think of plenty of reasons why I might be a giant pain in the ass.

"Say what you actually think. Say how you actually feel. I'm not convinced yet. If you want to get rid of me, own it. If you want to get rid of me, you better make me believe it."

She took her glasses off. There was now enough ambient sunlight to shine bright on the lenses. She tilted them back and forth as if studying the intricacies of old fingerprints.

"You frighten me," she said.

Something in her voice almost made it sound real.

Any thoughts I'd been storing up chose this moment to scatter like cockroaches chased off by a flashlight.

I turned my back on Wist. I moved like a zombie over toward a colorful couch near the magically protected edge of the roof. The hanging egg chairs arranged on either side of it looked like oversize birdcages.

Before I knew it, I was sitting down, gawping at the smooth couch fabric—a perfect cornflower blue—and wondering how it could possibly stay so clean and unweathered. Couldn't see any magic on it.

I kicked my shoes off and pulled my legs up.

"I frighten you," I said to Wist. "Do you know how ridiculous that seems?"

She'd followed me over, lagging a few steps behind. She didn't take a seat. She touched the woven basket-like frame of the hanging chair nearest the couch.

If it merely sounded stupid, I would've laughed at her. If I had no idea what she was talking about, I would've scoffed.

The problem was that I often felt frightening things when I looked at her. I just didn't see how she could've possibly sensed it herself.

Running into Yarrow yesterday had made me all too keenly aware of it. I remembered being a little kid and wanting so desperately to grow into someone big and sturdy, someone capable of cherishing Yarrow. I'd valiantly stretch my back whenever my parents measured my height. I'd stand on tiptoe in the mirror to imagine how a taller me would look standing next to her.

Cute. Innocent. Nothing wrong with that.

What had changed in me, and when? Did I get all bitter and curdled after being forced to attend the academy?

No. No point in pretending to speculate.

If there was a single moment to blame, it was the moment when I saw Wist on the verge of a breakdown. Months and months ago, in the middle of an empty street after dusk. Icy wild magic freezing the air. Her hunched back.

I'd healed her, sure. But ever since, there had been a part of me that said *more*.

I hugged my legs. "There's something wrong with me."

I still didn't plan on leaving Guralta. If Wist were disturbed enough to wish me gone, though, I might as well come clean with her.

"It's your fault," I added.

"I know."

"What? Of course it's not your fault. Don't just go along with whatever I say."

"You—"

"It's me," I told my knees. "The problem is me. I don't know where it comes from. I've never felt this violent."

My heart was sprinting as if pursued by shadows down a haunted corridor. I peeped sideways at Wist, then quickly looked away again. Too quickly to see the black eyes barren of judgment, of interest, of hunger.

"I want to tear you open," I said. "I want to see you cry. I want to see you destroyed."

The birds in the aviary sounded eerily far away.

From the other side of the couch came a light clatter. A hasty rustling. As if Wist had accidentally shoved at the swinging egg chair, then scrambled to steady it.

"I understand," she murmured.

The sheer force of my skepticism lifted my head. "You understand?"

"You didn't come to Guralta with any great love for mages."

"No, but—"

"My family and I have given you nothing but grief. When all you want is to be left alone to live your life. It's understandable that—"

"Wait." I reared up onto my knees. "You've got it all wrong. I don't hate you. That's the weird part. I don't hate you, and I don't think I'm a sadist. You know I've never been on board with animal torture.

"I see you and—and I want to unmask you. To slap the mask off. Rip it off. Reach inside you."

"This is my face," Wist said.

"I know. But you're human. You can get hurt. For that matter—you're hurting most of the time. All the time. You can fall on your knees. You can boil over with anger. I've seen it. That's how I know. It's like a drug. It feels *good* to see you crack. It makes me want more. More than I can ever possibly—"

I felt, at the exact same moment, a rush of heat and a rush of cold. My fingers pressed hard on the arm of the blue couch. I took a second to shut up and collect myself.

"I told you there's something wrong with me."

Wist's braid curled around her shoulders like a winter shawl. Then around her neck, covering her mage collar. Then around her chin and her mouth. I must've made her wish she had enough hair to wholly disappear inside it.

"You can stop trying to think of what's best for me," I explained. "You don't have any duty to protect me. If you're going to tell me to take your brother's bribe, tell me to do it because you want me wiped forever out of your sight. Doesn't mean I'll listen, obviously. Just saying. You don't have to disguise it."

"Go slower," Wist said. She tugged the coils of her braid down as if adjusting a scarf. "Please. I'm thinking."

I managed to hold my tongue for almost ten full seconds. Then I cracked. "My point is—on some level, I'm not so different from your brothers. Not different enough to claim the moral high ground, anyway."

Wist said nothing.

At first I assumed she was attempting to process what I'd thrown at her. Then the silence prolonged itself, over and over. I noticed her quivering. Her hands were on her face.

She didn't make a sound. Not a chirp. It didn't even seem as if she were struggling to keep quiet. There was no noise waiting to spill out in the first place. She shook like jelly, voiceless.

She was laughing.

My feelings flipped like a coin toss. Somehow that was all it took. I slumped back in my seat, loose and grinning.

"I know," I said. Although I had no clue what, in fact, had set her off. "I'm a real comedian."

Wist straightened up. She drank in a heavy breath. "You're nothing like my brothers."

"Whew. Good to know."

"You despise the academy. You want to stay here for a chance to shatter me?"

"No one said anything like that."

"Try it." Wist stood with her hands spread lightly at her sides, a formless invitation. "You're welcome to try any time. I bet you can't."

I almost choked.

On what?

On my own nervous spit, I guess.

In my head I jumped back to the start of it all, to the words that had sent me teetering over to this side of the roof.

"Wait. If you're so—then what did you mean? What the hell did I do to frighten you?"

This, of course, was the moment she chose to lose her voice again.

"Wist," I said. "I just admitted to having these monstrous urges to make you cry like a baby."

"Yes." She remained maddeningly deadpan. "I'd like to see you try."

"If that's not what frightens you, what does? Throw me a bone here."

"...You heal too well."

"Uh. What?"

Wist began walking off as if she'd remembered an errand. I chased her to the middle of the bridge between buildings.

The tightropes in the air on either side of us were the color of dying coals. The bridge to the mage wing—a straight and solid thing—vibrated underfoot. Almost to the point of bouncing.

I think it was supposed to do that. I think. I hope. Fingers crossed.

If Wist thought some mild architectural shaking would deter me, she thought wrong. I kept following her.

"You know I need a little more explanation than that," I told her shoulder blades.

The mage wing, too, seemed empty of people. Only masochists would come cavort around the library this early in the morning. But I kept my voice down. Just to play it safe.

Wist finally stopped attempting to flee. Not that she'd been trying very hard in the first place. She could simply port off into the ether if she really wanted to exit the scene in a rush.

She kept her eyes on the aviary on the other side of the rooftop-spanning bridge.

"If you healed me more," she said, "I might come to depend on it."

"So?"

The bridge had no physical railings. Only magic, nigh invisible. Wist's braid still found a way to wind like a vine through the protective mesh of cuttings.

She half-turned her head. "Are you happy as a healer? Do you always want to be known only as a healer?"

"You already know the answer to that."

"Then what I'm saying should make sense. You—with little experience, with no gentleness, with no technique—you heal me better than anyone I've ever met."

I crossed my arms. "Is that a compliment or an insult?"

"It's the truth. If I—you'll think I'm only after your healing. You'll feel used. And you'll be right. I'll need you, and I'll use you. That's what frightens me."

From what I could see of the side of her face, she was in prime form. That unshakable dark stare stripped of expectation or disappointment or hope.

The mask was Wist, too, as she'd said. The mask was her, as truly as whatever lay beneath.

"That's the stupidest thing I've ever heard," I said.

That got her to look at me.

"You're a high-class mage. You're supposed to use the rest of us peons like washcloths."

"For facial cleansing...?"

"Like dirty rags, then. You get my meaning. Don't pretend otherwise. Playing dumb is only cute when I do it."

I pointed straight at her. "I wouldn't say this to any other mage in the entire world. I'm annoyed that I even have to say this to you. A member of the goddamn Shien clan.

"You, of all people, can afford to be a little greedy."

She took one measured step back. Then another. "I am greedy. More so than most. That's why I have to be careful. You think you can break me? I'll—"

"Know who you sound like?" I asked. "You sound like your brother. Real easy to imagine him telling him how greedy you are. Telling you that you better watch out. You better restrain yourself.

"Well, you've got competition now. I'm greedy, too. I'd love to have an S-Class mage feel dependent on me. Get hooked on me. Could be a huge advantage. Heck, even just in terms of surviving the next few years of the academy."

Her lips parted to speak. I didn't let her. Not yet. "Consider our positions. Who's using who? Who's consuming who? Who's more likely to be called a leech? Use me as much as you want. No need to hold back. I'll bleed you dry."

The fog she'd filled the roof with had long since burnt to nothing. I urged her back over to the healer wing. We would be less visible here than out on the bridge.

Wist dug at her mage collar with the tips of her fingers. "If you really want to stay—"

"I do."

"That's your choice. I'll respect it."

"You better."

"My brothers won't give up so easily."

"Mm. It's not me they care about, though. I'm an ant in their path. It's you they want to strike at."

If we left it at that—if I tapped out here and sauntered off to grab breakfast—she'd revert to her default strategy. She'd curl up inside herself like a hermit crab and brace herself to silently endure whatever came. Hour by hour, day by day. Until it ended. Or didn't.

Wisteria Shien, I decided, needed a pep talk.

I did a quick perimeter check for nosy gulls. None in sight. Satisfied, I dragged Wist back over to the suspiciously clean-looking blue couch. I sat her down. I stood in front of her with my hands on my hips.

"Listen up," I told her. "Ne—what's his name? Nephrite?"

"Nerium."

"Nerium is the real problem, right?"

After a moment of contemplation, Wist nodded. "Ficus is more ... capricious."

"Right," I muttered, recalling how carelessly he'd lobbed acorns and cicadas at Wist, and steel-tipped darts at Tempus. "You could say that."

"He's less focused. More dangerous, maybe. But also lazier."

"Not the leader type. So let's talk about Shien Nerium. Someday you'll leave this brother of yours in the dust, and he knows it."

Wist blinked up at me. I did enjoy my chance to be taller than her. Plus, I was absolutely dead-on confident about what I had to say here.

"He's desperate to beat you down as much as possible while he still can. To block the future from your sight. To blind you to the fact that one day you'll be a full adult, and you'll still be an S-Class mage. Or even greater. But better educated than before.

"And you'll both still be Shiens. And people will start listening to you more than they listen to him.

"It's inevitable," I said, before she could protest. "The way I see it, he's always had two choices. He chose to try and break you like a horse. If he were less prideful, less self-protective, he might've chosen to cultivate you as an ally instead.

"Imagine it. He could've become your best friend growing up. The best big brother anyone's ever had. You would've loved him if he'd been good to you and those around you. Wouldn't you? You would at least have honored him, as he honored you.

"Whichever of you ended up as the clan heir in the end—well, the other could've been their right-hand man or woman. Their most trusted confidant.

"But he was too stuck up his own ass to consider that path. Truly a top-caliber idiot.

"We healers already know we can't get anywhere in life except by allying ourselves with those more powerful. Guess when you've got money and magic, the smart thing to do isn't always so obvious."

Wist's face remained still as a death mask. I strove to give her time to think it over.

"You may be correct," she said in the end.

"I know I am."

"But I don't know what to do about him now."

"We just have to make it not worth his while to keep coming after you. Clearly he does have other things going on in his life. We've been at school since April, and he only showed up on the island in August."

We pondered. We pondered for quite a while. No brilliant ideas to deter further interference came to mind.

I gave up. I threw myself down on the couch next to Wist. "How about this?"

"What?"

"Take his other leg. You already suggested it at the party."

"I'm tempted."

I sighed. I plunked the back of my head into the back of the couch. Nice and bouncy. My stomach gurgled loud enough that Wist attempted to offer me a flat tin of oil-packed fish. No, thank you.

"At least we agree on where things are headed," I said. "In the future, if not right away. Someday you'll be in a position to kick his ass without even trying. All the magic branches in you say so."

I sat up straighter. "Right now we should focus on speeding up that process. Getting you better positioned for that future. And a big part of that has got to be untangling your magic.

"So you get those clouds out of your head. So you can devote more thought to a world without your brothers looming up behind you. So you can acquire more and more skills. So you can prove to everyone that you have a lot of power *and* you know how to use it."

"To be clear," Wist said, "you're volunteering to heal me. A lot. All day and all night?"

"I don't work for free," I said on reflex.

I shook my head as I heard myself. Even I didn't know what I meant.

"Anyway. I would, yes, but the school rules are gonna cramp our style. It'll be hard to make significant progress if we risk getting in serious trouble every time we end up alone in a room together. The pro healers assigned to you might have a few complaints about it, too."

"Then—"

I held up a finger. "One thing at a time. First we survive your brothers' island vacation. Then we deal with whatever hurdles get posed by the school regulations."

"We," Wist said back to me, in a tone of puzzlement. It really was right there in her voice. Not just my imagination running wild.

"We," I repeated. "Like I said, better not worry about Asa Clematis. I'll use the hell out of you."

Suddenly her braid curled all the way around my shoulders. Full of the morning sun, it felt like a living thing, hotter to the touch than naked skin, thick and oddly muscular in shape.

For a second I thought she might reach for me with more than just her braid.

"Good," she said simply.

32

Wɪsᴛ ᴀsᴋᴇᴅ ᴍᴇ—more than once—if this was what I really wanted. I spit on your concerns, I told her. It almost got her to laugh again.

We decided to keep our distance from each other until the Shien brothers left Guralta Isle. A precautionary measure. Nerium's next step might not be decided yet. The two of them might not do anything at all to us.

Sometimes that was the whole point, Wist told me. Sometimes it was enough for them to show up and witness Wist's reaction. Her stony tolerance of the rabid anxiety about what they *might* do, to her or to others.

At such times, the joke of it was that they didn't have to lift a finger. Even if they did nothing, the mere possibility of it left her a mental wreck. Not that she let it show. But they were satiated by knowing it.

Wist and I stopped speaking. Just like after hunting season, and again after the originator exam.

This time, however, it felt different. This time it was a pact.

I did think it would behoove us to have some way to exchange messages. Nothing ostentatious. I mentioned this to Wist on the library roof. She made an ambiguous sound in response.

I assumed nothing would come of it.

Yet later that day, when I stopped by my room before dinner, the dorm steward passed me a flat package clumsily wrapped in stiff brown paper.

I briefly suspected it of being a booby trap sent by the Shien brothers. But surely their gift wrap would have a bit more flair.

When I opened the package at my desk, it turned out to be a notebook. The generic type you could buy at the school store. A subtle magic cutting clung to the lined pages.

On the back of the first empty page:

I have the same notebook. Anything you write here will also be written in mine.

For most of the following week, I had nothing special to share with her.

September crept into town, complete with unabating heat. The nighttime crickets grew bolder. The cicadas, though still boisterous, seemed ever so slightly more scarce. And not just because Wist had inadvertently culled a bunch of their cousins.

All I sent Wist were silly doodles drawn while taking breaks from mindless core subject homework. I had fun with it, but I'm not much of an artist.

All Wist sent me in return was the occasional question mark. Every so often, I took pity on her and jotted down a word or two to explain my creations.

I didn't catch a single glimpse of the Shien brothers, on campus or off.

After a week of doodling, it came time for us healer Rats to present our pipe cleaner dioramas in class. I'd almost forgotten what mine looked like.

I strolled into the workshop, swabbing sweat from my brow with a hand towel, grumbling to Saya about how I couldn't wait for true autumn. I strolled in there expecting to see Mr. Rift.

The healer dorm steward stood at the head of the room instead.

No one else seemed particularly rattled. This was the first time all year we'd had a substitute, yes, but the steward was a respectable healer in her own right.

I raised my hand to ask if Mr. Rift was okay.

"He isn't ill," said the steward. "He sends his apologies for missing out on your projects."

"He'll see them afterward, won't he? He has to help grade them."

"Of course." The steward turned and called for a different student to start presenting.

A sensation like the first rumblings of food poisoning crawled in my stomach.

I hung back after class. I would've asked Saya to stay, too, but she'd been exceptionally busy these days. She did belong to a bunch of clubs, to be fair. All of them had begun ramping up their activities in anticipation of the Guralta Cup at the end of the month.

While participation in the Cup itself was restricted to select upperclassmen, many clubs took it as an opportunity to run fundraisers—auctions, food or souvenir booths, special performances.

Others held mini-events to showcase their activities. Like the equestrian team doing show jumping, or letting little kids take pictures seated atop their horses. Meanwhile, there'd be a packed schedule of stage shows and concerts at Guralta Academy Hall, a professional-caliber venue better known among the student body as GAH.

So I couldn't begrudge Saya for leaving the workshop and immediately running off to her next thing. I went up to question the dorm steward alone.

At first the steward seemed inclined to shoo me off. When I persisted, she glanced up at the clock on the wall.

"Right now you might find Landon in his office," she said. "If you hurry."

I hurried.

It was the first time I'd seen his office door fully closed, forced all the way into its frame without the usual misshapen gaps. I nearly pulled a muscle wrenching it open.

Then, once I could actually see into the room, I froze.

It was clean.

No towels lining the windowsill. Nothing on top of the desk. The mini fridge stood wide open, empty and deactivated.

Mr. Rift, his back to me, rummaged deep in the cabinet where he normally kept snacks. He wore a dark navy blue shirt without any pattern on it.

He must not have heard me bang my way in. Either that, or he'd chosen to disregard me.

"Mr. Rift," I said. "What's going on?"

Only then did he emerge from the cabinet, hands swaddled in cleaning cloths.

"Asa." No real surprise in his voice.

He motioned for me to close the door. I did my best.

With so much sundry debris gone—trash bins full of paper, half-open cardboard boxes, ignominious stacks of books—the room felt less cramped than I remembered. The walls, too, were utterly bare, marked only by a night sky's worth of pinholes and the gluey remnants of half-dissolved tape.

I knew his walls had been covered in notes to himself. Letters from former students. Informational flyers. Foreign postcards. I'd spent many an afternoon squinting at them from my chair, trying to make out what all those letters said while he lectured me.

The strange part was how I couldn't recall anything specific that had been tacked up there. Not now that they were gone.

"You're leaving?"

I sounded worried. How embarrassing.

Mr. Rift straightened up, wiping his hands. He started to say something. Midway through he burst out sneezing. He apologized and turned to blow his nose.

"I've been getting up close and personal with a lot of dust," he explained.

"You were just going to disappear?" I demanded. "You seemed totally normal"—when had I last had class with him?—"the day before yesterday."

"Appearances can be deceiving," he stated, as if imparting a valuable life lesson.

"Oh, come on. Mr. Rift—"

"I've submitted my resignation."

"In the middle of the school year?"

"All that remains is to finish cleaning this room." He patted the corner of his bare desk.

"Did you get sick of me skipping class? I've been trying not to overdo it."

"Asa, class is much easier for me when you skip it."

Ouch. But the man had a point. I couldn't think of a single other healer Rat who argued with him as much as I did. I couldn't think of many other students who bothered to argue with him, period.

The Mr. Rift before me seemed relaxed. Maybe even relieved. If someone or something had attempted to push him out against his will,

I would've expected him to be irate. On the other hand, he'd never been one to proclaim how much he loved teaching. Whatever the reason for his abrupt departure, perhaps he was glad to be rid of us. Me especially.

But if he hated his students enough to quit on a moment's notice, he could've done that anytime. Why now?

I, for one, had given him plenty of grief over the past five months. And not just me, I'll have you know. He'd been a teacher here back when the Shien brothers were still in school.

Speaking of the Shien brothers—

I'm looking for Rift Landon's office, Shien Nerium had said as he fanned himself. Before I knew who he was.

I saw Nerium, Ficus, and Mr. Rift seated around a now-broken picnic table. Cicadas howling in the trees above. Mr. Rift with his mouth set in a grim line.

"This is because of them," I said. "Isn't it."

"That can be said of many things in this world." An unfamiliar gentleness had entered his tone. "There is alway a *them*."

My hands were in fists. "You know exactly what I mean. The Shien cl—"

Mr. Rift tossed a cleaning rag at my face. I caught it just in time to keep from inhaling it.

"If you're going to linger here," he said, "make yourself useful. There's still a lot of dust to take care of."

I stalked off to fetch a fresh bucket of water.

After returning, I started scrubbing the window glass. I had a lot of practice from helping out at the healer dorm.

Someone would have to circle outside the building to make a real difference. Old rain had dried to leave patterns like tiny brown scales all over the other side of the glass. But that was none of my concern.

"Why?" I asked Mr. Rift.

There was a whiny edge in my voice that even I could hear, and it grated on me.

"Are you asking why," he said, "or how?"

That tripped me up for a second.

I scrubbed harder as I thought. The far side of the glass stayed as dirty as ever. Over in mage territory, they probably had maids to do this stuff. Either that, or frivolous cuttings to eliminate the need for manual labor.

How must mean what the Shien brothers had done to force him to leave. A tempting incentive, like the money they'd offered me. Either that or the opposite: some sort of extortion.

I didn't know how they'd managed to secure Mr. Rift's resignation—but I could certainly guess at why. They were chipping away at anyone who seemed remotely close to Wist.

Not just anyone, actually. For now, they'd clearly homed in on us healers. They'd skipped past Azalea, the most obvious target.

Understandable. Other influential mages might not be too happy if the Shien brothers were known to have driven out a promising student of magic. Yet no one important outside the academy would raise a big fuss over the loss of a single healer student or teacher. Most of them regarded us as a fungible resource.

I considered an alternate possibility. The Wren family seemed far weaker than the Shiens. Wist's brothers might have recruited Azalea, just as they'd recruited Tempus. Just as they'd tried to recruit me. There might be an element of performance in her strident loyalty toward Wist.

Not that I would mention this. Wist knew her brothers better than I did. Wist understood the risks.

"Do you actually want to leave?" I asked Mr. Rift.

"I believe it's for the best."

"You know how they've treated their sister."

"I can guess."

I gave up on the window. I wrung out my cloth and draped it over the side of the bucket. "Wish I could—"

"Don't."

"I didn't even say anything yet," I objected.

"Don't plot revenge," said Mr. Rift. "Don't tackle them head-on. They aren't students here, and they haven't been students in years. They belong to a much larger world. You can't win."

"Is that what made you decide to leave? You looked at them and figured you couldn't win, so you immediately gave up? You'll just do whatever they say without a fight?"

"No." He began pulling open all the drawers of all his cabinets, as if doing a final check for forgotten paraphernalia. "Not entirely. It felt like the right time. It did help that Shien Nerium secured me an exit visa."

I started, and nearly kicked over my bucket of dirty water in the process. "You're leaving the country?"

"In a matter of days, yes."

I began to ask why.

Then I stopped.

Osmanthus was the harshest mageocracy on the entire continent. Maybe the only country that could even be called a true mageocracy, depending on how you defined it. My texts described most of our neighbors as being poorer, danger-ridden, plagued by natural disasters, locked in neverending skirmishes.

But if you didn't want to be ruled by mages for the rest of your life—

"There's another reason Shien Nerium recommended that I leave Osmanthus."

"What?"

Mr. Rift knelt on the floor to get to his lowest set of drawers. "I would rather have told you this when you were closer to graduating."

"Now there's no time left. Spit it out."

He twisted his neck to peer over his shoulder at me. He'd better be careful not to throw his back out with all this cleaning.

"There is no organized healer or subliminal resistance. There hasn't been any such resistance for decades."

"Yeah, too bad," I said under my breath.

"But there are healers with the ability to think and advocate for themselves. Some bonded to or otherwise affiliated with very powerful mages. Many of these healers happen to know each other. To be friendly, when circumstances allow it.

"Every so often, they manage to exert their influence on a mage in a pivotal position. Whispered suggestions. The subtlest of nudges. Sometimes it works as intended."

A circle created by Mr. Rift. New graduates meeting older alumni.

He probably had no say in what they did together, if they indeed got up to anything at all. If these healers chose to conspire against some mage—or to conspire against the government, even—he would still be able to swear total innocence.

If Shien Nerium suspected anything at all, though, it would give him yet another reason to want Mr. Rift out of the picture.

"There's a fundamental problem here." No longer pretending to help tidy up, I threw myself down in the familiar rickety rattan chair. "Gentle whispers? Subtle nudges? You think I have the patience for that?"

"Not at all."

"Then what's the point of telling me?"

"If you want to know more about what happened to previous healer movements, ask your roommate."

"Saya?"

"You're from a subliminal family, aren't you? You wouldn't have heard any of our history. None of it gets in textbooks. None of it gets in the news."

"Mr. Rift." I'd been keeping an eye on the window as best I could, but this conversation still made me antsy. "Aren't you afraid of the gulls?"

"After I leave campus today," he said, "I will never set foot here again. The gulls see and hear far more than you think. Just because you can't see the gulls doesn't mean they can't see you.

"Nothing I say here will make the administration report me or try to stop me. They understand that Shien Nerium has a hand in my departure. They won't interfere unless I walk outside and begin shouting made-up confessions of murder or molestation or high treason."

"Not sure it makes me feel better to know that the gulls are watching even more than I thought," I said.

"The mere existence of a rule doesn't guarantee that it'll be evenly enforced."

"That would be more comforting to hear if I were a mage student." I put my arms behind my head. "Never thought about leaving Osmanthus."

"Consider it a last resort." Mr. Rift rose to his feet, wincing. It was still strange to see him in such a drab and proper shirt. "Things aren't as dire as you might think, Asa. You aren't as trapped as you feel."

"That's not very convincing, coming from someone who's about to flee the country."

"You'll be free of the academy in three more years. No one will force you to attend university. Three years might sound like forever, but it's a very small portion of your overall life."

"Long as I don't die young," I muttered.

"If you keep up your current act—"

"What act?"

"If you keep pretending to be a barely adequate healer, you'll receive exactly the result you've been hoping for. The government won't send mage police to your door and demand that you work full-time as a healer once you graduate.

"You'll be able to get away with performing periodic community service, volunteering your time at government clinics. It's highly unlikely that you'll get courted for bonding. At least not by any mage of such great status that you feel incapable of refusing.

"So I won't tell you to stop. You're on the right track to have minimal—if not zero—healing duties in your adult life. It simply depends on whether that's still the outcome you most desire."

Why wouldn't it be?

Maddeningly, what came next happened at the exact moment that I started to protest.

Magic sparked in the middle of the room like the genesis of a forest fire. Mr. Rift and I scuttled in opposite directions, backs to the nearest walls. No strategy there—just pure cockroach instinct.

A Shien had entered the scene. Not the one we feared. But she'd ported in so messily that a shock wave slapped me in the face. It left a lasting sting. The open drawers rattled like chattering teeth. As a final insult, my bucket of slop water tipped itself over right onto the room's only floor rug.

Silence followed.

Once my paralysis lifted, I grabbed more cleaning rags and threw them down to soak up the spill. Wist had begun saying something to Mr. Rift. I'd never heard her speak so rapidly.

When she stopped to draw breath, Mr. Rift brought his hands together in a single sharp clap.

"You are not your brothers," he told her.

"Hi," I added belatedly.

Wist hadn't even seen me. Rather, she didn't seem to have consciously registered my presence. Now she faltered.

"You're already here," I said, before she could attempt to port away in another whirlwind. "The damage is done. Might as well stay and hang out. We'll never see Mr. Rift again after today." I glanced over at him for confirmation. "Will we?"

"Only if you become world travelers."

I shoved Wist into the lonely rattan chair he used for visitors. Her braid immediately wound around the arms and back as if tying her in place to be tortured. There was a peculiar purplish tint to her mouth. She looked very close to fainting.

I caught Mr. Rift's eye again. "You want to heal her? Last chance."

He motioned for me to go ahead.

I bent to make sure Wist saw me. "Can I?"

She nodded stiffly.

With Mr. Rift watching, it felt weirdly like some sort of unorthodox final exam. I worked quickly and roughly, wrenching at her magic to get the tangles out faster. Like doing someone else's hair without taking any care not to hurt them.

She was in bad enough shape that I honestly didn't think she would notice. The knots were so thick that they'd massed into a hard wall around her magic core, a barrier akin to the gnarled shell of a nut.

I stopped untangling once I'd cracked the nut, once I could glimpse most of the light of her core. Wist had her head in her hands.

"A word of advice," Mr. Rift said.

He appeared to be addressing me. But Wist, too, raised her head.

"Look at what you can do in Osmanthus before attempting to follow me—or anyone—out of the country."

"Mr. Rift, I can barely bring myself to do my homework."

He ignored this. "I agree that you shouldn't have to define yourself solely as a healer. I myself had other dreams once. But if you choose the path of a healer, it doesn't mean you've lost. And it isn't losing or giving up to care about a mage."

I couldn't resist talking back. "These words of wisdom would mean more if you were staying."

He shrugged. "Take from it what you will."

Wist joined us in scouring the last dusty corners of his office. Dappled sunlight poured in through the half-clean window glass. The tree fern outside stirred in the breeze, waving fronds like grasping fingers.

It had gotten quite stuffy in here, but I was too cautious to open the window and risk our voices leaking out willy-nilly. Even if Mr. Rift claimed there would be no consequences.

He, for one, didn't have to worry about what tomorrow on the island would bring us. Tomorrow, and the day after, and the day after. None of his concern. Must be nice, I thought.

As we finished up, I remarked that Shien Nerium seemed to be going easy on him. To the point of arranging a route out of the country. That was some real five-star service.

"He's younger than he looks," said Mr. Rift. "Younger than he wants to give the impression of being. Not everything he does is purely logical. Or even intelligent. He isn't infallible."

I turned to Wist. "How old is he?"

"Twenty-six."

"I mean ... that's pretty old," I said.

Mr. Rift snorted. "See how you feel when you're in your mid-twenties, Asa."

Once there was nothing else left to do, Wist and I picked up the sodden rug and draped it over the desk to finish drying. (I did ask her if she knew any magic to insta-dry it. Mr. Rift told her not to bother.)

He began redoubling his efforts to shoo us out of his bare-stripped office for good. I came up with excuses to stay. I picked diligently at the stubborn tape marks on the walls. My fingernails weren't at all suited to the task, but I made a good show of it.

"Fine," I said in the end. "Just one last thing."

I wanted to know if he had any memories of Yarrow. She'd been a student here well within his tenure. More recently than either of the elder Shien brothers.

"Right," said Mr. Rift. "You were childhood friends."

"You knew?"

"She mentioned you once or twice. Not by name. But the pieces fit."

Yarrow had described me, surely, as a sweet and docile kid. One who tried to imitate her in everything from hairstyle to clothing to dainty mannerisms while eating.

I didn't see how he could possibly have drawn a connection between that darling little angel and the Asa Clematis who gave him hell over every minor misprint in our textbooks.

I cast a sidelong look at Wist. Her lips were less sickly in hue than before. Her expression had reverted to neutral. Well, whatever Mr. Rift had to share, I guess I didn't mind her hearing it.

"Did Yarrow ever come to you for help?"

"Only once." Mr. Rift started to put his hand on his desk, as if to lean on it. He snatched his arm away as soon as he made contact with the still-damp rug hung there to dry.

Distaste written on his face, he continued: "She bonded a man from the Gwindel family, didn't she?"

"Did she want to know if there was any way to get out of it? What'd you tell her?"

"I told her she could flee the country," he said.

"Like you're doing now."

"Yes. But I warned her she might never be able to see her family again. Not for many years. And without the proper connections, she would forever have to live in fear of being deported."

A pause. For some reason, his eyes slid to Wist. "Originally she was being courted by Shien Ficus."

My brain stuttered. "Wait—what?"

"That was the time when she sought my advice. The whole Shien clan frightened her. With good reason."

Wist looked away, as if trying to give us some semblance of privacy.

Mr. Rift sighed. "When I suggested leaving the country, she asked me if there were any other options. I told her the only way to get Ficus to back down would be to align herself with a mage of higher status.

"A mage of equal birth, for instance, but older and more established. And preferably with more branches. I helped introduce her to the Gwindel clan."

"But—" I couldn't get my mind around this. "I saw Yarrow. Just last weekend. At a hoity-toity party hosted by the Shiens. Shien Ficus was there in person. If she rejected him for this other guy, wouldn't it be common sense not to show up at all?"

He shook his head at me. "Think like a mage, Asa. To mages, this is just business. Sometimes you win your bid. Sometimes you lose. In any case, it's been a couple of years since she bonded."

"Ficus is good at forgetting," said Wist. She herself had apparently forgotten that she was pretending not to listen to us.

Mr. Rift made a noise of agreement. "Once Shien Ficus gives up on something, he seems to have the ability to discard it utterly. I wouldn't be surprised if he no longer recalls her name."

So Yarrow had, under the sage advice of Mr. Rift, chosen an older and plainer and more powerful—and perhaps safer—mage.

She'd chosen him over someone closer to her age, and very beautiful.

And indisputably cruel. I recalled how Ficus had let his steel-tipped darts fly at Tempus. Who hailed from the same social class. Who openly adored him.

What kind of a choice was that?

OUR GOODBYES were unsentimental. Wist, in particular, seemed tongue-tied. At the last second, she blurted: "I'm sorry. Thank you."

I could tell she meant it. But her voice sounded dead. Mr. Rift gave her what struck me as being dangerously close to a look of pity.

"Don't apologize for your family," he said.

I urged him to tell us his destination. "You don't have to name the exact town," I said. "Where's the harm in saying which country?"

He wouldn't answer. I tried a different tack. "Will you still be somewhere along the coast? You said you came to Guralta to get a home by the sea."

Mr. Rift blinked. Then he laughed. "So you have retained some of the words that came out of my mouth," he said. "I was worried that none of it ever sank in."

I stood up straight. My most virtuous pose. "I'm always listening. I'm always learning," I informed him.

"Good." He sounded softer than I was used to, and unnervingly devoid of sarcasm. "Keep it up."

He warned us to stay away from the school gate. He didn't want anyone to see him off.

I wandered in a different direction, Wist in tow. By now I'd missed another afternoon class. That was nothing new, though.

It didn't really sink in until I saw the picnic table Wist had split in two last week. Still broken. Still surrounded by a crunchy carpet of upturned cicadas. Whole and perfect, from their crooked legs to their wingtips, and perfectly massacred. Repairs to the healer side of campus had never been the administration's utmost priority.

I inserted myself between Wist and the cicada cemetery. I steered her over to where the trees grew closer together, like fence posts for a giant. Here the paths had no paving or curly coral lining.

My brain showed me imagined footage of Mr. Rift, with the skeletal build of a greyhound, hauling a worn suitcase out through the silver-streaked front gate.

Wist and I had agreed to avoid loitering together like this. At least until her brothers packed up and left the island. But as we left Mr. Rift's office, she'd hinted at having something to tell me.

I scanned the trees. Some with deep dark bark, some so smooth and light that they looked obscurely unreal. Summer still had a hold of us, one powerful enough to make baths feel like an event of the distant past mere hours after you got out to dry yourself.

Hidden insects aside, our only living company appeared to be a pair of lost-looking ducks. I prodded her arm. "Well?"

"You'll hear the rumors soon," said Wist. "Before that—"

"What rumors?"

"About the reason for him resigning. Azalea told me. That's why I went to his office."

The brownish ducks lurking further down the path looked about sullenly. There was a clingy quality to the air, as if every inch around us were packed with invisible spiderwebs.

I swiped restlessly at my exposed forearms and neck. Nothing came off. But that didn't make it any less itchy.

"Azalea heard from Tempus," Wist continued. "He's been telling every mage student he sees today. Saying Mr. Rift killed his old bondmate. Saying he's the one who's been selling psychoactive cuttings to upperclassmen all year."

"That makes no sense." I was too baffled to feel any outrage. "If there were any proof he harmed a mage—I mean, even if there weren't proof—he'd have been jailed or executed years ago.

"And why would mage students have to procure illegal cuttings from a healer? They've got connections that Mr. Rift could never dream of. If Tempus were accusing him of dealing pharmaceuticals, that's one thing. But *magic*?"

We both kept our voices down, as if attempting to blend in with the last hurrah of summer insects.

"It doesn't have to make sense," Wist said heavily. "My brothers sent the same information to the Guralta Parent Association. If he didn't resign, he'd have been fired. If only to avoid a fight with the parental set. If only for the school to save face."

"You're telling me these mage parents are gullible enough to believe any nonsense your brothers vomit out their—"

"No," Wist said. "There's a grain of truth."

I had to remind myself not to yell. I had to remind herself that she was not the one who'd invented the rumors. She was not the one who'd goaded Mr. Rift to resign.

"You can't just leave it at that," I said, with all the self-restraint I could muster.

"I don't know everything. But I think—he was a junkie. A long time in the past. Not of his own accord. His late bondmate forced it on him, over and over. A much more malicious magic than the mood-lifter your friend took at the party. Or the hallucinogenic type Tempus used on you, back in hunting season."

"That one could've gotten me killed."

"It wasn't designed to be habit-forming."

"To sum it up, Mr. Rift used to have a bondmate," I said, "way back before he became a teacher. One who made him an addict."

This was my problem: I wanted to know about things that were best left well enough alone. "Then his bondmate passed away. And I guess he broke the habit. A lucky break, right? But how did his bondmate die in the first place? Probably not old age."

"In the version of the story told by my brothers and Tempus, Mr. Rift's bondmate was only trying to help him. Mr. Rift got addicted all on his own. He killed his bondmate out of desperation for his next fix."

"If Mr. Rift had anything to do with his bondmate's death," I said, "anything at all—it must've been the clearest-cut case of self-defense that ever went up in front of an Osmanthian court. So clear that it would've been some kinda international humanitarian scandal if they punished him."

I'd never heard of a healer laying hands on a mage and getting away with it.

Wist nodded. "I knew he had been bonded before. Today was my first time learning the rest of it."

"How'd you know he used to be bonded? He doesn't wear a thread."

She held her mouth shut long enough that I began to think she'd decided against saying anything more.

Then: "Once, months ago—I was there when Tempus told him no one wants a used healer."

"Bet Mr. Rift laughed him out of the room. Is that even true?"

"Maybe in some circles. Among younger mages."

"In fairness," I said, "used or otherwise, a healer would have to be completely off their rocker to want anything to do with the likes of Tempus."

Wist made a muted grunt of agreement. She was in uniform again today, but with her top mostly unbuttoned. I peeled my gaze off her undershirt.

"Wist. Is this all because I turned your brother down?"

As our silence stretched to the point of snapping, she put a hand on the base of my neck, the part exposed by my uniform.

I jerked in surprise. Her hand fled so quickly that it was like I'd imagined the whole thing.

Wist spoke as if nothing had happened. "Nerium must have already been laying the groundwork. Your answer wouldn't make any difference as to whether or not he spared Mr. Rift."

She was the expert on her own brother. Nothing to be gained by disbelieving her.

34

After the day Mr. Rift left Guralta Academy, Wist and I did a much better job of staying apart.

But first things first. That night, I borrowed a transceiver from the dorm steward.

This time she handed me a snail-shaped shell, an impeccable round whorl that wouldn't have looked out of place in Saya's hermit crab tank. The magic cuttings grafted to it hid deep in the heart of the spiral. Just like how hermit crabs keep their tender bits tucked well out of reach.

I spoke to my parents, giving them the usual assurances. I'd gotten remarkably good at it. Everything was fine and dandy. I complained vociferously about the humidity, the hints of grey mold beginning to invade our room.

They knew I had a roommate named Saya. Occasionally I entertained them with tall tales of Pepper's spice-ridden antics. But I'd never said a single word about Wist.

I redirected the conversation to bland talk of the neighborhood, their garden, the exact dates of the school's winter holidays. For my upcoming birthday, I requested more snack money. I stared at Shien Nerium's lighthouse on the windowsill as I rambled.

After finishing up with my parents, I took a few breaths. The night air wafting through the window felt cooler than usual. Almost like autumn was more than just a made-up dream.

I had to get through with this before Saya returned from the healer baths.

I gripped the shell harder. I tried to contact Yarrow. She'd told me how at the party, but I'd never actually gone through with reaching out to her.

It worked.

By the time Saya showed up, I'd long since given back the enchanted shell. From the corner of my eye, I watched her settle down in bed to plow through assigned reading.

If I didn't strike now, she'd switch on her half-broken melodium and tune me out until quiet hours kicked in.

"Saya."

"Hm?"

"You come from a long line of healers."

"Mm."

"I don't. My family is subliminals all the way back. On both sides."

At last she glanced over at me. Her hair was still damp, the exact color of wet sand. She'd pinned it back out of her face. "Something you want to ask me?"

"How'd you guess?"

Saya wasn't one to roll her eyes. Which was likely for the best. She had such prominent eyes that any exertion seemed liable to send them tumbling out of their sockets.

"Listen," I continued, low and quiet. "I'd like to know more about healer history. I'm clueless. Except for what they teach us in class. Which definitely isn't everything."

"You want to know everything?"

"With your help, yes."

"Sure. Let me fill you in," said Saya. "It can't possibly take more than a couple dozen hours."

Sometimes I suspected myself of rubbing off on her. I suppose that was sort of inevitable when you lived in close quarters with a roommate.

"I'll settle for a couple highlights," I offered. "I know this is a risky topic."

She pressed at her eyes as if they itched. She let out a short breath. She shoved her books aside and hugged her pillow to her chest.

Then she told me some of what she'd heard from her family.

Healers had always been fewer in number than mages. Of course, both were dwarfed by subliminals, who made up the vast majority of every country's population.

Up till about fifty years ago, high-scoring healers in Osmanthus were basically raffled off to be claimed by elite mages via lottery. This ended only after a number of top healers made a suicide pact. They started systematically dying—and sometimes killing each other.

I'd known about the old bonding lottery. But our history books offered a much blander explanation for why the lottery ended. They devoted more page space to acclaiming the current system as being profoundly free and enlightened.

I suppose it was, in comparison to how things used to be. Healers nowadays could ostensibly choose who to heal, who to bond. But what seemed like a willing choice on paper might not feel much like a genuine choice in reality.

Saya had blood relatives who'd participated in the suicide pact of half a century earlier. She had relatives who'd been among the very first healer students to attend Guralta Academy, right after it went co-ed. Which was only a couple of decades ago.

Why, Saya asked, don't most people care much about healers' rights?

What she said next sounded like something she must've heard from her family a thousand times over. Healer dogma.

Saya's answer: most people are subliminals. It simply doesn't affect them until they have a healer son or daughter. Even then, it's so rare to be a skilled healer, one meriting training, that it's like getting stricken by an awful childhood disease. Once it happens, you just have to take it as an immutable fact of life.

For those who really bought into the mageocracy, serving mages as a healer would be a deep and welcome honor. As for subliminals, many of them did cling to their nominal identity as mages or healers, despite their complete lack of meaningful magical power.

Who remained to fight for healers' rights? Healers themselves, the absolute smallest slice of the population? Those who already lacked legal protections? Who could look back to the world of fifty years ago and legitimately consider themselves to already be much better off?

Little by little, I realized that Saya had reached the same conclusion as me. Or rather, I'd reached the same conclusion as her. I'd been late to discover truths that she'd been keenly aware of all her life.

She'd arrived at the academy fully prepared to make enemies of her fellow healers (if she had to). As long as she ingratiated herself with mages, one day she would come out on top.

I couldn't speak to the degree of her success, or lack thereof. Co-ed classwork was deliberately kept very businesslike, and it wasn't like I had time to lounge around spying on her. If she ever got a chance to become more properly acquainted with mage students, it had to be happening during all those club activities of hers.

Either way, Saya's approach was the embodiment of what I'd said to Wist on the library roof. Long-term, the only way for us Osmanthian healers to win anything in life was by locking in the support of more powerful allies.

Wist came to mind, quite unprompted. She had a habit of barging in like that.

I soon stopped asking Saya about healer history. I'd heard enough. I understood the message Mr. Rift had been trying to send me.

I thought I did, anyway. If I was on the wrong track, well, too bad. Not like he'd ever show up to correct me.

I had trouble sleeping on these early September nights. Right as evening temperatures dropped to less ungodly levels of heat. Right when it should've gotten a little easier.

For once, gory nightmares weren't what kept me up. I kept looping back to the same question. What was my goal in being stuck at the academy for another three and a half years?

I must have some kind of goal. I hadn't chosen to enroll, but I'd looked Shien Nerium in the face and refused his money. I'd chosen to stay.

If you asked me a few months ago, I'd have said it was to survive. To somehow make it through. Certainly not to thrive. Certainly not to be noticed.

How about now?

Mr. Rift hadn't told me what to do with my life. That wasn't his style. Time to figure it out for myself.

Night after night, I sat at my desk under the guise of doing schoolwork. Instead of studying, I wrote in Wist's notebook.

Wist was much the same as me, insofar as you could ever compare a healer and a mage. Worlds apart, but with a few key points in common. Wist didn't necessarily aspire to be a great mage. She was stuck with her magic, though. No way to surgically remove it. And with her level of power, no one would ever expect or hope for her to be anything else.

At times when Wist too was there in her room, the answers came swiftly. I was always proud when I could pry more than a few one-syllable words out of her.

I'd root for you if you did want to do something else with your life, I wrote.

Like what?

The answer came to me at once. *Like start a company to sell artisan soap.*

???

Or spend all your time seducing girls on the beach, I added.

Wist: *Do I look like that's what I want to do with my life?*

Oh, sorry. Am I projecting? Never mind.

I looked at this last sentence and considered crossing it out. Or erasing it. But the words would have already appeared on her page.

Forget the soap, I wrote to her. *Forget the girls, too, if you want. You could just aspire to eat good food and look at the stars once in a while and try not to ruin anyone's life. Your personal mission doesn't have to be something noble.*

We joked a bit about what we could do if we ran away. Maybe we could follow in Mr. Rift's footsteps. Maybe we could find some distant unnamed place in the world where no one really cared if you were a healer or a mage.

My hand kept cramping from scribbling too fast. Somehow I never noticed until after I told her goodnight. Only when I curled up in bed afterward would it seize up, pain arcing through the muscle in jolts as quick as shooting stars.

Once I wrote, without any real context: *It's too bad there's no such thing as a chastity belt for bonding.*

A day later, I noticed that Wist had followed this up with: *Not for lack of trying. Nothing has ever been found to work perfectly.*

Given the absence of perplexed question marks, I could only assume she'd realized I was pondering the school code of conduct and its rules against mage-healer fraternization.

Someday I'll work the knots out of your magic better than ever before, I told her. *What would you be capable of if you weren't walking around in this fog of pain all day and all night?*

Wist's response came slowly. *Sounds like a lot of work for you.*

I wrote faster. *You might not want to use me. But remember—I want to use you. Normal mages don't feel like they owe healers anything, anyway.*

If you can't help feeling differently, then sure, pay me back. Give me royalties. Give me a percentage of whatever new power you can unlock by not having your magic branches be so cramped and cornered all the time.

What do you want it for? Wist asked.

I'm not going to put my genius plan in writing, you fool. Think about it. Healers can only ever hold power by proxy. Through others. With others. Not just talking about magic, of course.

If you don't aspire to anything great on your own, if you don't have any grand use planned for that power of yours—and if you don't want to start making artisan soaps instead—then give it to me.

She wrote in reply: *What makes you think I would?*

In my head, she sounded bemused.

I couldn't explain why, but I read Wist's writing as being more expressive than her spoken voice. Not that her penmanship showed obvious spikes of emotion.

Sometimes you surprise me, I wrote back. It was the best response I had.

The island had been lucky this summer. No notable typhoons. The first of the season came in the second week of September. It stayed far, far off shore: much too far for any evacuation orders.

The school faculty warned us not to swim, but students were still allowed to walk the beach. Though the wind wasn't strong enough to knock anyone over, we could see it pushing helpless seabirds backwards in the sky.

Sand lashed our ankles and calves hard enough to feel like rug burn. Clouds passing overhead cast dense shadows that flew across the ground at speeds seemingly faster than any airship.

I spoke with Yarrow several times as the Guralta Cup approached. Never in person, naturally. I had a whole lot of questions for her. The type of questions she couldn't possibly answer on the spot. But she did her best to oblige me later.

Her mage—the Gwindel mage, the one I'd resented and raged against for stealing her away—was plenty old enough to remember the circumstances around Wist's adoption.

Yarrow described him talking about how multiple families had competed to take custody of Wist. No one had ever seen a child like her, he said. Of course all the great mage clans wanted her. Gwindel complained that the Shiens had played dirty to get her. He blamed their matriarch, the current head of the clan.

Back then there had been jokes about Wist being a changeling. Her birth parents were relatively weak mages. Although magical strength was known not to be directly hereditary, no one could understand how a creature like her had been born out of the blue.

At the time, some also called her the second coming of the Kraken. In other words, the second coming of a fabled foreign enemy who'd helped the Blessed Empire oppress Osmanthus for centuries. Not exactly a compliment.

Then again, I thought, the Kraken had been a villain to Osmanthus (to the old monarchy, anyhow), but a godlike hero to her own empire. All depends on your standpoint.

Yarrow related how Gwindel, though not fond of the Shien brothers, had expressed some sympathy for Nerium's attitude toward Wist. How threatened he must have felt, Gwindel said. Eldest in the family. Right in line to inherit. And then they adopted a child with more magic branches than every other mage in the country put together.

This sounded like an exaggeration. But I did see his point.

"Would your mage have done the same?" I asked Yarrow. "Would she always have been treated like crap by others in line to inherit? No matter which clan adopted her? That makes zero sense. Are all mages idiots?"

It took Yarrow a few extra seconds to answer. In the meantime I heard only the breathy roaring of the silence inside my borrowed transceiver shell. Today the dorm steward had handed me an elegant striped whelk.

"He says he would have opted for a different approach."

Yeah, sure. It was all too easy to speak in hypotheticals.

"He also called you a mouthy little healer."

"Oh," I said weakly.

Of course Gwindel was listening. Perhaps in a literal sense, tilting his head toward Yarrow's hairpin. Or perhaps not. He didn't need to be in the same room with her to hear and feel and react to her thoughts.

"You seem more ... outspoken than a few years ago," I said to Yarrow.

Didn't want to get her in trouble. But curiosity consumed me. What had changed for her?

"True," she conceded. "We've reached a kind of equilibrium. Though there's nothing equal about it."

"How?"

"He sees what I've done for him. I'm in the top one percent of healers in the entire country."

I tried to listen with an open mind. I listened, and I heard genuine pride.

"He knows I pose no threat to him or the Gwindel clan. He's my livelihood. Nowadays, he's my whole family's livelihood. He doesn't hit me. In that sense, you could call us a team."

I was glad I couldn't see Yarrow's face as we spoke through the shell. Or rather, that she couldn't see mine.

If she and her bondmate got along so well now, perhaps I could risk pushing it a little further.

"You warned me about bonding once," I said. "Do you retract that?"

Yarrow took a sharp breath. I started falling all over myself to tell her that she didn't have to take it seriously. She didn't have to answer.

But she did. "Clematis."

"I'm sorry," I said wretchedly.

"I don't recommend bonding for you."

I thought she might close the subject there, but she kept going. Her tone was very even.

"You would have to love them in a way that—I don't know if it's right to love anyone that wholly. Even then, it would be frightening."

The essential qualities of her voice sounded the same as in my memory. Soft and high and soothing and whispery and utterly nonthreatening. Why did the words coming out of the shell still have the power to nail me down in place?

"Without love, you would at least need to be assured of them showing you the utmost respect." She stopped for a moment, as if to acknowledge that we both knew this to be a joke. "A soul-deep respect? What mage could honestly promise that? It's been trained out of them since birth."

"You—" I cleared my throat. I felt all out of words. "Doesn't seem like you would've been able to voice such thoughts in the past. Around the time when you first got bonded."

"Yes," said Yarrow. "I feel safer having independent thoughts now."

"So things really are better for you. That's—that's good. I had a hard time believing it."

"But it's like having those thoughts as a beast in a glass-walled cage at the zoo. Always being watched."

The eerie part was that I could hear a hint of a smile in her voice. That beautiful warm smile. Never again could I fully trust it. Having bonded, she would never again be completely and solely herself.

Out of respect for Yarrow, I kept the bulk of this out of my notebook.

I also wasn't quite sure how Wist would react, to be honest. She'd put on a very strange act around Yarrow at Nerium's party. Perhaps because she knew Yarrow was a healer for a rival clan? Yet Wist had displayed little to no interest in mage clan politics to date.

More importantly, I didn't want to incriminate anyone. And I didn't fancy myself a busybody. But I was already in deep. Way over my head. I could admit that.

I wrote to Wist: *If worst comes to worst, remember what we talked about on the mountaintop.* Hopefully she wouldn't be too muddled by magical agony to miss my hints.

35

ANOTHER TYPHOON, much larger and closer, was forecast for the week of my birthday. The last full week of September.

Torrential rain began pounding the island days before the wind picked up. The only saving grace was that the forecasters seemed quite confident it wouldn't make landfall.

The government didn't order anyone to leave the island. Even so, all students in off-campus housing got called back to stay in the dorms. Likewise, many beachfront vacationers decided to temporarily retreat over the bridge to Baneberry. I wondered if the Shiens and Gwindels had followed suit.

Mage seniors marched all over campus to prepare for the incoming typhoon. My classmates and I clustered awkwardly in the dorm lounge while they came by to briskly reinforce the roof and windows with magic, to shield the basement and first floor against flooding.

To my knowledge, no one had ever invented a magic skill capable of cleanly turning away a storm. Past attempts to do so had been accompanied by all sorts of ugly and unanticipated side effects (like somehow transforming the hurricane into a stampede of tornadoes).

But if they knew with a high degree of certainty that it would be nowhere near a direct hit, there was plenty magic could do to mitigate the effects.

I found myself having to repeatedly explain this to my parents. They wanted me to leave the island, to find my way home to the capital city till everything passed.

"I'll be fine," I told them. "We'll all be fine. They're keeping us corralled on campus for our own safety.

"Anyway—the island is locked down. Well, except for those with portal access. The tram won't be running for a while. If things get real bad, they'll evacuate us by porting."

Nothing I said seemed to staunch the worrying. Ah, well. At least I'd tried.

Orders to stay on campus turned into orders to stay indoors. Class got canceled for the rest of the week. Then they announced the postponement of the much-anticipated Guralta Cup.

All the while, the rain came down in sheets, in waterfalls, with intimidating and implacable force.

The only positive part of this, aside from not having classes, was that the last of the summer heat and stickiness fled before the driving rain. For the first time all season, I let down my long uniform sleeves.

One could only fold so many paper airships before the whole endeavor began to feel fruitless. Bored out of my mind, I sat cross-legged on my desk chair and tried to talk Saya into playing word games. When that failed, I started sketching my latest borrowed transceiver (a turban shell).

When someone rapped at our door, Saya and I exchanged uncomprehending looks. We'd just polished off a grumpy lunch. It was early afternoon, but already darker than twilight. Angry gusts kept rattling our rain-blasted window.

Saya seemed disinclined to move. I got up and answered the door instead.

The dorm steward stepped in before either of us could speak any words of invitation. She pushed the door shut behind her with her heel. Outside the building, the wind howled in rage.

"Asa," she said crisply.

"What?"

"You're suspended. Effective immediately."

I attempted to parse this. It seemed like the set-up for some sort of obscure prank.

"Class is canceled," I pointed out. Just in case it needed to be said. "What's there to be suspended from?"

She refused to address my airtight logic. "Try to be serious. You've been reported for fraternization."

In the space between heartbeats, I felt myself clench up. But my mouth was already moving in self-defense.

"I haven't broken any rules," I protested. "Not the serious ones. I'll swear anything. I haven't kissed anyone. I haven't—"

"Mage-healer fraternization is in the eye of the beholder," said the steward.

"What's that even mean?"

I knew without her telling me, though. It meant: *the rules can be anything we want.*

"Defend yourself at the tribunal." She beckoned. "Follow me."

"Now?"

"Now."

"Everything's shut down," I said, nonplussed. "We aren't allowed to go outdoors."

"You won't need to."

I stood frozen. The only part of me that kept working was that fist-sized muscle pumping away furiously in my chest, pumping as if fighting to bail out the bottom of a rapidly sinking boat.

"One moment," I managed. My voice sounded like someone else speaking.

I strode back to my desk. It was deep enough in the room that the steward might not be able to see the specifics of what I did with my hands. I grabbed the transceiver shell. I seized the black spiked lighthouse from the windowsill. I shoved them both in my uniform pockets.

I half-expected the steward to stop me, but she let it slide. I stuffed my feet in my battered school-issue shoes.

"You, too," the dorm steward said to Saya.

I blinked at Saya. "What'd *you* do?"

She shrugged one shoulder. Like ducklings, the two of us followed the dorm steward down to the laundry room.

I made a show of looking around. "I see how discipline works here. We're to get punished with a thorough washing?"

No one responded.

Don't judge me too harshly. This is how I cope.

The steward stopped before an unobtrusive locked door at the far end of the laundry room. It was painted a flat industrial yellow, and had a frame low enough that Wist would've banged her head if she tried walking straight through it. Not so much of a problem for the rest of us.

I'd noticed this door before, but I'd assumed it led to a storage closet. Or nowhere at all. The kind of door you'd open to reveal naught but an old unfinished wall.

The steward unlocked the wan yellow door. It creaked as it swung open. I tried to look through.

I couldn't see anything.

My brain told me there must be something on the other side. My brain acknowledged the existence of an open space beyond the threshold, a space that must've been filled. Yet my eyes understood nothing.

The dorm steward took out a jangling metal ring. The kind you might expect to see carried around by an old-fashioned jailer. Instead of keys, it held padlocks, all coated in a patina of magic cuttings. Too many different locks to count.

They were the type you could unlock by rolling set combinations of numbers. She selected one from the ring and held it up over the threshold as she opened it.

Magic rewrote the space beyond the door. It arrived in a flash so powerful that I found myself anxiously listening for a clap of thunder that never followed.

The dorm steward pushed us through.

The room for the disciplinary tribunal was perhaps less ostentatious than, in my stupor of shock, I'd expected.

What struck me above all else was the silence. As the door shut behind us, we were utterly cut off from any hint of building-slamming wind or potentially disastrous rain. Here in this windowless chamber, there might as well have been no seasons, no weather, no typhoon happening at all.

No. Windowless wasn't the right word for it. The walls bore opaque arched shapes that looked like they ought to be windows. Like they'd been windows in a past life. From them shone traces of magic and an imitation of blazing sunlight.

We could've been anywhere. I had no proof that we were even still on the island. If I had to guess, though—we might've been in one of the administrative buildings on the mage side of campus. The same building that housed the collar archives, for instance.

The Head Magister presided at the front of the room in formal mage robes, looking down on us.

I hadn't seen her in person in months and months. To an ordinary healer student, the head of school was so distant a figure that she might as well have been a silver-haired politician. A city governor. A Board member.

I recognized a few other mage faculty from around campus, as well as from the originator exam. I didn't know all their names. The dorm steward was the only healer staff member in attendance.

In my first few seconds after setting foot in this weirdly bright and soundless room, I battled to figure out my position.

It wasn't looking good.

On one side sat Wist, blank-faced, sandwiched between Ficus and Nerium. If this were a government courtroom, she'd be the plaintiff. Tempus lurked in the row behind them.

I was very slow to realize that Saya no longer lingered by the door with me and the steward.

Saya had gone over to take a seat in the same row as Tempus.

I didn't pay any attention to what happened next. The dorm steward must have led me over to the opposite side of the room. The side for me, the presumptive defendant.

The only other person here was—to my absolute astonishment—Azalea. I started to mouth my confusion at her. But I didn't know if we were allowed to speak. My brain felt like it'd been thrown in a food processor.

The steward made me sit diagonally below Azalea. I obeyed numbly.

The chairs on both sides, including mine, all had feet like naked human feet. Disturbingly realistic. And arms that ended in human-shaped hands.

They weren't bolted down. When I tried scooting my chair forward, the soles of its feet slid on the floor with an eerie velvety smoothness. No noise; no squeaking.

Each chair—empty and full alike—was a slightly different shade of wood. The hues varied from deep teak to bloodless birch. The more I scanned them, the more they looked like a faceless crowd, and the more the unvarnished wooden surfaces felt like skin.

Same as the driftwood couch back in the healer dorm common room. Had someone on the academy staff gone out of their way to procure the most ghoulish furniture they could find?

The Head Magister's seat was shaped to resemble an enormous pair of hands cupping her from behind. I immediately had visions of the colossal fingers curling down to squelch her like an overripe peach.

She spoke words that slid off me like typhoon rain off magically sealed windows.

I couldn't listen. I couldn't comprehend. I was too busy beating myself up for my own blindness. I'd suspected Azalea. Wrongly, it seemed.

I hadn't suspected Saya for a second.

Saya. Oh, Saya. She'd been so frazzled recently. She'd had plenty of good excuses. Now I wondered. Had she been busy preparing for Guralta Cup festivities with her school clubs—or busy feeding intel to Tempus, or the Shien brothers, or all three of them?

When I wasn't using Wist's notebook, I'd packed it at the bottom of a desk drawer, under a couple of wrinkled texts. I hadn't truly tried to hide it.

I tasted bile at the top of my tight-cinched throat. Not once had I made a conscious choice to trust Saya. It had been a given. Distrusting her had never even occurred to me as an option.

Why not? Because she didn't join forces with Tempus's other lackeys to harangue me during hunting season? She'd been gone for training camp the entire time, anyway. Because she so lovingly cared for her hermit crabs? I'd once put my own ass on the line to save them from what might've been a terrible fate.

This is how you thank me, Saya?

Yet my anger stopped short of fully erupting. I couldn't blame her. Not with my entire being.

She'd practically told me what she was doing. All I took away from it was that both she and I saw the necessity of winning over stronger allies. Mage allies.

I hadn't stopped to consider whose favor it might behoove her to seek, or who might benefit most from recruiting her. I'd only pictured Saya cozying up to fellow students. I hadn't thought at all beyond the confines of school.

Behind me, Azalea had risen to speak. She seemed to be defending me. Me and Wist both, in fact, though the tribunal was set up to pit us against each other.

She described the first time I'd healed Wist. Yes, they were alone, she said. But in an outside setting. And it was a real emergency. She said I'd saved Wist from going fully berserk.

This in turn raised a flurry of questions about why she and Wist had let me slink away in the dark afterward. Why they'd never mentioned my involvement. Why anyone would believe that a middling first-year healer student could pull off such a feat.

Props to Azalea for trying. I didn't know her too well, but I would never have expected her to face the Shien brothers and formally contradict their claims. It wouldn't have been fair to expect that. Didn't she come from one of the lower-ranked mage families?

I gradually came to understand that the Shien brothers had filed an official complaint with the school administration. Saya and Tempus offered additional reports to support their claims of inappropriate contact between Asa Clematis—a healer student—and Wisteria Shien. Their youngest sister.

Nerium wore layers of sandy linen. A summery garment. His hands rested, relaxed, atop the end of his cane. He talked so sincerely about how they only wanted to protect their sister from rash decisions and bad influences. Beside him, Wist touched her collar as if it choked her.

Saya wasn't done yet, either. I sat hard against the back of my chair when I heard her quote from my notebook. As if she'd memorized it. No—transcribed it.

She read steadily off a folded piece of paper. Briefly, my sight blurred. I could imagine Saya's small neat rows of handwriting more clearly than I could see my own weak curled fingers.

"I'd root for you if you did want to do something else with your life ... spend all your time seducing girls on the beach .... Someday I'll work the knots out of your magic better than ever before ... not going to put my genius plan in writing....

"If you don't aspire to anything great on your own, if you don't have any grand use planned for that power of yours ... then give it to me."

Only one thing kept me from covering my face with my hands.

Ficus had been toying with something too small for me to see from here. More scraps of paper, maybe. He appeared to be about a minute away from starting to make full-fledged spitballs.

As Saya droned on, he reached for Wist's left arm.

He twisted her forearm in both fists as if wringing water from a rag.

Wist didn't move. She didn't cringe.

I stared incredulously from Nerium to Tempus to the magisters arrayed in judgment. There was absolutely nothing to block their view of Wist and Ficus.

No one said a word.

They listened politely to Saya's testimony.

Was I losing my mind? What would he do next, start breaking Wist's fingers one by one right in front of the Head Magister?

I twisted around to make eye contact with Azalea. She was chewing her nails bloody.

I contemplated tipping my head back and screaming for Ficus to stop. By all appearances, no matter what anyone said from here on out, I was already well on my way to expulsion.

Nerium, smiling amiably, leaned over to whisper something. His glasses shone with a light not so different from that of the imitation windows.

After a few reluctant moments, Ficus let go of Wist. She brought her wrung-out arm back in front of her. It was shaking.

The school rules didn't matter, I thought. The truth didn't matter. What mattered was that adult members of the prestigious Shien clan had brought a formal complaint.

The content of the complaint could've been anything. Heck, they could've accused me of smelling funny. One way or another, the administration would've taken it just as seriously.

The Shien brothers wouldn't let Wist speak up. Look at her, trapped between them. Even if she tried, it would only backfire.

By arguing in my defense, she'd prove the exact points that Tempus had now risen to make. His delicate enunciation resounded through the room with the persuasiveness of a climactic speech in a play.

He painted a picture of me as a crudely manipulative social climber, laughable in my brazenness. But a real danger to a sheltered young lady like Wist, consumed by chronic pain, ignorant of the ugliness that awaited in the impure world outside the Shien family manor.

It took enormous strength of character for me not to look Tempus in the eye, open my mouth, and mime throwing up right there on the spotless echoing floor.

He continued. He described the bizarre lengths Wist went to in order to favor me. Following me on an unauthorized trip off the island. (No mention of how we'd gotten ported off the island in the first place.) Selecting me for her originator exam despite my indisputably abysmal grades.

"'Abysmal' is putting it a bit strongly," I said. "I fall right in the middle, thank you."

The Head Magister called for silence. Next, she asked for Shien Nerium to summarize his concerns.

Though I'd been blindsided by Saya's betrayal, I'd fully expected to see the Shien brothers here. I'd stuck the model lighthouse in my pocket because I'd had brief and grandiloquent visions of leaping up like a lawyer in a story.

I'd slam the tower down on a table and turn its crimson light up to the highest level. Surveillance gulls would come crashing into the windows in their eagerness to reach it. A dramatic demonstration of the miniature tower's power to create a distraction, to work mischief, to aid in violating the school code of conduct.

I got this from the Heap, I'd proclaim. Created and signed by the very Shien Nerium sitting right there across from me. He must've used it all the time, back in the day. No gulls ever saw him when he got up to bad shit. If you're going to punish someone for bending the rules, start with him.

Now those wild visions faded. For one thing, no one would be swayed by accusations of hypocrisy. They simply wouldn't care, and I couldn't make them.

I could imagine Nerium's response, too. He'd be supremely unruffled. He'd point out, ever so gently, that it no longer mattered who had first crafted the model lighthouse. Who possessed it now? Who was now most likely to have used it as a decoy?

Who now stood accused of flagrantly violating school rules?

Anyway, this chamber had no real windows. Even if it did, the surveillance gulls must've all been called to go shelter somewhere out of the reach of the typhoon winds.

Needless to say, I didn't take out the tower. Its spikes pricked me in the pocket as I sat wooden in my chair.

The turban shell on the other side of my body had spikes, too, knobby and irregular. I wormed my hand into my pocket to grip it.

Indignation resurged in me when Shien Nerium began to speak—very selectively—of our behavior at his house party. Half of what he described had occurred well out of his sight. The rest hadn't even happened to begin with.

My hand shot up. I didn't wait for anyone to call on me. "If someone needs to be blamed, then blame him," I snapped. "We're minors! We were on his property. We were outdoors half the time, and the rest of the time, there were plenty of people. Call more witnesses!"

As if additional witnesses would utter anything other than what the Shiens coached them to say.

"Your closeness is highly irregular," said the Head Magister.

"We've never even seen each other naked!"

Something jabbed me in the back. I twisted in my seat. *Not helping,* Azalea mouthed.

I shut up. In a way, it didn't matter whether my passionate declarations of innocence turned out to help or hurt my case. The so-called rules were soft putty to those with power, and a hard wall of cement to those without.

I wondered if Mr. Rift, too, had been obliged to sit through a similar farce before he wrote up his letter of resignation.

We were acting out Nerium's script now. All of us, willing or otherwise. At this point, there were only two possible outcomes.

No—not just at this point. Those two outcomes had been lying in wait ever since Saya and the dorm steward and I walked through the laundry room door into this falsely sunlit room.

Wist would be let off with a light rebuke. As for me, I'd be expelled. Shien Nerium left no room for doubt. He called my presence at school an unacceptable threat to Wist's integrity as a developing mage.

Whatever that was supposed to mean. What, precisely, did he intend to claim I threatened? Her purity? Her chastity? Her willingness to bond a more suitable healer some distant day in the future?

All sorts of arguments crowded my head. But I knew better than to voice them. Whatever I said now, I was already a goner.

The only question was what would happen after my expulsion. Would Shien Nerium renew his offer? Would he kindly volunteer to pay all my family's fees?

Of course not, you might think. Of course he would prefer to see me punished for my initial refusal. He would smile sadly and shake his head and tell me it was a true shame I had chosen so poorly.

Somehow, though, I had a premonition that he would give me the money.

Why? Because that'd be a foolproof way to guarantee I'd never be able to face Wist again. Not ever. Not even once she graduated.

After the tribunal ended, he would offer me the money once more. Don't worry, he would say. He'd be ever so discreet about it. He'd promise to cover the crippling expulsion and misconduct fees in full. Might even throw in some extra on top. As a gesture of charity. Noblesse oblige. A sign of friendship.

This time, I wouldn't be able to turn him down. I couldn't bring my parents to ruin out of my own stupidity and stubbornness and pride. I would bow and scrape and grit my teeth and take it.

I would take it all.

I would be his. I would owe him a lifetime's worth of loyalty. And you know what? He would only ask one little thing of me. It wouldn't be difficult at all, especially not after I departed the island.

He'd request for me to stay far away from his sister. I would obey him until the day one of us died.

I couldn't bring myself to look across the room at Wist. I was all out of ammunition. The jagged surface of the turban shell dug deep into my palm. I no longer knew what to say.

36

"FIVE MINUTES, PLEASE," said the Head Magister.

A noise-swallowing wall of magic encircled her and all the other staff at the front of the room, ceiling to floor. It looked like jelly, slick and prismatic.

After a few moments, a magister walked out. The transparent curtain rippled shut in their wake.

The magister went over to Nerium and Ficus and asked if they would care for refreshments. Even from here I could make out the full conversation. Must be something about the acoustics of the tribunal chamber, its pompous buttressed ceiling. Either that, or its coating of sound-shaping magic.

No one asked if Azalea or I wanted anything. Not that I could've answered. My throat felt too full.

As the magisters conferred, I watched the dorm steward wheel over a serving cart to bring the Shien brothers and Tempus tall glasses of sparkling water. Wist declined. Intentionally or otherwise, no one bothered offering a drink to Saya.

I dug the transceiver shell out of my pocket. It was an astonishingly ugly specimen, rough-surfaced and mottled and pointy. I held it cupped in my lap.

I wanted to stay.

Not necessarily here at school. Guralta Academy could go screw itself. My thoughts on that hadn't changed.

Maddening though she was, I wanted to stay with Wist.

This wasn't in my hands anymore. I'd laid the groundwork, to the extent that I could, but what happened next wasn't my choice.

Yet I still couldn't help thinking it: *Please, please, please.*

My eyes were painfully dry.

Nerium and Ficus clinked their glasses together.

I clutched the shell in my lap and forced myself to gaze straight across the room. Right into the dark dispassionate eyes of Wisteria Shien.

Outwardly, she offered no acknowledgment. But she was looking back at me. She'd been looking at me the whole time, come to think of it. Even when Nerium orated. Even when Ficus twisted her arm.

"Nerium," said Wist.

"Yes, my dear?"

I heard them as distinctly as I'd heard Nerium and Ficus toasting each other, as distinctly as I'd heard Tempus and Saya deliver their slanderous testimony.

Wist didn't turn to look at him when she spoke.

"If you get Clematis expelled," she said, slow and deliberate, "I plan to apply for emancipation."

I felt my blood jolt to life.

In the row behind me, Azalea sucked in a swift breath.

At first Nerium displayed no reaction whatsoever. Then he laughed a bit to himself. Just a quiet little huff. He handed Ficus his half-filled glass of sparkling water. Ficus regarded it quizzically, then set it down with a clank on the serving cart.

Nerium's hands clasped themselves once more over the head of his cane.

"Wisteria." His voice remained light, teasing. "You can't be serious."

Her voice, in contrast, remained as flat as windless waters. "I've prepared the paperwork. Grandmother might miss me. Will you? Thought you might be glad to see me go."

"Go where?" Ficus asked idly.

"Exactly," Nerium said. "Where would you go? You have no idea how to live on your own. You have no connections outside the clan. And you'll still have no power to stop Asa Clematis from being expelled. It's a simple matter of carrying the school regulations to their obvious conclusion. Fair treatment for all. No exceptions."

Funny, that. If the regulations were fair, we'd both be getting kicked out. Not just me. It takes two to fraternize.

Wist spoke at the same pace as before. Her brothers couldn't rush her. "If Clematis leaves, I'll leave, too. Both the academy and the clan."

Nerium studied her fixedly, as if attempting to compel her to make eye contact. Despite his own eyes being blotted out by the magic swaddling his high-end glasses.

"Why?"

All emotion had evaporated from his voice. It was like hearing a mockery of Wist. I hated it.

"...For her healing," Wist said, after a distressingly long pause. "I want Clematis for her healing."

I resisted the urge to cradle my head in my hands. She really needed to work on her acting skills.

To be clear, I saw and approved of what Wist was doing. She'd spoken in terms that people here in the tribunal chamber would understand. Of using and exploiting, of being used and exploited. Those were the dynamics of their world.

"You'll be stranded out on the streets in a week," Nerium told her.

"I've found a family willing to take me."

He let out a sharp bark of laughter. "Who?" He flung his arm out, finger pointed at Azalea. "Her? You're delusional. The Wrens wouldn't dare."

The sound-absorbing curtain around the magisters dissolved with the abrupt sizzle of water hitting a hot pan. They all seemed to be talking at once.

Except for the Head Magister, who had a hand raised to touch one of her magic-laced earrings. She put her other hand over her mouth and muttered as if speaking to herself. Or to someone unseen; someone using the skill called Transceiver.

This time, slow-bubbling triumph was what made my fingers curl harder around the homely turban shell. Finally.

"Not the Wren clan," Wist said to Nerium.

If I strained, I could make out the Head Magister's voice, even over the chatter coming from the rest of the faculty.

"Please," she was saying. "Don't trouble yourself. We'll arrange for an escort—"

A middle-aged man and a slim young woman materialized on the open floor of the chamber. Right at the midpoint between me and Wist. The man was stiffly bearded. He wore a waistcoat that strained to accommodate his belly.

His waistcoat also held in the aura of a haughty core. And twenty-two separate branches. Far more than any other mage in the room except Wist.

He'd ported himself and his healer with zero fanfare. No advance whiff of magic. No shining aftermath dusting the air around them. It was as if they'd been waiting there all along, quiet as you please.

That right there was one of the signs of a practiced mage. The more adroit they were with their power, the less noticeable its use became. The very best mages were supposedly the hardest to trace.

It still turned my stomach to watch him lead Yarrow around like he owned her. Yet this time—only this time—I was profoundly grateful to the Gwindel mage.

I jammed the borrowed transceiver shell back in my uniform pocket. Its job here was done. Now that they'd arrived in person, they wouldn't need to listen in.

Nerium looked pale. I wanted to laugh. If only I could peer inside his head. How it must be whirling. In a right tizzy. Ficus would be no help, either: he slouched in his chair and examined his nails.

Minutes ago, my gut had cramped up with stress, hard as stone. Now it cramped all over again, this time with the struggle not to burst out giggling.

"Hello, Wisteria," said the Gwindel mage.

Wist bowed her head at him. A gesture of thanks. He raised his hand in answer.

Yarrow said nothing. She bowed back in Wist's direction, albeit several degrees deeper than Wist herself. She had her hands clasped in front, her hair wound up in a smooth black knot at the nape of her neck. She could've been an attendant on one of the most expensive cross-country trains.

With his mouth hanging open, Tempus looked about as foolish as he did whenever I pictured him in my head. Which was never—I was too stingy to give him any mental real estate. But you get the idea.

Saya had her own mouth closed tight.

The Head Magister and her staff appeared to be striving and failing to maintain expressions of professional neutrality. Not failing in the sense that they betrayed a preference for one side over another, now that new sides had emerged and everything had gotten scrambled. Failing in the sense that they came off as having been thoroughly flummoxed.

Azalea kicked the back of my chair. I twisted my neck to see her visibly torn between outrage and grudging awe.

She glanced meaningfully from Wist to the Gwindel mage. "Did you—?"

This was around the time when Gwindel exchanged a few words of small talk with the Head Magister.

Then he said, without having offered any manner of greeting directly to Ficus or Nerium, "So long as all the proper procedures are followed, we would be delighted to welcome Wisteria to the Gwindel clan."

I couldn't honestly take much credit.

Through Yarrow, I'd confirmed that the Gwindel mage was open to hearing from Wist, Through my notebook, I'd suggested to Wist how she might get a hold of him. Without much context, and without writing any names.

I hadn't worried about Saya snooping. Even if I accidentally left the notebook open on my desk, I'd figured she'd think it was a diary. I'd figured she'd know to leave well enough alone. If it was just the two of us—no mages in town to curry favor with—I doubt she'd have read it.

But Saya herself had something of a paranoid streak. Perhaps that part of her had rubbed off on me. Or perhaps my experience during hunting season had left me wary.

Either way, I was lucky Wist hadn't been led completely astray by the vagueness of my hints about Gwindel.

The important part was that I didn't tell her what to do. She'd thought I would be better off taking Nerium's bribe, and I'd refused to listen.

I had to let Wist exercise the same right. To say no. To stay true to what she truly wanted.

During the originator exam, when Wist spoke of family emancipation on the mountaintop, she'd said:

Threatening to leave the Shiens is my last piece of leverage. Someday I might need to use it.

It wasn't my place to decide if her *someday* was now. Even if her last piece of leverage worked, after all, what would she get out of it? Nothing, really.

I was the one who would benefit most. I was the one who might get to stay in school, if she put her own family status on the line to fight for it. I was the one who'd be spared from a potential lifetime of kowtowing to my would-be post-expulsion benefactor, Shien Nerium.

Besides, I hadn't known if talks between her and Gwindel would go anywhere. Nor had I known how Nerium would strike at us next. I'd assumed he would wait until the typhoon passed.

I certainly hadn't expected to be sitting here as if on trial for crimes against the school, bathed in the oppressive yellow glow of faux windows.

I hadn't expected to be sequestered in a chamber that succeeded in the utter erasure of the typhoon rumbling offshore. Its wind and rain whipped every inch of the island, from the western caves to the eastern ruins. But not a trace of its presence managed to penetrate this stifled place.

I hadn't expected to twist my hands together as I wondered if Wist would ever say anything. If she was prepared to openly turn on the Shiens. If Yarrow would hear her speak through the shell. If the Gwindel mage would really be willing to show up in support.

Because if this gamble worked—

Nerium, cane in hand, stumped down to the part of the floor where Gwindel and Yarrow waited.

He stopped before the Gwindel mage.

"I find it difficult to believe," he said, "that the head of your clan would be so eager to antagonize us."

"Your treatment of your sister is an open secret in high society, boy." Gwindel sounded bored. "Few would be surprised by her transfer to another family.

"Few except, perhaps, the head of the Shien clan. Who might have been willing to overlook your capers, but only so long as you managed to keep the situation under control. And not risk outright losing your sister."

He winked at Wist. "Us S-Class mages need to stick together."

What a pretty sentiment. Those with power did so love to cling to each other.

Yes—let all the greatest mages ball up to form a rat king, ready to devour the rest of us. That was a perfect analogy for our glorious nation's mageocratic regime of government.

Not that I could afford to criticize the Gwindel mage out loud. Without evidence of his backing, Wist would've struggled to convince Nerium that she was sincere in her threat of emancipation.

I'd scoffed at Mr. Rift when he called Shien Nerium young. But now—as Nerium kept arguing—I understood. This felt like watching a calf trying to contest a bull.

Meanwhile, in the seats further back, Saya and Tempus appeared to have gotten locked in their own fierce debate.

Ficus balanced his glittering glass of water on the very tip of his forefinger.

Azalea's foot restlessly scraped at the back of my chair.

"Gentlemen," said the Head Magister. "Gentlemen!"

"This is a family matter," Nerium snapped.

"This is a school tribunal," said Wist.

Eyes hidden by his glasses, Nerium glanced at her. Then at Gwindel. Then at me. Then back to Wist.

Oh, I see. Trying to puzzle out the mastermind. Trying to determine who was most at fault.

The next time he looked at me, I smiled and waved.

Don't think I was making a mistake by calling attention to myself. Rightly or wrongly, he would never seriously think it was me. His mind was probably incapable of bending over far enough backwards to accommodate the fact that a know-nothing healer, a legal minor, had kicked his feet out from under him.

With plenty of borrowed help, of course.

The magisters seemed increasingly desperate to restore order, but their cries only added to the chaos. It didn't help that the room was designed to so generously convey every syllable of sound from end to end.

The Head Magister raised her voice. "We conferred. We reached a verdict." I'd never heard someone speak in such a booming tone while sounding so thoroughly defeated. "Allow us to—"

"My brother wants to withdraw his complaint," said Wist.

She stood up. A curious hush filled the chamber. She walked down into the middle, passing Gwindel with a nod. Then up to my side.

She sat next to me, sliding closer so that the carved arms and creepy wooden hands of our chairs touched. I would revisit these horrible chairs in my dreams, no doubt. Stiff fingers awakening. Growing into my flesh like roots or reaching up to woodenly strangle me. But I won't deny how good it felt to look over and see Wist there beside me.

"You will withdraw your complaint," she repeated, gazing down at Nerium. "Won't you?"

"First you threaten to leave the family." His voice had entirely lost its veneer of benevolence. "Now you demand concessions. Which is it?"

"I'll stay with the clan if you—all of you—stay off the island. Until after we graduate. And if none of you interfere with our lives at school the entire time. Directly or indirectly."

"You can't—!"

That was Tempus, almost howling. His cry cut itself short with the abruptness of a prey animal being slain in the night. Ficus must've ordered him to shut his damn mouth.

Nerium disregarded the ruckus. "We own property here," he said to Wist.

"Earn extra money by renting it out," I told him. "Hire a management company. No need to thank me for the idea. Just trying to help."

I saw his face twist. The magic on his glasses couldn't wholly conceal his expression.

He pivoted back toward the Gwindel mage. "You heard what my sister said. She won't take on the Gwindel name if I give her what she asks for.

"How can you be happy with the outcome of this? Your clan gets nothing from it. You've been used, my friend. Played for a fool. By juveniles."

Gwindel glanced at Yarrow. "What did I say about S-Class mages?"

"S-Class mages need to stick together," she murmured, eyes lowered.

"There you have it," he told Shien Nerium. "If your sister becomes a Gwindel, I've performed a tremendous service to my clan. If she remains a Shien, I've earned her personal gratitude all the same."

He adjusted his too-tight waistcoat. "I was merely taking a personal holiday on the island. Same as you, Shien. Shame about the weather lately. If I happen to make a powerful ally in passing—what's there to lament?

"I spoke to Wisteria a couple times before today. I see honor in her. Someday—ten years, twenty years, thirty years from now—I'll ask her a favor. A heavy favor, perhaps. I have full faith that she'll come to my aid. Consider it an investment in the future."

Wist's arm, on the arm of her chair, leaned against mine. Her fingers curled slowly around my wrist as if to take my pulse. I couldn't tell if she knew she was doing it. Her eyes stayed on her brother.

"You think I've lost this," Nerium said.

Gwindel clapped him on the shoulder. "You made a worthy effort. Save your strength for other battles."

The Head Magister cleared her throat. "If there is no longer a complaint to address, then there is no need for this tribunal. Let's adjourn."

"No."

The entire room looked at Wist.

"I have a complaint," she said. "A request. If you want me to stay enrolled at the academy."

She scanned each face in the chamber. "My brothers can go," she added. "All the witnesses can go. Except me and Clematis."

Tempus and Saya shuffled out in silence, escorted by a magister.

Ficus looked untroubled. As bored and beautiful as ever. When he rose to follow Nerium to the exit, though, he picked the water glasses off the serving cart and tossed them backwards over his shoulder, one by one, without looking to see where they fell.

The glasses shattered on the parquet floor. Neither Ficus nor Nerium winced or glanced back at the aftermath. They were gone by the time more magisters rushed down to take care of the shards.

The clean-up struck me as being a rather menial use of magic. But perhaps magic was the best way to ensure not a single speck of clear shrapnel remained.

Meanwhile, Yarrow came over to me. "Happy birthday," she said quietly.

"Thanks. I owe you. Best present I ever got was not getting expelled."

She wore a small smile. Couldn't tell if it was real. She bowed again to Wist before leaving.

Azalea tapped Wist on the shoulder to say goodbye.

"Hey," I said. "Thanks for vouching for us."

"I didn't do it for you," Azalea shot back.

I fought to keep a straight face. Far as I could tell, Wist had exactly one friend. But that friend of hers was a true one. Which was more than I could say for myself, considering Saya.

Azalea ended up departing with Yarrow and Gwindel. The Gwindel mage appeared to be in a terribly jovial mood. He kept joking with Azalea, who had no idea how to react.

It would've been a charming scene if Azalea and Yarrow were his daughters. But Yarrow was his bonded healer, tied to him till death.

He wouldn't always be such a munificent jokester. He wouldn't always be so triumphantly jolly. He believed to the bottom of his heart in the supremacy of S-Class mages.

This was the person I'd leveraged for a chance to stay with Wist.

37

Now the only students left in the chamber were me and Wist. The only adults were the magisters.

Wist still held my wrist. Her hand was very warm. Felt like it might start to melt into my skin.

The silence pressed at me as if to keep my lungs from fully expanding. I began to pull away from her. I thought about it, anyhow. Before I could make my move, Wist rose to her feet.

She tugged me down the steps to the open parquet floor.

The geometry of the inlaid patterns made them appear dangerously three-dimensional. I couldn't look where I walked, or I'd trip all over myself, my brain warning me I was about to stumble into a jagged hole or climb up a convoluted stack of cubes. All around the rest of the room, the empty chairs with their naked wooden limbs watched us.

We stopped before the Head Magister, mounted in her special seat made to look like the embracing hands of a giant.

The other magisters kept glancing at each other. The dorm steward stood off to one side like a household servant. That was quite likely what the mage faculty thought of her, in fact, though we healer students looked up to her as the ruler of our small domain.

"The issue at hand has already been resolved," the Head Magister told Wist. "Your brothers withdrew."

"The issue at *hand*," I repeated. "Clever."

No one thought this was funny.

The Head Magister remained adamantly focused on Wist. I may as well have been an autumn frog croaking in the campus underbrush.

"A typhoon is passing through," she said. "We have more pressing matters to attend to. This isn't an appropriate venue for personal—"

"My brothers wanted me to stay with the Shien clan," said Wist. "Do you want me to stay at the academy?"

This sent a murmur rippling through the staff.

A single student leaving—even a mage student with many branches—wouldn't normally deal that much of a blow to such a storied institution. Now, however, they might worry that crossing Wist would mean risking the wrath of not only the Shien clan, but also the Gwindel mage.

Gwindel had shown up in person to back Wist's claims. He'd all but declared himself willing to act as her patron. Moreover, he had the ear of a Board member. Not the school board—the Board of Magi that reigned over the entire country. (Although I'd bet on him having equally influential allies on the Guralta school board, too.)

Above all, his last few words in the chamber must've called the future to mind. He'd spoken of the coming decades. The Head Magister might find herself thinking ahead, considering anew who Wist might turn out to be ten, twenty, thirty years from now.

Perhaps the academy could afford to relinquish Wist the student. But did it make sense to give up any chance of support from the future

Wisteria Shien? By then she might have better mastered her unprecedented magical power. She'd already shown a willingness to outmaneuver her older brothers.

"State your complaint," the Head Magister said rigidly.

Wist started to let go of my wrist. Then, right where everyone could see, she took my hand instead.

I had to work very hard not to shoot her a startled look. I'd thought we were done for the day once Shien Nerium backed down. Yeah, we'd talked about wanting to relax the school rules, but I hadn't expected her to immediately start negotiating for it.

"Clematis will stay at the academy," Wist said. "For me to stay, too, I want an exemption from the anti-fraternization policy."

"We're not planning on bonding," I added hastily. "No way. Just don't want to worry about more people reporting me for saying hello to her in an empty hall."

"Yes," said Wist. "We want to fraternize. I want Clematis to be the only one healing me."

Okay. Maybe she needed some help with this.

I shot my hand up in the air and waved, as obnoxiously as possible, until all the magisters deigned to look at me.

"School is wonderful," I told them. "School is great for teaching us to heal the likes of Minashiro Tempus. But Tempus has nine branches. Wist … Wisteria has, what, thousands? The usual lessons about healing seem completely inapplicable."

Wist's hand anchored me, kept me from swinging my arms around and pacing as I spoke. Which was probably for the best. "Maybe the teachers here have more expertise than me when it comes to healing the average mage. Or an above-average mage. But not a single pro healer in the world is an expert when it comes to Wisteria Shien."

None of the decision-makers in the chamber were healers, either.

Would they understand what I meant?

"No one like Wisteria has ever existed in all the years since our textbooks were written. Since way before then, too. You can't tell me I'm wrong. So maybe there's a chance I could do a better job. I know my grades aren't the greatest, but maybe I'm uniquely well-suited to healing her, and her alone.

"She told me I heal her better than anyone else. That's why she wants me to be able to approach her without fear. Whenever she needs me. A very practical request."

The Head Magister said: "This isn't the first time students have attempted to carve out a special exemption."

Speaking of first times, today marked the first time this woman had ever directly addressed me.

"And you always reject them, I assume?"

"Correct."

Written or not, different rules already applied to healers and to mages. As well as to mages from different families. Which was why the faculty had overlooked a whole lot of heinous behavior from the Shien brothers, back in their day.

For now, Wist and I just needed to make it so that different rules applied to us. We didn't have to blow up the school's entire code of conduct. We'd fail if we tried.

A tacit exception, though? That seemed doable. Our job from here on out was to give the administration a hint of an incentive, plus the illusion of a pretext. Enough cloth, in other words, to make them feel like their asses were covered.

"Don't discount the wisdom of giving Wisteria Shien what she wants." I raised our joined hands for emphasis. "She hardly ever asks for anything. Someday Guralta Academy might have a bunch of new buildings with her name on it. Be it Gwindel or Shien or whatever else."

I took a breath. Just one or two more points to stick the landing. Behind her pursed lips, the Head Magister seemed impatient to be done with us. Or perhaps with me in particular.

I put on a sympathetic face. "Maybe you feel some hesitation about saying, 'Yes, go wild. Consort all you like, for all the rest of your days.' That's understandable.

"How about this. I'll gladly step aside if anyone else does end up healing her better than me. If you can't trust her word, try measuring the results. Make her retake the entrance exam. See how much better she does with me healing her.

"Or give us free rein for a limited time. Consider it a special trial. Take the rest of the school year to evaluate Wisteria's progress. Then judge whether giving us such a flagrant exception is worth it for a second year. I already know you all go much easier on fraternizing among seniors."

The Head Magister tapped her fingertips on one of the trunk-like thumbs of her unusual chair. "Your classmates might not consider such treatment to be fair."

"Nothing was fair from the start," I argued. "It isn't fair that I got locked into being a healer before I even knew how to speak. Fairness ought to be the least of your concerns.

"Wi—" I coughed. Kept wanting to say the shorter version of her name. But something about that seemed vaguely unprofessional. Here, at least, I would call her the same thing Nerium and Ficus and Gwindel called her.

"Wisteria has raw magic unlike anyone else in Osmanthian history," I continued. "Didn't have to do much research to see that. Why should she have to be tied down by the same restrictions as everyone else? It's like telling a horse to learn to run by following snails. No, worse—it's like making a horse wear a heavy shell on its back to fit in at the snail races."

In the back of my head it occurred to me that perhaps I ought to go a bit heavier on the buttering up and a bit lighter on the pedagogical criticism. But I'd been wanting to say this for such a long time. The words came out in a waterfall.

"How much of your mage curriculum even applies to her situation, anyway? How can you justify making her strip all her skills for an exam? It's not like she's shown any sign of running out of branches."

The Head Magister started to say something.

"No." That was Wist speaking. "Listen."

They looked nothing alike. Yet there was a similar hardness to their faces, one young and one old. The Head Magister wielded the force of an entire institution.

Unfortunately for the Head Magister, Wist didn't need any of that. Wist's own power was all packed inside her. Wist was used to losing things. Wist was altogether willing to walk away. From the Shiens. From the academy. But not, it seemed, from me.

I spoke into the silence Wist had paved for me.

"It can take hours, days, weeks to acquire a new skill," I said. "Can't it? Wisteria's catalog of skills—her ability to possess so many more at once than anyone else—that's her true wealth.

"You should be pushing her to build up that wealth. To test the limits of her parallel processing. You should be working to make sure she's capable of quickly accessing and fully exploiting all her skills even as her repertoire grows and grows."

I reached across my body with my free hand and slapped myself on the shoulder. "If you're so desperately concerned about us losing our minds and spontaneously bonding, stick another monkey on me. Worked fine at the originator exam, didn't it?"

Wist raised her chin and looked the Head Magister in the eye. "What she said."

Classic Wist. Perfectly steady. Perfectly cool. Perfectly empty. No one would be able to look at that face and convince themselves they had any idea what she was really thinking. No one would be able to look at that face and convince themselves they had any chance of getting her to yield.

"I consulted Mr. Gwindel about this," she added. "He seemed supportive. I can call him back to—"

"No need," the Head Magister said heavily.

That was when I knew we had together succeeded in grinding her down.

38

AFTERWARD, I left the tribunal chamber with Wist, instead of with the dorm steward. No one tried to stop me.

Wist said she would show me another way back.

When we stepped through the chamber door—one of several—it didn't magically transport us to the laundry room.

As I'd thought, we seemed to be in one of the administrative buildings over on the mage side of campus. Out here there were real windows, most of them many times taller than me, some slapped by wind and rain. The Head Magister would be relieved to discover that the island hadn't gotten swept away into the ocean while we debated.

Other windows looked out on scenery that appeared to be far removed from campus. Fields of tall cosmos flowers growing wild and tangled against an azure sky. Rice paddies shining yellow-gold, almost ready for harvest. The historical district in the capital that housed the Palace of Magi: cloudy and dark now, but not nearly so storm-tossed as the island.

Better not let those windows distract me. I looked around the hall for spies, for witnesses.

We were alone for as far as the eye could see. Just us and all the mystery cuttings woven into every nook and cranny of architecture in sight. Best to assume we were still being watched. But perhaps it didn't matter so much anymore.

"You won," I said.

"I barely said a word."

"We won, then. So why do you sound so grumpy?"

"I sound the same as always."

I elbowed Wist until she had no choice but to glance at me.

"Didn't know it was your birthday," she muttered.

At first I couldn't understand where she'd gotten this from. Then I recalled what Yarrow had murmured to me on her way out.

"Oh." I jerked a thumb back at one of the windows behind us. A window that showed the true state of the island. "What with the weather and your brothers, it didn't seem like a good time to celebrate."

Was it my imagination, or did she seem increasingly miffed?

"Let's be fair," I added. "I have no idea when your birthday is, either."

"February twenty-fifth. According to the Shiens."

"Better remind me next year."

Soft lights shaped like soap bubbles followed us through the corridor, unhurried, rising and falling at whim. They smelled distinctly of spica. I battled the urge to snatch one out of the air and crush it.

Victory felt equally fleeting, fragile, unreal. Maybe I just needed more time to get used to it. Maybe I was too preoccupied by Wist's fingers locked in mine. That seemed far more immediate.

In my memory, the tribunal chamber had already begun to sink like fragments of a bad dream.

Only one part remained afloat in blazing light and color: the part where Wist had risen and crossed the gulf in the middle of the room to join me.

That moment felt as if it had tattooed itself all over me, left marks so obvious that I couldn't believe no one else saw it, rolled my heart out thin as parchment and merged it with my skin. And she was still touching it. She still hadn't dropped my hand.

We passed the records room where they stored the output of all the mage student collars. Couldn't go in, of course. We passed a cavernous chamber full of black-headed gulls roosting like bats.

We didn't pass a single human soul. The mage students were supposed to be gathered in their dormitories.

Wist stopped in a circular vestibule filled with doors. Each appeared to bear the label of a different building, from the campus museum to the library to the gym.

"Mage students can't use this door." She tapped her knuckles lightly on the one labeled for my dorm. "But you should be able to pass."

"You'll have to let go," I said.

She looked down at me as if she'd forgotten our hands were joined. As if she thought I were making things up. Then she kept looking, eyes dark and searching.

The long, long end of her braid snuck along our merged shadow on the floor. It wound around my right ankle like a snake settling down to sleep. I couldn't tell if Wist even realized she was doing it.

"That was your roommate," she stated.

"Who, Saya? With the big eyes? What about her?"

"She said a lot of things. She read your notebook."

"Sorry." I was still kicking myself for that. "Should've protected it better."

"Now you have to go back and keep sleeping in the same room as her?"

"As if nothing ever happened," I said. "It'll be fine as long as your brothers are out of the picture. My other dormmates terrorized me much worse during hunting season. Lucky for you mages, never having to take roommates."

"Doesn't seem right," Wist said.

"Well, I'd love to angle for a single next year. Or at least a different roommate. But it isn't worth trying to switch now. Can't think of many others who would take me."

"I could—"

"Wist." I nailed her with my most incredulous stare. "They already gave us permission to openly trample a bunch of the school regulations. They aren't going to let us room together. Don't push it."

She didn't answer.

"On her own, Saya is harmless," I declared. "I can survive another half a year of awkward nights. Look at us—we just strong-armed the Head Magister into telling us we can cavort around without chaperones as much as we want. Let's be satisfied with what we've got."

"You did most of the talking."

"Would've been meaningless if I were standing there flapping my lips by myself," I said. "No one would've heard me out for more than a millisecond without you there to glower at them."

"The glowering worked?"

"Like magic."

"Then I'm glad I didn't wear my glasses."

"Exactly," I told her. "Nothing to shield them from the full force of your penetrating orbs."

"My what?"

"Never mind." I managed to keep my face neutral. It wasn't great form to always be the only one dissolving in laughter over your own jokes.

I turned my body toward the door.

"See you after the typhoon," I said.

Wist still wasn't letting go of my hand.

A faint alarm reared its head in me.

I lifted my right foot off the floor and wiggled it, shaking her braid—still clinging to my ankle—in the process.

"You'll trip me," I said accusingly.

Her braid unfurled and retreated. It kept lashing a hypnotic beat back and forth behind her. Its movements gave off the aura of an irritated cat.

She loosened her fingers slowly, with some difficulty. Once she released me, I flexed my hand to feel it again. To make sure it belonged to me.

While I was looking down, Wist touched the outer rim of my ear. Right next to the tiny white patch in my hair, the odd indelible spot that refused to grow in dark like the rest.

My breath went shooting down the wrong pipe. Which, in all likelihood, wasn't even possible. It was just pure air. But for an instant it stung like sea water going in all the wrong places.

Her touch was very light, almost light enough to tickle. Asking nothing.

I couldn't take it.

I tripped a step back. And then it was gone. And I regretted moving. The regret seized me like a cramp from running too fast. But this really wasn't the time or the place, was it? Not for whatever one or both of us did or didn't have in mind about—

To be strictly honest with you, it was always on my mind.

If I were going to reach for her, though, I didn't want it to be here in the cold mage building, with flocks of dormant gulls lurking down the hall.

Above all, I needed more time to unthaw. I'd spent too long not letting myself consciously acknowledge even the possibility of what her whispering touch on the skin of my ear suggested to me.

I forced myself not to say anything unnecessary. I blurted another quick goodbye. I reached for the magical door instead of reaching for Wist. I escaped to the familiar safety of the run-down healer dormitory.

39

THE SECOND TYPHOON of September left many a fallen branch in its wake. Thanks to the mage students' preparations, though, no windows shattered. In poorer parts of the island, basements flooded and trees came down. But not on campus. And the public wooden fishing piers, shielded by magic, survived the thrashing of the waves.

Several days passed before we got full clearance to roam freely. Until then, I had to spend a lot of time with Saya.

What irked me about Saya was that I couldn't puzzle out why I'd trusted her. I could conclude only that I'd been liable to assume the best of healers and the worst of mages.

I'd write off healers who gave me evidence of being shitty people—as had quite a few of my classmates. In the absence of any such evidence, I thought of us as fundamentally being on the same side. Arrayed against mages. Even if we had very different worldviews. Even if we weren't close friends.

Objectively, Saya wasn't a bad roommate. She was clean. She was quiet. She kept her stuff contained to her section of the room. She cared well for her hermit crabs. She didn't complain about my night terrors.

None of that had given her much of a reason not to stab me in the back.

After that farcical tribunal, we ended up waiting out the rest of the storm in close proximity. The only other people in the dorm I felt more comfortable with were Pepper and the steward. A number of the other Rats had already demonstrated their willingness to turn on me months and months ago.

Hanging out in my room with Saya didn't feel that much more unpleasant than it would've been to haunt the first floor lounge, or pester the steward till she told me to go do schoolwork.

A sad state of affairs? Perhaps. But part of me found it kind of funny.

"You know," I said to Saya, "I didn't think we were best friends. But I didn't think we were enemies, either."

She glanced up from the book in her lap. I had to give her credit for being able to look me in the eye without dithering.

"I have relatives who work for the Shiens," she said.

"How tragic."

"Not close relatives. Not the core family. A few of its offshoots."

"So that was one consideration for you."

"But not my main or only reason."

"Then why'd you double-cross me? Did Shien Nerium threaten you?"

"Not in so many words."

She cast her gaze down again, considering the page before her. She circled a paragraph. I'd bet the entirety of my measly pocket money that she hadn't actually read a word of it.

"You might be willing to gamble on the future potential of Wisteria Shien," Saya said carefully.

Outside, the wind groaned as if dying, as if begging for help.

"I prefer to decide based on the power balance right in front of me," she continued. "Shien Nerium personally requesting a favor. Versus Wisteria Shien, who sleeps through half the classes I've seen her in, and who's never spoken a word to me."

"And me?" I asked. "The target of your spying? Where do I come into this?"

I never got an answer.

Gradually, it dawned on me that there was no need for her to elaborate. Saya had spoken only of deciding which mage she ought to follow.

I had never been an option. I was too powerless, in her eyes, to exist as someone she could feasibly side with. Not when there were mages involved.

"Hope you know you picked the wrong side," I said.

We remained civil to each other for the rest of the school year (which ended the following March). When we were second-years, wearing our shiny new shrimp pins, I'd miss being able to peek in on her hermit crabs.

As far as I can recall, Saya and I never had another meaningful conversation again.

Not that I could resent her too deeply. From my perspective, she'd chosen the wrong person to ally with. On the most basic level, however, all she'd done was pull the same move as me.

Now I'd tasted a tiny morsel of success, honey on my tongue. I'd won something I'd never thought possible, and something I hadn't thought I wanted at all. The right to trot up to Wist in an empty classroom without looking over my shoulder to see if there were anyone watching. The right to stay here at the school I'd been determined to hate.

Call me ungrateful, but it made me want more.

I fancy myself a realist. My next grand ambition was simply to graduate in one piece. After that, I would do whatever I had to. Bend some rules—and laws—as far as they would go. Step right through the holes in others.

I would borrow power from those I admired, but also from those I found distasteful. Even those I might consider an enemy. That was the Clematis way now.

How else was a healer with no fame and no money supposed to even begin to make a dent in Osmanthian society?

Putting my burgeoning dreams into words would make me sound arrogant to the point of psychosis. But I thought maybe I could accomplish what Mr. Rift couldn't. What generations of healers (Saya's ancestors among them) had failed at.

Live long enough, and maybe I could make this country a place where growing up as a healer wouldn't feel like trying to claw through the bars of an ever-shrinking cage.

Why? Because I was confident there had never been a mage like Wist. Not in the history of Osmanthus as an independent nation, anyhow.

It would take her years to come anywhere close to making full use of her magical power. Just as I'd prophesied, though, one day everyone would know she outclassed everyone else alive. One day all the other mages would listen to her.

If—when that distant day came—she still listened to me, it would mean I secretly had the ear of every mage in Osmanthus.

Even at this early stage, we already had acquaintances in high places. Yarrow's bondmate worked for a Board member. I might despise everything he stood for, but I could appreciate his connections.

The school administration never made any kind of announcement about letting Wist and I fraternize to our hearts' content. That wasn't their way.

Students saw us walking together, eating together, skipping class together. No explanation. Tempus, at least, knew to leave well enough alone. I'm sure plenty of others tried to report us. Over time, when nothing came of it, they gave up.

The academy had its written code of conduct, but also numerous other rules that no one ever gave voice to. Never contradict an upperclassman. Stop asking the other teachers why Mr. Rift left. Stay away from the haunted shack on the far west end of campus.

Don't bother wondering why Wisteria Shien gets to use a fellow student—a Rat, at that—as her personal full-time healer.

If the rumors were true, generations of mages had gotten away with torturing their classmates. Mostly healers. At least since the school went co-ed. The Shien brothers may have perfected the art of the hunt in their time, but they weren't pioneers.

Anything I'd experienced was pretty light in comparison: after all, I'd come through hunting season with all my body parts intact. Thank god for Tempus being a wimp.

At any rate, Wist and I weren't even hurting anyone. Unlike her brothers. The more valuable she proved herself, the more inclined the administration would be to let us keep on getting away with our partnership.

Our worst obstacle in that first year of school had been the Shien brothers, and now they were gone. Ignobly banished from the island by Wist's threats to leave the clan.

I was enormously gleeful to find that, as a result, they ended up missing the Guralta Cup—the very reason their visit had originally been timed for August and September. With Wist insisting that they pack up to leave the island immediately, and the Cup rescheduled to October due to the weather, there was zero chance of them seeing it. Suckers.

Several years passed before the next time I encountered either brother in person.

And you know what? I didn't think about them once in the interim. I genuinely came very close to completely forgetting their faces and voices and names.

In my world, Wist was the only Shien who mattered.

When I met them again later, together with all the other sundry Shien siblings, we acted as if we'd never seen each other before in our lives. In Ficus's case, I kind of believed it. He seemed entirely capable of wiping my meager existence from his memory.

Nerium must've been different. Nothing he did could convince me he'd forgotten the scene of his defeat. Savoring that thought helped carry me though the unholy gauntlet of glassy stares and icy comments from every other Shien brother and sister.

40

BACK TO OUR FIRST YEAR at Guralta Academy. To the tail end of September, my sixth full month on the island.

Once the post-typhoon cleaning and safety checks came to an end, clubs and sports teams flung themselves back into preparations for the Guralta Cup.

Alumni families swarmed campus in flamboyant mage robes—more of them than ever before.

Colorful booths sprang up all over the grounds. Cut flowers flew through the sky, descending at night to rest and recover before soaring back up into the air again the following day. The gargoyles and other statuary struck poses I'd never seen before, pandering shamelessly to visiting children.

The healer classroom buildings and even the dormitory corridors played a mirrored version of the musical acts filling the grandiose Guralta Academy Hall. People apparently paid through the nose for tickets to see it in person. Not just parents of the performers, but plenty of unrelated island vacationers as well.

I was more interested in hiding from the crowds than paying attention to what happened at the Cup.

I'll have you know one thing, though. In her second year at Guralta, the first year she qualified for the Cup, Wist won every single challenge. She won the biannual mage pentathlons, too. She remained undefeated till graduation.

Poor Tempus. Got all that competitive spirit stomped clean out of him.

But we didn't plan on watching our very first Guralta Cup, the one that got pushed back. We devoted our energies to lurking a safe distance from the spotlight.

Wist invented yet another iteration of her porting skill. This one, fortunately, required neither piggyback rides nor the presence of poultry eggs.

She couldn't use it to cross ocean water, but her range covered the entire island. And as long as she touched me, she could take me with her.

For the first time, I saw the mouth of the sealed-off caves. I sat atop the eastern ruins, dangling my legs like a neighborhood kid sitting on one of the garden walls back home. It was a spot so high that the beachfront mansions looked like a pastel candy-colored diorama, curiously unimpressive. They wouldn't last nearly as long as these shambolic ruins, that's for sure.

Wist's braid wound around both of us to anchor us in place like a safety rope. I tipped my head back and watched airships cross the sea. No matter how high we ascended, those passing airships never looked much closer. Their distance and insectile angles made them seem like visitors from another world.

Wist liked roofs. She took a particular liking to the roof of the healer dorm, which wasn't supposed to be accessible even to us residents. I'd never been up there till she took my arm and ported me.

The roof had plenty of broad, flat areas to stand on. It was also covered in ivy that looked like it'd escaped from the garden of elephantine plants growing at the center of campus. The leaves were large enough that I could've sewn two together to make a sleeping bag.

"Picturesque," I said, "but we'll probably get ticks."

"We can inspect each other afterward."

In trying to determine if she were joking, I nearly forgot the reason we'd come here in the first place. I dug Shien Nerium's model lighthouse out of my inner pocket. It had gotten cool enough to wear my uniform jacket again, at least so long as we weren't roasting in unfiltered sunlight.

Wist took the lighthouse from me. She started to sit down right in the middle of the incredibly filthy roof. I stopped her and made her use one of the massive ivy leaves as a tarp.

I crouched nearby to watch her strip Nerium's cuttings from the model tower. With only Wist and the late afternoon sky and the hulking leaves visible, it felt like we'd shrunk to the size of crickets. Like we were the small ones, rather than the ivy being unusually big.

Wist split the tower in half down the middle. Since the tribunal, she'd already become a lot bolder about originating new skills whenever she wanted, and only explaining them to faculty after the fact.

She stuck one half in the end of her braid. The strands flexed to keep hold of it.

"You could put someone's eye out with that," I warned. "Looks like a weapon. It's basically a morning star, actually."

She handed me the other half. "Twist it if you ever need to summon me."

"It won't fall apart?"

"It won't fall apart."

"Something using Transceiver might've been more convenient."

I almost caught Wist frowning. Not quite, though. "Haven't learned Transceiver yet," she said. "It's extremely complex."

I raised my hands. "Never said it wasn't."

"We'll come up with something better someday," Wist concluded. "This will do for now."

She didn't stop at haunting rooftops, by the way. She took me up to the peak of the highest campus spires.

We had to peer way down to see the iconic floating sundial, the rough arch of the main school gate.

In doing so, we discovered that the stories were real. For no particular reason we could determine, there were brief moments when the flowing silver in the gate ran red.

In the evening, the tightropes binding building to building and the coral-lit footpaths formed shapes that seemed suspiciously different from the official campus maps. Only then did I realize, much to my outrage, that the paths weren't necessarily static.

No wonder my sense of direction got confused so easily.

"You didn't know?" Wist said.

I pulled a face at her. Wist patted me on the head.

The problem was that she used the tuft of her braid. Which meant she'd thumped me with her broken half of the spiky model lighthouse. Unintentionally, of course. But still.

As I yelped, roosting birds shot out from beneath the small stone overhang where we perched. I rubbed my skull. I moaned and groaned about it for the rest of the night. Wist, in fairness, did her best to apologize.

It was up in the spires that I came to see how frequently the campus gargoyles changed positions. Don't think I ever quite caught them in motion. But after each blink and each lapse in concentration, I'd refocus to see them in a new pose or a new location.

It was up in the spires that I told Wist, "If you come up to places like this to avoid people, you ought to look into acquiring a skill for going unnoticed."

And whether in the spires or on various rooftops or in mirror-lined classrooms or behind the gym, I healed her as much as we wanted. It got to the point where the patterns I saw when I closed my eyes began to resemble the interweaving of her branches.

Wist told me I didn't have to. She told me not to overdo it. I told her to shut up. I would stop when I got tired. I would stop when I lost interest.

The first time I used my half of the lighthouse to summon Wist ended up being during the height of the Guralta Cup. Early October.

I called her to join me on a nigh-empty stretch of beach. Empty not due to being underdeveloped, or less popular than any other slice of island shore. Empty simply because all the upperclassmen living in off-campus housing—and nearly all the vacationing families—had gone to the stadium to watch the Cup.

Formations of brown pelicans coasted nobly overhead. Sandpipers skittered past frothy smears of sea foam. Yet the whole time, we only saw a few other lonely human figures. All far in the distance.

As Rats, our presence in the Cup audience was encouraged. Assumed, even. But not strictly required.

Wist showed up on the sand in her school-regulation tracksuit. It had gotten breezy enough for me to fasten my jacket and hide my hands in my sleeves.

"Reminds me of the first time we met," I said. "Might've been colder back then."

One of Wist's branches twitched within her. A flicker like the brief light of a passing firefly. White fog swirled at our feet as if the sand itself were smoking.

I kicked at the magical fog. We watched it gutter and eddy until the wind tore it to bits.

"You like it here?" Wist asked.

"Here?"

"On the island."

"It's all right." Didn't want her to think I was soft.

She wasn't wearing her glasses, but they hung hooked on the front of her tracksuit.

"Thought you might get rid of those," I remarked.

"You seemed fond of them."

"What the hell gave you that idea?"

She started to answer. I backtracked. "No, wait. Let's not analyze how I feel about your glasses. If they bring up bad memories, don't let me be the reason you keep them."

"Bad memories?"

"You said—"

Wist glanced down at the glasses on her chest. "My brothers have done much worse. These hardly bring up anything. Except maybe the way you look at me when—"

"Not another word," I hissed.

I strode across the sand without looking to see if Wist would follow. My blood was pumping much too fast to stay at a standstill.

Annoyingly, Wist had little trouble keeping up.

"Might need real lenses someday," she said meditatively. "Sometimes I can feel my eyes getting tired."

"Good for you," I sniped.

"Good for you, too."

She had me there. I glared furiously at the sea.

We kept walking until we reached one of the piers. Sometimes bickering. Sometimes silent. We weren't missing any classes. And we had plenty of time.

Along the way, we crossed the sand in front of the Shien beach house. I tugged at Wist's arm.

Obscure figures bustled about the balconies and decks. I'd have thought it would be empty. Shuttered windows. Tumbleweeds bobbing in the infinity pool. But I guess a mansion like that needed to be cared for, even without anyone staying there. Perhaps the human labor to clean and maintain it came cheaper than the equivalent magic.

"Bring any eggs?" I asked Wist.

"No?"

"Guess that's for the best. I was gonna suggest egging it," I explained, "but your brothers aren't there to be bothered. We'd just cause trouble for the cleaners."

"Egging it?" Wist said blankly.

Which is how I ended up having to explain the concept of egging houses to the great Wisteria Shien.

Nerium and Tempus hadn't been entirely wrong when they claimed she was sheltered.

The pier, though solid enough to withstand turbulent waters—and smeared here and there with traces of magic—was a surprisingly crude-looking structure. Rough planks laid over muscular logs that loomed high out of the sea and sand, high enough to stroll beneath it as if passing below a wooden bridge.

Even if she raised her hand and jumped, Wist wouldn't come anywhere near brushing the bottom of the pier. The timber piling holding it up was thick enough that—if hollow—it could've housed our bodies like columnar coffins. With room to spare.

Pale growths dotted the places where wood met water. As well as the bases of the columns further back, all dry now, that would be submerged once the tide came in.

"Sometimes I wonder what they're actually afraid of." I keep my eyes on the barnacles. "With the anti-fraternization rules."

"Underage bonding," said Wist. The textbook answer.

"How often does that even happen? The general population might be one thing, but I'm talking about high-class mages enrolled at Guralta. Would a mage student who made it in here really throw everything away for some no-name brat? I mean, you wouldn't—"

"I would," Wist said suddenly.

The sea sloshed up against the wooden pilings.

"You would?"

Something inside me sloshed, too, as if tipped to one side. Defenseless. Right on the verge of spilling over.

I took a moment to reason with myself. I knew what I'd been talking about. Wist might mean something entirely different.

I stole a glance at her. Her hair had tied itself up in a comically elaborate series of nautical knots down her back. It looked like a pendulous cocoon to protect her half of the spiky lighthouse. Or to keep it from inadvertently stabbing anyone.

The wind tangled shorter wisps around her ears and her mage collar. She wore a cap with the school logo stitched on it, the brim shading her eyes.

I hated how good the tracksuit looked on her. I really did. It didn't even fit well. But she was long and relaxed and utterly unselfconscious. Unlike some of us.

"I told the Head Magister we wouldn't bond," I said, testing. "Never said we wouldn't do anything else."

Wist studied me in silence. Then her gaze went sideways, to the nearest of the logs that helped support the pier above us.

She addressed the log as if it were a valued third member of our conversation.

"But you don't want to," she said.

"Don't tell me what I want."

Wist reached toward my face. I dodged.

She didn't follow. "See?"

"That was a reflex!" I cried. "You know I—come on, you've seen how I ogle you. You have to know how much I—"

"No. I don't."

"You're kidding."

I quite earnestly contemplated flinging myself down and having a fit in the sand.

"You said you want to tear me open." Wist sounded the way she always sounded. Deathly serious. "You said you want to see me cry."

Not, perhaps, a love confession for the ages.

I thought about how to salvage this. I thought for what felt like a very long time. Wist didn't rush me.

The sea washed lazily up and down the shore. Birds quarreled in the distance.

Finally I told her, "Whatever I said, you've got to admit that I did sound pretty passionate saying it."

Wist didn't move.

She wouldn't move, not so long as I kept fleeing her.

"Half the reason my grades are so terrible," I said, "is because I want them that way."

"Well done."

"The other half is because you distract me out of my mind. Even when you're not there. Especially when you're not there."

I put a hand on her side, as if we were about to start dancing. Then my other hand. I could feel the movement of her breathing—far faster and unsteadier than I could ever guessed from listening to the rhythm of her voice.

For an instant, my throat was too tight to utter anything more.

"Maybe there's more than one way to make someone cry," Wist said thoughtfully.

"If that's what you're hoping for, the only thing you'll be crying from is disappointment." Boy, could I talk fast when I tried. "I've got all the experience of a—well, it's not zero. If you want to get technical. But I really wouldn't count it."

"You already touched the deepest parts of my magic."

"That's different. I just don't know what to—"

Her arms were around me, squeezing the breath out of me. I went on tiptoe without even meaning to, and she held me there.

"Clem," she said near the top of my ear, in a voice already cracked down the middle, "nothing you could do is wrong for me."

Her lips touched my temple. My lips touched her jaw. We bumped teeth.

I laughed, short and hysterical.

Our kisses were quick and shallow, then hungrier and deeper. Till both our necks hurt like hell and my feet started to cramp from staying up on my toes.

I tugged her jacket aside and bit her on the shoulder. Why? Because I could. I brought her fingers to my mouth and bit them, too. Not too hard. But perhaps harder than I should have.

Back on campus, over at the site of the Guralta Cup, the clapping and shouting must've been deafening. Here we only had the ocean to cheer for us. What more did we need?

I hadn't lost my desire to break her down. There were a lot of things I longed for. All contradictory. I wanted to destroy her, and I wanted to see her helpless smile when she cracked.

Was that really so strange?

Being destroyed didn't have to mean falling to her knees in despair every time, did it? Being destroyed could mean being stripped naked of the pain in her magic that had shrouded her heart and her thoughts all her life. Couldn't it?

Being destroyed could mean splintering beneath the force of her inability to hide herself from me. Being destroyed could mean getting chiseled open by an unrelenting joy.

There was definitely an abnormal part of me that very much wanted to see Wist sob with all the breath in her lungs. To see her collapse. To see her lose every last vestige of the self-killing self-control that Shien Nerium had taken such hideous pride in. That he'd worked so terribly hard to install in her.

But there was also a part of me that wanted to see her dismiss other mages with a flick of her finger. To freeze a crowd in place by giving them just a fractional glimpse of the full pulverizing weight of the magic inside her.

There was a certain indescribable quality to the depths of Wist's magic, to the convolutions of her branches. It seemed all wrong. Abominable. It could tickle primal human instincts in the same manner as the wriggling of countless maggots, as the churning of a landless ocean, as the vertigo from the crumbling edge of a cliff.

No single being was ever supposed to contain that much magic. If you didn't know her, it might feel like having your eyelids peeled open when all you wanted to was to squeeze them shut. It might feel like facing down the magical equivalent of the absolute worst kinds of body horror.

It was different if you knew her.

It felt different for me, at least.

The more I knew her, the more I wanted to help her reach her full glory. Wist's relative indifference to being glorious only made it more enticing. If she stretched herself to master her magic, I would know all the way to the meat of my bones that she did it for me.

So I'll admit it. Maybe I hadn't wanted to stay here with Wist just to use her. But if one day she seemed willing to let me milk her name and power, I wouldn't hesitate.

If we went into politics, if we climbed our way all the way up to the Board of Magi, there was a genuine chance we could make things better for other Osmanthian healers. Give them more choices. Real choices.

I still had no enthusiasm for being a generic healer of mages. For living out a life of service. Wist might seem different from other mages, but not everyone had a Wist. Reshaping the country for other healers— now that was a role I could embrace.

Wist would grow into her magic. With me there to help, she'd grow into it faster.

Who could stop us?

In calmer moments, we sat together on the sand below the pier, backs resting against a timber column. We'd picked one with fewer barnacles sticking out to poke us. The sky outside the shade of the pier was the sort of soul-deep blue that only seeps through on certain dry, cloudless autumn days.

I reached out to sift idly through the knots in Wist's magic.

"Feels nice," she said.

"What, this?" I tugged at a magic branch.

"That, and knowing my brothers are back on the mainland."

"That was all you," I said.

Wist disagreed. "You set me up to coordinate with Mr. Gwindel. His backing changed everything."

"Better thank Yarrow, too," I told her. (Naturally, we already had.)

I let Wist's branches slip through my fingers. "Listen, you know I won't stint on giving myself credit. I'm probably prone to taking more than I deserve.

"I can clear the clouds from your head. I can chase a lot of the pain out of your magic. At least temporarily. But I can't pull your magic like strings and make you stand up to your brother. That was you.

"You called his bluff—he can't speak for every Shien. He can't stand in for the head of your clan. Your grandmother, was it? The Shiens might've been willing to let him run rampant at home, but that doesn't mean they'd be nearly as willing to let you go without a fight.

"Which makes them even more terrible, in a way. They just want the prestige you might bring them. They want the promise of your future. They don't care how much you suffer in the meantime."

Wist had taken my hand and begun toying with my knuckles.

"It seems clear in retrospect," she said. "But at the time, I truly couldn't see how he'd react."

"The shitty part is that people outside you can stab you real deep, stab you to shreds, really mess you up. But someone on the outside can't just reach in and fix it all up in the same way. You're left on your own for that."

Wist leaned into me, a gentle weight. "Not completely."

I balked. "I haven't done anything. I can heal your magic. But I can't heal the rest."

"The rest?"

"You know. The mind stuff. The heart stuff."

"You still help."

She brought the base of my palm to her lips. What a sap.

"By the way," I said, "I brought that coin."

I wriggled it out of my jacket pocket. The imperial coin with the Kraken on it. I mimed flinging it at the water. "Is now a good time?"

We rose, dusting the sand off our butts.

I handed Wist the replica coin.

She tossed it lightly in her hand. Once. Twice. Then she laid it flat on her open palm, as if she planned to blow it off into the sea like blowing out a candle.

Her magic sparked with a sound like snapping fingers.

The coin went flying. Not as fast as a bullet, but close. It shot in a perfect straight line right down the center of the air below the pier, all the way past the point where the pier stopped and met open sea. It flew so far that I lost sight of where it dropped in the water.

Not my brother. Not my coin. Not my memories that needed exorcising. Yet a satisfaction much deeper than I'd expected curled up warm and content in my belly.

Wist's arms snuck around me. I felt her chin touch the top of my head. My entire body flared with an unprecedented awareness of its own existence.

At the same time, it seemed unbelievable that such closeness could come so easy to us. It felt like a trick. As if the sensation of Wist pressed up against my back would vanish—in the same way as her fog scattering— if I thought too hard about it.

Right up until a scant few minutes ago, the tiniest distance between fingertips and skin had gaped wide open between us, an insurmountable canyon.

We kept gazing down the open corridor formed by rows of tall wooden stilts below the pier. At the end of it lay the line where sky became sea.

It looked like something supernatural: a secret tunnel to another world. To our dazzling future. I turned back to Wist as the muted roar of the modest gray-green waves rolled in to applaud us, again and again and again.

A Note from the Author

How was your visit to Guralta Isle? Let me know with a rating or review—or by trying out other books in the series! Nothing inspires me more than seeing people read my work. It's as simple as that.

Above all, thank you for spending this time with Clematis and Wist. It was so much fun to write the story of how they first met: the very, very beginning.

Subsequent entries in the Clem & Wist series take place many years later, far away from the island. If it's your first time encountering these two, I hope you enjoy discovering how they change in the future (as well as how they don't!).

I'm already eager to work on my next book set in this world. I can think of no greater honor than the knowledge that there just might be people out there looking forward to reading it.

Follow my Author Page for future updates if you'd like to see more: **amazon.com/author/hiyodori**

Hope to see you again next time!

– Hiyodori

Novels by Hiyodori

The Clem & Wist Series

Book 1: The Lowest Healer and the Highest Mage

Book 2: The Reverse Healer Case Files

Prequel: No One Else Could Heal Her

Set in the World of Clem & Wist

The First and Last Demon (Standalone)